CHARLES DICKENS'S
OUR MUTUAL FRIEND

Even within the context of Charles Dickens's history as a publishing innovator, *Our Mutual Friend* is notable for what it reveals about Dickens as an author and about Victorian publishing. Marking Dickens's return to the monthly number format after nearly a decade of writing fiction designed for weekly publication in *All the Year Round*, *Our Mutual Friend* emerged against the backdrop of his failing health, troubled relationship with Ellen Ternan, and declining reputation among contemporary critics. In his subtly argued publishing history, Sean Grass shows how these difficulties combined to make *Our Mutual Friend* an extraordinarily odd novel, no less in its contents and unusually heavy revisions than in its marketing by Chapman and Hall, its transformation from a serial into British and U.S. book editions, its contemporary reception by readers and reviewers, and its delightfully uneven reputation among critics in the 150 years since Dickens's death.

Enhanced by four appendices that offer contemporary accounts of the Staplehurst railway accident, information on archival materials, transcripts of all of the contemporary reviews, and a select bibliography of editions, Grass's book shows why this last of Dickens's finished novels continues to intrigue its readers and critics.

Ashgate Studies in Publishing History

Offering publishing histories of well-known works of literature, this series is intended as a resource for book historians and for other specialists whose scholarship and teaching are enhanced by access to a work's publication and reception history. Features include but are not limited to sections on the text's composition, production and marketing, contemporary reception, textual issues, subsequent editions, and archival resources. The series is designed to allow for flexibility in presentation, to accommodate differences in each work's history. Proposals on works whose publishing histories are particularly significant for what they reveal about a writer, a cultural milieu, or the history of print culture are especially welcome.

Charles Dickens's
Our Mutual Friend
A Publishing History

SEAN GRASS
Iowa State University, USA

ASHGATE

© Sean Grass 2014

All rights reserved. No part of this publication may be reproduced, stored in a retrieval system or transmitted in any form or by any means, electronic, mechanical, photocopying, recording or otherwise without the prior permission of the publisher.

Sean Grass has asserted his right under the Copyright, Designs and Patents Act, 1988, to be identified as the author of this work.

Published by
Ashgate Publishing Limited
Wey Court East
Union Road
Farnham
Surrey, GU9 7PT
England

Ashgate Publishing Company
110 Cherry Street
Suite 3-1
Burlington
VT 05401-3818
USA

www.ashgate.com

British Library Cataloguing in Publication Data
A catalogue record for this book is available from the British Library

The Library of Congress has cataloged the printed edition as follows:
Grass, Sean, 1971–
  Charles Dickens's Our mutual friend : a publishing history / by Sean Grass.
      pages cm.—(Ashgate studies in publishing history: manuscript, print, digital)
  Includes bibliographical references and index.
  ISBN 978-0-7546-6930-2 (hardcover: alk. paper)—ISBN 978-0-7546-9659-9 (ebook)—ISBN 978-1-4724-0500-5 (epub)
  1. Dickens, Charles, 1812–1870. Our mutual friend. 2. Dickens, Charles, 1812–1870—Relations with publishers. 3. Literature publishing—England—History—19th century. 4. Authors and publishers—England—History—19th century. I. Title.
  PR4568.G73 2014
  823'.8—dc23
                                                                              2013035881

ISBN 9780754669302 (hbk)

Printed in the United Kingdom by Henry Ling Limited, at the Dorset Press, Dorchester, DT1 1HD

For Jean DePolis and Dollie Grass, whose histories I should also have written when there was time

Contents

List of Illustrations	*ix*
Acknowledgements	*xiii*

Introduction: *Our Mutual Friend*: "The poorest of Mr. Dickens's works"   1

1   The Man from Somewhere: Ellen Ternan, Staplehurst,
and the Remaking of Charles Dickens   9

2   The Cup and the Lip: Writing *Our Mutual Friend*   37

3   Putting a Price upon a Man's Mind:
Our Mutual Friend in the Marketplace   71

4   A Dismal Swamp? *Our Mutual Friend* and Victorian Critics   97

5   The Voice of Society: *Our Mutual Friend* since 1870   131

Appendix 1: Dickens, Ellen Ternan, and Staplehurst   159

Appendix 2: The Manuscript, the Proof Sheets, and the Berg Copy   165

Appendix 3: Contemporary Reviews of *Our Mutual Friend*   169

Appendix 4: Selected Bibliography of Editions of *Our Mutual Friend*   253

Bibliography	*257*
Index	*265*

List of Illustrations

Plates

1   A "typical" page from the manuscript of the novel.
    Our Mutual Friend by Charles Dickens, Original autograph
    manuscript with innumerable erasures and corrections.
    The Pierpont Morgan Library, New York; MA 1202, fol. 185r.
    Purchased, 1944.

2   Dickens's manuscript monthly number plan for No. 1.
    Our Mutual Friend by Charles Dickens, Original autograph
    manuscript with innumerable erasures and corrections.
    The Pierpont Morgan Library, New York; MA 1202, fol. 4r.
    Purchased, 1944.

3   Dickens's manuscript monthly number plan for No. 4.
    Our Mutual Friend by Charles Dickens, Original autograph
    manuscript with innumerable erasures and corrections.
    The Pierpont Morgan Library, New York; MA 1202, fol. 7r.
    Purchased, 1944.

4   Chapter 1, p. 3 of the Proof sheets. *Our Mutual Friend*
    by Charles Dickens, Proof sheets, with the author's ms. corrections.
    Henry W. and Albert A. Berg Collection of English and
    American Literature, The New York Public Library,
    Astor, Lenox and Tilden Foundations; vol. 1, p. 3.

5   Chapter 1, p. 3 of the first edition in 2 vols by
    Chapman and Hall. *Our Mutual Friend* by Charles Dickens
    (London: Chapman and Hall, 1865). Henry W. and Albert A. Berg
    Collection of English and American Literature, The New York
    Public Library, Astor, Lenox and Tilden Foundations; vol. 1, p. 3.

6   Dickens's manuscript monthly number plan for No. 2.
    Our Mutual Friend by Charles Dickens, Original autograph
    manuscript with innumerable erasures and corrections.
    The Pierpont Morgan Library, New York: MA 1202, fol. 5r.
    Purchased, 1944.

x   *Charles Dickens's* Our Mutual Friend

7   The end of Chapter 9, "A Marriage Contract," in manuscript.
     Our Mutual Friend by Charles Dickens, Original autograph
     manuscript with innumerable erasures and corrections.
     The Pierpont Morgan Library, New York; MA 1202, fol. 83r.
     Purchased, 1944.

8   The start of Chapter 10, "A Marriage Contract," in proofs.
     Our Mutual Friend by Charles Dickens, Proof sheets, with the
     author's ms. corrections. Henry W. and Albert A. Berg Collection
     of English and American Literature, The New York Public Library,
     Astor, Lenox and Tilden Foundations; vol. 1, p. 86.

9   The continuation of Chapter 10 in proofs. *Our Mutual Friend*
     by Charles Dickens, Proof sheets, with the author's ms. corrections.
     Henry W. and Albert A. Berg Collection of English and American
     Literature, The New York Public Library, Astor, Lenox and
     Tilden Foundations; vol. 1, p. 59 [87].

10   Dickens's note to Clowes on No. 5, in manuscript. *Our Mutual Friend*
     by Charles Dickens, Original autograph manuscript with
     innumerable erasures and corrections. The Pierpont Morgan Library,
     New York; MA 1202, fol. 120r. Purchased, 1944.

11   The beginning of Chapter 11, "Podsnappery," in manuscript.
     Our Mutual Friend by Charles Dickens, Original autograph
     manuscript with innumerable erasures and corrections.
     The Pierpont Morgan Library, New York; MA 1202, fol. 96r.
     Purchased, 1944.

12   Original pencil sketch of the monthly wrapper to *Our Mutual Friend*,
     Marcus Stone. *Our Mutual Friend* by Charles Dickens, Copy 4.
     Henry W. and Albert A. Berg Collection of English and
     American Literature, The New York Public Library,
     Astor, Lenox and Tilden Foundations.

13   The monthly wrapper of *Our Mutual Friend* as published for No. 11
     in March 1865, Marcus Stone. *Our Mutual Friend* by
     Charles Dickens, Copy 4. Henry W. and Albert A. Berg
     Collection of English and American Literature, The New York
     Public Library, Astor, Lenox and Tilden Foundations.

14   Pen-and-ink sketch (top) and published version (bottom) of
     "The Bird of Prey," Marcus Stone. *Our Mutual Friend* by
     Charles Dickens, Copy 4. Henry W. and Albert A. Berg Collection
     of English and American Literature, The New York Public Library,
     Astor, Lenox and Tilden Foundations.

List of Illustrations   xi

15 From "A Cry for Help," in manuscript, showing Dickens's
    instruction to Clowes. *Our Mutual Friend* by Charles Dickens,
    Original autograph manuscript with innumerable erasures
    and corrections. The Pierpont Morgan Library, New York;
    MA 1203, fol. 158r. Purchased, 1944.

16 Dickens's manuscript insertions A–E to Book the Fourth,
    Chapter 16. *Our Mutual Friend* by Charles Dickens,
    Original autograph manuscript with innumerable erasures
    and corrections. The Pierpont Morgan Library, New York;
    MA 1203, fol. 120r. Purchased, 1944.

Figure

A1.1 "Charles Dickens Relieving the Sufferers at the
      Fatal Railway Accident, Near Staplehurst,"
      Penny Illustrated Paper (front page), June 24, 1865.
      British Library, British Newspaper Library,
      19th Century British Library Newspapers Collection.   163

Acknowledgements

When I began working on this book more than four years ago, I could not have imagined where it—or my life—would have taken me since: to New York, over and over, as I combed the collections at the Morgan Library and at the Berg Collection of the New York Public Library; to Iowa, away from old friends and toward new ones, in a new professional setting; to new inquiries into the 1860s book market and Charles Dickens's place in it. At first I was thrilled just to participate in the scholarly effusion that Dickens's bicentenary promised, and to contribute one small verse to the magnificent celebration of his life and work. Now, I am profoundly excited and humbled by the stunning breadth of Dickens's achievement in *Our Mutual Friend*, an extraordinary novel that bred awe—but no contempt—as I grew more and more familiar with it, and that I have come to love as one of Dickens's crowning achievements. In the end, I am just childish and idealistic enough to believe that scholarly work is a labor of love, or that it ought to be, rather than just a slog toward tenure, or promotion, or the moment when nervous graduate students come to regard you yourself as one of the minor exhibits at a conference. The labor reflected in these pages has in the end been an immense joy, though it was not always so on the days when I hid in my study and, in my Trollopian way, forced myself to stay seated until I had made the daily shoes.

That labor was not unassisted, and I want here to acknowledge those who provided the necessary practical—and equally necessary impractical—help along the way. I am indebted, first and foremost, to the tireless work of the library staff at the Morgan Library and the Berg Collection, and most particularly to Alison Dickey, Head of Reader Services at the Morgan, who answered a flurry of emails and queries with extraordinary speed during the last stages of this project, and Anne Garner, Librarian at the Berg Collection, for first bringing the Berg copy of *Our Mutual Friend* to my attention and working patiently alongside me, and sometimes by telephone, as I asked questions, requested images, and ferreted through document after document in the reading room. At a late stage of the project Rebecca Filner and Isaac Gewirtz at the Berg Collection also proved to be enormous helps, and I thank them for making my last visit to the Berg a productive one. I am grateful, too, for the kind assistance of Donell Callender, Julia Iturrino, and Marilyn Garrett at the Texas Tech Library, as well as for the efficient work of the Interlibrary Loan staff there and the extraordinary energy of Monica Hicks, who shepherded me through the procedures for subventions and travel support. At Texas Tech I must also finally thank Lawrence Schovanec, then the Dean of Arts & Sciences, for supporting my work and for giving me, at a crucial time, the encouragement I needed to embark upon the next phase of my professional life. In the form of a Creative Arts, Humanities, and Social Sciences grant, too, Texas Tech was more than generous, and the university deserves richly any kind mention I can make of them here.

In the meantime, I would be remiss if I did not thank, too, my new colleagues at Iowa State and acknowledge the support of the Department of English and College of Liberal Arts & Sciences. Barbara Ching has been an excellent ally as my new chair, and Martin Spalding has been a helpful guide. My new colleagues were kind and patient enough to welcome me cheerfully at a time when this book was nearly finished, and when I tumbled into the office bleary-eyed and grumbling all too often owing to the agonies of the book's final throes. Though I was very new the College and other parts of the university assisted me with managing the final costs of images, permissions, and the other drudgery that comes at the end of a project like this one. I thank them all.

Others provided scholarly help when it was most needed and writing advice when it was most wanted, and the project is inexpressibly stronger for it. I am grateful to Robert Patten, Professor Emeritus at Rice University; to Dr. Catherine Seville at Newnham College, Cambridge; to Ann Hawkins and Jennifer Snead, former colleagues at Texas Tech; and to Ann Donahue and the erudite reader of the manuscript at Ashgate, all of whom offered brilliant suggestions with apparently unlimited tact and generosity. Just as important, I received timely, welcome, and purely unacademic support from a variety of people: at the very top of the list, my wonderful friends Ralph and Aileen, who took charge of me during my visits to New York and made sure that long days in the archives were balanced by fantastic dinners, good spirits, and incomparable company. In a broader sense I am indebted hopelessly to my parents, my wife's parents, and the many other relations and dear friends who provided so much kindness and support as I worked at this project, which turned out to be my life's greatest challenge—so far, at least—for reasons that I could not have predicted and never would have dreamed.

I must thank Mark Dickens, too, for his kind permission to publish freely from Dickens's manuscript materials related to *Our Mutual Friend*. His courtesy and promptness during the permissions-gathering phase of this work helped enormously. I am also grateful to Thomas Lisanti at the New York Public Library and David Sutton at the University of Reading for sending me Mark Dickens's way in the first place, and to William Moeck, who gave me the opportunity to present work from this book for the first time in November 2012 during the New York Public Library's "Charles Dickens: The Key to Character" Exhibition and public lecture series.

Finally I am indebted, now as always, to my wife Iris, whose strength and beauty and grace of character still leave me in awe after all these years. She is my Dora, my Agnes—occasionally even my daunting and breathtaking Estella (though, thankfully, without the apparent appetite for emotional cruelty). I could not have written this without her, cannot imagine my life without her and our bevy of four-footed children, most of whom spend their time drowsing portentously atop old copies of *Great Expectations* and drafts of chapters and piles of essays. I am endlessly grateful to live that life, and I thank her for making it and giving me a place in it. She is, like Bella Wilfer—but very unlike her, too—the true golden gold of both our lives, and I look forward to immortalizing her in another such acknowledgement very soon.

Introduction
Our Mutual Friend:
"The poorest of Mr. Dickens's works"

In December 1865, just a few weeks after Charles Dickens published the final monthly installment of *Our Mutual Friend* (1864–65), American critic Henry James wrote a grim and now-famous review of the novel for the weekly magazine *The Nation*. He did not mince words, opening with the severe verdict that *Our Mutual Friend* is "the poorest of Mr. Dickens's works. And it is poor with the poverty not of momentary embarrassment, but of permanent exhaustion."[1] James was young and brash, and he almost certainly thought far too much, far too early, of his own literary powers; the magazine was young, too, having published its inaugural issue in July that same year as the dust from the United States' Civil War settled. Decades later in his "Preface" to *The Tragic Muse* (1908) James would express his general distaste for the massive plots and superabundant prose of Dickens, Leo Tolstoy, and the other nineteenth-century literary giants by describing their novels as "large loose baggy monsters."[2] But in 1865 James confined himself strictly to enumerating Dickens's failings in this particular book, and these were apparently legion. He complained of the unreality of the novel's Jenny Wren, calling her "a little monster" and harrumphing that "she belongs to the troop of hunchbacks, imbeciles, and precocious children who have carried on the sentimental business in all Mr. Dickens's novels."[3] He complained, too, of the unmitigated—and therefore incredible—wickedness of Alfred Lammle and Fascination Fledgeby. He complained more generally that none of Dickens's characters in the novel, really, rose above caricature to offer complex psychologies, and that the novel therefore showed unequivocally that one of the "chief conditions of [Dickens's] genius [is] not to see beneath the surface of things."[4] He complained, frankly, a great deal for a 22-year-old aspirant who had published virtually nothing yet, and who was writing about the most beloved novelist of the age.

James's unrelenting attack on *Our Mutual Friend* is the best known and most frequently reprinted of the contemporary reviews, and for decades it has shaped our sense of what we know, or think we know, about the relative failures and merits of Dickens's last finished novel. Long after *Our Mutual Friend* was published, even Dickens enthusiasts and scholars often perceived the novel as a "bad book," or at least as an unpopular one, and even now, though its star

---

[1]   [Henry James], "*Our Mutual Friend*", *The Nation*, December 21, 1865, p. 786.

[2]   Henry James, *The Tragic Muse* (New York, 1908), vol. 1, p. x.

[3]   [James], "*Our Mutual Friend*", p. 787.

[4]   Ibid.

has been rising, it has little of the name recognition of *Oliver Twist* (1837–38), *David Copperfield* (1849–50), *A Tale of Two Cities* (1859), or *Great Expectations* (1860–61). This is an enormous shame, for *Our Mutual Friend* is certainly one of Dickens's most profoundly thoughtful and deliberately artistic books, and one very much worth critical and popular esteem. From the present vantage, the scorn that James heaped upon *Our Mutual Friend* looks like the product of a great many motivations—genuine distaste for the novel, certainly, but maybe, too, a dash of patriotism in the wake of Dickens's sympathy for the Confederacy, not to mention a healthy dose of the younger writer's natural desire to slay the dragon and so clear the field for the novels that he hoped someday to write, and that he and his generation did write during the last three decades of the nineteenth century. Ironically, though, James had no idea how close he was to the truth, at least in a way. Dickens was exhausted, whether or not this was evident in his art. His long physical decline began as he wrote *Our Mutual Friend* and accelerated when he traveled to America in 1867 for a grueling reading tour that sapped most of his remaining energy and strength. Though he lived for almost five more years after *Our Mutual Friend*—long enough, in his younger days, to write two or three new books—he never finished another novel.

James was probably right about other things, too, for *Our Mutual Friend* certainly has its flaws. Chief among these, perhaps, is a central marriage plot far too saccharine and unconvincing—upsetting, really, in the way that John Harmon and the Boffins take Bella Wilfer in, make her life into an appalling lie, then receive her self-abasing and immediate forgiveness because they have supposedly acted in the name of teaching her a trite "lesson" about the difference between money and true individual worth. Some readers find the opening chapters too ponderous and dark; others find them alienating, riddles to be solved rather than jovial Dickensian passages to be laughed over and enjoyed. In still other ways, *Our Mutual Friend* seems to show the artistic exhaustion that James describes, as when Dickens uses Betty Higden to have another halfhearted go at the Poor Laws, and when he fails to give her ungainly ward Sloppy anything like a credible name. Hablot K. Browne—Dickens's longtime illustrator "Phiz"—believed that Dickens knew his creative powers were waning, and he said as much when Dickens dropped him after 25 years of partnership and chose the much younger Marcus Stone to illustrate *Our Mutual Friend*. In a letter to a friend, Browne dismissed the move as sleight-of-hand, writing bitterly that "Dickens probably thinks a new hand would give his old puppets a fresh look."[5] True, several contemporary critics praised the novel warmly, among them Victorian reviewer *par excellence* E.S. Dallas, to whom

---

[5] Quoted in Valerie Browne Lester, *Phiz, the Man Who Drew Dickens* (London, 2004), p. 180. In this biography by Hablot Browne's great-great-granddaughter, she acknowledges that, in fact, Dickens probably made this change for mostly altruistic reasons, since Marcus Stone was the son of Dickens's old friend Frank Stone, who had died and left his family with very little. Lester surmises—as do several of Dickens's biographers—that Dickens probably hoped to give Marcus a chance to catch on more permanently with Chapman and Hall.

Introduction 3

an appreciative Dickens gave the novel's manuscript after his laudatory review appeared in the *Times*. But even now, and even for real enthusiasts of Dickens, *Our Mutual Friend* remains one of his least familiar works.

Yet if Dickens disappoints us occasionally in his last finished novel, he rewards us richly, too, and in ways that often carry *Our Mutual Friend* far beyond the achievements of his earlier books. He may never have drawn a character more psychologically credible than Eugene Wrayburn, more menacing than Bradley Headstone, or more compelling than Lizzie Hexam, each of whom is drawn with a subtlety that Dickens rarely approaches in his earlier fiction, and that his detractors often claimed he was simply incapable of. Likewise, his attack on "Podsnappery" and other upper-class hypocrisies cuts as deeply and cunningly as anything in *Little Dorrit* (1855–57), just as his portrayal of the dehumanizing power of capitalism broadens and deepens the critique he began in *Great Expectations*. And if the Bella/John marriage plot fails finally to move us, we nevertheless hurtle through the novel's closing chapters, propelled by Headstone's mounting rage, his savage attack on Eugene, and the grinding torments he undergoes at the hands of the novel's other consummate villain, Rogue Riderhood. Then there is the river, awash in human wreckage, the heart of both the modern metropolis and its capitalist project, sinister and sacramental, a pulsing and undulating presence that crouches at the dark center of the novel.

Our Mutual Friend is almost certainly too massive and strange ever to become popular now. Like other baggy monsters, including James's, it has outlived the taste for things of its kind. But Dickens's work in the novel is often masterful, as scholars began to recognize 40 years ago when they started returning to it persistently, dragging it out of the shadows, and admiring it more and more— not, perhaps, because it affords any distinct reading pleasure or exemplifies any particular aesthetic principle, but rather because it *is* so massive and strange, and because its massive strangeness is so very Dickensian. The Dust Mounds, the river, the Darwinian ecology, the social panorama, the psychological incisiveness, the linguistic play: these give the novel a stunning imaginative, thematic, and symbolic sweep. They make *Our Mutual Friend* seem to hold the world and everything in it. Meanwhile, the novel also strikes every note in the emotional scale, from the domestic absurdities of the Wilfers to the somber spirituality of Riah, and from the maudlin sentimentality of Little Johnny's death to the kind of physical brutality that Dickens almost never portrayed, and that he had not written of so intimately since the days of Sikes and Nancy. Returning to *Our Mutual Friend*, scholars have rediscovered an extraordinary work of literature, one that must be sounded to its critical depth if we are to understand its imaginative and ideological place within Dickens's remarkable oeuvre.

The purpose of this volume is to aid this ongoing critical reassessment and even provide a greater foundation for it by giving a publication history of *Our Mutual Friend*, by which I mean a comprehensive account of how Dickens came to write the novel, what choices he made while writing and revising, when and in what formats the novel first appeared, how it has appeared subsequently, how the novel fared financially and critically when it was first published, and how it has fared during the century and a half since. Dickens wrote *Our Mutual Friend* during a remarkable period in his life, when personal trials and physical illness exerted powerful influences upon several decisions he made about his literary work. In many respects, Dickens reinvented himself utterly in the years just before *Our Mutual Friend* by ending his marriage, breaking with old friends, and even setting aside the monthly format he loved best so that he could focus his attention on—and publish his fiction in—his own new literary and financial venture, the weekly magazine *All the Year Round*. After nearly a decade away from the form, Dickens expected, albeit somewhat nervously, that *Our Mutual Friend* would mark his triumphant return to monthly numbers. But he struggled to write installments to the proper length, to stay apace of the publishing schedule, and even, on one occasion, to rescue part of No. 16 from the splintered wreckage of a first-class railway carriage when he was nearly killed in the Staplehurst train accident. Even to expert readers, Mr. Venus seems now to belong quite organically to *Our Mutual Friend*'s thematic and symbolic concerns with reclaimed corpses and commodified subjects, yet he was an improvisation, born mainly because Dickens fumbled the length of his second installment and turned to his new illustrator for ideas. The novel's manuscript shows that Dickens often wrote easily and fluidly, as he did when describing the Wilfers at home or—more surprisingly—when he composed the fierce verbal sparring between Eugene and Headstone. At other times he labored doggedly over matters crucial to the plot, such as the specific terms of Boffin's masquerade as a miser, and over seemingly trivial things like Silas Wegg's declines and falls into mangled verse. During 1864–65, Dickens alternately wrote and struggled to write, crackled with energy and fell increasingly ill. Small wonder, then, that he produced in *Our Mutual Friend* a novel that readers have hated and loved, that sold well but not too well, and that reviewers variously called the best and worst thing he had ever done.

Working through biography, book history, and reception history, among other things, the following chapters explain in detail how these things came to be with *Our Mutual Friend* and, more broadly, how this remarkable novel came to be, as well. And while I do not necessarily aim here to celebrate or vindicate Dickens's last complete book, I confess, and even hope, that this may be an *effect* of my work. We scholars are still nearly a century behind in our critical assessment of this astonishing novel, which lingered mostly in the shadows for 75 years while critics, academic and otherwise, focused on celebrated titles like *The Pickwick Papers* (1836–37), *David Copperfield*, *Bleak House* (1852–53), and *Great Expectations*. These are important works, to be sure. Yet it is hard to imagine coming away from any serious read of *Our Mutual Friend* without coming away, too, with a marked appreciation for what the novel is, what it attempts, and what place it ought to occupy in an enduring assessment of Dickens's work. He almost certainly did not mean *Our Mutual Friend* to be a culmination. Worn out though he was by the time he finished writing it, he was already entertaining offers for a future novel, and by 1869 he was working busily at *The Mystery of Edwin Drood* (1870).

Introduction

For that matter, he so resented being reminded that he was seriously ill during the last years of his life that it is hard to see him sitting to write *Our Mutual Friend* and admitting even to himself that the novel might be his last, and that he had better use it to reckon up all of the artistic and pragmatic concerns that had, for 30 years, dominated his fiction. Still, the novel often *feels* like a culmination, concerned as it is with death and rebirth, life and afterlife, and the possibility of a glistening spiritual renewal amid the shocking realities of physical decay. More to the point, those who study Dickens have little choice but to regard *Our Mutual Friend* as a culmination. It simply came last, and it will always therefore remain the final example of Dickens's habits of writing and revision, his final striving after long-held artistic aims, his final point of contact with Victorian critics, and his final completed exchange—narrative and financial—with the innumerable readers who adored and sustained him. This publication history of *Our Mutual Friend* will, I hope, give scholars and readers a sense of that ending, and a beginning point, too, for new critical possibilities in his work.

Chapter 1, "The Man from Somewhere," gives a biography of Dickens's life during roughly the seven years before he wrote *Our Mutual Friend*, focusing principally upon those incidents and decisions that shaped Dickens's activities as an author 1857–61. At first blush, this may seem like an odd and unnecessarily long period to review; after all, Dickens wrote two novels during these years, *A Tale of Two Cities* and *Great Expectations*, and the present volume is about neither. But the start of Dickens's relationship with Ellen Ternan—Nelly, as he called her—in 1857 and the subsequent collapse of his marriage touched off a series of personal events and crises that impacted profoundly his subsequent professional course. Besides leaving *Household Words* in favor of creating *All the Year Round*—which, in turn, dictated the publication formats and artistic compressions of both *A Tale of Two Cities* and *Great Expectations*—Dickens also embarked upon a series of unprecedented and immensely profitable public readings, earning thousands of pounds and reaffirming his relationship with his adoring public at the very moment when his personal relationships were disintegrating around him. The period 1857–61 thus finds Dickens redefining himself as both a man and an author, and also banking on his work and reputation in radical new ways. *Our Mutual Friend*, which Dickens began brooding over in 1861, owes much of its shape to this period, and it may even be that the broken personal and professional relationships of these years account, at least partly, for the novel's frequent notes of isolation and despair, of lives warped and tainted by their relationship to money and exchange.

The second chapter, "The Cup and the Lip," turns from biography to textual study, providing an account of Dickens's writing activities during his months of work on *Our Mutual Friend*, then describing and providing photographic reproductions of some of the most striking elements of the novel's manuscript, held by the Pierpont Morgan Library in New York. No scholarly edition of *Our Mutual Friend* has yet been published, though one is currently in progress under the editorial direction of Leon Litvack at Queen's University, Belfast, and comparatively few scholars—Joel Brattin is the most notable—have even published essay-length textual studies. Taking its title from Dickens's epigraph for "Book the First," itself an allusion to the adage, "There's many a slip 'twixt cup and lip," this chapter argues particularly that the manuscript of *Our Mutual Friend* shows Dickens making a number of "slips" that mattered deeply to the eventual shape of the novel. Besides dealing extensively with the manuscript, the chapter draws evidence from and provides images of unique material held in the Henry W. and Albert A. Berg Collection of English and American Literature at the New York Public Library, including a volume of Proof sheets for the novel corrected partly in Dickens's hand and the remarkable Berg copy (as I call it here) of *Our Mutual Friend*, a first edition interleaved with rare and manuscript material, from the wrappers and advertisers of the original monthly numbers to the pen-and-ink drafts of Stone's illustrations, some of which bear captions in Dickens's hand. My purpose here is to show, as much as possible, Dickens at work, so that readers can see the decisions he made in planning, writing, revising, and finally publishing *Our Mutual Friend*. Partly, the chapter provides a sense of Dickens's creative process—a sense of how he transformed the original ideas for the novel into a powerful and provocative 20-number serial, and also of how he hoped to thread certain images and ideas through the whole. Mostly, it shows how profoundly and unexpectedly the material conditions under which Dickens worked ultimately shaped crucial elements of the novel.

"Putting a Price upon a Man's Mind," the third chapter, traces the novel's fate as a commodity designed for sale in the Victorian literary market. Beginning with an account of the unusual stipulation—a "death clause," for practical purposes— that Chapman and Hall worked out with Dickens in the contract for *Our Mutual Friend*, the chapter describes principally the formats in which the novel appeared during 1864–65 on both sides of the Atlantic, how these sold, and how successful the novel was commercially for Dickens and for Chapman and Hall. The publishers had plenty to lose with *Our Mutual Friend*, for they invested in it heavily: £6,000 for half copyright, plus hundreds more pounds to advertise Dickens's glorious return to monthly numbers. This, for a novel that would sell at 1s per number over 20 installments, and that probably would sell only modestly in collected form thereafter. Accordingly, the chapter tries to provide complete information about Dickens's contract with Chapman and Hall, their expenditures on Dickens's behalf, printing and sales figures for the editions of *Our Mutual Friend* brought out during the author's lifetime, and how sales of this novel compared with sales of other of Dickens's works. Robert Patten's *Charles Dickens and His Publishers* (1978) has been invaluable to this research, but I have tried also to reach beyond it to conclusions about this particular novel. One significant point that emerges from this attempt is that we must be careful in interpreting the meaning of printing and sales figures across Dickens's career, for it is not so simple as saying that *Our Mutual Friend* "failed" commercially because it did not sell as well as most of his other books. Sales certainly lagged, but they did so against the backdrop of an economic recession caused by the US Civil War, which injured the publishing

Introduction 7

industry in England and America. The question is not necessarily whether *Our Mutual Friend* sold as well as *Dombey and Son* (1846–48) or *Bleak House*; rather, it is whether it "failed" relative to other, contemporaneous works like George Eliot's *Romola* (1862–63), Anthony Trollope's *The Small House at Allington* (1864), or Wilkie Collins's *Armadale* (1865–66). Chapter 3 tries to answer that question, however cautiously and contingently.

The last two chapters—"A Dismal Swamp" and "The Voice of Society"— belong really to one extended project: chronicling *Our Mutual Friend*'s afterlife, first (in Chapter 4) by discussing the immediate responses of Victorian reviewers and readers, then (in Chapter 5) by describing the novel's century-long stay in the shadows of Dickens studies before undergoing a critical—and increasingly a popular—renaissance since roughly 1970. Predictably, Dickens's novel was reviewed by dozens of magazines and newspapers both during and immediately after its serial run. Chapter 4 discusses those reviews in detail, and all of them appear in full in Appendix 3. In its attempt to characterize and categorize the kinds of critical responses to *Our Mutual Friend* that appeared immediately upon its publication, though, Chapter 4 illustrates a major—and perhaps a surprising— point: that critical response to the novel, for all that James's attack has lived on so prominently, was mainly quite favorable. Many more contemporary reviewers agreed with our modern sense that the novel was immensely important and interesting than agreed with James and other detractors. I also use Chapter 4 to provide a longer view of the Victorian critical response to Dickens, so that opinions on *Our Mutual Friend* particularly can be understood within the context of a decades-long exchange between Dickens and his reviewers. Chapter 5, conversely, leaves Dickens's contemporaries behind in favor of what came after: a long period during which *Our Mutual Friend* was mostly neglected by critics, followed by a still-ongoing resurgence of interest in and appreciation for the novel. Much of this new attention, as I show, stems from the fact that the novel invites so many kinds of poststructuralist critical approaches, from Marxist to deconstruction to feminist and psychoanalytic theory, not to mention both historical and new historical studies of Victorian education, law, labor, and filth. Greater popular attention has followed, and from both predictable and unlikely sources, including two fine television miniseries produced by the British Broadcasting Corporation (BBC) in 1976 and 1998, a proliferation of available paperback editions, adaptations and appropriations like the 2009 20-part BBC Radio broadcast of the novel, and even reference to the novel at the Dickens World theme park.

The volume closes with four Appendices designed to provide additional resources and information for students and scholars of *Our Mutual Friend*. Appendix 1 provides transcriptions and reproductions of three items related to Dickens's relationship with Ellen Ternan and also to the Staplehurst accident. Appendix 2 describes the location and condition of the three major archival resources—the novel's manuscript, the Proof sheets, and the Berg copy—I have consulted in writing this volume and is designed to give information about the textual characteristics, usefulness, and accessibility of these materials so that scholars may undertake future studies that go beyond what I attempt here. Appendix 3 contains full transcriptions of all 41 reviews of *Our Mutual Friend* that appeared during or immediately after the novel's serialization, only 32 of which are identified in Brattin and Bert G. Hornback's excellent volume Our Mutual Friend: *An Annotated Bibliography* (1984) and almost none of which have been reproduced in their entirety in volumes like George H. Ford and Lauriat Lane's *The Dickens Critics* (1961), Philip Collins's *Dickens: The Critical Heritage* (1971), or Norman Page's *Charles Dickens:* Hard Times, Great Expectations, *and* Our Mutual Friend, *A Casebook* (1979). Last, and drawn heavily but not exclusively from Brattin and Hornback, Appendix 4 gives a comprehensive list of editions of *Our Mutual Friend* known to have been published in England and the United States during Dickens's lifetime, and a selected list of editions published after 1870.

James's criticism of *Our Mutual Friend* notwithstanding, it is just possible that this novel caught Dickens not benighted by creative poverty but rather at that breathtaking instant just before he dipped below the horizon and was lost. High noon is dazzling and brilliant, and during the middle decades of the nineteenth century, when he was at the zenith of his fame and productivity, no literary star burned more brightly or hotly than Dickens. He had flamed up suddenly with *The Pickwick Papers* and *Oliver Twist*, smoldered through the 1840s, then blazed away with unprecedented intensity through the 1850s and early 1860s as he wrote masterpiece after masterpiece—*David Copperfield, Bleak House, Hard Times* (1854), *Little Dorrit, A Tale of Two Cities, Great Expectations*—each novel winning more readers and raising him to a new height. But sunset is lovely in another way, for it is the time of impossible hues and shades, when the world shimmers with an unearthly beauty that makes everything sharp and distinct even as it presages the coming dark. *Our Mutual Friend* is both massive and unearthly, drawing us down into the primordial ooze of the river one minute and inviting us to "come up and be dead" the next.[6] It is the story of the world, a topography and archaeology of Dickens and his ever-undisciplined heart, a portrait of the artist as an old man. With apologies to James, *Our Mutual Friend* may be the very richest of Dickens's works. Two hundred years after his birth, these pages attempt to show how and why.

---

[6] Charles Dickens, *Our Mutual Friend* (London, 1997), p. 280.

Chapter 1
The Man from Somewhere: Ellen Ternan, Staplehurst, and the Remaking of Charles Dickens

Dickens glided purposefully among the dying and dead, administering what comfort he could to those lying injured at the bottom of the ravine. Minutes earlier he had been aboard the 2:38 tidal train from Folkestone to London, nestled comfortably in a first-class carriage and, just perhaps, talking amiably with his two female companions (one older, one much younger) or imagining the work to be done on *Our Mutual Friend*'s 16th monthly installment, most of which he was carrying back from his holiday in Boulogne. But a panic, then the scream of grating metal and a terrible wild careening, had changed all that in an instant, and he now moved through a nightmare of splintered wreckage and agonized groans. "No imagination," Dickens wrote to his friend Thomas Mitton a few days later, "can conceive of the ruin of carriages, or the extraordinary weights under which people were lying, or the complications into which they were twisted up among iron and wood."[1] As the *Times* described the scene the next day, "[t]he carriages that went down were so twisted, flattened, and turned upon their sides that it was impossible to say whether the unfortunate travellers inside had been killed outright by the shock or suffocated as they lay in the water and mud."[2] Ten passengers died in the accident at Staplehurst on June 9, 1865, and dozens more were injured. The great Dickens, the *Times* reported—"fortunately for himself and for the interests of literature"—walked away unharmed.[3]

The next week the inquest into the Staplehurst accident determined that railway workers had caused the problem as they attempted to replace rails on a small viaduct spanning the river Beult. In an unlucky moment, the foreman had consulted the timetable for the wrong day, so he expected no train for two more hours; meanwhile, the flagman, who should have been at least 1,000 yards from the site to warn oncoming traffic, had positioned himself scarcely 500 yards from the dismantled bridge.[4] Barreling downhill at nearly 50 miles an hour, the train

---

[1]   Charles Dickens, *The Letters of Charles Dickens* (Oxford, 1965–2002), vol. 11, p. 57.

[2]   "Dreadful Railway Accident at Staplehurst," *Times*, June 10, 1865, p. 9. The entire *Times* article is transcribed as Item B in Appendix 1.

[3]   Ibid.

[4]   Edgar Johnson, *Charles Dickens: His Tragedy and Triumph* (New York, 1952), vol. 2, p. 1018. Despite the more recent biography by Claire Tomalin (*Charles Dickens: A Life* [New York, 2011]), the most detailed accounts of Dickens's involvement in the Staplehurst accident appear in Johnson, vol. 2, pp. 1018–21; Peter Ackroyd, *Dickens* (New York, 1990), pp. 958–64; and Michael Slater, *Charles Dickens* (New Haven, 2009), pp. 534–6.

had no chance. The driver whistled desperately for the brakes when he saw the flagman, and a guard immediately applied them, but the engine still reached the bridge at around 20 miles an hour, jumped the 42-foot gap, lurched sideways, and rolled to a stop.[5] Only three cars back, Dickens's carriage nearly jumped the gap, too, but came to rest dangling precariously over the side of the ruined bridge, suspended by its coupling to the second-class carriage in front. Behind, all was chaos and ruin. The rear coupling to Dickens's carriage had broken, and the other first-class carriages had tumbled through the gap and down the riverbank, flipping and smashing to pieces in the muddy ground below. When Dickens realized that the immediate danger had passed, he calmed his female companions, then hailed the guard and demanded a key. In minutes, with the help of a workman and a makeshift ramp made of wooden planks, he had emptied his carriage and ushered its occupants to the safety of the riverbank, where he set about the grisly work of aiding the passengers lying bloodied and broken among the demolished cars. For three hours he administered brandy from his traveling flask and scrambled to and from the river's edge, retrieving water in his hat.[6] On June 24 the *Penny Illustrated Paper* gave a front-page sketch of Dickens tending the injured at Staplehurst, and the directors of the railway company sent him a "Resolution of Thanks."[7] Through the hours of dreadful toil, he told Mitton, he preserved his "constitutional (I suppose) presence of mind"—so much so that, in the middle of it all, he had a sudden realization and climbed back up into the still-dangling carriage. There, he retrieved from the pocket of his overcoat the unfinished manuscript of *Our Mutual Friend*'s 16th number.[8]

Time has erased any sign of the Staplehurst crash from the manuscript of *Our Mutual Friend*, but the story of the accident and all that led up to it still bears heavily upon the story of Dickens's last completed novel. Soon after the crash, Dickens's "presence of mind" gave way to clear signs of just how badly he had been shaken. He sent dozens of letters to friends on June 11, 12, and 13 to reassure them that he was unharmed, but he wrote very few of these himself, for he could scarcely hold a pen. His sister-in-law Georgina Hogarth wrote the lion's share, leaving Dickens merely to add the occasional postscript, or only to sign, mostly without even his usual flourish.[9] To his *All the Year Round* subeditor W.H. Wills and his friend John Forster, he confided that he would "turn faint and sick" after writing just a few notes, and three weeks after the accident he rejoiced that he had finally "even got [his] voice back," having "most unaccountably brought

---

[5] "Chapter of Accidents," *Examiner*, June 17, 1865, p. 383.

[6] The *Examiner*'s June 17, 1865, report on the inquest includes a passenger's eyewitness account of Dickens's efforts at the scene of the crash. See p. 383. The illustration, "Charles Dickens Relieving the Sufferers at the Fatal Railway Accident, Near Staplehurst," appears as Item C in Appendix 1.

[7] *Letters*, vol. 11, p. 65.

[8] Ibid., p. 57.

[9] See Dickens's various letters of June 11–13, 1865, in *Letters*, vol. 11, pp. 51–8.

The Man from Somewhere   11

somebody else's out of that terrible scene."[10] In London he could not bear the noise of the traffic, while at Gad's Hill, where it was quieter, he urged his eldest son Charley incessantly to "go slower" in the basket-carriage, even when they already crept along at a footpace.[11] One week after Staplehurst, with his characteristic will, Dickens did force himself back onto a train—a slow one, not an express—to begin conquering his fear, but he nonetheless suffered for the rest of his life from "sudden vague rushes of terror" during train travel, against which he fortified himself with brandy and sheer mental resolve.[12] Years later, in his memoir of his father, Charley called the accident "such a shock to the nervous system as [his father] never quite got over," and indeed, in a coincidence worthy of Dickens, he died on the fifth anniversary of the crash.[13]

Small wonder, then, that Dickens, having retreated to Gad's Hill on the evening after the accident, made it known to the authorities that he did not wish to testify at the inquest. Who could blame him? He was 53 years old and in declining health, and he had exerted himself furiously for hours amid appalling scenes on the day in question. More, to Dickens's unnaturally vivid imagination, the horrors of Staplehurst must have been present daily, hourly, constantly, unwelcome and unbidden. Yet Dickens did use June 12, the day on which the inquest began, to take care of one bit of crash-related business. He wrote to the manager at Charing Cross station on behalf of the younger of his female companions from that day, explaining that she had lost several "trinkets" in her struggle to get free of the carriage: "a gold watch-chain with a smaller gold watch chain attached, a bundle of charms, a gold watch-key, and a gold seal engraved 'Ellen.'"[14] A simple letter enough, but one pregnant with meaning. For "Ellen" was almost certainly Ellen Lawless Ternan, known familiarly as Nelly, the much younger woman with whom Dickens had carried on a clandestine relationship since 1857, and who, from that time, exerted a powerful influence upon his life and work. And Dickens had almost certainly refused to testify at the inquest for a reason that was *cliché* long before our postmodern times: he did not wish to explain publicly why he had been traveling with a pretty young woman who was not his wife.

To say that *Our Mutual Friend* owes much to the presence of Nelly is to say only what Edmund Wilson first made fashionable nearly 75 years ago when he published "Dickens: The Two Scrooges." Since then, biographical critics have looked for Nelly—and of course found her—in all of Dickens's later novels, though she seems to have been a rather inconsistent character. She is Lucie Manette in *A Tale of Two Cities*, young and gentle and pretty and replete with golden curls, and later she is Estella, the heartless gold-digging monster who

---

[10]   Ibid., pp. 58, 55, 65.

[11]   Charley Dickens, "Glimpses of Charles Dickens," in Norman Page (ed.), *Charles Dickens: Family History* (5 vols, London, 1999), vol. 1, p. 679.

[12]   *Letters*, vol. 12, p. 175.

[13]   Charley Dickens, vol. 1, p. 679.

[14]   *Letters*, vol. 11, p. 53.

blights Pip's life in *Great Expectations*. In *Our Mutual Friend* she is both Bella Wilfer and Lizzie Hexam, simultaneously another Estella reclaimed from the dust heap of sordid money-grubbing and an intrinsically worthy young woman rescued from poverty by a gentleman who cannot decide whether to make her his mistress or his wife. For all we know, during the period after 1857 Nelly may have been all of these, dispersed across the later fiction in the same way that Dickens dispersed himself across Sydney Carton, Pip , Eugene, John Harmon, and even the murderous Headstone. For Dickens, as for most writers, some things—the prison, the orphan, the angel in the house—simply became haunting refrains. Yet the biographical critics are not necessarily wrong when they suggest that Ellen mattered generally to Dickens's later work, or particularly to *Our Mutual Friend*. They have only misplaced their emphasis by suggesting that she did so in such tenuous ways. The story of Lizzie Hexam or Bella Wilfer *may* be some version of the story of Dickens's emotional life with Nelly during the 1860s. But the story of how Dickens came to write *Our Mutual Friend*—how he envisioned it, struggled with it, and eventually triumphed through it—is undeniably a story about Nelly, and about the ways in which their relationship drove Dickens to remake himself personally and professionally in the years leading up to the novel.

During a remarkable two-year period that began in August 1857, Dickens detonated his private life in a series of decisions that had enormous implications, too, for his life as an editor and novelist. He separated from his wife Catherine, initiated a secret relationship with Nelly, quarreled openly with old friends, and only narrowly escaped the kind of public scandal that would have laid waste to his reputation as the great novelist of Victorian morality and the pleasures of the domestic hearth. As a consequence, he also set about reinventing himself for the public, staking out a bold new professional course that fundamentally altered both the nature and form of his writing activities for the last decade of his life. He broke with his longtime publishers Bradbury and Evans after 15 years, abandoned the editorship of *Household Words*, and decided instead not only to create but also to finance his own weekly magazine, *All the Year Round*, which in turn caused him to leave behind for the better part of a decade the monthly publication format that had made his work accessible to enormous numbers of Victorian readers. Determined to face down the scandal and cement his relationship with his reading public, he also embarked upon an unprecedented and wildly profitable career as a public performer, giving readings from his old work and *becoming* his characters before packed houses in London, the provinces, and eventually the United States. In all of this he was carefully and consciously remaking himself and redefining the meaning of his "authorship": establishing new financial relations between his editorial work and the Victorian periodicals market, writing and publishing in new formats, and, by merging his identity publicly into the characters he had created, cultivating an unusual intimacy between himself and his readers. The history of *Our Mutual Friend* thus begins with the story of Nelly and how she came to be with Dickens on the day that the 2:38 tidal train crashed at Staplehurst.

I

So much has been written about Dickens's relationship with Ellen Ternan that it is hard to imagine doing justice to the subject without giving it a monograph of its own. Fortunately, Michael Slater has very recently done just that, to great effect, in *The Great Charles Dickens Scandal* (2012), where he updates not only the biographies of Dickens on this matter but also Claire Tomalin's indispensable *The Invisible Woman: The Story of Nelly Ternan and Charles Dickens* (1991). No biography of Dickens since the 1940s has failed to discuss at length the known details of this relationship, undoubtedly the most important one of the last decade of Dickens's life. For nearly 60 years after Dickens's death, common decency was enough to muzzle most speculation, and the affair that had been a *cause célèbre* in 1858 faded into obscurity. But this began to change when C.E. Bechhofer Roberts published his novel *This Side Idolatry* (1928), based on biographical details about Dickens—up to, but not quite including, the Nelly scandal—and casting him in a very unflattering fictional light.[15] Seven years later, when Thomas Wright published *The Life of Charles Dickens* (1935), in which he claimed to know from those who had been personally acquainted with Nelly later in her life that she and Dickens had a sexual affair, he resurrected a scandal that had nearly been forgotten and laid the groundwork for the questions that have most tantalized Dickens's biographers since.[16] Whether Dickens and Nelly ever really had a sexual affair, whether she bore him a child that died in infancy, whether Dickens's marriage finally collapsed when a piece of jewelry meant for Nelly was mistakenly delivered to his wife, whether Charley really discovered the affair when he stumbled upon his father and the pretty young actress walking alone on Hampstead Heath—these are questions that, barring some stunning evidentiary find, no biographer will ever answer with any certainty now. Dickens covered his tracks too well. He set out consciously and deliberately to craft a frenetic double life, intending to baffle the scrutiny of not only his contemporaries but also those like Wright and the others who have followed in his wake.

Having ended his marriage in a deplorably public way in 1858, Dickens remained, to most casual observers, the jolly *paterfamilias* of Gad's Hill, living with

---

[15] Michael Slater, *The Great Charles Dickens Scandal* (New Haven, 2012), pp. 56–9.

[16] Foremost of Wright's sources was William Benham, Canon of Canterbury, to whom (according to Wright) Ellen "told the whole story" of her time as Dickens's mistress "and declared that she loathed the very thought of this intimacy." See Thomas Wright, *The Life of Charles Dickens* (London, 1935), p. 356. In other papers, including in a letter to Dickensians J.W.T. Ley and Walter Dexter and in his unfinished autobiography *Thomas Wright of Olney* (published posthumously in 1936), Wright made other significant and unsubstantiated claims, including that Dickens and Ellen had children. For an excellent overview of Wright's role in provoking this line of inquiry and of the biographers who followed in his wake, see Slater's *The Great Charles Dickens Scandal* or, for a brief version, his Appendix B to *Dickens and Women* (Stanford, 1983), pp. 376–9. For a general summary of biographies of Dickens published 1870–1950, see T.W. Hill's two-part essay, "Dickensian Biography," *Dickensian*, 47 (1951), pp. 10–15, 72–9.

his sister-in-law Georgina and adult daughter Mamie (Mary) and welcoming his sons home from business exploits and terms of study abroad. But privately he was restive, oscillating constantly and warily between Gad's Hill, the London office of *All the Year Round*, and anywhere—Oxford Street, Ampthill Square, Slough, Peckham, Condette—he could steal time with Nelly. He would, as he wrote to intimate friends like Wills and Wilkie Collins, "vanish into space" for a few days or make a "Mysterious Disappearance" between dates of his reading tours.[17] Meanwhile, to many of his acquaintances, he gave contradictory accounts of his movements, then simply disappeared from view. Still, what we do know of Dickens's relationship with Nelly during these years—particularly at the beginning, when his infatuation with her drove him to extraordinary measures—is more than enough to show how profoundly she impacted his decisions about his writing during the last decade of his life, and especially in the years between *Little Dorrit* and *Our Mutual Friend*.

Dickens met Nelly in August 1857 when he hired her, her sister Maria, and their mother Frances to play the principal female roles for two performances of Wilkie Collins's play *The Frozen Deep* (1857) at the Free Trade Hall in Manchester. Dickens and Collins had collaborated extensively on the play during the autumn of 1856 while Dickens worked feverishly at both *Little Dorrit* and "The Wreck of the Golden Mary" (1856), the Christmas book he co-authored with Collins that year. Collins had done most of the writing for *The Frozen Deep*, but Dickens, with his typical zeal for all things related to the theater, had provided an endless stream of suggestions—so many that, according to Edgar Johnson, "[i]n its ultimate form … [the play] was almost as much his work as it was Collins's."[18] After a dress rehearsal on January 5, Dickens and company staged the play for the first time on January 6, 1857, as a night of amateur theatricals at Tavistock House, with Dickens and Collins themselves taking the lead roles and the rest of the cast including Georgina, Charley, Dickens's daughters Katey (Kate) and Mamie, and family friends like Forster, Mark Lemon, and Augustus Egg.[19] This initial performance was repeated on January 8, 12, and 14, each time for an audience of nearly 100 people who crammed themselves into the little schoolroom theater that Dickens had fitted up elaborately to that purpose. After the last performance, workmen descended upon the schoolroom and dismantled the temporary theater, and here things ended until the death in June of Dickens's friend Douglas Jerrold, an actor who left behind a wife and children in straitened circumstances. By midsummer, on behalf of the Jerrold Fund, Dickens had arranged a series of public performances of *The Frozen Deep* at the Gallery of Illustration on Regent Street and a private performance there for an enthusiastic Queen Victoria.[20] Then came the agreement to perform the play at Manchester.

---

[17] *Letters*, vol. 10, pp. 187, 409.

[18] Johnson, vol. 2, p. 866.

[19] Slater, *Charles Dickens*, p. 417.

[20] Victoria wanted Dickens and his company to come perform the play at Buckingham Palace, but Dickens objected on the grounds that his daughters had not yet been presented at court and ought not to appear there, in the first instance, as actresses. For accounts of this see Johnson, vol. 2, pp. 872–3; Slater, *Charles Dickens*, p. 427; and Tomalin, *Charles Dickens*, p. 282.

The Man from Somewhere   15

The difficulty with Manchester, Dickens realized immediately, was that the Free Trade Hall was immense, able to hold 2,000 people—far too large, he reasoned, for amateurs like his daughters and Georgina to make themselves heard.[21] He therefore approached his friend Alfred Wigan, manager of the Olympic theatre, to ask about professional actresses who might play the female parts. Wigan recommended the Ternans, two of whom—Nelly's elder sisters, Maria and Fanny—he had already engaged for the Olympic. Frances Ternan was an accomplished professional, having been on the stage since she was a child in the north of England.[22] Later, after marrying fellow-actor and theater manager Thomas Ternan in 1834, she toured in the United States before returning to England and gaining a strong reputation, acting with Dickens's eventual friend William Macready in various productions of Shakespeare and drawing favorable comparisons to Fanny Kelly and Fanny Kemble.[23] But Thomas died in 1845 after two years in the Insane Asylum at Bethnal Green, where he had likely been suffering from the final stages of syphilis.[24] He left behind his wife and three daughters, the youngest of whom, Nelly, was six, and for the next decade the Ternan girls struggled along, all of them on the stage, and all with reputations for the most perfect respectability despite contemporary prejudices against actresses. Late in 1846, Macready helped the Ternans with a gift of 10 pounds, and Tomalin points out that had Dickens not been in Geneva just then working on *Dombey and Son*, Macready might "have applied to him for further help for the Ternans" considering Dickens's habitual generosity with the families of artists.[25] He might then have met the seven-year-old Nelly; the future course of things might have changed. As it was, in 1857 Dickens took Wigan's suggestion and simply asked Mrs. Ternan, Maria, and the 18-year-old Nelly to appear in *The Frozen Deep* when it went to Manchester on August 21 and 22. They accepted, with the pretty but young and undemonstrative Ellen taking a minor role while her older, more vivacious sister acted the romantic heroine opposite Dickens.

The Ternans' effect on Dickens was electric—partly, no doubt, because of his fascination with all things related to the stage, which may have been heightened in this case by the vague romance of this household of women, vulnerable but struggling mightily and virtuously to make good. Part of Dickens's immediate emotional response must have stemmed, too, from the raw intensity of the play's final scene, in which Dickens, in the role of Richard Wardour, struggled onto the stage after weeks lost in the arctic only to die at the feet of the woman he loves, Clara Burnham (played by Maria), while also restoring to her the man

---

[21]   Ackroyd, p. 786.

[22]   For a detailed account of Frances Ternan's professional career and the lives and careers of her daughters, see Claire Tomalin, *The Invisible Woman: The Story of Nelly Ternan and Charles Dickens* (New York, 1991).

[23]   Johnson, vol. 2, p. 876.

[24]   Tomalin, *Invisible Woman*, pp. 45–6.

[25]   Tomalin, *Charles Dickens*, p. 186.

she loves but has feared dead. To modern readers *The Frozen Deep* may seem like little more than above-average Victorian melodrama. But those who saw Dickens perform as Wardour during 1857 were stunned by his power. Maria had seen him do so at the Gallery of Illustration earlier in the summer, and she confided to him during rehearsals her fear that she would not be able to control her emotions during the final scene. She could not, nor could Lemon ("the softest hearted of men"), nor could the rest of the cast, all of whom wept together at the end of the play and had to be comforted before the start of *Uncle John*, the farce that followed *The Frozen Deep* after an intermission.[26] Of the second night at Manchester, Collins later said that Dickens performed "a magnificent piece of acting. He literally electrified the audience."[27] Initially, as a letter from Dickens to his friend Angelina Burdett Coutts on September 5 suggests, he may have been have been fascinated by Maria rather than Nelly.[28] But it was Nelly, the youngest, with her golden hair and retiring personality, to whom Dickens eventually turned, perhaps because she was so precisely like the romantic heroines he had idolized since the death of his young sister-in-law Mary Hogarth in 1837.[29]

But something else was also at work—something that made Dickens all the more susceptible to Nelly's inadvertent charms, and that explains the violence of feeling with which he responded to events in the months that followed. For nearly three years, Dickens had confided to friends his unhappiness with the life he was obliged to lead. He had grown restless and dissatisfied, having risen to the very top of the literary world, but having also reached middle age and, as David Copperfield might say, found something wanting. "Why is it," he wrote to Forster in early February 1855, "that as with David, a sense comes always crushing upon me now, when I fall into low spirits, as of one happiness I have missed in life, and one friend and companion I have never made?"[30] Though he began confessing it openly only around this time, much evidence suggests that his domestic unhappiness, or at least his restlessness, was of much longer standing. The comparison to David implies that he felt this want, however vaguely, as early as 1849, and even before this he had occasionally cultivated intimacies with and developed attachments for other women in ways that made Catherine unhappy. As Lillian Nayder points out, during the mid-1840s Catherine had objected to Dickens's intimacy with their Genovese friend Madame de la Rue, and in 1844 he had become infatuated suddenly with a young woman named Christiana Weller, who reminded him—but apparently

---

[26]   See Dickens's letter to Angelina Burdett Coutts on September 5, 1857, in *Letters*, vol. 8, pp. 432–4.

[27]   Quoted in Johnson, vol. 2, p. 878.

[28]   *Letters*, vol. 8, pp. 432–4. Slater makes this point as well. See *Charles Dickens*, p. 435.

[29]   For more on Dickens's strange obsession with Mary Hogarth, see Johnson, vol. 1, pp. 195–204; Ackroyd, pp. 212–43; and Tomalin, *Charles Dickens*, pp. 78–80.

[30]   *Letters*, vol. 7, p. 523.

no one else—of the dead Mary Hogarth.[31] By 1855, this discontent seemed to be building toward some indefinite crisis that found its way into his letters with greater and greater regularity, and that would soon erupt into action.

On February 7 Dickens discovered that the house at Gad's Hill Place had come up for sale, rife as it was with memories of his father and the ambitions of his youth. And on February 9, after more than a decade, he heard from Mrs. Henry Winter, formerly Maria Beadnell, the first love who had rejected him two decades before. He responded eagerly—and secretly—to her letter and eventually agreed to meet her, but he was disappointed to find her old, fat, and toothless, and characterized by the vapid garrulity that he lampooned in Flora Finching in *Little Dorrit*.[32] Catherine, too, had grown heavy after 12 pregnancies in 15 years, and Dickens regarded her family—Georgina excepted—with growing distaste and scorn. As he approached middle age, Dickens found Catherine's weight and lassitude to be useful foils against which to consider his own still-youthful energy, even though, as Nayder points out, Catherine was nothing like as indolent as Dickens often claimed.[33] Still, his marriage was failing. His children were disappointments. Old friends like Jerrold were dying. His early life was passing away. As he prepared to start *Little Dorrit* in 1855, he wrote to several friends that they might eventually hear of him having run off to the North Pole or having locked himself away in a secluded chalet in the Alps where he could lead his rich imaginative life in isolation.[34] In April 1856 he wrote to Forster, "The old days—the old days! Shall I ever, I wonder, get the frame of mind back as it used to be then? Something of it perhaps—but never quite as it used to be. I find that the skeleton in my domestic closet is becoming a pretty big one."[35] It had become so big, in fact, that it is difficult now to tell whether Dickens's sudden and intense infatuation with Nelly was the cause or only a consequence of his failing marriage.

Either way, the end of the Manchester performances left Dickens crushed. For a few days he busied himself with work associated with *Household Words* and supervised laborers digging a new well at Gad's Hill, which he had bought. But to Hannah Brown on August 28 he wrote describing his "restlessness," saying, "I feel as if the scaling of all the Mountains in Switzerland, or the doing of any wild thing until I dropped, would be but a slight relief."[36] The next day he wrote Collins in "grim despair" to propose that the two of them "go anywhere—take any tour—see

---

[31] Lillian Nayder, *The Other Dickens: A Life of Catherine Hogarth* (Ithaca, 2011), p. 118; Tomalin, *Charles Dickens*, pp. 151–2. Nayder's biography of Catherine explores carefully and cogently Dickens's emotional attachments to a number of women during the course of his marriage, most of them long before the trouble with Nelly began in 1857.

[32] See Nayder, p. 236.

[33] Ibid., pp. 236–7.

[34] See for instance Dickens's letters to Mrs. Winter on April 3, 1855, and Forster on January 20, 1856. *Letters*, vol. 7, p. 584 and vol. 8, p. 33.

[35] Ibid., vol. 8, p. 89.

[36] Ibid., p. 422.

18 *Charles Dickens's* Our Mutual Friend

any thing—whereon we could write something together ... For, when I *do* start up and stare myself seedily in the face, as happens to be my case at present, my blankness is inconceivable—indescribable—my misery amazing."[37] In a letter to Forster a few days later, he finally and for the first time confessed his misery at home, as if somehow the dizzying experience of performing at Manchester with the alluring Ternans had driven him to a breaking point. Telling Forster that he wished to give himself the "relief of saying a word of what has long been pent up in my mind," Dickens wrote:

> Poor Catherine and I are not made for each other, and there is no help for it. It is not only that she makes me uneasy and unhappy, but that I make her so too—and much more so. She is exactly what you know, in the way of being amiable and complying; but we are strangely ill-assorted for the bond there is between us. God knows she would have been a thousand times happier if she had married another kind of man ... It mattered not so much when we had only ourselves to consider, but reasons have been growing since which make it all but hopeless that we should even try to struggle on. What is now befalling me I have seen steadily coming, ever since the days you remember when Mary was born [in 1838]; and I know too well that you cannot, and no one can, help me.[38]

Striking here is the absence of recrimination: at this early stage, Dickens seems to have understood that his failing marriage was at least as much his fault as his wife's. Two days later, continuing his exchange with Forster, he revived an old idea of earning money by traveling the country and giving paid readings from his books. Clearly he could not rest. For Dickens—perhaps because here, as in so many other things with him, writing it seemed to make it so—all appears to have been over with his wife by September 4 or 5, 1857. Then, on September 7, Dickens and Collins set out, nominally to "see any thing" they might write about in five installments for *Household Words*, but really to Doncaster in pursuit of the Ternans, who were engaged at the Theatre Royal there for the week of the St. Leger's Day race.

In this sense, though she did not know it, Nelly's impact on Dickens's writing was immediate, for the travelogue that emerged from this trip, "The Lazy Tour of Two Idle Apprentices" (1857), would not have been written if not for her, the trip never taken.[39] More, the strange contents seem often to be about Nelly, either because of Dickens's real experiences with her at Doncaster or because of the taut emotional life his infatuation was obliging him to lead. For the most part, "The Lazy Tour" is a bizarre pastiche made up alternately of real incidents, ghost stories, and flights of imaginative fancy narrated through the eyes of Dickens's and Collins's alter egos, Francis Goodchild and Thomas Idle. Dickens took the names from William Hogarth's *Industry and Idleness*, of course, but something

---

[37] Ibid., p. 423.

[38] Ibid., p. 430.

[39] Co-authored by Dickens and Collins, "The Lazy Tour" appeared in *Household Words* in five weekly installments October 3–October 31, 1857.

curious and ominous underlies his decision to assume the persona of a "good child" in the very act of pursuing Nelly and abandoning his wife. In "The Lazy Tour" only Chapter 5, the final installment, details the week that Dickens and Collins spent at Doncaster, and here the narrative rages against drunken "gentlemen" who interrupt the theater—and who perhaps had interrupted Nelly—by putting "vile constructions on sufficiently innocent phrases in the play."[40] Later, Goodchild falls into a deliberately sentimentalized rapture, recorded as part of the last day of the St. Leger, about "little lilac gloves" and a "winning little bonnet, making in conjunction with her golden hair quite a Glory in the sunlight round the pretty head."[41]

Earlier chapters hint at a different, much darker kind of emotional intensity, particularly Chapter 4, where Dickens crafts a ghost story involving a man who marries a woman whom he does not love—named Ellen—then kills her simply by appearing before her and ordering her, day after day, to "Die!"[42] As with Dickens's later novels, we cannot possibly know how much of this writing he meant as explicit commentaries on his real life, with Nelly or with Catherine. Clearly, though, the new relationship with the former had seized his entire being. On September 17 he wrote to Wills from Doncaster, saying that he had gone there "along of his Richard Wardour!" and continuing, "Guess *that* riddle, Mr. Wills!—"; three days later he wrote again to say that he intended to "take the little—riddle—into the country this morning."[43] These were the first sallies in what became a decade-long practice of concealing his movements and writing in code. A few days later he was back at Gad's Hill, his feelings having become "more complex, more painful and more intense," and he spent the next two weeks studiously avoiding his wife and her family, who had come to stay with her at Tavistock House.[44] In early October he did finally try to stay at Tavistock House with Catherine and his in-laws, with the result that a quarrel drove him out upon the streets at 2 A.M., when he walked the entire 30 miles to Gad's Hill.[45] On October 11, never really having returned to Catherine, he took a decisive step: he wrote to his trusted servant Anne Cornelius and gave her instructions for sealing up the doorway between his and Catherine's rooms, effecting his permanent removal from their marital bed.

For the next several months, things seem to have continued in this impossibly tense state. Dickens often behaved indefensibly, and, as Johnson puts it, "Tavistock House, during these months, was an unhappy home. There were no children's theatricals on Twelfth Night. Kate wept in her lonely room, Georgina kept the house going, and Dickens debated trying to begin a new book" instead of embarking upon the paid readings he had begun to contemplate in September.[46]

---

40   Charles Dickens, "The Lazy Tour of Two Idle Apprentices," in *The Dent Uniform Edition of Dickens' Journalism*, ed. Michael Slater, 4 vols (London, 1994–2000), p. 472.

41   Ibid., p. 471.

42   Ibid., p. 455.

43   *Letters*, vol. 8, pp. 449, 450.

44   Tomalin, *Invisible Woman*, p. 105.

45   Slater, *Charles Dickens*, p. 438.

46   Johnson, vol. 2, p. 912.

20   *Charles Dickens's* Our Mutual Friend

He was simultaneously paralyzed by the gulf between what he wanted and what he thought possible and goaded nearly to madness by his need to *act*, somehow. To Forster he wrote, "Too late to say, put the curb on, and don't rush at hills—the wrong man to say it to. I have no relief but in action. I am become incapable of rest," while to his old friend Mrs. Richard Watson he confided:

> I wish I had been born in the days of Ogres and Dragon-guarded Castles. I wish an Ogre with seven heads ... had taken the Princess whom I adore—you have no idea how intensely I love her!—to his stronghold on the top of a high series of Mountains, and there tied her up by the hair. Nothing would suit me half so well this day, as climbing after her, sword in hand, and either winning her or being killed.—*There's* a state of mind for you, in 1857.[47]

So Dickens, in his imaginings, turned himself into the potential hero of chivalric romance, and in a letter remarkable, too, for its extended description of the Manchester performances four months earlier. Meanwhile, he had also begun rewriting the history of his marriage, now blaming Catherine for her inability ever to be happy, her excruciating jealousy, and her incapacity even for getting on with their children.[48] God knows what Dickens wanted at this time. He was a mercurial compound of romantic intensity and bitterness. But certainly he did not want to be at Tavistock House with Catherine and the Hogarths. He made extended trips away from home and, for the first time, refused to write to Catherine while away.[49] Throughout March he made inquiries and sought Forster's approval for the idea of a public reading tour, and on April 29 he delivered the first such reading, *The Cricket on the Hearth*, in London at St. Martin's Hall.[50] During the next three months he gave 15 more. But he was no nearer to having either Nelly or the domestic happiness he had now convinced himself he had always missed.

Then, like a thunderclap, the storm finally broke. Perhaps this was the time of the incident with the misdirected jewelry, or perhaps the time when Charley encountered Nelly and his father walking on Hampstead Heath.[51] Perhaps Dickens

---

[47] *Letters*, vol. 8, pp. 646, 488.

[48] Ibid., pp. 471–2.

[49] Nayder, p. 248. See also Slater, *Charles Dickens*, p. 436.

[50] Malcolm Andrews, *Charles Dickens and His Performing Selves: Dickens and Public Readings* (Oxford, 2006), p. 269. Andrews's study is an excellent biographical and critical account of what Dickens hoped to do with his public readings. Among other things it includes a complete schedule of the readings Dickens gave 1853–70. See pp. 267–90. For texts of the readings—and for Philip Collins's excellent introduction to them—see Charles Dickens, *The Public Readings* (Oxford, 1975).

[51] In *The* Punch *Brotherhood: Table Talk and Print Culture in Mid-Victorian London* (London, 2010), Patrick Leary traces the story of the jewelry back as far as an entry in Richard Bentley's diary for March 23, 1859, before pointing out helpfully that Tomalin mentions the incident, traced to other evidence, in *Invisible Woman*. See Leary, p. 88 and note 35; Tomalin, *Invisible Woman*, pp. 110–11 and note 23; and Slater, *The Great Charles Dickens Scandal*, chs. 1 and 2. The story of Charley encountering the pair is also given in Slater, *The Great Charles Dickens Scandal*, pp. 25–6; Tomalin, *Invisible Woman*, p. 111; Ackroyd, p. 827; and Nayder, p. 260.

The Man from Somewhere 21

could no longer tolerate things as they were and decided to act. Or perhaps the Hogarths, fully aware of Dickens's growing contempt for them, finally persuaded the normally easygoing Catherine that she deserved better from her straying husband, literary genius though he was, and that she ought to disbelieve his constant assertion that he had.only an innocent interest in the poor fatherless girl. We cannot know for sure. But on May 9, 1858 Dickens wrote to their mutual friend Miss Coutts to announce his separation from his wife. In the days ahead, Dickens would claim that Catherine had "for some years past ... been in the habit of representing to [him] that it would be better for her to go away and live apart."[52] At this early stage, however, he simply told Miss Coutts, "We have been virtually separated for a long time. We must put a wider space between us now, than can be found in one house."[53] He also continued to elaborate the thesis that Catherine had never had a good relationship with the children—an allegation that the evidence certainly does not support—writing,

> If the children loved her, or ever had loved her, this severance would have been a far easier thing than it is. But she has never attached one of them to herself ... never attracted their confidence ... never presented herself before them in the aspect of a mother ... No one can understand this, but Georgina, who has seen it grow from year to year.[54]

He was at this time "like a madman," his daughter Katey later recalled, "this affair brought out all that was worst—all that was weakest in him."[55] He was now determined to throw off his wife, and he set about justifying it any way he could.

Plans for a formal separation proceeded easily at first, with Forster acting as Dickens's agent and family friend Lemon—and later Dickens's publisher Frederick Evans—representing Catherine. Even before Dickens announced the separation to Miss Coutts, he and Catherine had reached a tentative settlement in which he would pay her an annual maintenance of £400 and provide her with a brougham.[56] Charley, the eldest, would live with his mother, while Georgina (to the dismay of the Hogarths) and the other children would continue to live with Dickens—an apparently unequal division until we remember that, at the time, the father customarily retained all rights to his children. And indeed, despite Dickens's assertions about Catherine's inadequate mothering, he instructed his solicitor Frederic Ouvry to strike from the Deed of Separation a clause that would have restricted her right to see the children on the grounds that the "exception seemed to ... convey an unnecessary slight upon her."[57] But by the middle of the month the agreement had collapsed. Dickens had discovered that the Hogarths—

---

[52] *Letters*, vol. 8, p. 740.

[53] Ibid., p. 558.

[54] Ibid., p. 559.

[55] Gladys Storey, *Dickens and Daughter* (London, 1939), p. 94.

[56] *Letters*, vol. 8, p. 739.

[57] Ibid., p. 602.

particularly Catherine's mother and youngest sister Helen—were spreading word about Dickens and Nelly, and that, owing either to their carelessness or to simple scandalmongering, whispers had begun linking him sexually to Georgina as well. The weekly *Court Circular* did so in an editorial, and Patrick Leary concludes that, given the evidence, the fact that "such rumours were spreading rapidly is beyond question."[58] Most likely, in their anger with not only Dickens but also their *other* daughter who had chosen to stay with him, Mrs. Hogarth and Helen apparently told people that Catherine could sue for divorce under the new Matrimonial Causes Act if she chose. But the 1857 Act permitted a wife to sue for divorce only if her husband's adultery were aggravated by some grosser offense. They may have misunderstood it. By insisting that Catherine might legitimately sue, the Hogarths would have implied—probably unintentionally—that Dickens was having sexual relations with Georgina, which would have been classed as incest.

Dickens raged, furious at the gross insult to his character, to Georgina's, and to Nelly's. At this early stage Dickens's relationship with Nelly probably was not sexual, whatever it became in later years, and such was Georgina's admiration for her brother-in-law that she submitted to a gynecological examination and was found to be *virgo intacta*.[59] But such rumors had the potential to sully both women and to annihilate the reputation that Dickens had crafted so earnestly during 20 years in the public eye, and upon which he depended for the goodwill of his readers and for his financial livelihood. He responded angrily and decisively, breaking off all negotiations toward a settlement and demanding through Ouvry that Mrs. Hogarth and Helen sign a written retraction of their slanders. When Miss Coutts tried to intervene on Catherine's behalf, he replied,

> [N]o consideration, human or Divine, can move me from the resolution I have taken. And one other thing I must ask you to forgive me. If you have seen Mrs. Dickens in company with her wicked mother, I can not enter—no, not even with you—upon any question that was discussed in that woman's presence.[60]

He also wrote to Arthur Smith, the business manager for his planned reading tour, enclosing to him a letter that offered considerable details about the reasons for his separation from his wife, reiterating and expanding his assertions about Catherine's failures as a mother and writing for the first time that the idea of separating had originated with her. This letter, filled with unfortunate recriminations against his wife, Dickens incautiously authorized Smith to show "to any one who wishes to do me right, or to any one who may have been misled into doing me wrong."[61] On May 26, with the settlement agreement still pending and rumors continuing to fly about London, Dickens wrote to Ouvry and urged him to be "relentless" with his wife's relations.

---

[58] Leary, p. 83. For the incident of the *Court Circular*, see Leary, p. 88.

[59] Ackroyd, p. 813.

[60] *Letters*, vol. 8, p. 565.

[61] Ibid., p. 568.

The Man from Somewhere 23

He also set about preparing a more public defense. Concerned by the start of June that the rumors plaguing him in England might also reach the United States, Dickens consulted with Forster about how best to defuse them. Forster apparently urged Dickens to authorize some American friend to contradict such rumors publicly, but as Dickens wrote to Ouvry, the plan was "altogether untenable. Surely on your knowledge of human nature ... you cannot think it feasible that I should write to any distinguished man in America, asking him to do for me, *what I have not done for myself here*! It is absurd."[62] He therefore began drafting a statement, intending to take the unusual step of having it appear in as many newspapers and magazines as possible, including in *Household Words*. On May 29, the exasperated Hogarths reluctantly signed the required retraction, at last paving the way for a settlement. The details now mostly arranged, on June 4 Dickens enclosed to Catherine a copy of the statement he meant to publish, asking her to confirm to Wills that she did not object to its contents. He was weary, or so it sounds, for although he wanted to be rid of his wife, he did not necessarily want to be rid of her on the terms of cruelty and reprisal that had characterized recent weeks. "Whoever there may be among the living," he wrote to her, in perhaps the last tender words she ever had from him, "whom I will never forgive alive or dead, I earnestly hope that all unkindness is over between you and me."[63] Three days later his "Personal" statement appeared in the *Times*, and on June 12 it occupied the entire front page of *Household Words*.[64] It also appeared in several other magazines and newspapers, but Dickens was angered and dismayed that neither the editor, Lemon, nor the publishers—*his* publishers—Bradbury and Evans, printed the statement in *Punch*. This, though Dickens apparently never asked them directly to do so.[65]

In this way, the end of Dickens's marriage and the start of his new life with Nelly signaled the end of several relationships that had, for a great many years, been among the most important in his life. He never forgave Lemon or Evans for not printing his "Personal" statement in their magazine, and it may be, too, that their work on Catherine's behalf—though he himself had asked them to assist her—made their editorial decision appear to be a tacit indictment of his conduct.[66] He also quarreled openly with William Thackeray, first because he believed that his sometime rival had helped to spread the scandal, and subsequently in defense of his friend, the younger writer Edmund Yates, who had offended Thackeray and was eventually dismissed from the Garrick Club.[67] But Dickens lost other old

---

[62] Ibid., p. 577.

[63] Ibid., p. 578.

[64] I provide as Item A in Appendix 1 a complete transcription of the statement as it appeared in the *Times*.

[65] For a cogent and intelligent discussion of this, see Leary, pp. 89–90.

[66] Slater, *Charles Dickens*, p. 455.

[67] For accounts of Thackeray's role in the scandals surrounding Dickens and Catherine's separation, see *Letters*, vol. 8, p. 573n; Johnson, vol. 2, p. 922; Nayder, p. 277; Ackroyd, pp. 815–21; and Slater, *Charles Dickens*, pp. 452–3. For the best accounts of the "Garrick Club affair" involving Dickens, Thackeray, and Yates, see Leary, pp. 92–101; *Letters*, vol. 8, pp. 589–603; Johnson, vol. 2, pp. 930–35; and Ackroyd, pp. 826–7.

friends, too, in some cases because they sided with Catherine after the separation, and in other cases, perhaps, because he either would or could not trust them with the knowledge of his new life with Nelly.[68] He gradually fell away from both Miss Coutts and her widowed companion Brown, both of whom had been among Dickens's most frequent correspondents during the middle of the 1850s. He even withdrew somewhat from Forster, spending time instead with Collins—who had his own unconventional domestic situation—and other younger men, mostly from among the frequent contributors to *Household Words*. For Dickens, the break from his wife meant other breaks, too, and a new life that might restore to him the charms of his romantic bachelorhood and the "frame of mind" of the days gone by. Having defeated the Hogarths, Dickens signed a Deed of Separation granting Catherine £600 annually and settling her in an establishment of her own at 70 Gloucester Terrace, Regent's Park. Then, on August 1, he went off to Clifton to begin his first provincial reading tour. Even with Catherine gone he could not rest.

II

Dickens's 1858 reading tour inaugurated a crucial new professional course. For the rest of his life he worked at least as much as a public performer as he did as an author, and he certainly earned far more money from reading than he did from writing novels. For the last 25 years of his life, Dickens earned an average of £2,900 annually from his writing, but from the beginning the public readings were an even greater financial success: from 1858 to 1870 he earned around £45,000 from the readings, nearly half of the £93,000 he left behind at the time of his death.[69] From April 1857 to October 1859, he read 124 times in London, Scotland, Ireland, and cities and towns across England.[70] He undertook a second, less demanding tour during 1861–63, after finishing *Great Expectations*. And upon finishing *Our Mutual Friend* in 1865, though his health was failing, Dickens committed himself first to two extensive tours of England, Scotland, and Ireland and then to a six-month trip to the United States in 1867, where he delivered 76 readings. He had considered going to America to read in 1859 for the princely sum of £10,000, but he hesitated and then rejected the offer only to find soon after that the Civil War had closed America to him for several years to come. In 1862 he also considered and then declined an offer to give a six-month reading tour in Australia, from which he estimated he might earn as much as £12,000.[71] Even in the letters he wrote during his first reading tour in 1858, Dickens often sounds overawed by the sums involved, filling his letters home—now directed to Georgina and Mamie—with accounts of the enormous crowds and "frantic prices

---

[68] According to Nayder, Catherine remained friends with Lemon, Evans, Thackeray, Dallas, John Leech, John Everett Millais, and longtime *Household Words* contributor Shirley Brooks. See pp. 288–96.

[69] Andrews, p. 45.

[70] Andrews, pp. 269–74.

[71] Fred Kaplan, *Dickens: A Biography* (New York, 1988), p. 449.

The Man from Somewhere 25

for stalls."[72] Only one month into the provinces, Dickens estimated that the first 25 readings would earn him, after deductions, a "handsome Thousand Pounds."[73]

In a way, Dickens's public readings were not exactly new. He had read on dozens of earlier occasions on behalf of charitable and workers' societies, starting with *A Christmas Carol* (1843) on December 27, 1853, on behalf of the newly founded Birmingham and Midland Institute.[74] Over the years he had raised thousands of pounds in this way for a variety of causes, yet even so, when he had broached with Forster the possibility of reading publicly on his own account, Forster had tried to dissuade him, arguing that "[i]t was a substitution of lower for higher aims" and a great blow against the respect that he owed to his calling as a writer and his position as a gentleman.[75] Dickens retorted that he received 20 or more requests each week inviting him to read publicly at some venue or on behalf of some cause, and that these showed that people anyway already believed that he was paid for such work. It could not, therefore, be of any moment to the public whether or not he began seeking remuneration for reading. To Forster he wrote on March 20, 1858, that he was not yet decided, and that he would propound the matter to two "*distinguished ladies of his acquaintance*" and take their advice.[76] Really, he had already taken his own advice, having written confidentially several days earlier to ask Evans, with whom he was then still on good terms, whether he could see any objection to the plan and laying out his proposed schedule of summer readings in London followed by a provincial tour.[77] Evans was no doubt delighted by the prospect of the publicity that Dickens would bring to his older works, for during 1857–58 Bradbury and Evans undertook a Library edition of Dickens's novels and updated their Cheap edition by incorporating *Dombey and Son*, *David Copperfield*, and *Bleak House*. Still, though Evans seems to have responded enthusiastically, it hardly mattered. Dickens knew what he wished to do, and he had already set about doing it with his customary energy.

Dickens's motives for embarking upon this new professional course were complex, but they all originated in the common causes of his dissatisfaction at home and the new life he meant to live with Nelly. Early in 1858, as he planned the first tour, he remained driven by his need to keep moving, to exhaust himself with action. Even as he tested the waters with Forster and Evans, he wrote to Collins on March 21:

> The Doncaster unhappiness remains so strong upon me that I can't write, and (waking) can't rest … I have never known a moment's peace or content, since the last night of the Frozen Deep. I do suppose that there never was a Man so

---

[72]   *Letters*, vol. 8, p. 640.

[73]   Ibid., p. 643.

[74]   Johnson, vol. 2, pp. 790–91.

[75]   John Forster, *Life of Charles Dickens* (London, 1928), p. 641.

[76]   *Letters*, vol. 8, p. 535. The editors point out that these ladies were Miss Coutts and Mrs. Brown.

[77]   Ibid., pp. 532–3.

26   *Charles Dickens's* Our Mutual Friend

seized and rended by one Spirit. In this condition, though nothing can alter or soften it, I have a turning notion that the mere physical effort and change of the readings would be good, as another means of bearing it.[78]

Recent events had also heightened his perennial anxiety about money, and he planned the tour with that concern in mind, too. In March 1856 he had paid nearly £1,750 to buy Gad's Hill Place—another attempt to recapture some of the romance of his youth—and in September 1857, even as he wrote to Forster of his unhappy marriage, he proposed the idea of the public readings as a way of "paying for [the] place."[79] Thereafter he paid for costly improvements at Gad's Hill—most particularly a new well—though he still intended to live in London at Tavistock House and either to let his new "Kentish freehold" or to use it as a periodic escape.[80] Meantime, Charley had required an expensive setting-up in his new career with Baring Brothers, and Dickens had purchased for his second son Walter a military commission and paid his passage to Calcutta as a cadet.[81] He had also become Nelly's unofficial patron, sending £50 to John Buckstone—manager of the Haymarket theater—apparently to persuade him to engage Ellen upon her return from Doncaster.[82]

More important, by the time Dickens began planning his first tour in earnest in March 1858, the possibility of a permanent and expensive separation from Catherine may already have been in his mind, and so, too, might the expense of elevating the Ternans from their position as a family of struggling actresses to one more on the level with his own. His letters home to Georgina, Mamie, and Katey during his 1858 provincial tour emphasize, over and over, the enormous profitability of his new work, often even eliding the real human presence of his audience in favor of an account of how many stalls saw him perform or how many pounds the room held.[83] After reading at Exeter on August 3, for instance, Dickens wrote to Georgina that he only "regretted" that they "could not squeeze more than £75 into the room."[84] Likewise, from Liverpool Dickens wrote of having had an enormous crowd, 2,300 people, "[o]ver £200 in money," and more than £100 on each of the two nights before.[85] At Limerick he remarked having read in a small but charming theatre to "an admirable audience. As hearty and demonstrative as it is possible to be. ... I am very glad we came," he continued, "though we could

---

[78]   Ibid., p. 536.

[79]   Ibid., p. 435.

[80]   Ibid., p. 597.

[81]   Johnson, vol. 2, p. 875.

[82]   *Letters*, vol. 8, p. 465.

[83]   Not surprisingly, the passages that do this rhetorical work were among those characteristically omitted from the three-volume collection of Dickens's letters that Georgina and Mamie edited and published 1880–82. See Dickens's various letters to Georgina and Mamie in *Letters*, vol. 8, pp. 617–94.

[84]   Ibid., p. 617.

[85]   Ibid., p. 629.

have made heaps of money by going to Dublin instead."[86] He had added to his repertoire now, reading not only from the Christmas books but also taking great care to make scenes from his longer books into shorter pieces: *Little Dombey*, *Boots*, *The Poor Traveller*, and *Mrs. Gamp*.[87] He also discovered early on that he could supplement his profits from ticket sales by selling reading copies of his works.[88] All told, by the end of October, Dickens estimated his "clear profit" from the tour "after all deductions and expences [*sic*]" to be more than 1,000 guineas a month—far more than he would have earned by writing a new book.[89] Indeed, though Dickens finished only two novels during the last decade of his life, he had lost neither his creativity nor his vigor. He was working as hard as ever, and again he was the Inimitable, mapping out a course that no other novelist could follow.

But the reading tour was not entirely about the money for Dickens. He had always had a love for the stage and might have become an actor in 1835 had a terrible cold and some "inflammation of the face" not kept him from appearing for his audition.[90] In later life, even his busiest seasons as a novelist and editor did not keep him from going to the theater at every chance, directing and acting in amateur productions, collaborating with Collins, Tom Taylor, and others in writing both original plays and adaptations, or keeping lifelong friendships with actors like Jerrold and Macready. He loved to act and—as reactions to his performance as Wardour suggest—was exceptional at it. Thackeray attended a performance of *The Frozen Deep* in 1857 and remarked, "[I]f that man would now go upon the stage, he would make his £20,000 per year"—a prediction, as Peter Ackroyd points out, "which was closer to the truth than he could then have realized."[91] Now, working from his own novels, Dickens did more than just read: he *became* his characters night after night before enormous crowds. Voices, facial expressions, peculiar postures and mannerisms all were varied as Dickens welcomed each new character onto the scene. This had always, after a fashion, been part even of Dickens's writing process. On one occasion when Mamie was a child, she recalled, Dickens permitted her to rest quietly in his study while he worked. "I was lying on the sofa endeavouring to keep perfectly quiet," she wrote,

> while my father wrote busily and rapidly at his desk, when he suddenly jumped from his chair and rushed to a mirror which hung near, and in which I could see the reflection of some extraordinary facial contortions which he was making. He returned rapidly to his desk, wrote furiously for a few moments, and then went again to the mirror.[92]

---

[86] Ibid., p. 647.

[87] Andrews, p. 270.

[88] See *Letters*, vol. 8, p. 633n.

[89] Ibid., p. 689.

[90] Forster, *Life*, p. 60.

[91] *Letters*, vol. 8, p. 261n; Ackroyd, p. 776.

[92] Mary Dickens, "My Father as I Recall Him," in Norman Page (ed.), *Charles Dickens: Family History* (5 vols, London, 1999), vol. 1, p. 48.

For Dickens the line between visual performance—physical embodiment, we might even say—and narrative invention had always been razor-thin. Now, as a public reader, while he delighted in his ability to perform scenes so that they elicited the appropriate sympathetic response, he took even greater joy from the audience's recognition of the characters—Sam Weller, Mrs. Gamp, Scrooge, Tiny Tim, Paul Dombey—he brought to life from the pages of his fiction.[93] After a performance at Harrogate he wrote to Georgina of a "young fellow ... who found something so very ludicrous in Toots that he *could not* compose himself at all, but laughed until he sat wiping his eyes with his handkerchief. And whenever he felt Toots coming again, he began to laugh and wipe his eyes afresh;" in the presence of such merriment, Dickens himself could not keep a straight face.[94] And when Dickens performed the trial scene from *Pickwick* in Birmingham in October 1858, he was gratified to find that "when Mr. Sergeant Buzfuz said 'Call Samuel Weller!,' they gave a great thunder of applause, as if he were really coming in."[95]

Ultimately, too, it was the applause that mattered, and the need for applause that drove Dickens to take to the stage amid the chaos of his extraordinary personal trials. To be sure, as Malcolm Andrews writes, part of what drove Dickens to the stage was the opportunity it afforded him for a "kind of vagabond flight from the domestic hearth" and into the more stirring bohemian life of the mid-Victorian theater.[96] But he was also driven by uncertainty and by the sudden loss of the emotional support he always craved. In 1858 his relationship with Catherine was ending, and he could not know for certain what relationship he would cultivate with Nelly or how long it might last. Consequently, not just amid scandal but in defiance of it, and perhaps to console himself for the much wider destruction he had wrought in his personal life, he used his public readings to deepen in unprecedented ways his relationship with contemporary readers—the relationship that had always mattered to him most, and the only relationship in his life that endured. As I have argued elsewhere, there is a sense in which Dickens's deliberate public reinvention of himself through his public readings might be understood as a practical culmination of the logic inherent in the law of copyright, which had, as Mark Rose argues in *Authors and Owners* (1993), enforced a closer and closer identification of the author with his or her intellectual work, so that "the commodity that changed hands when a bookseller purchased a manuscript or when a reader purchased a book was as much personality as ink and paper."[97] In this sense it is

---

[93] At intermission of a reading in 1863, the normally taciturn Thomas Carlyle remarked to Dickens, "Charley, you carry a whole company under your own hat." Quoted in Johnson, vol. 2, p. 1009.

[94] *Letters*, vol. 8, p. 659.

[95] Ibid., p. 682.

[96] Andrews, p. 41.

[97] Mark Rose, *Authors and Owners: The Invention of Copyright* (Cambridge, 1993), p. 121. I discuss this at greater length in "Commodity and Identity in *Great Expectations*," *Victorian Literature and Culture*, 40/2 (2012), especially pp. 625–7.

somehow appropriate, and even predictable, that by 1860 Dickens was making himself quite deliberately into "portable property" by writing autobiographically in *Great Expectations*. Meanwhile, in May 1858 news of his separation from Catherine began to spread, and by month's end he was fuming at the gossip linking him with Nelly and Georgina. But the series of London readings continued unabated, and Dickens's letters from these months routinely express his pleasure at finding himself met, performance after performance, with enthusiastic applause. By the end of August, a month into the subsequent provincial tour, he had a new reason for concern: the ill-advised letter about Catherine that he had sent to Smith months earlier—with instructions that he should show it "to any one"—had found its way into the press.

The "Violated Letter," as Dickens subsequently called it, created a new and more intense crisis, first in America and then at home in England. Smith may have believed that Dickens's exhortation to show the letter "to any one" meant that he ought to publicize it in whatever way he could. Whether innocently or not, Smith at some point shared the letter with the London correspondent of the *New York Tribune*, where it appeared in its entirety under the heading "The Dickens Domestic Affair" on August 16, 1858.[98] Two weeks later, on August 31, the *Morning Chronicle* and *Morning Herald* both published the letter in England, along with Dickens's letter of authorization to Smith and a copy of the retraction that Dickens had wrenched from Catherine's family. Many who had sympathized with or even pitied Dickens after his personal statement in *Household Words* two months earlier now turned on him, indignant at not only his allegations against his unhappy wife but also his apparently deliberate and unmanly conduct in having them published. Distraught, Dickens wrote urgently to Ouvry, asking him at once to communicate with Catherine and assure her that he had not consented to publication of the letter, and that it "ha[d] shocked and distressed [him] very much."[99] But this time, despite being derided and condemned in the pages of *John Bull* and the Liverpool *Mercury*, among other papers, Dickens mounted no public defense. He simply continued reading and reporting gleefully at every turn that the audiences were large and enthusiastic—that, in short, they implicitly reassured him at each performance that his domestic troubles had not blunted their adoration for him or his work, and that he might yet emerge unscathed into the new life he meant to create.

Dickens's remarkable career as a public performer of his fiction was the first major professional innovation to emerge from the tumult of his ruined marriage and infatuation with Nelly. The second was his decision, late in 1858, to leave Bradbury and Evans and *Household Words* to create his own weekly magazine *All the Year Round*, a decision that altered fundamentally the form that Dickens's novels would take for years to come. In the autumn of 1858, Dickens remained

[98] *Letters*, vol. 8, p. 648n. For a full transcription of the "Violated Letter," see *Letters*, vol. 8, pp. 740–41.

[99] Ibid., p. 648.

icily furious with Evans for having refused—so Dickens thought—to allow his "Personal" statement to appear in *Punch* six months before. On November 9, his provincial tour nearly over, Dickens wrote to Bradbury and Evans to request a special meeting of the partners in *Household Words* for the following week "for the consideration of a Resolution I shall have to propose."[100] The meeting was duly called, but Dickens did not attend. Instead, he sent Forster, armed with power of attorney, to propose on his behalf that the partnership be dissolved "by the cessation and discontinuance of that publication on the Completion of the Nineteenth Volume" in May 1859.[101] Wills seconded the proposal, giving it the only additional vote that it required to pass, but Bradbury and Evans declined to act, as they disbelieved Forster's ability to represent Dickens at the proceedings under the contractual arrangements of the partnership.[102] Though Evans claimed that he never fully understood what he had done to offend Dickens, he could not possibly have been surprised that Dickens held the grudge, having seen while working on Catherine's behalf during the negotiations for the separation how easily Dickens could take offense and how slowly his anger subsided once worked to any pitch.[103] Still, the suddenness with which Dickens proposed to annihilate their very profitable joint property—*Household Words* earned around £1,700 profit in both 1857 and 1858—must have come as an unwelcome shock.[104]

But Dickens was determined to break with the publishers, and here, as in most things, he eventually got his way. On November 27 he communicated to them through Forster his willingness to purchase their interest in *Household Words* and reiterated that the publication would be "discontinued Six months hence"; on December 14 he offered them £1,000 for their share in the copyright and an additional sum, to be determined by a valuation, to purchase their share in the stock and plates.[105] They refused, convinced despite Dickens's majority ownership and the vote of the partners that he could not legally put an end to *Household Words*. Undeterred, Dickens simply began making the necessary arrangements to begin printing and publishing his own new magazine, and to do so in the way that would most rankle his old employers. During January 1859 he consulted with Forster and

---

[100] Ibid., p. 700. The partners in *Household Words* at the time of its creation in 1850 had been Dickens (1/2 share), Forster (1/8), Wills (1/8), and Bradbury and Evans (1/4), and the contract stipulated that "[t]hree out of four proprietors (the firm counting as one) constituted a quorum, and disputes were to be settled by vote." In February 1856 Forster made over his 1/8 share to Dickens, who then divided it between himself and Wills, giving Dickens a 9/16 share—in other words, majority ownership—of the magazine and effectively making Dickens and Wills together a quorum. For more on these arrangements, see Robert Patten, *Charles Dickens and His Publishers* (Oxford, 1978), pp. 240, 462–3; and *Letters*, vol. 8, p. 730.

[101] *Letters*, vol. 8, p. 700n.

[102] Ibid.

[103] Leary, p. 92.

[104] Patten, *Charles Dickens and His Publishers*, p. 464.

[105] *Letters*, vol. 8, pp. 711, 719. Patten gives an excellent account of Dickens's final break with Bradbury and Evans and the founding of *All the Year Round*, pp. 267–71.

The Man from Somewhere 31

Collins about possible titles, initially proposing (apparently with no touch of irony) "Household Harmony"—which Forster delicately put down, suggesting to Dickens that it might not be "accepted as a happy comment" on the recent occurrences in his private life—before settling on "All the Year Round."[106] The following month Dickens took new offices at 26 Wellington Street North, Strand, only a few doors down from the old offices of *Household Words*, and he made arrangements for paper, printing, and what he called "an immense system of advertising."[107]

In March, he struck his blow. Having been warned off by Ouvry from a more audacious plan of advertising his new magazine directly in the pages of *Household Words*, Dickens instead had half a million handbills printed up and distributed across London. Bradbury and Evans filed suit in Chancery on March 21, alleging that Dickens was doing irreparable harm to their joint property and asking the court to restrain him by injunction from issuing any advertisements or notices announcing the discontinuance of *Household Words*.[108] The court refused the injunction, leaving Dickens free to pursue his plans. *All the Year Round* published its first issue on April 30, 1859, and, in a matter of weeks, had doubled the circulation of its predecessor, which limped along until its last issue on May 28. There, Dickens took one last dig at the defeated Evans, reminding the public that he had "announced, many weeks ago, that [the magazine] would be discontinued on the day of which this final Number bears date. The Public have read a good deal to the contrary, and will observe that it has not in the least affected the result."[109] Beginning with the May 28 issue of *All the Year Round*, he added to its title "with which is incorporated *Household Words*."[110] In the end, Dickens even got his way with the remains of *Household Words*, which the court had declared must be sold before it would render a final decision on costs. At the auction of the property on May 16, Dickens, who did not attend, planted the unknown Arthur Smith among the bidders, and Smith bid for the property—with the foreknowledge of Dickens's ally, the publisher Frederic Chapman, of Chapman and Hall—against both Chapman and Evans. Evans was entirely bewildered, as he had expected competition on Dickens's behalf to come from Chapman himself. Taking advantage of the confusion, Smith won the bidding at £3,550, some £1,600 of which represented Dickens's valuation of *Household Words*' stock on hand; the other £2,000 was essentially for the copyright. As 3/4 owner of the magazine, counting Forster's and Wills's shares, Dickens had managed to buy Bradbury and Evans out of the copyright for just £500, or half of what he had offered them six months before. He then turned around and sold the stock to Chapman and Hall for £2,500—and laughed, no doubt, all the way to the bank.[111]

---

[106] Forster, *Life*, p. 671.

[107] *Letters*, vol. 9, p. 30.

[108] Patten, *Charles Dickens and His Publishers*, p. 268.

[109] Quoted in Johnson, vol. 2, p. 946.

[110] Ibid.

[111] Patten, *Charles Dickens and His Publishers*, p. 269.

With its short topical pieces, occasional poems, light political commentary, and serialized fiction, *All the Year Round* resembled *Household Words* and other contemporary magazines in many of its particulars. It had, to be sure, a more international feel, which Dickens cultivated by making the magazine less reliant on English topics *du jour* than *Household Words* had sometimes been, largely to accommodate the American readers he expected to reach by selling the right of publication in the United States to New York journalist Thomas Coke Evans for £1,000.[112] But the new magazine's more fundamental differences from its predecessor mattered profoundly to Dickens's own writing during and after 1859. For one thing, *All the Year Round* placed a much heavier emphasis on long works of fiction, always reserving the journal's first several pages for serialized work from the leading novelists of the day.[113] Throughout the first decade of its existence, circulation of *All the Year Round* tended to rise and fall in direct proportion to the public's interest in its leading serials, which included blockbusters like Collins's *The Woman in White* (1859–60), *No Name* (1862), and *The Moonstone* (1868) and less successful works like Charles Lever's *A Day's Ride* (1860–61). Just as significant, after his experience with Bradbury and Evans—and for that matter with Richard Bentley 20 years earlier as the editor of *Bentley's Miscellany*— Dickens had had enough of publishers. He funded *All the Year Round* himself, devising a contract that granted him 3/4 share of the copyright and profits and awarded the other 1/4 to Wills, who continued to work under him as subeditor. Meanwhile, to Chapman and Hall, to whom Dickens now nominally turned to publish his future novels, he granted only rights of distribution, allowing them to serve as his commissioned agents for all sales of *All the Year Round* outside of London. If *All the Year Round* succeeded, then, Dickens would reap the lion's share of the rewards. If it failed he would bear the losses.

Dickens therefore took pains to guarantee success, and these pains ultimately changed the pattern of his writing and publishing activities during the next several years. He planned his next novel, *A Tale of Two Cities*, for weekly serialization to give *All the Year Round* a proper sendoff, beginning publication of the novel in the inaugural issue. Five years earlier Dickens had written *Hard Times* in weekly portions for *Household Words*, and he had also tried the format in 1840–41 with *Master Humphrey's Clock*. But he had never liked it, and even as he neared completion of *A Tale* in August 1859 he was still complaining to Forster of the "time and trouble of the incessant condensation."[114] Still, the novel did the needful by generating immediate interest in the new magazine. By mid-June Dickens was reporting to Forster that *All the Year Round* had already repaid him, "with five per cent interest, all the money [he] advanced for its establishment ... and yet [left] a good £500 balance at the banker's!"[115] But Dickens understood that in this

---

[112] Slater, *Charles Dickens*, p. 473.

[113] Slater also makes this point in his "Introduction" to volume 4 of Charles Dickens, *The Dent Uniform Edition of Dickens' Journalism* (4 vols, London, 1994–2000), p. xii.

[114] *Letters*, vol. 9, p. 112.

[115] Ibid., p. 78.

switch to weekly serialization in the pages of a magazine, he risked losing touch with the longtime audience for his novels in parts. In an attempt to accommodate those readers, Dickens had Chapman and Hall collect the weekly installments of *A Tale* at the end of each month so that they could be reissued as the more familiar monthly numbers, complete with the familiar green wrapper and original new illustrations by Browne (*All the Year Round* never contained illustrations). But these sold indifferently—only around 5,000 copies a month—and each month's collected chapters did not necessarily coalesce around and accentuate the periodic crises of action that readers had come to expect of the form. For all practical purposes, Dickens had left behind the format that had won him so many readers during a career of 20 years, and that had so often guaranteed his financial success.

Worse, in 1859 Dickens was again anxious about money, in spite of the success of his recent reading tour and the promising start for *All the Year Round*. He still owned both Tavistock House and Gad's Hill Place, but he was now spending much more of his time at the latter, away from London, and consequently he was also continuing to pour money into renovations, now having hired contractors to dig a tunnel beneath the high road to connect the Gad's Hill grounds with the picturesque shrubbery on the other side. In fact, he had all but decided to move permanently to his country estate, and in January 1859 he consulted with Wills about the possibility of letting Tavistock House, apparently to the Ternans.[116] Wills seems to have talked him out of such a rash proceeding, but the following month Dickens issued an unusual directive to his bankers, instructing them to sell £1,500 of his "New 3 per Cents ... & take out a Power of Atty. for Sale of all that fund at present in my name."[117] He clearly had a sudden need for cash, perhaps related to that month's initial business arrangements on behalf of *All the Year Round*, but quite possibly having instead to do with the fact that two weeks later the humble Ternans bought the 84-year lease of a four-story townhouse at Ampthill Square. In other words, by the middle of 1859 Dickens was almost certainly supporting four establishments, if one counts his maintenance for Catherine, and his sons Francis and Alfred would soon come of age. Small wonder, then, that in the middle of his work on *A Tale of Two Cities*, he agreed nevertheless to write a short story for Richard Bonner at the *New York Ledger* for the tidy sum of £1,000.[118]

Nor had he any intention of taking chances with the success of *All the Year Round*. On July 2 Bradbury and Evans had launched their own competitor to Dickens in the form of *Once a Week*, founded much upon *All the Year Round*'s plan but also featuring lavish illustrations, and in December the field became more crowded still when George Smith launched the more luxurious *Cornhill* magazine as a monthly with Thackeray at the helm. With *A Tale of Two Cities* nearing its conclusion—it finished its serial run on November 26—Dickens was

---

[116] Ibid., pp. 10–11 and n.

[117] Ibid., p. 29.

[118] Ibid., p. 44n. The story, "Hunted Down," appeared in the *Ledger* in three installments on August 20 and 27 and September 3, 1859.

already planning for a way to guarantee his readership by keeping his writing present in the magazine. In the narrative guise of an "Uncommercial Traveller," Dickens contributed 16 new pieces to *All the Year Round* during the first 10 months of 1860, and he returned to the model in 1863 and 1868 for a second and third series of essays. Of course, in 1860 he need not have worried. *A Tale of Two Cities* was followed by Collins's *The Woman in White*, which drove circulation still higher. Fueled by these two novels, sales of *All the Year Round* during its second and third half-years (November 1, 1859–October 31, 1860) netted Dickens and Wills nearly £3,500 in profits in addition to the salaries they already paid themselves for their editorial posts.[119] As a result, despite the financial demands pressing upon him, and because he had already lined up new fiction for *All the Year Round* from Lever and his old friend Edward Bulwer-Lytton, Dickens felt able during late summer 1860 to begin planning his next novel, *Great Expectations*, as a return to monthly numbers and as an attempt, too, to penetrate for the first time the lucrative market for three-volume novels that had been created by Charles Mudie and the other proprietors of the circulating libraries.

But the plan to publish in monthly numbers was short lived.[120] By early October, with Lever's *A Day's Ride* failing in *All the Year Round*, Dickens called "a council of war at the office" to address the magazine's slumping sales:

> It was perfectly clear that the one thing to be done was, for me to strike in. I have therefore decided to begin the story as of the length of the *Tale of Two Cities* on the first of December—begin publishing, that is. I must make the most I can out of the book. … The name is GREAT EXPECTATIONS. I think a good name?[121]

As he explained a few days later to Forster, though he had already begun writing his new novel, he had no choice but to redesign the story for a different format, for "[t]he property of *All the Year Round* is far too valuable, in every way, to be much endangered."[122] In a kind letter to Lever, Dickens broke gently the news of the declining sales and explained to him that, thenceforth, for as long a time as *A Day's Ride* continued in the magazine, "we must go on together."[123] *Great Expectations* thus began its serial run on December 1 and was, by any measure, the commercial success that Dickens had wanted. It arrested, then reversed, the slide of *All the Year Round*, and by negotiating a separate contract for US publication in *Harper's Weekly*, Dickens earned an additional £1,000. The novel still also appeared as a triple-decker, passing through four three-volume printings and selling nearly 3,500

---

[119] Patten, *Charles Dickens and His Publishers*, p. 464.

[120] For an excellent discussion of Dickens's plans for writing and publishing *Great Expectations*, see Edgar Rosenberg's essay "Launching *Great Expectations*," in Charles Dickens, *Great Expectations* (New York, 1999), pp. 389–423.

[121] *Letters*, vol. 9, pp. 319–20.

[122] Ibid., p. 320.

[123] Ibid., p. 321.

The Man from Somewhere   35

copies, mostly to the circulating libraries that Dickens had wanted to reach.[124] This time, though, Dickens made no pretense of collecting the novel into monthly installments, leaving it instead to appear only in the weekly format he had never liked and the three-volume format he had never tried. Somehow, in three years, in a stunning burst of acumen and audacity provoked by the greatest emotional trial of his life, Dickens had detonated and then utterly reinvented his personal and professional lives. And—professionally, at least—he had emerged the richer for it.

III

By late 1861 the violent personal and professional upheavals that had begun at Manchester four years earlier had finally subsided. With *All the Year Round*, with Chapman and Hall, with his adoring readers, with Nelly, Dickens had created a remarkable array of new relationships that he would retain until the end of his life. On the other hand, he neither recovered nor really even attempted to recover the ruined relationships that had come before. He never mended his friendships with Lemon, Evans, or Miss Coutts, and he might never have reconciled with Thackeray, either, had Katey not interceded, persuading Thackeray that he ought to approach her father and strike up a conversation the next time they met: "[H]e is more shy of speaking than you are," she told him, "and perhaps he mightn't know you would be nice to him."[125] Not long after, the two great novelists exchanged words and shook hands at the Athenaeum Club—a moment for which Dickens was soon enormously grateful, since Thackeray died of apoplexy just a few weeks later, in December 1863. With Catherine he never reconciled, writing to her just three times after 1858: once to provide information about a family burial plot when her mother died; again, and somewhat more kindly, in reply to her note of concern after the Staplehurst crash; and one last time before he left for America in 1867. Even then, Dickens could not bring himself to write a single word of reminiscence regarding their trip there together 25 years earlier, instead remarking blandly, "Severely hard work lies before me, but that is not a new thing in my life, and I am content to go my way and do it."[126] Three years earlier Miss Coutts had tried one last time to restore Dickens and Catherine at least to cordial terms. He had replied, appropriately, with a metaphor of authorship: "I do not claim," he wrote to her, "to have any thing to forgive … [but] a page in my life which once had writing on it, has become absolutely blank, and … it is not in my power to pretend that it has a solitary word upon it."[127] Dickens had simply erased the old times—had broken with them cleanly and irrevocably, with brutal emotional force. After four years of struggle, he had simply willed himself into another life.

---

[124] Patten, *Charles Dickens and His Publishers*, pp. 290–92.
[125] Quoted in Johnson, vol. 2, p. 1013.
[126] *Letters*, vol. 11, p. 472.
[127] Ibid., vol. 10, p. 356.

He had finally settled, in other words—not down, exactly, for that would have been impossible for a man of Dickens's energy and unflagging ambition. Rather, he had settled into something like a new groove, of energy poured into creating and performing his public readings, of proprietorship rather than mere editorship of *All the Year Round*, of 12-mile walks through the Kentish countryside, and of "mysterious disappearances" and that restless, ceaseless flitting to Slough, to Peckham, and to Condette. To Boulogne, and then home again on the 2:38 tidal train with the manuscript pages from *Our Mutual Friend*'s No. 16 in his pocket. In 1859, even as so much of his life swirled in chaos, Dickens sat several times for a portrait by William Frith, with results that grated upon Dickens's friend Edwin Landseer. "I wish," Landseer told Forster after seeing the portrait, "he looked less eager and busy, and not so much out of himself, or beyond himself. I should like to catch him asleep and quiet now and then."[128] Few ever caught him so at any time of his life. But like all seismic events, Dickens's chance meeting with Nelly in August 1857 had created fundamental shifts, making Dickens into a very different novelist than he had been a decade before. He had learned to capitalize on his imaginative work in new ways, using both his public readings and the suggestively autobiographical *Great Expectations* to fashion himself, quite literally, into a literary commodity. Indeed, most critics agree that *Great Expectations* and *Our Mutual Friend* offer Dickens's most incisive critiques of capitalism, and this may be precisely because he had, during these years, entangled himself so profoundly in the dictates of the market. Yet in another way, Dickens's transformation during 1857–61 had rendered him particularly ill-suited to write *Our Mutual Friend*. He had a demanding second career now as a reader of his own work, was both proprietor and editor of a weekly magazine, and lived a complicated and restless double life. When he signed the contract for the novel with Chapman and Hall in November 1863, moreover, he had not—owing to the demands of *All the Year Round*—even attempted a novel in 20 numbers since finishing *Little Dorrit* in June 1857. In this sense, and in others, he was about to take on the greatest artistic challenge of his long career.

---

[128] Forster, *Life*, pp. 668–9.

Chapter 2
The Cup and the Lip:
Writing *Our Mutual Friend*

On a winter evening in February 1864 Marcus Stone accompanied Dickens to the theater where, at intermission, the novelist asked his new young illustrator an unexpected question: did he happen to know of some "peculiar avocation" that he might feature in *Our Mutual Friend*?[1] Dickens was then working on his third monthly installment, and though he had already introduced readers to the corpse-dredging Hexams in the first chapter, he had apparently decided that he needed another bizarre occupation for the story. Happily, Stone knew just the thing. He had been working on a new painting showing an arrested man being marched down a public thoroughfare, and he had wanted to introduce into the composition a begging dog. In want of a model for the dog, he consulted a fellow-artist who in turn recommended that he visit Mr. Willis, a taxidermist, in St. Andrew's Street near Seven Dials. Through Willis, Stone acquired a stuffed dog that served the purpose, then he attended the theater with Dickens that same night. When the novelist asked him about a peculiar avocation, Stone immediately suggested to an eager Dickens that they visit Willis's shop together the next afternoon. Though Willis was absent when they arrived, Dickens, with his customary quickness of observation, took in the entire shop at a glance—"the dingy interior, with its 'bones warious; bottled preparations warious; dogs, ducks, glass eyes, warious'"—and when he returned home set about reproducing it for *Our Mutual Friend*.[2] In the place of Willis, whom Stone said the novelist never saw, Dickens created the near-sighted, lovelorn Mr. Venus, "Preserver of Animals and Birds ... [and] Articulator of human bones," one of the most original characters in the novel and perhaps even in Dickens's larger body of work.[3]

As it turned out, Dickens's introduction to Willis's strange shop on St. Andrew's Street could not have come at a better time. For just around the time of his visit to Willis—likely within two days before or after—Dickens received from the printer his proof sheets of *Our Mutual Friend*'s No. 2 and learned, to his consternation, that he had overwritten the installment by more than five printed pages, a margin so wide that he could not hope to correct matters, as he often did in such cases, by lining out bits of dialogue or otherwise compressing his prose. Requiring a more drastic solution, Dickens removed No. 2's original final chapter—the very long "A Marriage Contract" describing the Lammles ill-favored match—and substituted for it the chapter introducing Venus, "Mr. Wegg Looks After Himself," in the

---

[1] Frederic G. Kitton, *Dickens and His Illustrators* (London, 1899), p. 199.

[2] Ibid., p. 200.

[3] Dickens, *Our Mutual Friend* (London, 1997), p. 89.

process shortening the second installment from 37 pages to the required 32. "A Marriage Contract" became instead the final chapter of No. 3, postponing by 30 pages and 30 days Dickens's return to the Veneerings and the rest of the "Social Chorus." Nor was this the only significant error that Dickens made as he tried to return to the monthly number format. The surviving proofs show that he also overwrote No. 1, and the manuscript and proofs alike show that he overwrote No. 4, too. In a letter to Collins on January 25, 1864, he celebrated having "done the first two Nos" and said he was "now beginning the third," but after nearly a decade away from monthly installments, he also complained of feeling "at first quite dazed in getting back to the large canvas and the big brushes; and even now, I have a sensation as of acting at the San Carlo after Tavistock House."[4] As he began writing *Our Mutual Friend* during the winter of 1863–64, then, Dickens was struggling mightily to work himself back into the groove of the format he had practically created three decades before. Worse, he was doing so with a novel so massive and unwieldy that it probably defied at every turn the practical need to compress it into perfectly regular portions.

It is hard now to imagine *Our Mutual Friend* without Mr. Venus. Arthur Waugh remarked phlegmatically in 1937 that "the 'Venus' business generally is a superfluous excrescence on the plot," but probably very few critics of the present day would agree.[5] Dickens's melancholic taxidermist seems now to belong intrinsically to the novel's symbolic concerns with death, Dust, rebirth, the grotesque traffic in human matter, and the anatomization and articulation of both individual persons and the gloomy world in which they move. Yet we probably must wonder how different the novel might be had Stone taken Dickens to see some other peculiar avocation—to see a night-soilman, for instance, or some singed and ruddy limeburner, or the ringmaster to a flea circus. Or we might at least wonder how different the novel would be had the overlong proofs for No. 2 come back a week earlier or later, when Dickens's need to solve the problem might well have led to some other result. Since Dickens may have asked Stone about a peculiar avocation before receiving the proofs, it is not necessarily true, as short-hand accounts sometimes allege, that Venus exists in the novel only because of Dickens's overwriting. But the incident nevertheless reveals a great deal about the way that *Our Mutual Friend* owed its final content and shape, in significant ways, to a remarkable combination of careful planning, unexpected error, sheer accident, and the imaginative leaps and creative genius of Dickens at his best. When Dickens began writing *Our Mutual Friend* during the autumn of 1863, he meant the title of Book the First, "The Cup and the Lip," to foreshadow the fates of many characters' early hopes, most of which are dashed by the end of the novel. But the title might be applied, too, to Dickens's writing, for he slipped often as he wrote *Our Mutual Friend*. He overwrote and underwrote numbers, he fell dangerously ill, he lost a son and a dear old friend, he survived the crash at Staplehurst, and, for

---

[4]   *Letters*, vol. 10, p. 346.

[5]   Arthur Waugh, "Charles Dickens and His Illustrators," in Arthur Waugh and Thomas Hatton, *Retrospectus and Prospectus: The Nonesuch Dickens* (Bloomsbury, 1937)—often called *Nonesuch Dickensiana*—p. 45.

The Cup and the Lip   39

many months, he worked doggedly yet fell further and further behind the pace of publication. In certain ways, the novel bears the scars. But Dickens's letters, his manuscript, and other surviving materials show that this is not the whole story of *Our Mutual Friend*. Rather, through 24 remarkable months of dogged work and frenzied creativity, each time Dickens slipped he managed somehow—as with Venus—to arrive at surer imaginative ground.

I

Our Mutual Friend first appeared in England from Chapman and Hall in 20 numbers, published as 19, from May 1864–November 1865, each one in a green paper wrapper bearing Stone's cover design and accompanied by two of his illustrations. The first 18 numbers consisted of 32 pages of the novel each, and the last—the "double number"—of 53 pages of fiction accompanied by 11 pages made up of the Postscript and the front matter for the novel. No. 1 carried 32 pages of advertisements, the two illustrations, then the 32 pages of fiction, followed finally by more advertisements. As a curious sign, perhaps, of Dickens's supreme anxiety regarding the early numbers, No. 1 also carried a printed slip inserted between the plates and the start of the novel declaring, "The Reader will understand the use of the popular phrase Our Mutual Friend, as the title of this book, on arriving at the Ninth Chapter (page 84)."[6] Subsequent numbers were identical except that they omitted this slip and began with 16 pages of advertisements rather than 32, and also except that No. 19/20, the double number, carried four illustrations rather than two. In the United States, Harper and Brothers published the installments in *Harper's New Monthly Magazine* June 1864–December 1865 and reproduced all but four of Stone's illustrations, though delays with John McLenan's reengravings of Stone meant that the illustrations for part one appeared in part two, and those for part two appeared in part three. To catch up, for the fourth part *Harper's* included four illustrations, but publication of the illustrations continued to be erratic, with two, four, or none appearing in parts thereafter.[7] In *Harper's* the

---

6   Thomas Hatton and Arthur H. Cleaver, *A Bibliography of the Periodical Works of Charles Dickens* (London, 1933), p. 349. According to Walter E. Smith's *Charles Dickens in the Original Cloth: A Bibliographic Catalogue* (Los Angeles, 1982), some copies of the first volume edition from Chapman and Hall also have this slip tipped in at the first page. See vol. 1, p. 107.

7   Walter E. Smith points out in *Charles Dickens: A Bibliography of His First American Editions* (Calabasas, 2012) that Harper and Brothers' first two-volume edition omits six illustrations entirely—"The Boofer Lady," "A Friend in Need," "Lightwood at Last," "Mr. Boffin Does the Honours of the Nursery Door," "Not To Be Shaken Off," and "The Dutch Bottle"—because McLenan's reengravings for Volume 1 were not all finished when Harper and Brothers rushed the volume to press, fearful that they might not beat their competitors to the punch despite their outlay for American rights. Two of these, "The Boofer Lady" and "A Friend in Need," were finished in time for inclusion in No. 10 on February 20, 1865. But Volume 2 simply omitted the other four illustrations until subsequent editions. See pp. 390–92.

text was also laid out in two columns per page, unlike the single-column English edition. One further "first edition" also bears mention here: the edition published in Germany by the publisher Baron Bernhard Tauchnitz, who secured rights to the novel from Dickens and printed *Our Mutual Friend* in four volumes as Nos. 730, 760, 780, and 800 in his "Collection of British Authors" series. The volumes included 20 of Stone's illustrations, and Tauchnitz also issued them as monthly installments simultaneous with those in England, though extraordinarily few of these installments have come to light.

Chapman and Hall and Harper and Brothers each also published the novel in two volumes during, not after, its serial run. In England Volume 1 appeared just before No. 10 on January 20, 1865, and Volume 2 appeared on October 21, 1865, just before publication of the closing double number; book publication in America came slightly later, on February 2 and November 11, 1865, just as the serialization did, but the two volumes still preceded Nos. 10 and 19/20 in *Harper's*.[8] More, as the novel's British ending date—October, not November, 1865—reminds us, with *Our Mutual Friend* as with all of Dickens's 20-number novels, we must understand both the number of installments and the dates upon which they appeared, as Dickens might say, in their Pickwickian sense. From the time of *The Pickwick Papers* in 1836–1837, Dickens had used the idea of "20 monthly numbers" as a kind of short-hand to mean 20 numbers published over 19 months, with the installment for month 19 comprising a double number of 19 and 20 combined to finish the novel. He also, in his novels in parts, observed the periodical tradition of publishing in advance of the nominal issue date—sometimes at least—so that numbers of *Our Mutual Friend* typically appeared either on the first day of the month of issue or late in the month prior. No. 8 for December 1864 appeared on December 1, then, but No. 1 for May 1864 appeared on April 30, No. 17 (for September 1865) on August 31, and the final double number not in November 1865 but rather late in October.[9] Still, as a practical matter, scholars (including this one) generally refer to installments as Dickens did, according to the month for which they were dated and issued.

These are not irrelevant details for one studying *Our Mutual Friend*, for they reveal just how far ahead Dickens needed to write if he wanted to remain comfortably in advance of publication, and how easily he might "slip" if he suffered illness, accident, or other delay. For instance, since No. 19 and No. 20 had to be ready together at the time for the 19th installment, Dickens had always to write at least one extra month in advance, unless he intended eventually to write 19 and 20 together in a single month in a dizzying rush. More, Dickens typically took three to four weeks to work through sets of proofs for each number, which

---

[8]   Ibid. No. 10 appeared in *Harper's* on February 20, and Nos. 19/20 not until the December issue.

[9]   Identifying certainly the actual issue dates of parts of Dickens's serials is always tricky. I base the information here on advertisements Chapman and Hall placed in the *Athenaeum*, which often indicate on which particular date a new monthly part became available for purchase.

means that he needed really to be drafting material at least two months ahead, not one. Add to this the continuous editorial work that Dickens performed for *All the Year Round*, and the extraordinarily heavy seasonal work he did each October for the magazine's perennially successful Christmas number, and a picture begins to emerge: of Dickens, as desperately busy as always, facing in the summer of 1863 the daunting challenge of planning his first novel in 20 numbers since creating *All the Year Round* four years before. Consequently, though he began negotiating a contract for *Our Mutual Friend* with Chapman and Hall in September 1863, he said from the outset that he did not intend to begin publishing installments until the following spring. He wanted, he told Forster, five numbers written by the time the first appeared in May 1864—a quantity that, given the double number he intended, amounted to a lead of four months on publication and three months on the correction of proofs.

According to Forster, Dickens had chosen the title of *Our Mutual Friend* in 1861, perhaps not long after finishing *Great Expectations*.[10] He had used the expression "mutual friend" occasionally in his work as far back as *Pickwick* and "our mutual friend" first in *The Old Curiosity Shop* (1840–41) and, more recently and frequently, in both *Bleak House* and *Little Dorrit*. As Forster writes, during 1861–63 Dickens held to the phrase as his title for the new novel "through much objection."[11] Yet it is not clear that the title played much role in his conception of the story, or that, by choosing the title, he hastened his ability to plan and write his new book. In fact, though Dickens wanted to begin a new novel shortly after finishing *Great Expectations* in April 1861, he took nearly three years to begin writing again, a time during which he returned to old notes and scraps of ideas to find the characters and events upon which the new book would turn. Forster insists that the "three leading notions" of *Our Mutual Friend* are all mentioned in Dickens's letters during these years, and he takes these notions to be: first, the Hexams and Riderhood and their "ghastly calling"; second, John Harmon, "a man, young and perhaps eccentric, feigning to be dead, and *being* dead to all intents and purposes"; and third, the various actors in the "Social Chorus," from the Lammles with their matrimonial impostures to the "Perfectly New" Veneerings, all over varnish as if they have just come home from their manufacturers.[12] Forster also points out helpfully that Dickens's intention to "use somehow ... the uneducated father in fustian and the educated boy in spectacles whom Leech and [Dickens] saw at Chatham" finally took shape in *Our Mutual Friend*'s Gaffer and Charley Hexam.[13] For the most part Dickens's *Book of Memoranda*, where he began jotting down writing ideas in 1855, agrees with Forster's account—but at times it agrees so closely with phrases that appear verbatim in Forster's biography that it seems likely that either Dickens transcribed ideas from the *Memoranda* book into letters to Forster or that Forster, who had access to the book while writing his biography,

---

[10]   Forster, *Life*, p. 740.

[11]   Ibid.

[12]   Ibid.

[13]   Ibid.

42 *Charles Dickens's* Our Mutual Friend

attributed to Dickens's letters the things he had really found among these rough notes. Still, the *Book of Memoranda* shows that Dickens did indeed develop many of the ideas for *Our Mutual Friend* during 1861–63, even including a bit of dialogue that Forster does not mention, but that contains an early draft of Eugene's request, "Let me die, my dear," after he is attacked by Headstone.[14]

But other aspects of Dickens's novel owe instead to earlier influences, or in some cases to ones that were more immediate when he began writing. Perhaps the earliest of these was the article "Dust: or Ugliness Redeemed" by Richard H. Horne, an account of London's Dust-mounds that Dickens had published in *Household Words* in 1850.[15] *Book of Memoranda* entries dating back to 1855, meanwhile, show that even before Dickens began writing *Little Dorrit* he had devised preliminary ideas that he eventually used for Podsnap ("And by denying a thing, supposes that he altogether puts it out of existence"), Young Blight ("for ever looking out of window, who never has anything to do"), and even the Hexams ("Found Drowned. The descriptive bill upon the wall, by the waterside," and in a separate entry on that page, "A 'long shore' man—woman—child—or family ... connect the Found Drowned Bill with this?").[16] He also drew upon the *Memoranda* for many of *Our Mutual Friend*'s names—Tippins, Twemlow, Harmon, Lammle—a thing he had done for all of his novels since *Little Dorrit*. Throughout the winter of 1861 and spring of 1862, Dickens tried to assemble these imaginative scraps into the novel he had already named *Our Mutual Friend*, but in April he wrote to Forster, "Alas! I have hit upon nothing for a story. Again and again I have tried."[17] Then, during the summer of 1863 as he began again to consider *Our Mutual Friend* in earnest, a letter from Eliza Davis, the wife of the Jewish solicitor to whom Dickens had sold Tavistock House, prompted another decision about the book. Davis's letter asked Dickens to donate to a Jewish memorial and, by way of encouragement, blamed him for having helped to inspire "vile prejudice against the despised Hebrew" with Fagin three decades before and implied that by donating he should "atone for a great wrong" to the Jewish people.[18] Though Dickens defended himself gently but firmly in his reply, he introduced Riah into *Our Mutual Friend* only months later—"to wipe out," Forster acknowledges, "a reproach against his Jew in *Oliver Twist*."[19]

Yet early in August 1863, he still had not begun. "I am always thinking of writing a long book," he confided to Collins, "and am never beginning to do it."[20]

---

[14] Charles Dickens, *Book of Memoranda* (New York, 1981), p. 24.

[15] [Richard H. Horne], "Dust: or Ugliness Redeemed," *Household Words*, July 13, 1850, pp. 379–84.

[16] Dickens, *Book of Memoranda*, pp. 4, 5, 8. Michael Cotsell discusses these materials, too, in his introduction to *The Companion to* Our Mutual Friend (London, 1986), pp. 5–6.

[17] *Letters*, vol. 10, p. 75.

[18] Ibid., p. 269n.

[19] Forster, *Life*, p. 740.

[20] *Letters*, vol. 10, p. 281.

The Cup and the Lip

But it is possible to trace another major influence on *Our Mutual Friend* back to precisely this time, and to the novel then being serialized in *All the Year Round*. Though it has not, to my knowledge, been noted by other critics, Dickens seems to have borrowed brazenly from Charles Reade, whose August 1 installment of *Very Hard Cash*—which describes the residents of Barkington who are ruined by the failure of the town's bank—lingers briefly over the story of "Old Betty," who

> had a horror of the workhouse. To save her old age from it she had deposited her wages in the Bank for the last twenty years; and also a little legacy from Mr. Hardie's father. She now went about the house of her master and debtor, declaring she was sure he would not rob *her*, and, if he did, she would never go into the poor-house. "I'll go out on the common, and die there. Nobody will miss *me*."[21]

Here, it seems, is the germ of *Our Mutual Friend*'s Betty Higden, who flees in terror from the specters of the poor-house and a pauper burial and in the process constitutes Dickens's final seething attack on the Poor Laws. However much Reade's novel irritated Dickens with its heavy-handed caricatures of lunacy doctors and commissioners—and however much Dickens chafed at the circulation of *All the Year Round* being "rather dropped by Reade" during the summer and fall of 1863—this bare suggestion of "Old Betty" seems to have taken its place in the imaginative miasma that was leavening into *Our Mutual Friend*.[22] Late in August, having in the meantime "evaporated for a fortnight" to France, Dickens wrote to Forster to say that, at long last, he was "full of notions ... for the new twenty numbers."[23]

If Dickens struggled more than usual to begin writing his new novel, he certainly had reasons. Initially, in March 1862, he blamed his lack of invention on the residence he had taken in town for the spring season, "an odious little London box" that, he wrote to his friend William de Cerjat, "I so thoroughly detest abominate and abjure."[24] Later in the year troubles of a more serious nature began to press upon him as well. His mother was entering the final months of her long and pitiable mental decline and was being cared for at a house in Grafton Terrace by Helen Dickens, the widow of his brother Alfred. Early in the summer, too, Georgina was stricken suddenly with chest pains and fell gravely ill, terrifying Dickens and leaving him to wonder what might become of the children—and him—if they lost their devoted aunt's attentions. "No one," Dickens wrote to Macready in early July, "can ever know what she has been to us, and how she has supplied an empty place and an ever widening gap, since the girls were

---

[21] Charles Reade, *Very Hard Cash*, in *All the Year Round* (August 1, 1863), p. 534.

[22] *Letters*, vol. 10, p. 348. For discussions of how *Very Hard Cash* fared in *All the Year Round*, see Malcolm Elwin, *Charles Reade* (London, 1931), pp. 172–3; and John Sutherland, "Dickens, Reade and *Hard Cash*," *Dickensian*, 81 (Spring 1985), pp. 5–12.

[23] *Letters*, vol. 10, pp. 281, 283.

[24] Ibid., p. 52.

mere dolls."[25] Principally for Georgina's health—though partly, perhaps, so that he might steal time with Nelly—Dickens spent much of the second half of the year in France, finally situating Georgina and Mamie in a residence in Paris in October and flitting back and forth ceaselessly between London, Gad's Hill, and the continent. By December Georgina had mostly recovered, but in February of the new year Dickens had again to find a town residence for the London season, and in April he learned that his old beloved friend Egg, who had acted with him and Nelly and Collins in *The Frozen Deep*, had died unexpectedly while traveling abroad. "Think what a great Frozen Deep lay close under those boards we acted on!" Dickens wrote to Collins of the news, "my brother Alfred, Luard, Arthur, Albert, Austin, Egg—even among the audience, Prince Albert and poor Stone—all gone! ... However, this won't do. We must close up the ranks and march on."[26] Through the summer Dickens renewed his efforts to plan *Our Mutual Friend* and on September 8 he finally broached the possibility of a new novel with Chapman and Hall. Then, on September 12, his ailing mother died, reinvigorating every galling memory that Dickens had spent decades trying to forget.

Of course, Dickens's personal difficulties were not the only things hindering his writing. He was, as always, impossibly busy with work, just not the work of beginning *Our Mutual Friend*. During spring 1862 he had again given a series of readings in London, many of them incorporating new selections developed from *Nicholas Nickleby* (1838–39) and *Copperfield*.[27] Then, while abroad with Georgina and Mamie in October, he planned and chose the contributors for *All the Year Round*'s upcoming Christmas number "Somebody's Luggage," in the end writing three of the number's eight stories himself. In France that winter he also gave four readings at the British Embassy, then another series of London readings March–June 1863. When he finally began work on *Our Mutual Friend* in earnest in October of that year, he was already slaving at the 1863 Christmas number, "Mrs. Lirriper's Lodgings," which would turn out to be one of *All the Year Round*'s most resounding successes. As a consequence his letters from September 1863 are a fascinating mishmash of indications for the Christmas story, arrangements related to his mother's death, and contract negotiations with Chapman and Hall for the new novel. As he put it to Forster in March 1864 while laboring over the last of the five numbers he wanted to finish before publication began in May, "I have grown hard to satisfy, and write very slowly. And I have so much—not fiction—that *will* be thought of, when I don't want to think of it, that I am forced to take more care than I once took."[28] Perhaps this explains why Dickens responded so gratefully the following year when Dallas reviewed *Our Mutual Friend* for the *Times* and called

---

[25]   Ibid., p. 100.

[26]   Ibid., p. 238.

[27]   See Andrews, p. 277. Collins gives the full texts of these readings as *David Copperfield* and *Nicholas Nickleby at the Yorkshire School* in *The Public Readings*, pp. 219–48, 253–77.

[28]   *Letters*, vol. 10, p. 377.

especial attention to Dickens's "care" in writing the novel.[29] Dickens had never worked so meticulously before, nor so doggedly and determinedly amid a legion of other concerns.

Our Mutual Friend may well owe much of its somber tone to Dickens's troubles during these years—to his broken marriage, to lost friends, and to the herculean effort that preserving his professional life had required. Indeed, given the tenor of Dickens's life in the years that preceded *Our Mutual Friend*, we need not wonder why the novel is such a bleak wasteland of corpses and dust only fitfully redeemed by the warmth of loving relationships that are always too few and too far between. Though he refused to admit it, Dickens had grown old, his face seamed, his hair gray and wispy, and his natural buoyancy much compromised by worry, fatigue, and intermittent illness. Yet he was not incapable of hard work, and through the early 1860s he not only continued tirelessly to deliver readings and to work at *All the Year Round* but also to serve as the guiding force for his children and the various other dependents—Nelly, Catherine, his mother, his sister Letitia, his sister-in-law Helen—who demanded so much of his money and time. *Our Mutual Friend*, too, is a product of this labor. But to admit this is not to say, with James, that the novel is therefore deeply labored rather than deeply felt, for the two propositions are not mutually exclusive. If anything, Dickens felt too bitterly the frustrations and disappointments of which he wrote, and too eagerly the slender possibility of an ideal, romantic love like Bella's for John Harmon, or Lizzie's for Eugene. Dickens worked at *Our Mutual Friend* not with the imaginative infertility and exhaustion with which one wields a pickaxe but rather with the intensity of the master-craftsman, the painter mixing the precise hue, the sculptor chiseling the perfect line. Certainly he agonized and labored over *Our Mutual Friend* in ways that he never had over *Pickwick*. Equally certainly, *Our Mutual Friend* is the richer, more complex, more extraordinary novel.

Dickens finally began writing *Our Mutual Friend* in October 1863 when he escaped, on or around October 15, to Gad's Hill so that he could work unmolested on the opening chapters. He was, he told Forster, "determined not to begin publishing with less than five numbers done," and he worked through the fall and winter with this idea in mind.[30] But he had also "Mrs. Lirriper's Lodgings" to write for Christmas, and he seems generally to have made only slow progress on the novel. He was delayed somewhat by his shock and sadness over Thackeray's death in December, which in turn occasioned him to spend part of January writing "In Memoriam" of his brother-novelist for the *Cornhill*. To Sir William Russell he wrote, as he had to Collins when Egg died, of the "constant closing-up of the ranks and marching on"—which, predictably, is just what Dickens did, finishing No. 2 by the last week of January and beginning work on No. 3.[31] Still, and though Dickens did not know it, the pattern had been set, for his work on *Our Mutual Friend* would be punctuated repeatedly by obstacles and interruptions of this kind.

---

[29]   [E.S. Dallas], "*Our Mutual Friend*," *Times*, November 29, 1865, p. 6.
[30]   *Letters*, vol. 10, p. 300.
[31]   Ibid., p. 335.

Early in February he continued to write but was also, again, negotiating for a place in London to take Georgina and Mamie to for the spring. Then, on February 7—his 51st birthday—he learned that his son Walter had died suddenly in India on December 31 of an aneurism of the aorta. Even so, the next day Dickens was again focused on his work, for he wrote to Georgina from the *All the Year Round* office, "I have been interrupted again today, and am almost beside myself."[32] On February 13 he moved his household from Gad's Hill to his new London residence at 57 Gloucester Place, and a few days later, still hard at work on No. 3, he went with Stone to St. Andrew's Street to visit Willis's taxidermy.

During these early months, in fact, Dickens worked extensively with Stone even while he also tried to work himself back into the groove of writing monthly installments. In *Victorian Novelists and Their Illustrators* (1971) John R. Harvey famously asserted that by the 1860s Dickens had lost interest in illustrations generally and certainly had none in Stone's for *Our Mutual Friend*.[33] But as Jane Cohen, Michael O'Hea, and others have since shown, this was far from the case.[34] Dickens coached his novice illustrator painstakingly during the early months, recommending subjects and critiquing drafts, and only later giving him more flexibility as Dickens's energy flagged and his faith in Stone grew. In 1863 Stone was just 23 and relatively new to book illustration. He was, or at least wished to be, principally a painter, but he had been grateful for the work in 1861 when Dickens gave him the chance to illustrate the Cheap edition of *Little Dorrit*. The next year he provided illustrations for the Library editions of *Great Expectations*, *Pictures from Italy* (1846), *American Notes* (1842), and *A Child's History of England* (1851–53).[35] But this was all very different from drawing alongside the great novelist and conforming, as best he could, to the requirements of the monthly format. These were demanding, since he could begin drawing for a number only once Dickens had finished drafting that part of the story; for hints regarding the novel's future events, he had no key but Dickens himself. During February 1864, Dickens therefore spent considerable time coaching his protégé, meeting with him and providing advice on the draft sketches he was already completing. On February 14 Dickens sent Stone proofs of No. 1 and said that he hoped also to have them for No. 2 soon. "It will be best," Dickens told him, "for you to read the 1st. two Nos. before we take counsel together. We will then settle in the first place, what little indication of the story we will have on the cover."[36] He even sketched for Stone an illustration of where the title, author, illustrator, and publisher information would

---

[32] Ibid., p. 354.

[33] John R. Harvey, *Victorian Novelists and Their Illustrators* (New York, 1971), pp. 164–5.

[34] See for instance "Chapter 16: Marcus Stone" in Jane R. Cohen's *Charles Dickens and His Original Illustrators* (Columbus, 1980), pp. 203–9, and Michael O'Hea's "Hidden Harmony: Marcus Stone's Wrapper Design for *Our Mutual Friend*," *Dickensian*, 91 (Winter 1995), pp. 198–208.

[35] Kitton, pp. 201–2.

[36] *Letters*, vol. 10, p. 357.

The Cup and the Lip   47

appear on the monthly wrapper, to show him the content he would be obliged to draw around when he began work.[37] By February 23, Stone had finished his draft of the wrapper design, which Dickens called "*excellent*" and then critiqued in virtually every detail.[38] By then Dickens had also "done the St. Andrew place," he told Stone, and "made it the last Chapter of the 2nd No."[39] In short, by the close of February Dickens had managed to correct his overwriting of Nos. 1 and 2 and was working his young illustrator into proper shape for the months ahead.

Dickens's pains to supervise Stone's work can be understood partly as an impulse to control the drawings of his much less experienced—and almost certainly subservient—partner. Stone was no Browne, even if his art was as good, for Browne had made a long career as an illustrator of serial fiction and periodicals and had worked closely with Dickens for nearly a quarter century. Also, where Browne worked in steel engraving, Stone preferred wood, a difference that threatened to ruin some of the finer points of the younger man's work given the heavy printing demands of a new monthly-number novel by Dickens.[40] In short, Dickens had practical reasons for wanting to help Stone along, but it seems likely, too, that he took such trouble because he hoped genuinely to assure the young man's success. For the early numbers he recommended to Stone which subjects he should draw, and he still occasionally gave constructive advice. On March 2, despite beginning to feel desperately behind with his novel, Dickens wrote coaxingly to Dalziel Brothers, the wood engravers who would prepare Stone's drawings, remarking that he was "anxious to give Mr. Stone's illustrations ... every possible chance" and that he should "feel really obliged ... if [they] will have the kindness to take the engraving of them under [their] especial protection."[41] Later that month he campaigned to have Stone elected to the Garrick Club. Once he was sure that Stone understood both the pace of and intent for his work for the monthly numbers, Dickens seems to have had very little else to say about the drawings. By the time he sent Stone proofs of No. 6 in July, Dickens was letting him choose his own subjects for the illustrations, and he typically confined his remarks to compliments on their quality and to providing the captions (or "Letterings") for each one. By the summer of 1864, Dickens and Stone seem to have settled into an easy routine, with Dickens providing proofs to Stone six to eight weeks prior to publication, and Stone completing drawings in about 10 days and sending them on to Dickens for captions and approval.

---

[37]   The Editors of the *Letters* provide a facsimile reproduction of this sketch in vol. 10, p. 358.

[38]   Ibid., p. 361.

[39]   Ibid., p. 362.

[40]   As William Vaughan has recently noted, "wood-engraving could never match metal engraving (in its various forms) or lithography in finesse, [but] it could nevertheless be used with sufficient refinement and distinction to manifest an aesthetic of its own." See Vaughan's "Facsimile Versus White Line: An Anglo-German Disparity," in Paul Goldman and Simon Cooke (eds), *Reading Victorian Illustration, 1855–1875: Spoils of the Lumber Room* (Farnham, 2012), p. 34.

[41]   *Letters*, vol. 10, p. 366.

48   *Charles Dickens's* Our Mutual Friend

But the easy routine of Dickens's correspondence with Stone underscores nevertheless just how difficult and complex his activities were as he worked through the monthly installments of *Our Mutual Friend*. At virtually all times from January 1864 to September 1865, besides reviewing Stone's illustrations, Dickens usually was drafting one installment, correcting initial proofs of another, and working through a combination of intermediate and final proofs for one or even two more. Furthermore, Dickens's mentions of "Nos." in his correspondence often use only that short-hand rather than identify which particular number of *Our Mutual Friend* he means, and sometimes—as when he is writing to Wills about "Nos." of *All the Year Round*—he is not talking about *Our Mutual Friend* at all. The complications of both the work and Dickens's sometimes vague references to it thus make assembling a chronology of his writing surprisingly hard. In June 1864, for instance, as Dickens neared the publication of No. 3 for July, his schedule of work appears to have looked like this. On June 10 he was planning No. 7 but had not yet begun to write it. On June 14 he reviewed Stone's final illustrations for No. 4 and suggested subjects for the plates to No. 5. On June 18 he sent Stone captions for No. 4. And on June 26, he wrote to Wills to say that the initial proofs of No. 6 should arrive to the *All the Year Round* office very soon. Then, at the end of the month, Dickens made a "Mysterious Disappearance" to France where he intended to consider not *Our Mutual Friend* but rather whether the next Mrs. Lirriper (for Christmas 1864) "might have a mixing in it of Paris and London."[42]

To date, the Editors of Dickens's *Letters* have provided by far the best chronology for *Our Mutual Friend*, though they necessarily do so only piecemeal through the excellent footnotes to his letters during this time. But the complications of Dickens's work mean that even their chronology needs occasional correction. For instance, in a note to Dickens's letter of February 24, 1865 to Marcus Stone providing the captions for "Bibliomania of the Golden Dustman" and "The Evil Genius of the House of Boffin," the editors identify the former as an illustration to No. 11 and the latter as an illustration to No. 12.[43] But both appeared in No. 12 for April 1865, which makes sense since Dickens's letters typically provided captions only for illustrations that would appear in the same month. Likewise, on April 13, 1865, Dickens wrote to Stone to enclose a set of unidentified proofs, telling him, "This is not corrected, but is legible. You will find plenty of subjects in it. Whether one of the two should be Mr Boffin behind the Alligator's smile, I leave to you."[44] The Editors identify the proofs in question as No. 13 for May 1865, but they are almost certainly for No. 14, for the three chapters of the earlier number—Book the Third, Chapters 8–10—never mention Boffin in Venus's shop, instead detailing Betty Higden's death, Bella and John's visit to Lizzie, and the "grinding torments" of Headstone's endless nocturnal pursuit of Eugene.[45] Boffin does not hide behind

---

[42]   Ibid., p. 409. The reference is to "Mrs. Lirriper's Legacy," the Christmas number of *All the Year Round* for 1864.

[43]   Ibid., vol. 11, p. 19.

[44]   Ibid., p. 32.

[45]   Dickens, *Our Mutual Friend* (London, 1997), p. 533.

The Cup and the Lip 49

the "Alligator's smile" until Book the Third, Chapter 14, the final chapter of No. 14 for June. But these are relatively minor points. The Editors of the *Letters* have truly done yeoman's work with the chronology, and I have relied heavily upon their work in creating my own chronology in the following pages.

By the time *Our Mutual Friend*'s No. 1 was published in May 1864, Dickens does seem to have written his five-number advance—even though, through much of April, Wills was ill and threw a heavier share of *All the Year Round* onto him. On March 18 Dickens had proofs of Nos. 1, 2, and 3 in hand, so he was presumably working on No. 4 at mid-month and on No. 5 as the first number went to press. But the evidence suggests that throughout the months of *Our Mutual Friend*'s serialization, he almost continuously lost ground, sometimes at a rate that alarmed him. During June 1864 he should already have been drafting No. 7, but he was still just planning that number on June 10, and the fact that the proofs for No. 6 were not ready even near month's end suggests that he began working on No. 7, at best, only near the start of July. He had nearly finished that number a few weeks later, but to Forster he confided that he knew he was falling behind. He was "unwell," he told Forster, and "out of sorts":

> Although I have not been wanting in industry, I have been wanting in invention, and have fallen back with the book. Looming large before me is the Christmas work, and I can hardly hope to do it without losing a number of *Our Friend* [*sic*]. I have very nearly lost one already, and two would take one half of my whole advance."[46]

He rallied, however, and probably finished No. 7 late in the month, and he certainly finished No. 8 during the third week of August. On October 1 he wrote to Wills, "Mrs. Lirriper is again in hand. I had flown off from the finish of No. IX of our Mutual, to perch upon her cap."[47] He therefore began his Christmas work having drafted nine numbers of the novel—and having given up, as he had predicted in July, one month of his advance.

Not surprisingly, Dickens dashed off his work on Mrs. Lirriper as quickly as he could manage and then, with "No. 10 ... unborn," made off to Dover for a short time to work without interruption. Perhaps because of the pressures of *All the Year Round*, or the pressures of social engagements, or simply the desire to spend time with Nelly, Dickens escaped from London and Gad's Hill increasingly during the next several months, as if he needed the solitude—not of his study at home—in order to write. Late in October he wrote to his friend Cerjat of being driven

> to cross the channel perpetually. Whenever I feel that I have worked too much, or am on the eve of over-doing it, and want a change, away I go by the Mail Train, and turn up in Paris, or anywhere else that suits my humour ... So I come back as fresh as a Daisy, and preserve as ruddy a face as if I never bent over a sheet of paper.[48]

---

[46] *Letters*, vol. 10, p. 414.

[47] Ibid., p. 431.

[48] Ibid., p. 445.

50   *Charles Dickens's* Our Mutual Friend

His rush to Dover suggests that he was trying to escape October without losing a number to his Christmas work, and perhaps he nearly managed. But then his old friend Leech died suddenly of a heart attack on October 29. A few days later Dickens wrote miserably to Forster, "I have not done my number. This death of poor Leech ... has put me out woefully. Yesterday and the day before I could do nothing; seemed for the time to have quite lost the power; and am only now by slow degrees getting back into the track to-day."[49] In a few days he had steeled himself against this new unhappiness, and by the middle of November he had finished writing No. 10. But the Christmas work and Leech's death had together cost him another half-month of his advance. He was now, it is true, halfway through *Our Mutual Friend*. But he had wrenched just five numbers from himself in the last six months, and he would have to write the last ten in just ten months if he wanted to finish in time to correct proofs of his double number.

Dickens's letters go nearly silent on *Our Mutual Friend* during December 1864. He mentions the novel just once, in a letter to Frederic Chapman on December 30 that accompanied the title page, dedication, table of contents, and table of illustrations for the collected Volume 1, which would appear roughly simultaneously with No. 10 near the end of January 1865. He had clearly finished drafting No. 11, meanwhile, either in December or in the very early days of the new year since he wrote to Stone on January 10 to suggest subjects for the illustrations to the number—a hint that Stone already had, or soon would have, at least the initial proofs in his hand. At mid-January, he was also planning his research for Boffin's transformation into a miser, for he wrote to George Holsworth at the *All the Year Round* office on January 18 asking him to get a copy of F.S. Merryweather's *Lives and Anecdotes of Misers* "or any thing else that will give the means of reference I want."[50] This detail may suggest that Dickens had not yet begun drafting No. 12, since the chapter for which Dickens was researching ("The Golden Dustman Falls Into Bad Company") was the first for that installment. But he must then have begun, and written quickly. By February 14 he had already corrected and returned proofs for No. 12, so during most of February and into early March he was likely drafting No. 13. He still had very little margin for error, but at least he had lost no more ground since November.

In another way, though, February 1865 was momentous for Dickens, for at mid-month he suffered the first severe and sustained attack of the illness that eventually killed him. On February 21 he sent off several letters complaining of "a wounded foot," a malady that he explained in greater detail 10 days later, writing to Forster:

> I got frost-bitten by walking continually in the snow, and getting wet in the feet daily. My boots hardened and softened, hardened and softened, my left foot swelled, and I still forced the boot on ... At length, going out as usual, I fell lame on the walk, and had to limp home dead lame, through the snow, for the last three miles—to the remarkable terror, by the bye, of the two big dogs.[51]

---

[49] Ibid., p. 447.

[50] Ibid., vol. 11, p. 7.

[51] Ibid., p. 23.

The Cup and the Lip 51

As Ackroyd points out, "[t]here can be no certainty in any medical diagnosis so long after the event," but the likelihood is that Dickens was experiencing the first major symptoms of arterio-sclerosis or even blood clots in the leg.[52] He was in agony at Gad's Hill and kept to the sofa for several days, but he soon rallied enough to make the trip to London to seek out a house for the coming spring season. By March he was situated at 16 Somers Place near Hyde Park, but the pain in his foot had not really subsided, and he began complaining late in the month to his physician Frank Beard that despite resting the "confounded foot [was] as bad as ever again."[53] For weeks, the inflamed foot disrupted Dickens's beloved routine of concentrated writing followed by ferocious walks where he could arrange his ideas for the work to come. Ironically—and perhaps suggestively, too—he may well have been suffering his first pangs of frustration and immobility even as he wrote "Scouts Out," the last chapter of No. 13, which describes Eugene's cunning plan to enrage and exhaust Headstone through tireless nocturnal traversals of London. Throughout March and April, Dickens was almost housebound at Somers Place; he did not even go out to dinner for the first time until April 27. Yet he managed somehow to write No. 14 by the first week in April and No. 15 by very early May. He was suffering, though, and frightfully worn—working himself, he told his daughters, "into a damaged state."[54] By late May, though he was still hobbled, he was finally well enough to travel, so he escaped to France to convalesce and begin work on No. 16. "Work and worry, without exercise, would soon make an end of me," he wrote to Forster before leaving. "If I were not going away now, I should break down. No one knows as I know to-day how near to it I have been."[55] He was also now perilously near to giving up any semblance of an advance on *Our Mutual Friend*—No. 16, for August, would appear on July 29, but Dickens had still not quite finished it on June 9 when his train crashed at Staplehurst.

Though Dickens escaped the accident uninjured, Nelly apparently did not, and her health became a new source of anxiety as he tried to finish the novel. She had sustained injuries to her arm and neck and lost the jewelry that Dickens later tried to claim from the manager at Charing Cross station.[56] For more than two months, Dickens referred to the "Patient" in his letters to Wills, and on June 25 he sent instructions to his servant John Thompson to "[t]ake Miss Ellen tomorrow morning, a little basket of fresh fruit, a jar of clotted cream … a pair of pigeons, or some nice little bird. Also on Wednesday morning, and on Friday morning, take her some other things of the same sort—making a little variety each day."[57] In later years, according to Ackroyd, Nelly's friends recalled her left arm and

---

[52]   Ackroyd, p. 957.

[53]   *Letters*, vol. 11, p. 28.

[54]   Ibid., p. 48.

[55]   Ibid.

[56]   Tomalin, *Charles Dickens*, p. 332.

[57]   *Letters*, vol. 11, p. 65. For references to the "Patient" see also *Letters*, vol. 11, pp. 70, 86.

shoulder being intermittent sources of pain to her, and occasional talk that she had supposedly in earlier life been injured in some unspecified accident.[58] Even with this new cause for anxiety, and despite being so unnerved that he could hardly hold a pen, Dickens enclosed part of an installment to William Day at Clowes on the day after the accident, noting in the letter, "There are 3 more pages of this No. to follow. You shall have them shortly. Proofs to Gad's Hill, as I have left town."[59] The Editors to the *Letters* suggest that Dickens was returning corrected proofs of No. 15, but it seems more likely that he was sending Day the nearly complete manuscript of No. 16, since he is clearly requesting "proofs" from them rather than "revises" as he often called them in their intermediate stages. Indeed, in *Our Mutual Friend*'s "Postscript, in Lieu of a Preface," in which he writes about his narrow escape at Staplehurst, Dickens states that he rescued from the train "Mr. and Mrs. Boffin (in their manuscript dress of receiving Mr. and Mrs. Lammle at breakfast) ... Bella Wilfer on her wedding day, and Mr. Riderhood inspecting Bradley Headstone's red neckerchief as he lay asleep."[60] If Dickens was being at all precise beneath this playful tone, this would mean that he rescued three of No. 16's four chapters, which may explain why he was prepared to send all but three pages of the number to Day. As for the fourth chapter, "The Golden Dustman Sinks Again" may just not have been finished, or a few pages may have been disfigured in the crash. Either way, by June 21 Dickens had received, corrected, and returned to Clowes the proofs of No. 16, though he had been surprised to see, he told Forster, that he had "under-written number sixteen by two and a half pages—a thing I have not done since *Pickwick!*"[61]

By the end of June, then, Dickens had just three months to write his last four installments if he wanted to have even part of October to handle the proofs of the final double number. He was under enormous pressure, his nerves stretched to breaking by Staplehurst, Nelly's injuries, and a wave of unrelenting summer heat. He responded by erupting in a two-month creative frenzy, not just finishing the novel on time but finishing it a month *early*, writing the last 13 chapters of the novel in a stunning eight-week burst. At the start of July Dickens had "but just begun" No. 17.[62] But by the middle of the month he had obviously finished it, for he wrote to Stone on July 19 telling him to expect proofs from the printer "directly."[63] He then began working furiously at the final three numbers, his letters to friends bursting with hyperbolic allusions to the labor he was now pouring into the book. To Ouvry he wrote of *Our Mutual Friend* having him "by the throat," and to Wills he remarked that he was "[d]isturbed in mind by Our Mutual, and in body

---

[58]   Ackroyd, p. 962.

[59]   *Letters*, vol. 11, p. 49.

[60]   Dickens, *Our Mutual Friend* (London, 1997), pp. 799–800.

[61]   *Letters*, vol. 11, p. 67. Forster points out in *Life* that Dickens's assertion is not entirely true: he had, on one occasion, also underwritten a number of *Dombey*. See p. 743.

[62]   *Letters*, vol. 11, p. 66.

[63]   Ibid., p. 72.

by myriads of minute flies."[64] To another friend he wrote an even more playful letter in late July, proclaiming, "I am as right as a man can be who is working his head off—beginning with the hair."[65] But he was clearly working himself to the point of exhaustion just as he had in May, his work on the novel punctuated, he told Dallas in mid-August, by "a little festival of Neuralgia in the face."[66] On August 22 he wrote to Day telling him to expect "some MS of the double No. 19 & 20 from me tomorrow" and also to George Russell declaring that he was in the "agonies" of finishing the book.[67] "No news," he told Wills on August 27, "except that I am working like a Dragon, and that I hope something near a week may bring me through it."[68] A week did bring him through it. On September 2 a weary Dickens wrote triumphantly to Day enclosing "the whole conclusion of the text of Our Mutual Friend," including the "Postscript," the front matter for Volume 2 of the book edition, and the proofs of No. 18 corrected and ready for press.[69] He asked Day to send the proofs along to Stone when they were ready, and he wrote to Stone, too, to tell him that the novel was finished and give him instructions for the proofs and illustrations of the double number. Then he vanished into space.

II

The manuscript that Dickens left behind when he departed for France in September 1865 is, for obvious reasons, the most significant resource available to scholars who want to study Dickens's creative processes and writing practices in *Our Mutual Friend*. It is a fascinating text, rife with evidence of Dickens's persistent problems with overwriting and underwriting and of his painstaking work on particular characters and scenes. Held by the Pierpont Morgan Library in New York, the manuscript is 443 slips of cramped, much corrected, sometimes nearly illegible prose, most of it in dark blue ink with lines sloping downward gently to the right. The typical slip consists of a single column of writing on one side and a page number at the top center (sometimes top left-center) in Dickens's hand, starting over again at 1 with each new monthly number. For its purposes, the Morgan has numbered the folios, too, in pencil in the upper right corner, restarting at 1 only at the beginning of No. 11 (the novel's Volume 2). By this time in his life Dickens's penmanship was not always the best, nor was it helped probably by his bouts of facial neuralgia or, in later numbers, by his unnerving experience at Staplehurst. He seems to have preferred to end chapters at the bottom of a page rather than carry them over—a problem sometimes, since it led him often

---

[64] Ibid., pp. 74, 76.
[65] Ibid., p. 77.
[66] Ibid., p. 84.
[67] Ibid., pp. 84, 85.
[68] Ibid., p. 86.
[69] Ibid., p. 88.

54   *Charles Dickens's* Our Mutual Friend

to cramp his writing even more than usual to squeeze in his concluding lines. To make matters worse, Dickens revised his manuscript so actively that the typical page of *Our Mutual Friend* contains upwards of 25 canceled words and interlinear additions, many of them so cramped that they are nearly indecipherable (Plate 1). Infrequently, writing appears on the verso of a finished slip as well, in some cases because Dickens made an abortive start to the page and flipped it over to begin again, and in others because he used the verso to write or paste in new material meant for insertion in the page that follows. The complications of the manuscript explain, at least partly, why Clowes reserved a special team of compositors for Dickens throughout *Our Mutual Friend*'s serial run. Still, for all its challenges, the manuscript remains an irreplaceable resource for any scholar of the novel.

But it is not the only resource, nor even the only one left from 1864–65. On the contrary, scholars interested in the rich textual history of *Our Mutual Friend* can also use two other resources—one of them described in detail here for the first time, so far as I know—that supplement Dickens's manuscript in crucial ways. The first of these, and the more familiar, is the set of Proof sheets held in the Berg Collection at the New York Public Library, a single bound volume (two volumes as one) that contains a full run of proofs for the novel—excepting the illustrations, which do not appear—some of them bearing corrections in Dickens's hand. Generally, the Proof sheets are most useful for what they reveal of Dickens's problems with overwriting in the early numbers of *Our Mutual Friend*, since these were, as it happens, more extensive and persistent than the manuscript shows. The proofs show precisely how much Dickens needed to cut from No. 2 when he substituted Mr. Venus for "A Marriage Contract," for instance, and they show that he overwrote No. 1 by a wide margin as well. Beyond such details the proofs have only limited utility for scholars, except to confirm that Dickens completed most of his imaginative revisions while his chapters were still in manuscript, using the proofs only to correct punctuation errors, missing words, and occasional misspellings introduced by compositors driven half mad by his difficult scrawl. In one instance in No. 20, one of Dickens's marginal corrections to the proofs is rendered illegible by the binding, further evidence that he corrected the proofs as loose sheets, one number at a time, and that they were bound only sometime after the novel's serial run.[70]

More, though the proof sheets are nominally "complete," only those for Nos. 1, 2, 8, 9, 11, 14, and 19/20 bear editing marks, and the marks in No. 9 are so scanty that they are not verifiably in Dickens's hand, nor are they in his accustomed blue ink.[71] Nor, as it turns out, are even the marked proofs necessarily decisive, for some

---

[70]   Proof sheets of *Our Mutual Friend* by Charles Dickens, New York Public Library, Henry W. and Albert A. Berg Collection, vol. 2, p. 269.

[71]   In fact, the question marks inked occasionally into the margins in No. 9 are not shaped like those in the numbers Dickens definitely worked on. It is worth pointing out, too, that while the proofs for No. 3 also bear Dickens's editing marks, nominally at least, this is only because the last two pages of No. 2's proofs, which Dickens worked through thoroughly, were moved to No. 3 during revision. For an example of the uncertain editing marks for No. 9, see for instance the Proof sheets, vol. 1, p. 258 or 278.

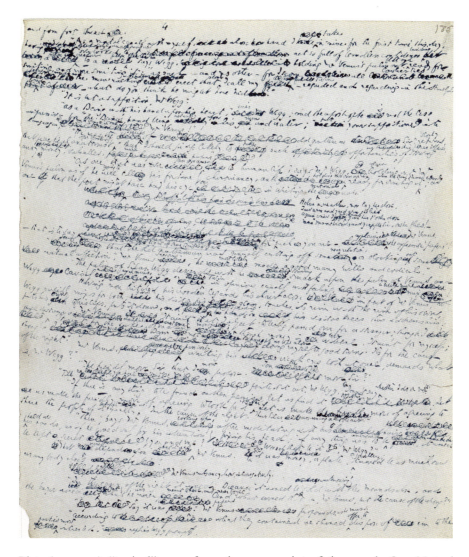

Plate 1   A "typical" page from the manuscript of the novel. *Our Mutual Friend* by Charles Dickens, Original autograph manuscript with innumerable erasures and corrections. The Pierpont Morgan Library, New York; MA 1202, fol. 185r. Purchased, 1944.

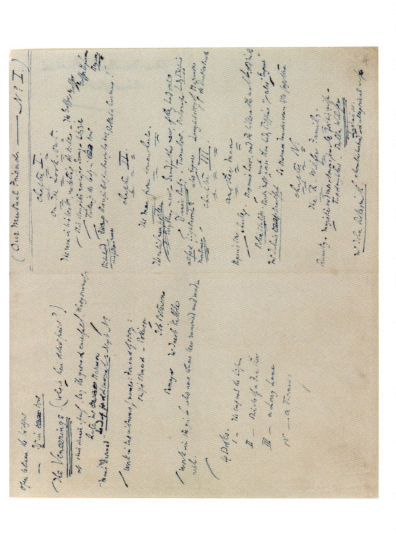

Plate 2 Dickens's manuscript monthly number plan for No. 1. *Our Mutual Friend* by Charles Dickens, Original autograph manuscript with innumerable erasures and corrections. The Pierpont Morgan Library, New York; MA 1202, fol. 4r. Purchased, 1944.

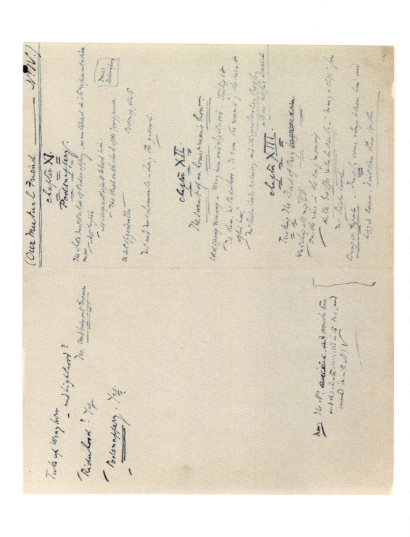

Plate 3   Dickens's manuscript monthly number plan for No. 4. *Our Mutual Friend* by Charles Dickens, Original autograph manuscript with innumerable erasures and corrections. The Pierpont Morgan Library, New York; MA 1202, fol. 7r. Purchased, 1944.

3

"Take that thing off your face."
She threw it back.
"Here! and give me hold of the sculls. I'll take the rest of the spell."
"No, no, father! No! I can't indeed. Father!—I cannot sit so near it!"
He was moving towards her to change places, but her terrified expostulation stopped him and he resumed his seat.
"What hurt can it do you?"
"None, none. But I cannot bear it."
"If I had laid into you at ten year old, you'd have taken kinder to your water-side life."
"O no, father, and I am sure you could never have touched me in anger, for you never did."
"The more fool me, ~~child~~. It's my belief you hate the sight of the river."
"I—I do n't like it, father."
"As if it wasn't your living! As if it wasn't meat and drink to you!"
At these latter words the girl shivered again, and for a moment paused in her rowing, seeming to turn deadly faint. It escaped his attention, for he was glancing over the stern at something the boat had in tow.
"How can you be so thankless to your best friend, Lizzie? The very fire that warmed you when you were a baby, was picked out of the river alongside the coal barges. The very basket that you slept in, the tide washed ashore. The very rockers that I put it upon to make a cradle of it, I cut out of a piece of wood that drifted from some ship or another."
Lizzie took her right hand from the scull it held, and touched his lips with it, and for a moment held it out lovingly towards him; then, without speaking, she resumed her rowing, as another boat of similar appearance, though in rather better trim, came out from a dark place and dropped softly alongside.
"In luck again, Gaffer?" said a man with a squinting leer, who sculled her and who was alone. "I know'd you was in luck again, by your wake as you come down."
"Ah!" replied the other, drily. "So you're out, are you?"
"Yes, pardner."
There was now a tender yellow moonlight on the river, and the new comer, keeping half his boat's length astern of the other boat, looked hard at its track.
"I says to myself," he went on, "directly minute as you hove in view, Yonder's Gaffer, and in luck again, by George if he ain't! Scull it is, pardner—don't fret yourself—I didn't touch him." This was in answer to a quick impatient movement on the part of Gaffer, the speaker at the same time unshipping his scull on that side, and laying his hand on the gunwale of the Gaffer's boat and holding to it.
"He's had touches enough, not to want no more, as well as I make him out, Gaffer! Been knocking about with a pretty many tides, ain't he pardner? Such is my out-of-luck ways, you see! He must have passed me when he went up last time, for I was on the look-

B 2

Plate 4   Chapter 1, p. 3 of the Proof sheets. *Our Mutual Friend* by Charles Dickens, Proof sheets, with the author's ms. corrections. Henry W. and Albert A. Berg Collection of English and American Literature, The New York Public Library, Astor, Lenox and Tilden Foundations; vol. 1, p. 3.

OUR MUTUAL FRIEND. 3

"Here! and give me hold of the sculls. I'll take the rest of the spell."

"No, no, father! No! I can't indeed. Father!—I cannot sit so near it!"

He was moving towards her to change places, but her terrified expostulation stopped him and he resumed his seat.

"What hurt can it do you?"

"None, none. But I cannot bear it."

"It's my belief you hate the sight of the very river."

"I—I do not like it, father."

"As if it wasn't your living! As if it wasn't meat and drink to you!"

At these latter words the girl shivered again, and for a moment paused in her rowing, seeming to turn deadly faint. It escaped his attention, for he was glancing over the stern at something the boat had in tow.

"How can you be so thankless to your best friend, Lizzie? The very fire that warmed you when you were a babby, was picked out of the river alongside the coal barges. The very basket that you slept in, the tide washed ashore. The very rockers that I put it upon to make a cradle of it, I cut out of a piece of wood that drifted from some ship or another."

Lizzie took her right hand from the scull it held, and touched her lips with it, and for a moment held it out lovingly towards him; then, without speaking, she resumed her rowing, as another boat of similar appearance, though in rather better trim, came out from a dark place and dropped softly alongside.

"In luck again, Gaffer?" said a man with a squinting leer, who sculled her and who was alone. "I know'd you was in luck again, by your wake as you come down."

"Ah!" replied the other, drily. "So you're out, are you?"

"Yes, pardner."

There was now a tender yellow moonlight on the river, and the new comer, keeping half his boat's length astern of the other boat, looked hard at its track.

"I says to myself," he went on, "directly you hove in view, Yonder's Gaffer, and in luck again, by George if he ain't! Scull it is, pardner—don't fret yourself—I didn't touch him." This was in answer to a quick impatient movement on the part of Gaffer: the speaker at the same time unshipping his scull on that side, and laying his hand on the gunwale of Gaffer's boat and holding to it.

"He's had touches enough not to want no more, as well as I make him out, Gaffer! Been a knocking about with a pretty many tides, ain't he pardner? Such is my out-of-luck ways, you see! He must have passed me when he went up last time, for I was on the look-out below bridge here. I a'most think you're like the wulturs, pardner, and scent 'em out."

He spoke in a dropped voice, and with more than one glance at Lizzie who had pulled on her hood again. Both men then looked with a weird unholy interest at the wake of Gaffer's boat.

"Easy does it, betwixt us. Shall I take him aboard, pardner?"

"No," said the other. In so surly a tone that the man, after a blank stare, acknowledged it with the retort:

B 2

Plate 5   Chapter 1, p. 3 of the first edition in 2 vols by Chapman and Hall. *Our Mutual Friend* by Charles Dickens (London: Chapman and Hall, 1865). Henry W. and Albert A. Berg Collection of English and American Literature, The New York Public Library, Astor, Lenox and Tilden Foundations; vol. 1, p. 3.

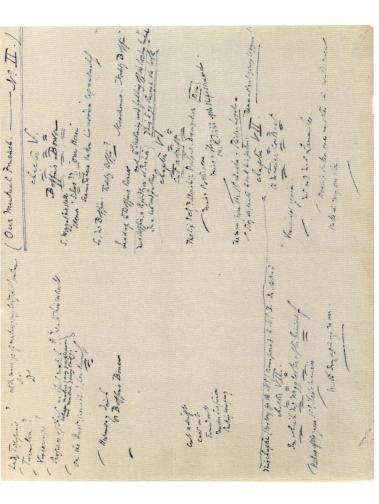

Plate 6 Dickens's manuscript monthly number plan for No. 2. *Our Mutual Friend* by Charles Dickens, Original autograph manuscript with innumerable erasures and corrections. The Pierpont Morgan Library, New York; MA 1202, fol. 5r. Purchased, 1944.

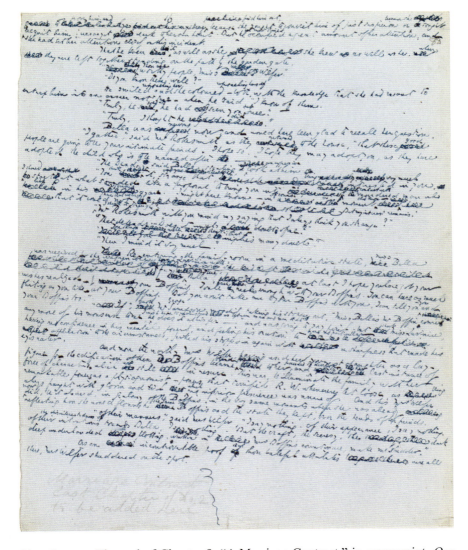

Plate 7 The end of Chapter 9, "A Marriage Contract," in manuscript. *Our Mutual Friend* by Charles Dickens, Original autograph manuscript with innumerable erasures and corrections. The Pierpont Morgan Library, New York; MA 1202, fol. 83r. Purchased, 1944.

OUR MUTUAL FRIEND.

character, which was still in reserve. This was, to illuminate the family with her remarkable powers as a physiognomist; powers that terrified R. W. whenever let loose, as being always fraught with gloom and evil which no inferior prescience was aware of. And this Mrs. Wilfer now did, be it observed, in jealousy of these Boffins, in the very same moments when she was already reflecting how she would flourish these same Boffins and the state they kept, over the heads of her Boffinless friends.

"Of their manners," said Mrs. Wilfer, "I say nothing. Of their appearance, I say nothing. Of the disinterestedness of their intentions towards Bella, I say nothing. But the craft, the secrecy, the dark deep underhanded plotting, written in Mrs. Boffin's countenance, make me shudder."

As an incontrovertible proof that those baleful attributes were all there, Mrs. Wilfer shuddered on the spot.

CHAPTER X.

~~A MARRIAGE CONTRACT.~~

~~There is excitement in the Veneering mansion. The mature young lady is going to be married (powder and all) to the mature young gentleman, and she is to be married from the Veneering house, and the Veneerings are to give the breakfast. The Analytical, who objects as a matter of principle to everything that occurs on the premises, necessarily objects to the match; but his consent has been dispensed with, and a spring-van is delivering its load of blooming plants at the door, in order that to-morrow's feast may be crowned with flowers.~~

~~The mature young lady is a lady of property. The mature young~~

~~CHAPTER VII.~~

A MARRIAGE CONTRACT.

There is excitement in the Veneering mansion. The mature young lady is going to be 'married (powder and all) to the mature young gentleman, and she is to be married from the Veneering ~~halls~~, and the Veneerings are to give the ~~marriage~~ breakfast. The Analytical, who objects as a matter of principle to everything that occurs on the premises, necessarily objects to the match; but his consent has been dispensed with, and a spring-van is delivering its load of blooming plants at the door, in order that to-morrow's feast may be crowned with flowers.

The mature young lady is a lady of property. The mature young gentleman is a gentleman of property. He invests his property. He goes, in a condescending amateurish way, into the City, attends meetings of Directors, and has to do with ~~dealings~~ in Shares. As is well known to the wise in their generation, ~~dealing~~ in Shares is the one thing to have to do with in this world. Have no antecedents, no established character, no cultivation, no ideas, no manners; have

---

Plate 8   The start of Chapter 10, "A Marriage Contract," in proofs. *Our Mutual Friend* by Charles Dickens, Proof sheets, with the author's ms. corrections. Henry W. and Albert A. Berg Collection of English and American Literature, The New York Public Library, Astor, Lenox and Tilden Foundations; vol. 1, p. 86.

Shares. Have Shares enough to be on Boards of Direction in capital letters, frequently oscillate mysterious business between London and Paris, and be great. Where does he come from? Shares. Where is he going to? Shares. How does he do it? Shares. Perhaps he never of himself achieved success in anything, never originated anything, never produced anything? Sufficient answer to all doubts, Shares. O mighty Shares! to set these flaring images so high, and to cause us smaller vermin, as under the influence of henbane or opium, to cry out, night and day, "Relieve us of our money, scatter it for us, buy us only extensively, and sell us, ruin us, take rank among the powers of the earth, and fatten!

While the Loves and Graces have been preparing this torch for Hymen, which is to be kindled to-morrow, Mr. Twemlow has suffered much in his mind. It would seem that both the mature young lady and the mature young gentleman must indubitably be Veneering's oldest friends. Wards of his, belike? Yet that can scarcely be, for they are older than himself. Veneering has been in their confidence throughout, and has done much to lure them to the altar. He has mentioned to Twemlow how he said to Mrs. Veneering, "Anastatia, this must be a match." He has mentioned to Twemlow how he regards Sophronia Akershem (the mature young lady) in the light of a sister, and Alfred Lammle (the mature young gentleman) in the light of a brother. Twemlow has asked him whether he went to school as a junior with Alfred? He has answered, "Not exactly." Whether Sophronia was adopted by his mother? He has answered, "Not precisely so." Twemlow's hand has gone to his forehead with a lost air.

But two or three weeks ago, Twemlow sitting over his newspaper, and over his dry-toast and weak tea, and over the stable-yard in Duke Street, St. James's, received a highly-perfumed cocked-hat and monogram from Mrs. Veneering, entreating her dearest Mr. T., if not particularly engaged that day, to come like a charming soul and make a fourth at dinner with dear Mr. Podsnap, for the discussion of an interesting family topic—the last three words duly underlined and pointed with a note of admiration. And Twemlow, replying, "Not engaged, and more than delighted," goes, and this takes place—

"My dear Twemlow," says Veneering, "your response to Anastatia's unceremonious invitation is truly kind, and like an old, old friend. You know our dear friend Podsnap?"

Twemlow ought to know the dear friend Podsnap, who lately covered him with so much confusion, and he says he does know him, and Podsnap reciprocates. Apparently, Podsnap has been so wrought upon in a short time as to believe that he has been intimate in the house many, many, many years. In the friendliest manner he is making himself quite at home, with his back to the fire, executing a statuette of the Colossus at Rhodes. Twemlow has before noticed in his feeble way how soon the Veneering guests become infected with the Veneering fiction. Not, however, that he has the least notion of its being his own case.

"Our friends, Alfred and Sophronia," pursues Veneering the veiled prophet, "our friends Alfred and Sophronia, you will be glad to hear,

Plate 9   The continuation of Chapter 10 in proofs. *Our Mutual Friend* by Charles Dickens, Proof sheets, with the author's ms. corrections. Henry W. and Albert A. Berg Collection of English and American Literature, The New York Public Library, Astor, Lenox and Tilden Foundations; vol. 1, p. 59 [87].

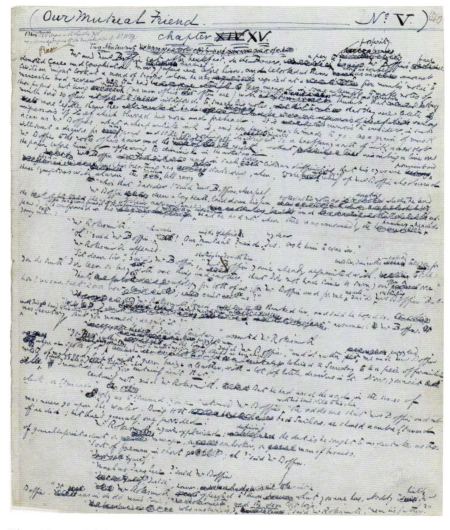

Plate 10 Dickens's note to Clowes on No. 5, in manuscript. *Our Mutual Friend* by Charles Dickens, Original autograph manuscript with innumerable erasures and corrections. The Pierpont Morgan Library, New York; MA 1202, fol. 120r. Purchased, 1944.

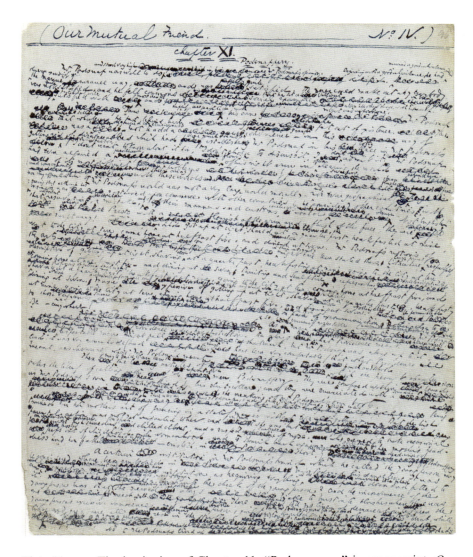

Plate 11   The beginning of Chapter 11, "Podsnappery," in manuscript. *Our Mutual Friend* by Charles Dickens, Original autograph manuscript with innumerable erasures and corrections. The Pierpont Morgan Library, New York; MA 1202, fol. 96r. Purchased, 1944.

Plate 12   Original pencil sketch of the monthly wrapper to *Our Mutual Friend*, Marcus Stone. *Our Mutual Friend* by Charles Dickens, Copy 4. Henry W. and Albert A. Berg Collection of English and American Literature, The New York Public Library, Astor, Lenox and Tilden Foundations.

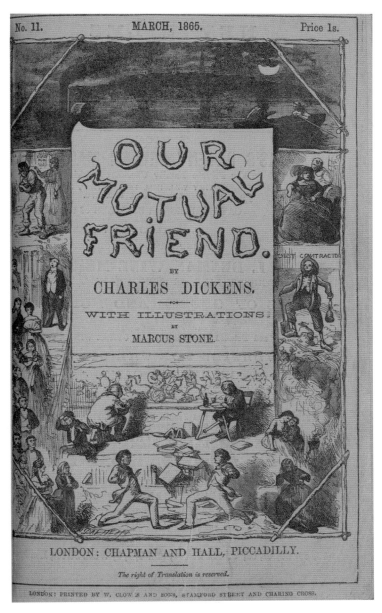

Plate 13   The monthly wrapper of *Our Mutual Friend* as published for No. 11 in March 1865, Marcus Stone. *Our Mutual Friend* by Charles Dickens, Copy 4. Henry W. and Albert A. Berg Collection of English and American Literature, The New York Public Library, Astor, Lenox and Tilden Foundations.

Plate 14   Pen-and-ink sketch (top) and published version (bottom) of "The Bird of Prey," Marcus Stone. *Our Mutual Friend* by Charles Dickens, Copy 4. Henry W. and Albert A. Berg Collection of English and American Literature, The New York Public Library, Astor, Lenox and Tilden Foundations.

Plate 15 From "A Cry for Help," in manuscript, showing Dickens's instruction to Clowes. *Our Mutual Friend* by Charles Dickens, Original autograph manuscript with innumerable erasures and corrections. The Pierpont Morgan Library, New York; MA 1203, fol. 158r. Purchased, 1944.

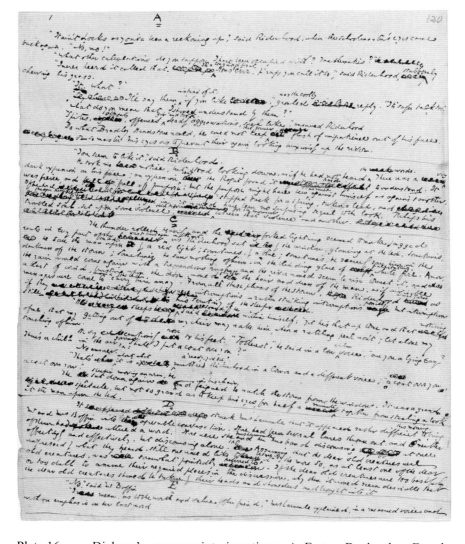

Plate 16 Dickens's manuscript insertions A–E to Book the Fourth, Chapter 16. *Our Mutual Friend* by Charles Dickens, Original autograph manuscript with innumerable erasures and corrections. The Pierpont Morgan Library, New York; MA 1203, fol. 120r. Purchased, 1944.

The Cup and the Lip   55

things that appear in the first edition from Chapman and Hall apparently postdate the included sheets, while in other instances the corrections indicated in the proofs were never made at all. For instance, page 50 of the proofs gives Bob Gliddery's name as "Glibbery" three times, though the page features other corrections and though Dickens must have corrected the repeated error in some later set.[72] Too, a collation of the corrected proofs for Nos. 19/20—which are entirely untouched after Book the Fourth, Chapter 13—with the first edition shows that Clowes made just 29 of the 50 corrections that Dickens marked, though most of these were as simple as inserting commas, canceling stray letters, and adding or deleting single words. At best, then, the volume of Proof sheets contains various intermediate sets collected, completed, and bound only after the fact, perhaps by some enterprising employee at Clowes. As a result, but for the instances in which Dickens overwrote his early numbers, the proofs tell us very little about his work on the novel.

The third and perhaps least familiar major resource available to scholars is an item that I call here the Berg copy of the novel, identified by the New York Public Library simply as "Copy 4," a grangerized two-volume first edition that has been turned into a stunning repository of materials related to *Our Mutual Friend*. At its core, the Berg copy is a standard first edition from Chapman and Hall. But it also contains a monthly wrapper from each of the novel's 20 installments and a complete "Advertiser" from almost all, with materials from Nos. 1–10 compiled at the end of Volume 1 and those from Nos. 11–20 at the end of Volume 2. Better yet, the Berg copy contains several manuscript items: all 40 of Stone's pencil and pen-and-ink illustrations to the novel, some bearing captions in Dickens's hand; Stone's original pencil sketch and pen-and-ink draft for the monthly wrapper; studies of several subjects that Stone incorporated into the illustrations; and 15 additional illustrations, not by Stone, for an unidentified later edition of *Our Mutual Friend*. Needless to say, Stone's sketch and draft for the wrapper design and his manuscript illustrations are the most fascinating items for scholars, and both Cohen and O'Hea have published the sketch wrapper and discussed it in detail.[73] The sketch wrapper and the pen-and-ink illustration for "The Bird of Prey"—which appeared in No. 1 and then served as the frontispiece for Volume 1 in January 1865—differ markedly in manuscript from the version published in 1864. Though we can only conjecture whether Dickens objected to elements of the original "The Bird of Prey," Dickens's letter to Stone on February 23, 1864, requests very specific revisions to his wrapper design. The presence of that original design in the Berg copy allows us to see precisely what Dickens objected to, how Stone revised the wrapper to satisfy Dickens's conceptions of the novel's major threads, and how much of those threads Dickens wished the wrapper to reveal

---

[72] See the Proof sheets, vol. 1, p. 50. "Glibbery" was in fact the original name for the character in the manuscript, that name having been carried forward from a list of names in Dickens's *Book of Memoranda*, p. 3 verso.

[73] See Cohen, p. 205, and the entirety of O'Hea. Cohen also reproduces the pen-and-ink illustration for "Eugene's Bedside," p. 209.

to his readers. A comparison of Dickens's letter against the wrapper's various versions also shows us, a bit surprisingly, that the revisions to the wrapper, like those Dickens made to the early numbers, were designed partly to accommodate the physical format of the novel.

Together the manuscript, Proof sheets, and Berg copy of *Our Mutual Friend* thus give us a composite and comprehensive view of Dickens at work on his last finished novel. Most obviously, the manuscript and Proof sheets show Dickens's several moments of practical crisis in the early numbers, where his persistent overwriting forced him to undertake large-scale revisions to the content and structure. He cut extensively on several occasions, in one instance divided a chapter, and twice shifted content between months. He bent *Our Mutual Friend*, his most powerful indictment of capitalism, repeatedly to the requirements of his 20-number format and, in a larger sense, to the Victorian literary market. Yet even as he did so, these same documents show, he committed himself much more broadly and painstakingly to his imaginative and creative aims. He labored over not just the plot but also its most powerful symbolic resonances, and he reworked heavily his most significant characters and incidents throughout his revisions, worrying over every detail of Boffin's masquerade, Eugene's pursuit of Lizzie, and Headstone's murderous fulmination. His labor in the novel tended generally, in other words, toward greater and greater creative purposiveness, even when he revised mainly (or at least ostensibly) to shrink installments to the necessary length. In this sense, though Dickens's work on the early numbers gives us the sense of *Our Mutual Friend* poised uneasily between his imaginative aims and the practical requirements of his serial format—with the balance tilting often to the latter—the collective evidence offered by the manuscript, the Proof sheets, and the Berg copy gives a different view: of practical requirements subsumed into a comprehensive imaginative vision, and of that convergence giving rise to an extraordinary novel.

Dickens's creative intentions for *Our Mutual Friend* are recorded most explicitly, in many ways, in the monthly number plans he composed for the novel. As organized by the Morgan—and perhaps as organized by Dickens, when he presented it to Dallas in January 1866—the manuscript of *Our Mutual Friend* is divided into its traditional two volumes, each of which is preceded by Dickens's monthly plans for that half of the novel. Dickens had used such plans for his 20-number novels beginning with *Dombey and Son*, and they had allowed him generally since then to create more complex and cohesive plots, or at least to keep track of them once he had set them in motion. For *Our Mutual Friend* each number plan consists of a single page turned edgewise with two distinct columns of writing. On the right, Dickens headed the column by giving the novel's title and indicating the number of the installment, and below this he provided a list of the installment's chapter numbers and titles as well as scanty notes regarding the content of each chapter. The left side he reserved for less formal musings: questions to himself, notes regarding things to emphasize, and memoranda respecting the contents of the previous number or ideas that he needed to carry forward to the next one (Plate 2). In 1987 Harry Stone edited *Dickens' Working*

The Cup and the Lip 57

Notes for His Novels, a collection of all Dickens's monthly number plans, and the current Oxford World's Classics and Penguin editions of *Our Mutual Friend* each print the plans for the novel in an Appendix. Thus, a comprehensive account of the plans is unnecessary here. But it is worth pointing out that the plans do tell us certain things about the novel, including, quite often, what Dickens wanted to emphasize within a certain chapter or number, and even how he attempted to build thematic and symbolic resonances across the novel as a whole.

This is particularly true of Dickens's intentions for Headstone, Eugene, and Lizzie, which reappear in his notes several times and with increasing emphasis. No. 6 introduces Headstone in its first chapter, "Of an Educational Character," and Dickens's plan for it includes the phrases "selfish boy" as well as "and selfish schoolmaster"—a clear indication of the parallel he wished to draw between Charley and Headstone—and also a reminder to be "Very Particular within Smith Square, Westminster," the location he gives later in the chapter for Lizzie and Jenny's home.[74] He also goes through the possibilities "Amos Headstone," "Amos Deadstone," and "Bradley Deadstone" before settling finally on the name "Bradley Headstone," double underlined, an uncertainty that is also reflected in the first few pages of the manuscript for No. 6.[75] In his plan for No. 9 Dickens reminds himself to "Work up the scene in next No. between Lizzie, her brother, and Bradley Headstone," and in the plan for No. 16 he writes of Headstone, "often at Plashwater Weir Mill Lock, and prepare for the attack on Eugene."[76] Then, for No. 17, which includes "A Cry for Help," Dickens writes in his left-hand notes, "The attack on Eugene / Lizzie saves him / *Back to the opening chapter of the story*," and on the right side under the chapter heading he draws a box around the words, "Back to the / Opening chapter / Of the book, *strongly*," and underlines the final word three times.[77] What Dickens has in mind, of course, is his desire to construct one of the novel's most suggestive moments, when Lizzie must use her experience as a corpse-dredger's daughter to pull her gentleman lover's senseless body from the river, thereby becoming the savior who makes possible his rebirth into a higher sense of moral purpose. Dickens took similar—though less extensive—pains with other parts of the novel, too: Boffin's masquerade, for instance, Wegg's nefarious plotting, and the Lammles' designs on Georgiana Podsnap. His close and persistent work on these elements of the novel in his monthly plans illustrates the extent to which he used the plans not only to organize the plot but also to craft the novel's more significant thematic and symbolic content.

---

[74] Original autograph manuscript of *Our Mutual Friend* by Charles Dickens, Morgan Library, MA 1202, fol. 9.

[75] Ibid., fols 139–40. Joel Brattin discusses this uncertainty regarding Headstone's name, too, in "Dickens' Creation of Bradley Headstone," *Dickens Studies Annual*, 14 (1985), pp. 147–8.

[76] MA 1202, fol. 12; Original autograph manuscript of *Our Mutual Friend* by Charles Dickens, Morgan Library, MA 1203, fol. 6.

[77] MA 1203, fol. 7.

The monthly number plans tell us much about Dickens's creative work on the novel, then, but we must be careful not to overestimate their significance, at least with respect to how much formal planning Dickens really did before beginning to write in October 1863. He had, certainly, thought through his main incidents and characters and many details of the plot. But because the Morgan's organization has the monthly number plans precede each half of his manuscript, and because when they are published the plans always appear in collected form, reviewing the monthly number plans inevitably conveys the wrong idea about how and when Dickens composed them. He did not write them all at once—did not, at the outset, plan all of the numbers as a preliminary to writing the novel. Rather, Dickens composed a monthly plan only as a starting point for his work on that particular number, and perhaps, as he got further along, to remind himself which topics and characters he had handled in each month's installment. His monthly number plan for No. 1 therefore tells us virtually nothing about the novel as a whole, beyond a brief note on the left side of the page where Dickens lists the titles for *Our Mutual Friend*'s four Books (Plate 2). Likewise, the plan for No. 5 shows no sign of Dickens's reorganization of material stemming from his overwrite of No. 4, which caused him to split his original Chapter 13 ("Tracking the Bird of Prey") into two shorter chapters and to carry over the second ("The Bird of Prey Brought Down") into No. 5, where it became that installment's first chapter. Dickens did return to the plan for No. 4 to note, "*Mem*: The No. [xxx] overwritten / and this chapter divided into two, and carried on into No. V" (Plate 3).[78] But in the plan for No. 5 he had neither to adjust chapter numbers nor make other corrections, though he does write in his left-hand notes, "Mem: *for the No.* / 6 pages of the No. brought forward _ 26 left to write."[79] He seems, then, to have written the plan only after he knew of the problem with No. 4 and thus to have planned and written No. 5 with that problem already in mind.

In the early numbers of the manuscript and Proof sheets, instances of overwriting like this one originate the most obvious and extensive of Dickens's revisions to *Our Mutual Friend*. They were, in many ways, the source of his most radical changes to the novel, particularly in its structure. He clearly was not exaggerating when he wrote to Collins of feeling "dazed" by his return to 20 numbers, nor did his struggles with the length of installments begin or end with the familiar story of Venus's creation. On the contrary, Dickens overwrote three of his first five numbers—1, 2, and 4—and it may be that he only escaped the same error with Nos. 3 and 5, his other "advance" installments, because each had already been designed to compensate for his overwriting in the others. The evidence of the manuscript suggests that to fill 32 printed pages, Dickens needed to write 23–25 by hand, but he seems not to have known this early on. As a result, No. 1 stretches to 29 manuscript pages, which the proofs show as an overrun of four printed pages. In the proofs, page 32—nominally the last page of No. 1—is

---

[78] MA 1202, fol. 7.

[79] Ibid., fol. 8.

thus followed not by 33 but rather by a page headed "Overmatter of No. 1 of the New Serial" and then renumbered to 1. But even the proofs do not show what deletions Dickens made to shrink the installment to the proper length; rather, one must discover these by comparing the proofs of No. 1 against chapters 1–4 of the first edition. On page 3, for instance, Dickens excised five lines of dialogue from the exchange between Lizzie and Gaffer (Plates 4 and 5), and he made similar cuts, also often to dialogue, elsewhere in Chapter 1 and in Chapter 3. More, he appears to have focused on dialogue for an eminently practical reason: cutting dialogue, because of its spacing, would shorten the installment to the proper length typeset line by typeset line rather than just a word at a time. Still, he did cut ruthlessly from Chapter 4 as well, partly from its dialogue but also by condensing his account of the Wilfers at home. None of these cuts was particularly crucial on creative grounds. But the mere fact of them underscores how badly Dickens struggled after his long absence from the format, and how assiduously he worked to fit his creative labor to his practical needs.

These struggles continued with Nos. 2 and 4, with the result that Nos. 2–5 were all shaped in important ways by his efforts to make them the requisite length. Dickens's overwriting of No. 2 is the more familiar instance because of his invention of Venus. But in the manuscript, Chapter 7 introducing Venus bears no sign of the complication—there, Dickens simply numbered the new chapter "VII" and inserted it as necessary. The evidence of trouble appears in three other places: in a left-hand correction to the monthly number plan for No. 2 (Plate 6), in a faint pencil notation at the close of Chapter 9 that reads, "A Marriage Contract last chapter of No. 2 to be added here" (Plate 7), and in a deletion and correction to the first page of Chapter 10, which shows the original chapter number "VII" lined out and replaced by "X" and also the original page numbers 21–28 canceled and replaced by 17–24, this last because the chapter's new position in No. 3 meant four fewer pages of material prior to its start.[80] In this instance, Dickens's repagination seems to have puzzled even the Morgan's curators, for their folio numbers for "A Marriage Contract" indicate mistakenly that four folios are missing—their pencil notation on folio 90 reads "(86–89 omitted) 90"—presumably because Dickens's own numbers seem to show an unspecified cancellation of four pages.[81] In fact, though, the bottom of folio 85 is perfectly continuous with the top of folio 90: "And now Veneering shoots out of the study, wherein he is accustomed, when contemplative, to / give his mind to the carving and gilding of the Pilgrims going to Canterbury."[82] More to the point, the absence of any revising mark to the chapter number at the start of Chapter 7 suggests that, even if Dickens began imagining his strange taxidermist before he knew of the overwriting in No. 2, he never began

---

[80] Ibid., fols 5, 83, 84.

[81] Ibid., fol. 90.

[82] Ibid., fols 85–90. Given that Dickens's original page numbers are canceled for folios 84 and 85 as well, it is not clear why the "omission" is only noted in the Morgan's numbering beginning at folio 86.

60   *Charles Dickens's* Our Mutual Friend

writing "Mr. Wegg Looks After Himself" until he knew that it would be Chapter 7. The Proof sheets show other signs of this same trouble, for the corrected proofs for "A Marriage Contract" that begin after page 86 (in No. 3) have been pasted overtop of the original sheets and still even bear the pagination from their original location in No. 2: pages 59–64 for the first six pages, and "Overmatter New Serial No. 2" cut apart and pasted onto blank sheets for the rest (Plates 8 and 9).

Mercifully for Dickens, No. 4 appears to have been the last monthly installment that he flubbed in this way, and here he came up with yet another new solution. This time, he split the number's concluding Chapter 13 into two chapters, one that would close No. 4 and another, Chapter 14, that would begin No. 5. To make the new chapter division work, Dickens wrote new material as an introduction to the newly created number and chapter. In the first edition and in the Proofs, Chapter 14 ("The Bird of Prey Brought Down") begins with two short paragraphs of narration interspersed with a heated exchange between Riderhood and Eugene, which closes with the narrator's remark that Mortimer is "[a]stonished by his friend's unusual heat."[83] But this chapter beginning—from the opening words "Cold on the shore" to the phrase "Lightwood stared too, and then said"—does not appear in the manuscript, which runs continuously from Riderhood's, "he's in luck agin, by George if he ain't!" to Mortimer's rejoinder, "What can have become of the man himself?"[84] Nor does the manuscript even bear a precise notation as to where this new material might be inserted, since a large horizontal arrow drawn near the right margin, as if to indicate an insertion or deletion, is not quite in the right location.[85] He did, however, note the restructuring after the fact by amending his monthly plan for No. 4 (Plate 3), and also by making a correction to Chapter 15, which would have been Chapter 14 and begun No. 5 if not for the error. On the first page of Chapter 15, Dickens canceled "XIV" for the chapter's number and added "XV" in its place, and he gave instructions to Clowes to explain the desired change: "Printer / This No. to begin with Ch. XIV / as returned—Originally the last chapter of No. IV CD" (Plate 10).[86]

By the time No. 1 of *Our Mutual Friend* appeared on April 30, 1864, Dickens's persistent problems with overwriting were behind him. But the considerable revisions he completed to the beginning of No. 5 remind us that these revisions, though undertaken for practical reasons, had particular imaginative effects. In his newly configured Nos. 4 and 5, Dickens interrupts the conversation between Eugene, Mortimer, and Riderhood in a way that would be awkward and unusual even as a chapter break, and that is infinitely more so as a break between monthly installments. Yet the interruption creates suspense, too, that is carried over from No. 4 to No. 5 as the three men and the reader alike wonder what can have become of Gaffer. More, the material that Dickens added to create his new start to

---

[83] Dickens, *Our Mutual Friend* (London, 1997), p. 172.
[84] MA 1202, fol. 116.
[85] Ibid.
[86] Ibid., fol. 120.

The Cup and the Lip

No. 5 includes a stinging exchange between Riderhood and Eugene, which ends with the latter commanding Riderhood, "Hold your tongue, you water-rat," and consequently "astonishing" Mortimer.[87] The revision may, in other words, have been pressed upon Dickens for practical reasons, but he uses it to give the exchange greater intensity, allowing us to glimpse far earlier than we otherwise would that something unusual underlies Eugene's fiery response—to Riderhood, nominally, but really to Lizzie's plight. In the same way, even Dickens's substitution of Mr. Venus for "A Marriage Contract" in his earlier revisions changes the novel in subtle ways. The introduction of Venus reinvigorates early on the novel's initial concern with Dust, commodification, and cycles of waste and renewal, giving them a prominence they might lack if they were not kept before the reader in Nos. 1 and 2. Meantime, the figures in the "Social Chorus" are deferred not just spatially by three chapters but also temporally by a month—a difference that must have appeared far greater to Dickens's serial readers than it appears to us now, reading the novel as a single volume. Even Dickens's inevitable practical revisions to the novel tended to allow him to intensify what he already wished to convey.

To say that Dickens revised practically, then, is not to say that he did so carelessly or without attention to his creative aims, nor is it to say with James that the book is *labored* because it required meticulous work. True, in these several instances of overwriting he was adjusting content to form, but he was less betraying his artistic intentions than adapting them, almost organically, to the concrete realities of their textual environment. Nor were these the only revisions he made to the early installments of his novel, many of which are rife with traces of his imaginative work. In the manuscript—where, presumably, we find Dickens revising for purely creative reasons, since he was doing so before he knew his numbers were overwritten—Dickens labors heavily over Boffin's first meetings with Mortimer and Rokesmith in Chapter 5, and, in the same chapter, over the precise language of Wegg's comical declines and falls into terrible verse. He also worked and reworked the scene in which the Boffins meet Betty Higden in Chapter 16. Meantime, the beginning of Chapter 11, "Podsnappery," may be edited more heavily and illegibly than any other page in the novel (Plate 11). He also seems to have agonized over both character and chapter names: "Amos" instead of Bradley and "Deadstone" instead of Headstone; Miss "Pitcher" instead of Peecher; "Conversation" instead of Fascination Fledgeby; and "The Six Jolly Fellowship-Porters" for Chapter 6 instead of its eventual title, "Cut Adrift." No detail was too small to attract Dickens's notice. Perhaps this explains why, when Bulwer-Lytton wrote to Dickens in November 1865 praising the novel but also critiquing it, Dickens replied somewhat defensively that he worked "slowly and with great care, never giv[ing] way to [his] invention recklessly, but constantly restrain[ing] it."[88] That care is evident throughout the manuscript, even in the early numbers when he had to revise for other purposes.

---

[87]   Dickens, *Our Mutual Friend* (London, 1997), p. 172.

[88]   *Letters*, vol. 11, p. 113.

It is evident, too, in the Berg copy of *Our Mutual Friend*, which shows just how carefully Dickens worked with Stone to plan the first several illustrations even amid the problems of the early installments. When Dickens wrote to Stone about the draft wrapper and called "the design for the cover, *excellent*," he nevertheless asked him gently to make a "slight alteration" to accommodate "a business consideration not to be overlooked":

> The word "Our" in the title, must be out in the open, like Mutual Friend; making the Title three distinct long lines—"Our" as big as "Mutual Friend." This will give you too much design at the bottom. I would therefore take out the Dustman, and put the Wegg and Boffin composition (which is capital), in its place. I don't want Mr. Inspector or the Murder Reward bill, because those points are sufficiently indicated in the River at the top. Therefore you can have an indication of the Dustman, in Mr. Inspector's place. Note, that the Dustman's face should be droll, and not horrible. Twemlow's elbow will still go out of the frame as it does now, and the same with Lizzie's skirts on the opposite side. With these changes, work away![89]

Dickens may have softened his criticism by calling it a "slight alteration," but the letter goes well beyond the "business consideration" of giving greater prominence to the first word of the title. Here, as in the cases of his practical revisions to the early installments, Dickens uses revision as an opportunity to intensify the novel's creative content even as he adapts it, too, to the practicalities of the literary market. Whatever he told Stone, he wanted—and got—a significant reorganization of the composition, principally along the lines that his letter describes.

The most striking differences between the draft illustration and the published wrapper are indeed the ones that Dickens proposes (Plates 12 and 13). In the published wrapper, "Our" appears in the central frame for the title instead of being tucked under the arches to the bridge, and Mr. Inspector and the Murder Reward bill have been removed entirely from their original position on the right side. Along these same lines, Stone made the additional change of removing the "Found Drowned" bill that appears in the draft just to the left of the larger sign "Dust Contractor." The effect is to provide fewer hints for the early plot incidents involving John Harmon, though it is hard to blame Stone for having made these so prevalent since he was obliged to draft the wrapper after reading only Nos. 1 and 2. Probably for this reason, the figures in the draft and published wrappers come all from the first seven chapters: Lizzie and Gaffer on the river; Mrs. Boffin with Mr. Boffin leaning over her; Old Harmon, who appears as a skeletal dust contractor with a large bell; Lizzie comforting Charley and looking into the fire; Bella on her father's lap; John Harmon doubled, perhaps only symbolically or perhaps as George Radfoot, at the bottom of each composition; Wegg reading to Boffin; the "Social Chorus," overlooked by the flummoxed Twemlow; Riderhood turned out by Abbey Potterson. Meanwhile, pivotal figures from later in the novel—

---

[89] Ibid., vol. 10, p. 361.

The Cup and the Lip 63

Headstone, for instance, and Riah—never appear at all.[90] Dickens's concern that Stone would have "too much design at the bottom" once "Our" had been moved was mended by Stone himself, who shortened vertically the river scene at the top of the illustration. Even so, Dickens clearly did not want Old Harmon to have pride of place at the bottom center, as if he was somehow the key toward which all of the novel's action tended. In the published illustration, he appears just where he should: adjacent to the Boffins, a cause but not a result of the novel's action.

Yet Dickens's letter to Stone does *not* recommend the illustration that appeared in Old Harmon's place. Rather, while Dickens's letter suggests that Stone allow Wegg and Boffin to take up the entire space below the frame, the published wrapper shows instead a much expanded view of John Harmon encountering himself, so to speak, in a hint at the secret identity plot that the novel unmasks. The draft deemphasizes this revelation by placing it beside Old Harmon, whose foregrounding makes the Harmon composition appear to recede into relative insignificance. But there is no mistake about Stone's desire to emphasize the doubled John Harmon in the published wrapper. The figures are larger and more prominent, and they appear as the conclusion toward which everything else in the composition tends. The "Social Chorus" on the left and the Boffins and Hexams on the right both belong visually to storylines that flow downward and into the center, and in a subtle but decisive touch, the published wrapper also has Wegg and Boffin's books tumbling down through the bottom of the horizontal frame and into the space between the two Harmons, as if in acknowledgement that the pair's relationship will end in the revelation of identity that culminates the main thread of the plot. All of the final composition's action—and, by implication, all of the novel's—belongs to the discovery of Harmon's double identity.

We cannot know for certain what role Dickens played in deciding upon this new design for the monthly wrapper, or whether he rather than Stone suggested that the dual Harmons be emphasized in this way. True, Dickens's letter of February 23 proposes another alternative. But Dickens may have sent Stone other letters that have not survived, and he sometimes met Stone in person to discuss the novel, as on the night when he asked Stone about a "peculiar avocation"—a night that came, incidentally, while Stone was preparing the draft of the wrapper. More, another manuscript illustration from the Berg copy suggests the extent of Dickens's control over Stone's work, particularly in these early months when Dickens was so anxious for the success of his new illustrator. No letter survives in which Dickens asks Stone for revisions to "The Bird of Prey," but the manuscript illustration is captioned in Dickens's hand—so he undoubtedly saw it—and it differs markedly from the illustration published with No. 1 on April 30, 1864 (Plate 14). All of Stone's pen-and-ink drawings are reversed in their published versions since they were first carved into wood as exact reproductions, then flipped over to be impressed

---

[90] O'Hea argues—unconvincingly, in my view—that the doubled character at the bottom of the illustration is meant also to refer to the conflict between Eugene and Headstone. See pp. 206–7.

upon the printed page.[91] But "The Bird of Prey" reflects another difference, too, that Dickens probably requested. In the draft Gaffer looks carelessly down past his right elbow, almost as if he is glancing down into the back of the boat rather than into the water beyond. The published illustration changes this, giving Gaffer an attitude of taut fixity that accords much better with the somber, menacing mood of the novel's beginning. He is turned entirely to the back of the boat, and he grips the boat's sides and stares back into the water, his eyes following the tow rope to a cargo or destination that remains tantalizingly beyond the scene. More so than the draft, the published illustration underscores Gaffer's separation from his daughter, his alert intensity, and the presence of some important mystery in the water below. Like Dickens's revisions to the text of the early installments, the revisions he demanded of Stone tended to reinforce his imaginative intentions for the novel.

After his extraordinary care with the early installments and illustrations, Dickens seems generally to have settled into discernible patterns with his writing and revisions. It is hard to say with any accuracy that he revised more at some times than at others, at least in the strict sense of chronology. Rather, Dickens revised most heavily at points in the novel when he was trying to get key elements of his plot and themes as he wanted them, and he generally revised least in those parts of the novel that mattered less. Just as he struggled mightily to write Harmon's first meeting with Boffin in Chapter 8, he revised heavily, too, the scene in Chapter 15 in which Boffin hires Harmon as his Secretary and also the scene in Book the Third, Chapter 15, when Boffin and Harmon have their final showdown and Bella runs off to her family again. Each of Betty Higden's appearances in the manuscript also came with a shower of ink, as Dickens struggled to mount a final, crushing attack on the Poor Laws. This is especially true in Book the Third, Chapter 8, when Betty dies in Lizzie's arms, though one phrase in particular—"*Now* lift me, my love"— must have sounded in Dickens's ears before he began writing, since it appears almost verbatim as "Now lift me my dear" in a note to the monthly number plan for No. 13.[92] Certain key chapters also come in for particularly painstaking work, "A Solo and a Duett" (Book the Second, Chapter 13), for instance, and "A Cry for Help" (Book the Fourth, Chapter 6). Very little is surprising here. Generally speaking, Dickens took pains with those things that were worth the trouble. But one category of heavy revisions does not seem to fit this category, though it is consistent throughout: repeatedly and unaccountably, even after the very early numbers, Dickens continued to take pains with Wegg's awful verse.

By the same token, other parts of the novel seem to have required no effort at all to write, or perhaps they were not significant enough to Dickens's main purposes to deserve much care. The domestic scenes featuring the Wilfers appear to have emerged in all their good humor directly from Dickens's still-fertile

---

[91] For an excellent discussion of the process by which wood engravings became book illustrations, see Vaughan, particularly p. 34.

[92] Dickens, *Our Mutual Friend* (London, 1997), p. 506. See for comparison MA 1203, fol. 3.

The Cup and the Lip 65

imagination, just as his cutting satire of the "Social Chorus" seems—with the exception of "Podsnappery"—to have come to him with astonishing ease. He rarely had to revisit the scenes featuring Lizzie and Jenny, though in several instances this changes the moment some interloper enters the scene. The pages of "Still Educational" (Book the Second, Chapter 2) are very, very clean until Eugene enters, while "Mercury Prompting" (Book the Second, Chapter 5) is quite heavily edited until its final paragraphs focusing on Jenny, where she several times invites Fledgeby to "come up and be dead." Surprisingly, Dickens also seems to have written very easily in most of the scenes featuring Headstone, particularly in "A Riddle without an Answer" (Book the Second, Chapter 6), "The Whole Case So Far" (Book the Second, Chapter 15), and even "What Was Caught in the Traps That Were Set" (Book the Fourth, Chapter 15)—as if, we might conjecture, Dickens had Headstone so firmly in mind that he wrote fluidly in these chapters despite their emotional intensity. This is not to suggest that he did not write and revise Headstone with care; on the contrary, Brattin has shown the reverse.[93] But he labored less over Headstone than over many key elements in the novel. If there is anything like a brief chronological trend to Dickens's revisions, it may simply be that by the time he wrote the double number, he was focused so intently on the work of finishing the novel and could see the end so clearly before him that some chapters in Book the Fourth show little revision at all. Only "Showing How the Golden Dustman Helped To Scatter Dust" and "Checkmate to the Friendly Move" bear signs of heavy revision, and understandably so: they are the chapters in which Dickens concludes what some regard as his most complicated plot.

Beyond these features of the manuscript, a few more require mention. One of these, the most significant, is a bit of formatting that Dickens intended to have in the novel but that has been omitted almost invariably from later editions and does not appear in the current editions from Oxford World's Classics, Penguin, or Vintage. In "A Cry for Help," Dickens indicates in the manuscript "(Printer. Two white lines here)" after the paragraph that ends, "After dragging at the assailant, he fell on the bank with him, and there was another great crash, and then a splash, and all was done" (Plate 15).[94] The intention, clearly, was to close the scene of the attack by disrupting and deferring the narrative, which resumes in the next paragraph with Lizzie's desperate attempt to save Eugene. Clowes did indeed supply the requested spacing, which is evident in the Proof sheets, just as he had earlier complied with other formatting requests—for Wegg's business advertisement to appear in a box in Book the First, Chapter 5, for instance, and for Jenny's to appear the same way in "A Respected Friend in a New Aspect" (Book the Third, Chapter 2).[95] But as Brattin points out, in the proofs the introduced spacing in "A Cry for Help" fell at the bottom of the page where it apparently looked unintentional, and it has been

---

[93] See Brattin, "Dickens' Creation of Bradley Headstone."

[94] MA 1203, fol. 158. See for comparison Dickens, *Our Mutual Friend* (London, 1997), p. 682; and Dickens, *Our Mutual Friend* (Oxford, 1983), p. 698.

[95] MA 1202, fol. 43; MA 1203, fol. 19.

missed by compositors and editors since.[96] Dickens also noted "(white line here)" in Chapter 10, "A Marriage Contract," at the close of the paragraph ending, "and even the unknowns are painfully and slowly strained off, and it is all over," presumably to suggest the lapse of time between the end of the Lammles' wedding celebration and the start of their miserable honeymoon on the Isle of Wight.[97] But this, too, has been lost from current editions of the novel. Though it appears correctly in the proofs, the first edition shows the break between those lines coming, as in the case above, at the end of a page; consequently, editors since have failed to notice and preserve it.[98] Even in an American edition of 1864–65, that blank line does not appear.[99] Finally, scholars interested in Book the Third, Chapter 14, should save their money and time rather than visit the Morgan to see it: the manuscript chapter looks as though it was written in disappearing ink, leaving nothing legible but the heading for the first page. Those looking for textual curiosities about Wegg, Venus, and Boffin must turn their attention to the other chapters in which they appear.

As Dickens neared the end of *Our Mutual Friend*, he did encounter one other unexpected problem: in a reversal of his trouble in the early installments, he actually underwrote Nos. 16 and 18 during his final, frenzied months of work. The first of these, No. 16, may well have been a result of Staplehurst. It was the installment that Dickens had rescued from the train, and that he later remarked having underwritten by more than two pages. The second, No. 18, may be explained simply by the sheer volume of work Dickens was trying to complete during an astonishingly short time in August 1865. In each case, Dickens remedied the problem by drafting passages of new material to be inserted into the original chapters, often focusing particularly on dialogue to add lines of text more quickly, just as he had focused on removing dialogue when he needed to cut early numbers down to size. All but one of the seven large-scale revisions to No. 16 appear on two pages of text that Dickens wrote separately, and that the Morgan has organized simply by inserting them as the first two pages of the installment. The new passages are labeled A–F and all appear properly inserted in the first edition, but the absence of marks in the manuscript to show where they should be inserted suggests that Dickens indicated the proper locations in some copy of the proofs that has not survived (Plate 16). Revisions A, B, and C were added to Book the Fourth, Chapter 1, D and E to Chapter 2, and F—by far the longest—to Chapter 4. Meanwhile, another multiline addition to the end of Chapter 4 appears as a cut-in to the manuscript itself rather than on these two pages, running from Bella's, "Pa, dear!" to the narrator's description of Bella beseeching him "in the prettiest manner."[100] Another indication that Dickens was attempting to lengthen the number appears in the proofs for No. 16, where the unnumbered facing page to 192—the end of Book the Fourth, Chapter 4—has

---

[96] Brattin, "Dickens' Creation of Bradley Headstone," p. 159. See Charles Dickens, *Our Mutual Friend* (London, 1865), vol. 2, p. 213 for evidence of the blank lines.

[97] MA 1202, fol. 92.

[98] Proof sheets, vol. 1, p. 65; Dickens, *Our Mutual Friend* (London, 1865), vol. 1, p. 92.

[99] Charles Dickens, *Our Mutual Friend* (New York, 1864–65), vol. 1, p. 185.

[100] MA 1203, fol. 142A.

The Cup and the Lip   67

pasted into it as an addition the last several lines of the chapter as they appear in the published novel, beginning with Bella's, "Did I pinch your legs, Pa?" and running through the end of the chapter. Revisions D and E draw more explicit attention to the Lammles' conniving as they try to draw out the Boffins over breakfast, and F inserts the good fun of the hopelessly romantic young waiter who attends John, Bella, and her father during their wedding dinner at Greenwich—a pure innovation that, as we shall see, found considerable favor with some contemporary critics. All told, the addition to the proofs and revisions D, E, and F make for more than two pages in manuscript and perhaps nearer to three in print; despite the initial deficit, they produced an overrun in proofs of some 21 lines.[101]

But A, B, and C are the shorter and more important creative revisions, for they work brilliantly to heighten the tension of the emerging cat-and-mouse between Riderhood and Headstone as the latter begins lurking around Plashwater Weir Mill Lock. The first addition, in which Riderhood asserts openly that Headstone has been giving his mind to "[s]pites, affronts, offences giv' and took, deadly aggravations, and such like," hints at the extent to which the older villain has read Headstone's heart and seen the violence lurking there.[102] The second, B, hints at the eventual end of their deadly collaboration, for the narrator remarks something like Headstone's suicidal thoughts as the schoolmaster stares into the water in the lock below: "If he had stepped back for a spring, taken a leap, and thrown himself in, it would have been no surprising sequel to the look. Perhaps his troubled soul, set upon some violence, did hover for the moment between that violence and another."[103] The third revision to this chapter lingers over Riderhood's scrutiny of the sleeping Headstone, suggesting his long consideration of the other man's intentions and the meaning of the red neckerchief, half hidden around Headstone's throat and looking so much like his own. Together, the revisions work persistently toward making Riderhood seem more than a match for Headstone, turning the tension into more than just a matter of how and when the schoolmaster will attack Eugene. They also show that Dickens's late revisions, like his early ones, tended to serve his creative aims as thoroughly as his practical ones.

The additions to No. 18 are less extensive but generally follow the same pattern, for here again Dickens simply composed an entire sheet—again arranged by the Morgan as the first page of the installment—of four revisions divided by horizontal lines and designated A–D. The first, A, is a long addition to the middle of Book the Fourth, Chapter 8, running from "Miss Wren had a reasonably good eye for smiles" to "no trace of amazement" and describing Jenny's strange encounter with Mrs. Lammle, in which she sizes up the older woman while the sounds of Fledgeby's caning go on upstairs.[104] B and C are additions to the next chapter and work together to underscore the mended relationship between Riah and Jenny, first as Jenny tries to take care of Riah after his departure from Fledgeby's (from Jenny's "Where are

---

[101]   Proof sheets, vol. 2, p. 192 and facing.

[102]   MA 1203, fol. 120.

[103]   Ibid.

[104]   Ibid., fol. 167.

you going to seek your fortune?" to the narrator's "she mistrusted his making the journey"), and then as Riah cares for her at the moment that her unconscious "child" is discovered in the street (from "Belongs to you?" to Riah's whispered explanation, "It's her drunken father").[105] There is in these revisions a touching reciprocity—a symmetry that reinforces the emotional and physical care that these two outcasts take of each other in the colder, broader world of the novel. The last revision, D, comes in Chapter 10 and does little more than attenuate one of Eugene's faltering lapses into senselessness, his imploring of Mortimer in the original to "[s]top my wandering away" being supplemented by another snippet of dialogue, beginning with Eugene's "Keep me here" and ending with the narrator's remark that Eugene's "appeal ... affected his friend profoundly."[106] Despite the poignancy of the scene between Jenny and Riah, none of these revisions has the force of Dickens's additions to the Riderhood and Headstone scene in No. 16. Perhaps Dickens, working furiously and simultaneously at Nos. 18, 19, and 20, was merely too caught up in the race to the finish to do more with these last additions. But of course, as the novel wound down, there was anyway less tension to sustain, less symbolism to be reinforced, and less explicitly creative work to be done. Dickens's play was nearly played out. But for a few scenes—principally those in which Harmon and Boffin unwind the complexity of the plot—even in manuscript the final double number shows Dickens working quickly and surely to conclude the novel.

III

Until nearly the end of the novel, then, Dickens continued to "slip" in writing *Our Mutual Friend*. But amid his slips, and even when he had to revise principally for length, his grueling labor remained fundamentally creative rather than practical, or at least both creative *and* practical. Dickens did not write *Our Mutual Friend* effortlessly. But then, he had written none of his novels effortlessly, no matter the airy mythology that has sprung up over the years about the endless imaginative outpourings of the early part of his career. He burst upon the scene almost magically with *The Pickwick Papers* and followed it impossibly quickly with *Oliver Twist* and *Nicholas Nickleby*, all while writing journalism, *The Memoirs of Joseph Grimaldi* (1838), and a host of other works that are now mostly forgotten. They were, every one of them, the product of both imaginative fertility and Herculean labor, his boundless energy expressing itself in the creative restlessness that characterized his life. In 1836, one of the overwhelming characteristics of his letters to his then-fiancée Catherine Hogarth was their tendency to apologize for his being unable to see her, so utterly overwhelmed was he with his writing. March 20 of that year brought to "dearest Katie—"

> A note, and not me. I am very—very—sorry. I am tired and worn out to-day, mind and body; and have that to do, which will certainly occupy me 'till 1 or 2

---

[105] Ibid.

[106] Ibid.

The Cup and the Lip   69

o'Clock. I did not get to bed till 3 o'Clock this morning; and consequently could not begin to write, until nearly one.[107]

He had also apologized the day before, and he did so again the day after, and again the day after that. All the while, he was writing *Pickwick* but not yet simultaneously engaged upon *Oliver Twist*, as he would be by the end of the year. To say that Dickens *labored* over *Our Mutual Friend*, then, is not to issue a pejorative assessment of the novel. It may lack the explicit linguistic vivacity of Alfred Jingle and Sam Weller and the high good humor of Nicholas Nickleby beating Wackford Squeers. It may be less lively a story. But *Our Mutual Friend* is undoubtedly the more complex novel, the more ambitious, the more subtle in its characters, the more sophisticated in its use of symbol, plot, and narration. Only a very few of Dickens's novel—*Little Dorrit*, perhaps, *Bleak House*, and *Great Expectations*— even approach *Our Mutual Friend* in these respects. So while Dickens labored painstakingly at his novel, it is perhaps worth asking whether there is another way to produce a book of this magnitude and vision, shot through with the unsettling and uncanny insight that everything is Dust, yet able to raise the quiet romance of modern life from the ashy ruins.

By the time Dickens escaped to France in September 1865, he had very nearly killed himself with the labor of writing *Our Mutual Friend*, though of course he would not admit it. On September 13 he wrote to Yates from Paris to say that he was leaving that city the next day and making his slow way back to Gad's Hill and the *All the Year Round* office. "The heat has been excessive on this side of the Channel," he told him, "and I got a slight sun-stroke last Thursday, and was obliged to be doctored and put to bed for a day. But thank god I am all right again."[108] He almost certainly was not "all right"—almost certainly was suffering from "sun-stroke" in the same way that, six months before, he was suffering from "frostbite." The signs of his increasing illness were upon him now as they had been then, the severity of the illness suggested by, if nothing else, the rarity of Dickens ever keeping to bed for a day and allowing himself to be doctored rather than taking solace in one of his notorious walks. Even before leaving for Paris he had written half-jokingly to Forster of the lingering trouble in his left foot, saying that he had managed to get a boot on that day only because it had been "made on an Otranto scale."[109] Death did not come for Dickens in 1865, though. He survived his sun-stroke in Paris, just as he had survived frostbite and Staplehurst—and, for that matter, just as he had survived his infatuation with Nelly, the disintegration of his marriage, the public humiliation of the "Violated Letter," and the other private griefs and professional vicissitudes that had transformed his life and art since *The Frozen Deep*. And he survived them all to write a novel of extraordinary power and resilience, fully as able to defy the odds and the critics as Dickens ever was himself.

---

[107] *Letters*, vol. 1, pp. 140–41.

[108] Ibid., vol. 11, p. 91.

[109] Ibid., p. 89.

Chapter 3
Putting a Price upon a Man's Mind:
Our Mutual Friend in the Marketplace

In its concluding double number, *Our Mutual Friend* closes the mystery of the Harmon fortune by having John Harmon finally undeceive Wegg, who is crushed to learn that his copy of the will is worthless and that, consequently, he cannot extort even a brass farthing from Boffin. With his typical generosity of spirit, though, Boffin tells Wegg, "I shouldn't like to leave you, after all said and done, worse off in life than I found you. Therefore say in a word, before we part, what it'll cost to set you up in another stall."[1] Insolent to the last, Wegg uses a great many words and names a great many things he claims to have lost by serving Boffin—his ballads, his gingerbreads, his umbrella, his stool and trestles—before arriving at one final complaint. "[I]t's not easy to say," he tells Boffin, "how far the tone of my mind may have been lowered by unwholesome reading on the subject of Misers ... All I can say is, that I felt my tone of mind a lowering at the time. And how can a man put a price upon his mind!"[2] *Our Mutual Friend* is no comic masterpiece, but surely this line qualifies as one of Dickens's most preposterous jokes. For hundreds of pages no mind has been lower than Wegg's, whether in his coarse desire to "collect [him]self like a genteel person" by reacquiring his amputated leg or in his increasingly infamous designs upon Boffin, who has literally taken Wegg off the street and given him a home and comfortable work.[3] Wegg's villainy ends in attempted blackmail, but it is worth noting that it begins in an apparently innocuous but closely analogous enterprise: making a sham of mental work, charging the Boffins five shillings a week for the absurdity of hearing him read texts ranging from street ballads to Edward Gibbon's *History of the Decline and Fall of the Roman Empire* (1776–89). Wegg's mental labor consists, that is, not of *producing* but rather of *reproducing*, and doing so badly. From first to last his frauds are merely misappropriations of others' words and texts; they parody legitimate authorship. And this, more than anything, is what the novel seems to punish him for, since we last see him being dumped into a scavenger's cart by Sloppy, who has spent years reading to Betty Higden for free. Wegg may make a sham of intellectual work, then, but the novel's final joke is on him.

But Wegg is not the only—nor even the most telling—product of the novel's thematic engagement with intellectual work. Rather, he is a comic *doppelgänger* of the sinister Headstone, who has turned his mind so doggedly into a "wholesale

---

[1] Dickens, *Our Mutual Friend* (London, 1997), p. 768.
[2] Ibid., p. 769.
[3] Ibid., p. 88.

warehouse ... always ready to meet the demands of retail dealers" that he becomes nearly inhuman, a volatile compound of foaming fits and breathtaking violence.[4] In part, Headstone is another in a long line of Dickens's failed teachers—Squeers, Mr. Creakle, Mr. Gradgrind, Mr. Wopsle's great-aunt—but he is much more fully drawn, his inhumanity offered as the product of a mental inflexibility that treats the intellect as a strictly acquisitive and reiterative thing rather than as productive or creative. As the narrator says:

> He had acquired mechanically a great store of teacher's knowledge. He could do mental arithmetic mechanically, sing at sight mechanically, blow various wind instruments mechanically, even play the great church organ mechanically. From his early childhood on, his mind had been a place of mechanical stowage.[5]

Conceiving intellectual work as a menial task that can carry him from pauperism to respectability, Headstone leads a mental life that is fundamentally transactional, buying and selling—rather than producing—mental wares and so turning the intellectual work of others to account. In this sense he resembles Wegg, but whereas Wegg only does violence to language, Headstone is psychologically terrifying and physically dangerous. His attack on Eugene is no preposterous joke. Instead, it is one of the most brutal scenes in Dickens, just as his suicide and the simultaneous murder of Rogue is one of the most emotionally taut. While Wegg encourages us to laugh at the idea of putting a price upon a man's mind, Headstone shows us the potential horrors of such mental arithmetic when its misapplication results in a thoroughly economized subject.

If the problem of intellectual work does not remain a mere joke in *Our Mutual Friend*, it may be because for Dickens putting a price upon his mind had never really been a laughing matter. Blighted by his family's insolvency and his father's imprisonment in the Marshalsea, Dickens's sad childhood cast its shadow over the rest of his life and drove him not just to Warren's Blacking in 1823 but also, from age 15, to learning shorthand, climbing the ranks as a Parliamentary reporter, and devoting himself with frenzied energy to a career as a writer and editor that would place him far beyond any possibility of renewed financial disgrace.[6] But his financial success came largely because he forced himself to become not only an extraordinary novelist but also an exceptionally shrewd man of literary business. At the dawn of his career when he needed money and exposure, he overextended himself grossly through a series of contracts with several publishers—John Macrone, Bentley, Chapman and Hall—typically for far less than his work turned out to be worth by the time he finished writing. By November 1836, though he had already resigned the *Morning Chronicle* and turned down Thomas Tegg's offer of

---

[4]   Ibid., p. 218.

[5]   Ibid.

[6]   Biographies have usually given the start of Dickens's employment at Warren's as 1824, but Michael Allen presents a convincing case for this earlier date in *Charles Dickens and the Blacking Factory* (St. Leonards, 2011), pp. 92–5.

£100 for a short Christmas book entitled "Solomon Bell the Raree Showman," he faced at least a half-dozen writing commitments, including those for *Pickwick*, a second series of *Sketches by Boz*, the editorship of *Bentley's Miscellany*, and the novels that would eventually become *Oliver Twist* and *Barnaby Rudge* (1841).[7] Aided by Forster, he therefore spent much of 1837–40 wringing concessions from publishers, partly so that he could manage his impossible workload, and partly so that he could share more entirely in the rewards of his labor. With Bentley, for instance, Dickens had signed a contract in August 1836 obliging him to write two three-volume novels, then three months later signed another contract agreeing to provide an article every month for the *Miscellany* at a rate of £21 per sheet. But in the end, Dickens forced Bentley—despite having no real legal grounds to do so—to accept *Oliver Twist* as both the monthly article and a three-volume novel, getting paid for it twice. He also ignored the provision for a second three-volume novel for Bentley, at least temporarily, while he wrote *Nicholas Nickleby* for Chapman and Hall under a contract that he did not sign until January 1838.[8]

He also gained an unprecedented level of control over his copyrights, first by consolidating them under Chapman and Hall in 1840 and then, when he took his work to Bradbury and Evans four years later, by arranging things so that the houses would have to collaborate—under his direction—on cheap editions, reissues, and other attempts to work the copyrights. Here Dickens was blazing a new trail. His battles with Richard Bentley in 1837–39 were, Patten observes, "symptoms of a larger crisis in early Victorian print culture" in which publishers, authors, and attorneys were establishing legal frameworks for entirely new situations.[9] During his trip to the United States in 1842, too, Dickens was so loud upon the subject of international copyright that he passed quickly from being fêted to being reviled by the American press, and he came home embittered and dispirited by his time in the young republic. Still, the net results of this continuous wrangling were worth the trouble—not, or at least not immediately, with respect to international copyright, but certainly when it came to his footing with publishers in England. When Dickens started *Pickwick* for Chapman and Hall in 1836, he agreed to receive nine and a half guineas per 24-page monthly installment but left the entire copyright to the publishers, who cleared £14,000 from the novel in parts.[10] In 1844, when Dickens

---

[7]   See Robert Patten, *Charles Dickens and "Boz": The Birth of the Industrial-Age Author* (Cambridge, 2012), p. 138; and also Patten, *Charles Dickens and His Publishers*, p. 34. In *Charles Dickens and "Boz"* Patten argues incisively that Dickens's overwhelming commitments actually show that "he had enough experience with publishers already to know that some promises weren't kept," p. 141.

[8]   See Patten, *Charles Dickens and His Publishers*, pp. 75–90.

[9]   Patten, *Charles Dickens and "Boz,"* p. 143.

[10]   Ibid., p. 149. Chapman and Hall raised this remuneration voluntarily as readership and profits soared: to £21 for 32-page installments beginning in June 1836 and then to £25 in November 1836. They also presented him with a one-time bonus of £500 in April 1837 on the anniversary of the first number and eventually made his total remuneration for the book £2,000.

moved to Bradbury and Evans, the contract awarded them only 1/4 share in his works plus a 10 percent commission on sales for the next eight years, a privilege for which they paid £2,000.[11] Despite their modest share, the contract—which eventually covered *Dombey and Son*, *David Copperfield*, and the early numbers of *Bleak House*—enriched Bradbury and Evans by nearly £15,000.[12] Dickens made nearly twice that much.

By the time Dickens broke with Bradbury and Evans in 1858, he had, for practical purposes, placed himself beyond the need for publishers, entirely in the case of *All the Year Round* and quite nearly in the cases of his novels, too. Though he "returned" to Chapman and Hall in 1859, really he published *A Tale of Two Cities* and *Great Expectations* himself, in his own magazine, leaving Chapman and Hall to handle only the novels' reissue in other editions. For the monthly parts issue and single-volume editions of *A Tale*, Chapman and Hall handled the printing and accounting in exchange for a 10 percent commission on sales—which they reduced voluntarily to 7.5 percent as a show of good faith—and they repeated this arrangement for the three-volume *Great Expectations* in 1861.[13] With the one-volume edition of *Great Expectations* the following year, Chapman and Hall finally got a 50/50 split. By then, Dickens had made £5,000 from publishing the two novels in collected form, while Chapman and Hall had made more like £500. Surely Frederic Chapman had something grander in mind when he coaxed Dickens into returning. But he did not complain, and when Dickens bought up Bradbury and Evans's 1/4 share in his novels for £3,000 in 1861, Chapman dutifully agreed to purchase the share from Dickens for £3,250. Apparently 25 percent, 10 percent, or even 7.5 percent of Dickens was far better than no Dickens at all.

After three decades of struggle, in other words, Dickens had reached the enviable point at which he could dictate terms, and he did just this in September 1863 when he approached Chapman and Hall—at long last, they must have thought—about the possibility of a new novel in 20 numbers. On September 8 Dickens wrote to them to say that he had "carefully considered past figures and future reasonable probabilities" and concluded that he could give them half-copyright in *Our Mutual Friend* for £6,000.[14] Nor, apparently, was he disposed to negotiate terms. He closed the letter by writing:

> Of course you will understand that I do not press you to give the sum I have mentioned, and that you will not in the least inconvenience or offend me by preferring to leave me to make other arrangements. If you should have any misgiving on this head, let my assurance that you need have none, set it at rest.[15]

---

[11] Patten, *Charles Dickens and His Publishers*, p. 155.

[12] Based upon the half-yearly totals provided in Patten's Appendix A in *Charles Dickens and His Publishers*.

[13] Ibid., p. 278.

[14] *Letters*, vol. 10, p. 287.

[15] Ibid.

Putting a Price upon a Man's Mind 75

The offer was, as Patten writes, very much "on a 'take it or leave it' basis," but Dickens must have known that Chapman and Hall were unlikely to miss their chance.[16] They had, Dickens's letter makes clear, approached him before about writing a new novel, for he remarks that the timing of their payments for the new novel could follow the schedule they mentioned "in [their] last letter to [him] on the subject."[17] More, though Chapman and Hall had already taken steps toward publishing a People's edition of Dickens's works—the first volume of which, *Pickwick*, appeared in June 1865—no such project would do financially, at least in the short term, what a novel in 20 numbers would, especially since Dickens had been absent so long from his old audience and could be counted upon to make a triumphant return. The delay had all been on Dickens's side, partly perhaps because of fatigue, failing health, or sluggish invention, but principally because *All the Year Round* and his lucrative public readings kept him extraordinarily busy and provided him with a handsome income.[18] Now, however, he was ready to strike in, but only after calculating to a nicety what his novel was worth and asking confidently for his price. After a few weeks' consideration, Chapman and Hall gave it to him.

Whether they should have done so—and whether *Our Mutual Friend* lived up to their or Dickens's expectations—is a puzzle of literary history. The simple facts show that despite much excitement and publicity, *Our Mutual Friend* never became the commercial phenomenon they all anticipated, and it may well be that our general awareness of this shortcoming has gone a long way to creating the impression that it was a "bad," or at least unpopular, book. In *Charles Dickens and His Publishers*, still the standard scholarly work on the subject, Patten points out that Chapman and Hall lost £700 on *Our Mutual Friend* and calls the novel a "relative commercial failure," though he remarks, too, that for Chapman and Hall it still may not have been a bad deal.[19] By not haggling over the price, Frederic Chapman kept Dickens happy and so secured his continued cooperation for any new works, the People's edition, and nearly £10,000 of back stock, as well as for the immensely profitable Charles Dickens edition of his works that they brought out beginning in 1867. But these details tell us little about whether, on its own merit, *Our Mutual Friend* failed or, if it did, what that failure might mean. Unquestionably, the novel in parts sold worse than *Little Dorrit*, *Bleak House*, or *Dombey and Son*; unquestionably, it failed, too, to repay Chapman and Hall's £6,000. Yet the reasons for this are complex and have, in the main, very little to do with the novel itself. They are bound up instead with the broader patterns of mid-century publishing and book buying and the difficult economic conditions England faced during the second half of the US Civil War. Compared with what

---

[16] Patten, *Charles Dickens and His Publishers*, p. 302.

[17] *Letters*, vol. 10, p. 287.

[18] Patten makes this point, too, writing, "money delayed rather than hastened the appearance of the novel," *Charles Dickens and His Publishers*, p. 301.

[19] Ibid., p. 309.

76   *Charles Dickens's* Our Mutual Friend

Dickens or Chapman and Hall hoped the novel would do, *Our Mutual Friend* fell short. But it was in other ways one of the most successful novels of Dickens's career, and perhaps one of the most successful of the 1860s. Putting a price upon a man's mind is no easy thing, it turns out. The story of *Our Mutual Friend*'s commercial failures and successes deserves a serious hearing before we toss the novel, alongside Wegg, into the scavenger's cart.

I

The contract that Dickens signed with Chapman and Hall for *Our Mutual Friend* laid out, for the most part, only the basic features of publication and payment. It stipulated that the novel would be a serial in 20 monthly parts, that publication would commence by the end of 1864, and that Dickens would receive his £6,000 in increments of £2,500, £2,500, and £1,000 payable upon the appearances of Nos. 1, 6, and 20. Chapman and Hall would keep the accounts and, in exchange, receive 5 percent commission on gross sales, leaving all the profits to be divided evenly with Dickens. Certain other details were not in the contract, though they must have been matters of plain understanding between the parties. For instance, Dickens undoubtedly intended to publish his 20 numbers over 19 months, and presumably both parties understood that monthly installments would cost the customary shilling. The contract never mentions, either, the arrangements for publishing in two volumes; rather, one of Dickens's letters from August 1864 suggests that plans for the two-volume edition evolved during that summer, when Chapman apparently suggested that *Our Mutual Friend* might depart from Dickens's usual pattern by being collected into volumes *during*, not after, its serial run. Dickens approved the scheme, pointing out that "[t]he construction of the story is particularly favorable to it, for No. Ten will end the second book."[20] Consequently, Volume 1 comprising Nos. 1–10 appeared concurrently with No. 10 late in January 1865, while the remaining numbers appeared as Volume 2 in late October. Possibly the departure from custom was meant to accelerate sales for Chapman and Hall by putting the receipts for Volume 1 in their pockets nine months earlier than otherwise. After all, besides the £5,000 they had paid to Dickens by January 1865, they were on their way to spending nearly £1,000 more for advertising and £5,378, 4s, 1/2d for printing, binding, and other production costs.[21] Meanwhile, as Patten reminds us, "[t]he only certain income for [them] … was the 5 per cent commission on gross sales, excluding payments for translation and advertising revenues."[22] Those sales would have to be brisk. Despite list prices of 1s for monthly installments and 11s per volume for the collected edition, industry discounts and price breaks for bulk purchases meant that major players like Charles Mudie and W.H. Smith paid

---

[20]   *Letters*, vol. 10, p. 423.

[21]   Gerald Grubb, "Some Unpublished Correspondence of Dickens and Chapman and Hall," *Boston University Studies in English*, 1 (1955), p. 121n.

[22]   Patten, *Charles Dickens and His Publishers*, p. 303.

Putting a Price upon a Man's Mind 77

more like 9s per dozen for parts and 7s, 6d per bound volume.[23] After deducting for costs, the profit per shilling number was razor thin. Chapman and Hall got their commission plus half of around 5d of profit per copy. To recoup their £6,000 payment for half copyright of Dickens's novel, they needed to sell nearly 600,000 parts in 19 months, perhaps fewer depending upon the success of the two-volume edition.

Even so, Chapman and Hall's decision to pay Dickens's asking price for *Our Mutual Friend* was probably relatively easy, not just because they had waited four years for the chance but because, at the time, Dickens's popularity appeared to have reached new heights, so that even a significant investment was likely to be repaid at compound interest. In May 1859 *All the Year Round* had launched to a circulation of 120,000 before settling in at the consistent—and still extraordinary—figure of 100,000 throughout *A Tale of Two Cities* and *The Woman in White*. Thereafter, Charles Lever's *A Day's Ride* dropped the magazine somewhat, but *Great Expectations* reversed the slide, prompting a delighted Dickens to observe in May 1861 that his magazine's circulation exceeded even that of the *Times*.[24] By July, too, he was complaining to Macready that "a compound of bungling on the part of the publisher and of the printer" had caused *Great Expectations* to be out of print for a fortnight, since two printings totaling 1,750 copies had already sold out; by October, the novel had passed through five printings and sold 3,500 copies of its lavish three-volume edition, priced 31s, 6d, attracting greater and greater numbers of readers as it circulated through Mudie's.[25] As for Dickens's last novel in 20 numbers, *Little Dorrit* had sold in excess of 650,000 parts during 1855–57 and earned £22,500 from its sale as a serial, while five years earlier *Bleak House* had sustained even higher sales and earned a thousand pounds more.[26] Chapman and Hall thus had every reason to expect that *Our Mutual Friend* would rise to the occasion, and certainly that it would make back their investment. By September 30 they had agreed in principle to Dickens's proposal, and Dickens sent Ouvry a letter including "the heads of an Agreement" and instructing him to draft a contract based upon the same.[27]

Immediately the agreement hit a snag. One of Ouvry's partners, William Farrer, wrote to Dickens the same day, apparently to ask what would happen to any money that he had already received if he died before finishing the novel.[28] It is not entirely clear whether Chapman and Hall or rather Dickens's solicitors raised this concern first, or precisely why they did so. Perhaps those who knew Dickens personally were worried already about his health, or perhaps Chapman and Hall wanted a provision simply because of the unusually large sum involved.

---

[23] Ibid., pp. 404–5.

[24] *Letters*, vol. 9, pp. 412–13.

[25] Patten, *Charles Dickens and His Publishers*, p. 290.

[26] Ibid., pp. 391, 355.

[27] *Letters*, vol. 10, p. 294.

[28] Ibid., p. 295.

78 *Charles Dickens's* Our Mutual Friend

The tone of Dickens's reply to Farrer suggests that his own legal team may have originated the question as they began preparing the contract. On October 1 Dickens wrote:

> I had thought of the point you mention in your note of yesterday, but did not know what to do about it. In former similar agreements between Chapman and Hall and myself, it has not been recognized. Would it be well to refer it to them, and ask them if they have any suggestion to offer on that head?[29]

Of course, there had been no "similar agreement" with Chapman and Hall for decades, and the sum of money involved meant that, really, Dickens and his publishers alike were in uncharted waters. As Dickens suggested, Farrer referred the question to Edward Chapman, who replied that he could not "hit upon any scheme which answers the purpose. The simplest is the one we discussed, viz., his insuring his life for £2,000, but then comes the question how is that to be allotted into 'times' and 'sums'"—how, that is, the contract might make proper provision for the quantity of work Dickens had finished versus the quantity of payment he had already received.[30]

In the end the parties agreed essentially to defer the issue, signing a contract on November 21 that retained the original language regarding how Dickens would be paid and that turned the matter over to Forster to settle in the event of Dickens's death or incapacity. The penultimate paragraph of the contract for *Our Mutual Friend* thus reads:

> That if the said Charles Dickens shall die during the composition of the said work or shall otherwise become incapable of completing the said work for publication in twenty monthly Numbers as agreed it shall be referred to John Forster Esquire One of Her Majesty's Commissioners in Lunacy or in case of his death incapacity or refusal to act then to such person as shall be named by Her Majesty's Attorney General for the time being to determine the amount which shall be repaid by the said Charles Dickens his executors or administrators to the said Edward Chapman and Frederic Chapman as a fair compensation for so much of the said Work as shall not have been completed for publication and the said Charles Dickens his executors or administrators will immediately after the said award or determination shall be made pay to the said Edward Chapman and Frederic Chapman the sum of money so to be awarded or determined to be unpaid.[31]

In the event, the legal hand wringing turned out to be irrelevant, but the proviso returned—more usefully, unfortunately—in the contract he signed in 1869 for

---

[29] Ibid., pp. 295–6.

[30] Ibid., p. 476.

[31] Agreement between Dickens and Edward and Frederic Chapman, for the writing and publishing of the serial Our mutual friend, for the sum of £6000, dated Nov. 21, 1863, New York Public Library, Henry W. and Albert A. Berg Collection.

Putting a Price upon a Man's Mind 79

The Mystery of Edwin Drood.[32] The details settled, Dickens was finally poised to return to 20 numbers, and Chapman and Hall were prepared to make his return the literary event of the decade.

To that end, during the winter and early spring of 1864 Chapman and Hall launched an advertising campaign so extensive that no Londoners—and probably precious few Britons—could have failed to know that Dickens was preparing a new novel, that it would appear in 20 numbers beginning in May, and that its title was *Our Mutual Friend*. They printed more than a million 8vo and 16mo handbills, 145,000 demy 8vo catalogues, and enough posters and placards to saturate major cities all over England.[33] They also spent £550 to advertise the novel in every major newspaper and journal throughout its first six months of publication.[34] On March 15 Frederic Chapman wrote to Dickens to say that he had arranged with W.H. Smith to have them distribute 200,000 of the small bills and to place large placards—30 long frames for four months—at Smith's major railway stands.[35] "I sent out the [newspaper] advts as you desired," Chapman also told him, "but I am sorry to say that the Times has not yet put it in—They promised me yesterday that they would try to commence as today [*sic*]."[36] Enormous advertisements were also placed in train stations at Birmingham and Bristol, and posters appeared not only at Camberwell and Kennington Gates but also on the sides of a hundred omnibuses and several steamboats—"perhaps," Patten surmises, "exploiting the importance of the Thames in the novel."[37] To any literate passerby along the Strand or boarding a train at Victoria or Paddington or King's Cross, London must have seemed bursting with Dickens. In all, Chapman and Hall spent £868 on advertising, bringing their total investment in the novel to almost £7,000. Looking back, it is unclear whether any novel could have lived up to the massive expectations.

Early on, Chapman and Hall's aggressive marketing campaign seems to have produced considerable excitement and an excellent chance for financial success. For one thing, as Thomas Hatton and Arthur Cleaver point out, the advertising sheets in *Our Mutual Friend* were more extensive than in any other of the original novels in parts.[38] The novel's advertising revenue, in fact, more than compensated Chapman and Hall for what they had spent in that regard, for in total they received

---

[32] Patten, *Charles Dickens and His Publishers*, p. 316. For *Drood*, which Dickens planned for 12 monthly installments, he received a payment of £7,500 from Chapman and Hall in exchange for the right to all profits on the first 25,000 copies. Patten notes that payments totaling £4,000 are the only evidence of sums that Chapman paid to Dickens and may be "the only payments he was ever required to make." Patten, *Charles Dickens and His Publishers*, p. 317.

[33] Ibid., p. 307.

[34] Ibid.

[35] Grubb, p. 121.

[36] Ibid.

[37] Patten, *Charles Dickens and His Publishers*, p. 307.

[38] Hatton and Cleaver, p. 345.

£2,750, 12s, 10d—£600 more than Bradbury and Evans had gotten for *Bleak House* and £750 more than they had gotten for *Little Dorrit*.[39] Likewise, printing records show that Chapman and Hall were preparing for brisk sales, partly, no doubt, on the basis of mere projections, but partly also based upon preorders for the novel, which were presumably considerable. They had William Clowes and Sons print 40,000 copies of No. 1—2,000 more than for *Little Dorrit*'s first number—and 35,000 of these were stitched.[40] Less than a week after No. 1 appeared, Dickens wrote delightedly to Forster, "Nothing can be better than *Our Friend* [*sic*], now in his thirtieth thousand, and orders flowing fast."[41] He also wrote enthusiastically to Wills to say that "[a]ccording to present appearances you seem to be in the way of winning our bet upon *Our Mutual*!" which makes it sound as though Wills had encouraged a nervous Dickens by wagering on the eve of publication that his long absence from monthly numbers would not impede the success of *Our Mutual Friend*, and that the novel would sell every bit as well as those that had come before.[42] According to Forster, sales of *Pickwick*'s monthly parts had crested at 40,000 by No. 15, and *Nickleby* had eventually topped 50,000.[43] Since those early days, however, *Little Dorrit* had been the high water mark, and even its print runs had never reached the 40,000 of *Our Mutual Friend*'s first number.

These were heady days for Dickens, and he must have been enormously relieved. Like an ageing virtuoso, he had returned to the stage to discover that he was still beloved, irreplaceable, at the very top of the tree. For months he had struggled with the length of installments, the inexperience of his new illustrator, and the dazzling effect of his return to the "large canvas." His marriage was broken, his friends were dying, and he was beginning to feel his age. Yet apparently none of this mattered. Out of practice and out of spirits and unaccompanied by Phiz, he was still the same inimitable and impossibly popular Dickens, and—most importantly—the money was still pouring in. By summer 1864 he had already received his first £2,500 from Chapman and Hall, and another such sum was due to him before Christmas. Better yet, sales receipts and advertising income had netted him another £1,977, 6s, 4d in profits by the end of the year, and he had also found other means of capitalizing on the novel.[44] In May 1864 Tauchnitz paid Dickens £75 for the right to print *Our Mutual Friend* in Germany.[45] In America, meanwhile, Harper & Co. agreed to give Dickens £1,000 for advance proofs so that the novel could appear in *Harper's New Monthly Magazine* simultaneously with publication in England, then follow in a two-volume "paper" edition priced

---

[39] Patten, *Charles Dickens and His Publishers*, pp. 405, 355, 391.
[40] Ibid., p. 446.
[41] Forster, *Life*, p. 742.
[42] *Letters*, vol. 10, p. 390.
[43] Forster, *Life*, pp. 91, 109.
[44] Patten, *Charles Dickens and His Publishers*, p. 405.
[45] *Letters*, vol. 10, p. 360 and n.

$1.00 and a one-volume edition in cloth at $1.50.[46] For *Little Dorrit*, Dickens had made around £4,500 on his 3/4 copyright during the first eight months of serialization, plus another £75 for early sheets to America.[47] Eight months into *Our Mutual Friend*, he was already in pocket £8,200.

Chapman, on the other hand, could not have helped being nervous. Wills almost certainly lost his bet regarding sales of *Our Mutual Friend*'s first number, for only 35,000 of the 40,000 copies printed were eventually stitched, leaving the novel 3,000 copies short of *Little Dorrit*'s initial sales. Chapman adjusted accordingly, printing only 35,000 copies of No. 2—not an unusual drop-off for Dickens's serials, most of which had their starting print runs cut as the publisher adjusted to the demands of the market. But the number of copies stitched for No. 2 fell again, to 31,000, then to 27,000 for No. 3 and 25,000 for No. 4.[48] In four months, the print run had declined by more than a third, prompting Dickens to send a reassuring letter to Frederic Chapman. On August 28 he wrote:

> I regard No. 4 as certain to pick up, and I have the strongest faith in the book's doing thoroughly well. I believe it to be GOOD, full of variety, and always rising in its working out of the people and the story. (I know I put into it, the making of a dozen books). The circulation is already larger than that of Copperfield or of Chuzzlewit, as I remember without looking into the accounts.[49]

Maybe so. But *Martin Chuzzlewit* (1843–44) was among Dickens's worst-selling novels in parts, never surpassing more than 23,000 copies a month and certainly not commanding £6,000 for half-copyright.[50] Too, though *Dombey and Son* and *Bleak House* had succeeded brilliantly as serials, the novel that came between them—Dickens's favorite child, *David Copperfield*—had not, opening at 30,000 printed in May 1849 but dropping to just 22,000 by October and remaining at the lower figure through the closing number. Gone, apparently, were any exuberant comparisons to *Little Dorrit*. Dickens could only point to the labor he was pouring into the novel, as if to remind Chapman and himself that he was earning, by the sweat of his brow, the enormous sums flowing into his bank accounts. Considering how important his readers' adoration always was to Dickens, the money may not have consoled him much in the face of obviously declining sales.

In his biography Forster notes the drop-off between Nos. 1 and 2 of *Our Mutual Friend* and asserts that "the larger number was again reached, and much exceeded,

---

[46]   Patten, *Charles Dickens and His Publishers*, p. 308. Pricing information for the one- and two-volume American editions from Harper is taken from an advertisement in *The Round Table: A Saturday Review of Politics, Finance, Literature, Society*, 9 (November 18, 1865), p. 176.

[47]   Patten, *Charles Dickens and His Publishers*, p. 391.

[48]   For printing and stitching figures for Dickens's novels in parts, see Patten's Appendix B in *Charles Dickens and His Publishers*. The particular figures for *Our Mutual Friend* appear on pp. 446–7.

[49]   *Letters*, vol. 10, p. 423.

[50]   Forster, *Life*, p. 302.

before the book closed."[51] But the evidence is against it. Sales continued to decline all the way until No. 6, for October 1864, when they stabilized at a print run of 28,000 with 24,000 stitched. There they stayed through the Christmas season, surprisingly, despite competition from "Mrs. Lirriper's Legacy" in *All the Year Round*. Since its inception in 1862, the special Christmas number of *All the Year Round* had been a popular phenomenon, so much so that the magazine's half-yearly accounts after 1861 invariably show much higher profits for the period November–April than for May–October.[52] In 1862 "Somebody's Luggage" sold 185,000 copies by December 22, and the next year Dickens boasted to Collins that "Mrs. Lirriper's Lodgings" had surpassed its predecessor by selling 220,000.[53] The Christmas number for 1865, "Dr. Marigold's Prescriptions," also reached sales of 200,000 by early January and eventually topped a quarter of a million, and in 1866 "Mugby Junction" sold 256,000 copies in a month.[54] The sales figures for "Mrs. Lirriper's Legacy" in 1864 are not mentioned in any of Dickens's letters, but Dickens's total profits from *All the Year Round* do show a marked decline for the half-year ending in April 1865, to £1,370, 9s, 9d compared with £2,069, 14s, 0d and £2,142, 16s, 6d for the half years ending April 1863 and 1864.[55] Still, it is hard to know exactly what this decline means, for even in the wake of the remarkable sales of the 1865 Christmas book, Dickens's half-year profits on the magazine remained surprisingly low. It may be that the normal circulation of *All the Year Round* excluding the Christmas number had declined, or that he was paying out greater sums to authors or printers. If the 1864 Christmas number really did suffer, however, it may mean that its competition with *Our Mutual Friend* hurt its receipts rather than injuring sales of the novel. Only once, in 1860, had Dickens issued a Christmas story in *All the Year Round* while also publishing a novel in parts, and then it was an unwelcome result of his sudden decision to serialize *Great Expectations*. If anything, the presence of both *Great Expectations* and "A Message from the Sea" in *All the Year Round* that winter probably made for higher sales of both works. That *Our Mutual Friend*'s monthly sales remained stable throughout the Christmas season may testify to the loyalty of its readers and to the momentum the novel had gained after its unsettled start.

During the spring of the new year, though, the print run for the novel dipped still lower, to 25,000, beginning with No. 13 in May 1865. Readership may have begun falling off again, perhaps in February and March, since the decision to reduce the print run must have been made in advance of No. 13's appearance at the end of April. Meantime, Volume 1 of the novel, collecting Nos. 1–10, together with the half-title, title, dedication, contents, and list of illustrations, was published in January 1865 at a price of 11s. Patten believes that this innovation in the scheme for volume publication "made little difference in sales," but it is very hard to know

---

[51]   Ibid., p. 742.

[52]   See Patten's Appendix D in *Charles Dickens and His Publishers*, p. 464.

[53]   Patten, *Charles Dickens and His Publishers*, p. 301; *Letters*, vol. 10, p. 346.

[54]   *Letters*, vol. 11, pp. 133, 295.

[55]   Patten, *Charles Dickens and His Publishers*, p. 464.

for sure.[56] In the past, the early numbers of Dickens's novels in parts had continued to sell many months into the serial run—sometimes even requiring additional printing—as new readers were drawn to the story. New copies of *Dombey and Son*'s first three numbers from October–December 1846 were still being printed and stitched during the second half of 1847, and for *Bleak House* Bradbury and Evans printed a total of 8,000 additional copies of Nos. 1–4 late in 1852, though the novel had begun appearing serially in March.[57] Readers interested in beginning *Our Mutual Friend* late in 1864 would not have been much inclined to go back and purchase the old shilling numbers when they could get them, in January 1865, collected into Volume 1. And those same readers, if they liked the novel, may well have chosen to wait 10 more months for the matching Volume 2 rather than buy the second half of the novel in monthly parts. Total sales of the novel might have been unaffected by the new publishing scheme, then, but the sale of monthly parts cannot have been helped. On the other hand, the two-volume edition sold briskly. Though he was always reluctant to stock novels that were not triple-deckers, Mudie took 832 two-volume sets, and W.H. Smith took 500 for sale at his railway stalls. All told, by the end of 1865, Chapman and Hall had sold nearly 2,700 copies of the two-volume edition for a total of £1,864, 13s, 0d in receipts.[58]

Hopefully, the performance of the two-volume edition consoled Frederic Chapman somewhat for the disappointing sales of the serial, which continued to lose readers until the story concluded in November 1865. Though the print run continued at 25,000 until the end, the number stitched dwindled to just 59,000 for Nos. 16–18 combined and to just 19,000 for the closing double number.[59] Not since *Chuzzlewit* had one of Dickens's final double numbers sold so anemically, and not since then, at least, had one of his publishers had buyer's remorse. Chapman and Hall's last significant reckoning of the half-yearly account for the novel in parts shows that, by June 1866, *Our Mutual Friend* had sold approximately 380,000 parts—just 2/3 of the break-even point—while the records for 1867 show that sales of the two-volume edition rose eventually to 3,030.[60] Total receipts for the novel by June 1867 were therefore £12,539, 14s, 9d with another £2,750, 12s, 10d in advertising revenues, for a total income of £15,290, 7s, 7d.[61] After deducting for costs and Chapman and Hall's commission, Dickens got more than £5,000 of these receipts, to which he could add his £6,000 for half-copyright and £1,075 for his separate contracts in Germany and the United States. He made, in other words, more than £12,000—a princely sum, though still less than the £19,000 he would earn two years later for his American reading tour.[62] For Frederic Chapman the

---

[56]   Ibid., p. 309.
[57]   Ibid., pp. 427, 419.
[58]   Ibid., p. 405.
[59]   Ibid., p. 446.
[60]   Ibid., p. 405.
[61]   Ibid.
[62]   Andrews, p. 45.

news was much worse. The house had taken just £740, 10s, 5d in commission and £4,608, 14s, 8d in profits. They may have had their £10,000 of Dickensian back-stock to console them, but even two years after the novel finished its serial run they had made back only around £5,350 of their £6,000 investment. Surely it was not the return they expected from the author they had waited 20 years to reacquire.

These are the plain facts of *Our Mutual Friend*'s commercial failure. But they are not the only facts, nor do they tell us all that we need to know. On the face of things, they tell the story of a novel that was marketed heavily, that appeared to great enthusiasm and extraordinary early sales, and that failed almost dismally to find favor with and keep the attention of Victorian readers. They tell the story, that is, of an unpopular book, or at least of a book that begins so grimly and ponderously on the Thames that readers accustomed either to Dickens's lively humor or the decade's sensational fiction quickly set it aside in favor of other fare. In this sense, too, they may even tell the story that James tells, of Dickens the ageing novelist failing in invention and imagination, and of a novel so labored and tired that, by the time of the double number, only half of its original readers remained. Yet the story is not so simple as this, either, for Dickens made more money from *Our Mutual Friend* than he had ever made from a novel in his life, and it is possible, moreover, that the novel suffered far more from England's troubled economic climate during the mid-1860s than from any lack of enthusiasm among its readers. Certainly Dickens was disappointed by the novel's sales. He had always been sensitive to the size of his audience, and he had tried to calculate shrewdly but fairly what the novel would be worth before he proposed terms to Chapman and Hall. But it does not necessarily follow that because Dickens made money and his publishers did not, the novel failed commercially. After all, had Dickens simply published *Our Mutual Friend* under the standard terms of his old contracts with Bradbury and Evans, asking for no money up front but granting the house a 1/4 share plus 12.5 percent commission, Chapman and Hall would have made £2,500 and Dickens would still have gotten more than £7,000. It would have been, in other words, a runaway success, particularly compared against other novels published during these same years, which happened to be the worst years for the publishing industry since the railway bubble and financial panic of the 1840s. Patten's formulation—that *Our Mutual Friend* was a "relative" commercial failure—is ultimately the right one, then, but of course it begs the question: relative to what? That, it turns out, is another story altogether.

II

Our Mutual Friend was not *Bleak House* or *Little Dorrit*, to begin with. There is no doubt whatever about that. Those two novels, separated only by the serialization of *Hard Times* in *Household Words* in 1854, constituted the popular high-water mark for Dickens's post-1840 fiction, as he took great pleasure in pointing out to his readers. In the "Preface" to the first two-volume edition of *Little Dorrit*, published just after the novel's serial run, Dickens wrote:

Putting a Price upon a Man's Mind

> In the Preface to Bleak House I remarked that I had never had so many readers. In the Preface to its next successor, Little Dorrit, I have still to repeat the same words. Deeply sensible of the affection and confidence that have grown up between us, I add to this Preface, as I added to that, May we meet again![63]

In March 1852 *Bleak House* had opened with a print run of 38,000, more than 34,000 of which were stitched, and by December Bradbury and Evans had undertaken an additional printing of 2,500 copies of the early numbers.[64] Though the audience slipped somewhat, as it always did for his serials, the print run never fell below 34,000, and by the time the story ended in September 1853 Dickens had sold nearly 700,000 monthly parts for a profit to himself of well over £10,000.[65] Encouraged by these figures, Bradbury and Evans ordered an even larger initial print run—40,000—for *Little Dorrit*'s first number, and by the time the double number appeared 19 months later, 3,000 more copies of No. 1 had been printed to accommodate continued sales.[66] Readership fell off a little more steeply for *Little Dorrit* than for *Bleak House*, and only 29,250 copies of its double-number were stitched; nevertheless, the novel still sold more than 650,000 monthly parts and earned Dickens what Patten calls "the best figures of his career," around £11,500.[67] To be precise, these were second best, considering his total take on *Our Mutual Friend*.

More than anything, the enormous sales figures for *Bleak House* and *Little Dorrit* testify to Dickens's immense popularity during the 1850s, but it is worth remembering that literary commerce, like other kinds, does not happen in a vacuum. Dickens achieved these successes during a decade when an expanding economy led to unprecedented growth in the British book trade. By 1851, England had emerged from a prolonged economic slump that began with a depression in 1843 and continued through the railway bubble and subsequent banking crisis during the period 1844–48. Thereafter, amid greater prosperity and rising literacy rates, the British publishing industry entered a decade of sustained and spectacular growth, helped along by the gradual removal of the "taxes on knowledge" that had long been a barrier to the acquisition of reading materials and also by certain external events—the Great Exhibition, the death of the Duke of Wellington, the Crimean War—that inspired both more titles and larger readerships.[68] Alexis Weedon has demonstrated, too, that the "peak in titles in the early 1850s ... is also evident in the quantity of books manufactured"; in other words, the number of titles grew because the aggregate demand for books did, not because publishers

---

[63] Charles Dickens, *Little Dorrit* (Oxford, 1979), p. xl.

[64] Patten, *Charles Dickens and His Publishers*, p. 419.

[65] Ibid., p. 355.

[66] Ibid., p. 251.

[67] Ibid.

[68] Simon Eliot, *Some Patterns and Trends in British Publishing 1800–1919* (London, 1994), pp. 8–10.

86   *Charles Dickens's* Our Mutual Friend

chose to publish more titles in smaller print runs.[69] To the extent that we can rely upon the numbers from contemporary sources like the *Publishers' Circular* and *Bent's Literary Advertiser* and from modern databases like the *Nineteenth-Century Short Title Catalog*, book production appears to have begun rising sharply in the late 1840s and to have continued to do so until 1854, when it reached a plateau that lasted until the middle of the next decade. In 1848 George Routledge inaugurated his enormously successful Railway Library, and W.H. Smith opened his first railway stall at Euston Station on November 1 of that same year. By 1856 the number of books produced in England annually had nearly doubled from 10 years earlier—to 14.49 million from 8.72 million—and newspapers were established during the 1850s at triple the rate of the decade before. "According to the best judgment we can make," John Sutherland has observed, "the great Victorian reading public and the mass market that went with it were formed in the early 1850s."[70] Dickens was both a minor cause and major beneficiary of that formation, as the remarkable sales of his two monthly serials from the 1850s attest.

Our Mutual Friend was published at a very different time, and it cannot have helped the novel's commercial prospects that it appeared amid England's worst economic conditions since the mid-1840s. Literary scholars may know the 1860s best for sensational novels and the massive readerships they attracted. But the 1860s— and particularly the years 1863–66—were difficult for the book trade, principally because the US Civil War wreaked such devastation on the American economy and, in turn, crippled British exports. Weedon contends that neither the depression of 1843 nor the economic downturn of 1857 had the kinds of repercussions for British publishing that the Civil War produced. It affected, she writes, "both sides of the Atlantic. This was compounded in Britain shortly after by the liquidity crisis of 1866–67 which reached its zenith on 12 May 1866 when the bank lending rate soared to 10 per cent."[71] At the time the United States accounted for one-third of British book exports, and during 1861–64 these plummeted in value from more than £150,000 annually to scarcely £50,000.[72] In January 1863 Sampson Low, who represented Harper & Co. in England, wrote to Wills to alert him that Harper, in its financial distress, could not renew its agreement to pay £250 per annum for advance sheets of *All the Year Round*.[73] With Dickens's blessing, Wills replied that they would send the sheets anyway, "for no other return than the gratification it will, I am sure, afford."[74] After the war ended in 1865, the American market rebounded quickly, to the great relief of British publishers. By March 1866 Frederic Chapman

---

[69]   Alexis Weedon, *Victorian Publishing: The Economics of Book Production for a Mass Market, 1836–1916* (Farnham, 2003), p. 49.

[70]   John Sutherland, *Victorian Novelists and Publishers* (Chicago, 1976), p. 62. Weedon makes a similar point on p. 49.

[71]   Weedon, p. 158.

[72]   Ibid., p. 40.

[73]   *Letters*, vol. 10, p. 202n.

[74]   Ibid.

Putting a Price upon a Man's Mind 87

was writing hopefully to Dickens to say of the half-yearly accounts that "[t]he expenses of paper & print for Library and Cheap editions has been very heavy, considerably over £3,000," because the house had found it necessary to keep more stock on hand to accommodate "frequent orders from America."[75]

Though hard to quantify precisely, the effect of America's troubles on the British book trade appears to have been substantial. After what Simon Eliot calls a "steady, relentless rise" during the 1850s and early 1860s, paper production in England fell sharply during 1864–65 before recovering slightly and reaching a plateau by the end of the decade.[76] But whereas paper production had risen more than 54 percent during the 1850s, it rose by just 17 percent during the next decade, and it did so entirely in the early years, for the mid-decade fall was so sharp and the recovery so slow that paper production in 1869 was still slightly lower than it had been in 1863.[77] Meanwhile, after a decade of profuse growth, the number of new periodicals and newspapers founded annually leveled off, too, and even the smaller number founded during the 1860s tended to fail twice as frequently as those that had been founded during the decade before.[78] The most popular periodicals suffered during the first half of the 1860s, too, likely from a combination of England's general economic slump and the ferocity of the competition in an increasingly crowded field. Founded in 1860 by George Smith and featuring Thackeray as its editor, the *Cornhill* magazine opened, like *All the Year Round*, to a circulation of around 100,000. But by the end of 1864 the circulation had fallen all the way to 40,000, and two-thirds of the decline came even before Thackeray resigned the editorship in April 1862.[79] Likewise, Bradbury and Evans's *Once a Week* lost readers quickly during the early part of the decade, selling 570,000 total copies during its first half-year but dropping to less than 420,000 for the first half of 1860.[80] Thereafter the magazine shed around 35,000 readers a year, except in 1862 when it carried Ellen Wood's *Verner's Pride*, the successor to her smash success *East Lynne* (1861).[81] Of the major literary periodicals, only *All the Year Round* enjoyed uninterrupted success during the early 1860s. Apart from fleeting moments of concern during the serial runs of Lever's *A Day's Ride* and Reade's *Very Hard Cash*, circulation held at or near 100,000 throughout the decade, with much larger totals for the Christmas numbers. From 1860 to 1867, *All the Year Round* failed just once to yield at least £3,400 in annual profits.[82] Here as in other things, Dickens was apparently inimitable.

---

[75] Grubb, p. 122.

[76] Eliot, p. 10.

[77] Ibid., pp. 10–11.

[78] Ibid., p. 85.

[79] John Sutherland, "*Cornhill*'s Sales and Payments: The First Decade," *Victorian Periodicals Review*, 19/3 (1986), p. 106.

[80] William E. Buckler, "*Once a Week* under Samuel Lucas, 1859–65," *PMLA*, 67/7 (1952), p. 938.

[81] Ibid., p. 939.

[82] Patten, *Charles Dickens and His Publishers*, p. 464.

Given the evidence, Eliot concludes that we must "take seriously the proposition that the period between the late 1850s and early 1870s consists of a very considerable leveling off of literary production" and that publishers especially felt the financial pinch.[83] In some ways, as Sutherland points out, there "seems to have been a lot of money floating around the publishing world at this period," for George Smith at Smith, Elder and Co. began paying enormous sums for new fiction—£2,500 for Anthony Trollope's *The Small House at Allington*, £5,000 for Collins's *Armadale*, and £10,000 for George Eliot's *Romola*—and in 1864 several publishers rushed in to help Mudie, buying up better than £50,000 of stock to save him from financial difficulty.[84] But Smith's diverse business interests had made him enormous sums overseas, so he could afford to invest in long-term relationships with authors rather than in individual titles. Moreover, it is possible and perhaps even wise to read such events as signs of trouble, for they may have been prompted mostly by the nervousness of publishers who wanted to stabilize the industry while securing their individual positions in it. As the literary market eroded, major publishers like Smith, Bentley, and Chapman and Hall may have been quite willing to pay high prices for novelists who were guaranteed to sell or to help prop up Mudie, the nation's single most important buyer of new fiction. But the availability of cash for some publishers does not diminish the fact that the industry as a whole was hurting. Bentley struggled mightily to remain solvent from the mid-1850s, first because of competition from Routledge's Railway Library and subsequently from the effects of the US Civil War, and Samuel Beeton simply went out of business, selling his copyrights to Ward, Lock & Tyler to pay off his debts.[85] On two occasions, in 1861 and 1866, Frederic Chapman wrote apologetically to Dickens about the "state of the trade" and the smallness of the proceeds from various back editions.[86] Chapman and Hall were in no danger of failing, but several publishers went bankrupt in 1866 from the combined effects of the sluggish trade and the national monetary crisis.[87] This may be another reason why Chapman and Hall were willing in 1863 to pay so dear for *Our Mutual Friend*: trapped in a down market, they were, like other houses, looking around them for a sure bet. Dickens may have looked very much like the trump card they required.

Considering the economic climate and the state of the British book trade, then, Dickens could hardly have picked a less propitious time to issue a new 20-number novel, and these conditions probably account for at least some of *Our Mutual*

---

[83] Eliot, p. 106.

[84] Sutherland, *Victorian Novelists and Publishers*, pp. 67–8. Sutherland makes the figure for Trollope's novel £3,500 for absolute copyright, but according to the editors of Trollope's letters he rejected this larger offer and accepted instead an offer of £2,500 for serial rights and "an eighteen months' license to issue two kinds of book editions," after which point copyright reverted to Trollope. See *The Letters of Anthony Trollope* (Stanford, 1983), vol. 1, p. 156n.

[85] Weedon, pp. 47–8.

[86] Grubb, pp. 79, 122.

[87] Weedon, p. 48.

Putting a Price upon a Man's Mind 89

Friend's commercial struggles. But Dickens's new novel was also contending against more specific obstacles, most of them stemming from the direct competition the novel faced in the literary market. Part of the problem, Patten argues, was the shilling-number format, which had by 1864 "pretty well run [its] course":

> [Shilling numbers] did not collect conveniently into three volumes for the lending libraries; they were too big for the commuter customers; they were a poor bargain for the average book buyer, who could get several stories for the same price or less by purchasing a shilling magazine, or a story complete in one instalment by ordering the Christmas number of *All the Year Round. Doctor Marigold's Prescriptions* sold a quarter of a million copies where *Our Mutual Friend* sold 19,000.[88]

The point is well taken, for a relatively small number of best-selling Victorian novelists had ever really attempted the format, and though Dickens was foremost among them, he was one of the last to continue to use it.[89] Yet the publication of "Mrs. Lirriper's Legacy" in December 1864 had made no difference to the sale of *Our Mutual Friend*'s monthly parts, for by the 1860s the Christmas buying season was already well established as a cultural and economic phenomenon. Twenty years after *A Christmas Carol*, Dickens's Christmas offerings almost certainly attracted a wider, and somewhat different, group of buyers and readers than did his novels. Indeed, the emergence of a defined Christmas season—which paralleled popular developments like the Christmas tree and Christmas card—was, Eliot writes, "one of the most distinctive features" in monthly publication patterns beginning from the late 1830s.[90] During the 1860s, the number of titles published every month during January–September declined compared with the same months during the more vigorous 1850s. Conversely, the number of titles published October–December rose, both in absolute quantity and as a proportion of the annual market. They are the only months that counter the 1860s' general trend toward decline.[91]

Our Mutual Friend could therefore have coexisted peacefully and profitably with "Mrs. Lirriper's Legacy" in 1864, and it probably could have done so, too, even with the growing number of weekly and monthly magazines that appeared during the early 1860s. During the 19 months of *Our Mutual Friend*'s serialization, the *Cornhill* published not only Thackeray's unfinished *Denis Duval* from February–July 1864 but also Elizabeth Gaskell's *Wives and Daughters* (1864–66) and Collins's *Armadale*, the latter of which pitted Dickens against his enormously popular protégé from *Our Mutual Friend*'s No. 6 through its concluding double number. The appearance of *Denis Duval* even gave the *Cornhill* a brief lift, from around 41,000 readers at the start of 1864 to 45,000 during the spring, though it returned to the lower circulation by the end of the year.[92] *Once a Week*, meanwhile,

---

[88]   Patten, *Charles Dickens and His Publishers*, pp. 309–10.

[89]   Sutherland, *Victorian Novelists and Publishers*, pp. 23–4.

[90]   Eliot, pp. 33–5.

[91]   Ibid., p. 35.

[92]   Sutherland, "*Cornhill*'s Sales and Payments," p. 107.

90 *Charles Dickens's* Our Mutual Friend

had Ellen Wood's *Lord Oakburn's Daughters* (1864) and Thomas Trollope's *Beppo* (1864), while Dickens had George Augustus Sala's *Quite Alone* (1864), Percy Fitzgerald's *Never Forgotten* (1864–65), and Amelia Edwards's *Half a Million of Money* (1865) in *All the Year Round.* From most of these competitors, at least in the abstract, Dickens should have had nothing to fear: whatever some critics had always thought of his work, he had spent his career outdueling even the great Thackeray in the market, and among the others perhaps only Collins, fresh from his successes with *The Woman in White* and *No Name*, could even approach Dickens's popularity. But the periodicals market to which Dickens returned in 1864 was not the one he had left seven years earlier. With *All the Year Round* and the competitors it spawned, he had himself helped to remake it, and in ways that were choking off the novel in parts.

But Dickens's fiercest competitor by 1864 was the one that, of all others, was the most formidable and most unexpected, not to mention the most likely to draw money away from his new novel: himself. Apart even from "Mrs. Lirriper's Legacy" or *All the Year Round* and its rivals, Dickens was competing, by the time he wrote *Our Mutual Friend*, against the vast array of his own immensely popular novels, which were available continuously in both Cheap and Library editions and continued to sell tens of thousands of copies each year. This had been the case in a modest way even during the 1850s, for Chapman and Hall had first started issuing a Cheap edition of Dickens's works in 1847—including *The Pickwick Papers, Nicholas Nickleby, Oliver Twist, The Old Curiosity Shop, Barnaby Rudge, Martin Chuzzlewit, American Notes, Sketches by Boz* (1836), and the *Christmas Books*—at a price of 1-1/2d per weekly part, 7d per monthly part, or anywhere from a half-crown to 4s for sets of unbound numbers and 5s to 6s, 6d for volumes bound "in half-morocco, marbled edges."[93] From April 1847 to September 1852, Chapman and Hall reissued an old novel roughly every six months, and it may be more than coincidence that the single new novel in parts that Dickens produced during these years, *David Copperfield*, was one of the worst sellers of his career.[94] For almost the next 20 years, Chapman and Hall sold between 200,000 and 350,000 of these parts annually, providing Dickens with a steady income of around £175 per year.

The potential impact of these business activities on *Our Mutual* Friend is clear. During the months of *Our Mutual Friend*'s serial run, sales of the Cheap edition's weekly and monthly parts hit 172,900 for just the second half of 1864 and a whopping 630,000 during 1865, while sales of bound volumes reached 21,500.[95] In 1858, too, the Cheap edition had been updated to include *Dombey and Son, Copperfield*, and *Bleak House*, and it was joined in that same year by a Library edition that included all of Dickens's works through *Little Dorrit.*

---

[93] Patten, *Charles Dickens and His Publishers*, p. 191.

[94] The Cheap edition of *The Pickwick Papers* overlapped Nos. 7–20 of *Dombey and Son*, while the Cheap edition of the *Christmas Books* overlapped Nos. 1–7 of *Bleak House. Copperfield*, on the other hand, competed variously with *Chuzzlewit, Oliver Twist, American Notes*, and *Sketches by Boz* throughout its serial run. See Patten, *Charles Dickens and His Publishers*, p. 191, for the table showing the dates of publication for the Cheap edition.

[95] Ibid., p. 362.

Putting a Price upon a Man's Mind 91

During 1864–65 the Library edition sold 15,000 volumes at 7s, 6d.[96] Then, simultaneously with the appearance of *Our Mutual Friend*'s No. 14 in June 1865, Chapman and Hall launched its new People's edition, beginning all over again with the always popular *Pickwick* at 2s per volume, and of course it advertised the People's edition with full-page notices in the "Advertiser" to *Our Mutual Friend*. Where better? By year's end the People's edition had sold more than 135,000 volumes and earned £1,358, 17s, 4d in profits.[97] *Our Mutual Friend* was the first of Dickens's novels in parts to compete with so many editions of his other fiction, and it may have suffered even though the Dickens industry was booming. During the 19 months that *Our Mutual Friend* appeared, copies of Dickens's other works sold some 800,000 weekly and monthly parts and 170,000 bound volumes, earning gross receipts of more than £15,000.

In the meantime, and also during *Our Mutual Friend*'s serial run, Chapman and Hall made small additional printings of the shilling numbers for *Pickwick*, *Chuzzlewit*, *Dombey*, *Copperfield*, and *Little Dorrit*—typically 500 copies per part—presumably because these continued even in 1864–65 to sell modestly in their original monthly format.[98] We cannot know precisely what effect these may have had, for while we have information about printing, we have none about sales. For most of Dickens's novels such small printings took place every two to three years, which suggests that we might estimate sales at roughly 200 full copies of each monthly serial each year. In the year and a half of *Our Mutual Friend*'s serial run, then, we might assume that 300 full copies of each novel were purchased this way, not just for those novels that were reprinted in 1864–65 but also for those that had been reprinted in 1862–63 and would sell out in time for a similar printing by 1865–66. It is not unreasonable to suppose, therefore, that 2,500 full copies of Dickens's monthly serials were purchased while *Our Mutual Friend* was appearing, accounting for a total of 50,000 monthly parts. Had just this money been spent on *Our Mutual Friend* instead—though, admittedly, there is no guarantee that it would have been—the novel would have outsold both *Chuzzlewit* and *Copperfield* despite the enormous sums being spent on the Cheap, Library, and People's editions. Chapman and Hall may have made just £5,350 from *Our Mutual Friend*, but from June 1864 to December 1865 they made another £3,550 from their other Dickensian ventures, or what would have been the income from another quarter of a million monthly installments. When *Our Mutual Friend*'s first number appeared to enormous fanfare in May 1864, Dickens was already everywhere, not just Inimitable but Inexhaustible, an entire sector of a British book trade of which *Our Mutual Friend* was only a part. That trade as a whole was hurting in 1864–65, but Dickens remained extraordinarily big business.

Viewed in this context, *Our Mutual Friend*'s sluggishness in monthly parts begins to appear less like a popular referendum on the novel and more like a consequence of complex circumstances over which Dickens had little control.

---

[96]   Ibid., pp. 364, 389.

[97]   Ibid., p. 407.

[98]   See Patten's Appendix B in *Charles Dickens and His Publishers*.

The one thing he might have done differently, in Dallas's opinion, was begin the novel in a less grim and alienating way. Though he praised the novel warmly as one of Dickens's best, he remarked in his review for the *Times* its unfortunately cool reception with the Victorian public:

> Novels published in parts have the advantage and disadvantage that their fortunes are often made or marred by the first few numbers; and this last novel of Mr. Charles Dickens, really one of his finest works … labours under the disadvantage of a beginning that drags. … never before had Mr. Dickens's workmanship been so elaborate. On the whole, however, at that early stage the reader was more perplexed than pleased. There was an appearance of great effort without corresponding result. We were introduced to a set of people in whom it is impossible to take an interest, and were made familiar with transactions that suggested horror.[99]

The problem, Dallas goes on to say, is not just the obscure beginning on the Thames but also the novel's early chapters dealing with the "Social Chorus," since these lead readers to assume—wrongly—that the characters all will be vapid, boorish, and unsympathetic; as a consequence, impatient readers put the novel down without arriving at the more engaging content to come. This was so much the case, Dallas writes, that many London libraries "contented themselves with a short supply" of the novel, prompting Chapman and Hall to issue a complaint to that effect in the press.[100] A decade earlier, before *All the Year Round* and the *Cornhill*, and sensational fiction, and the slumping economy, it might not have mattered that Dickens's new novel only begins creating obvious dramatic tension in No. 4 where it finally brings Rogue and Eugene together over Gaffer's death, develops Eugene's infatuation with Lizzie, and sets John Rokesmith to work for the Boffins. But in 1864, with so much else available in the literary market—and so much, even, of Dickens—*Our Mutual Friend* could ill afford to begin slowly.

That sales dropped off so quickly, from a print run of 40,000 for No. 1 all the way to 30,000 for No. 3, suggests that Dallas was right. But it would have required an almost unimaginable level of impatience among the novel's early readers to think that a quarter of them simply abandoned the novel after two installments. All of Dickens's novels in parts experienced some such drop-off, particularly between Nos. 1 and 2 when the publisher was still gauging the gap between preorders and total demand. *Bleak House* and *Little Dorrit* dropped by 2,500 and 3,000, respectively, and *Copperfield* by 6,000.[101] But none of these continued to fall so precipitously between Nos. 2 and 3 as *Our Mutual Friend*. Perhaps the real problem lay with Chapman and Hall, who may have overestimated grossly the likely sales because of some combination of wishful thinking and their massive ad campaign, then been reluctant to adjust their print order immediately to the realities of the market. They had not, after all, handled one of Dickens's novels in parts for 20 years, while

---

[99] [Dallas], "*Our Mutual Friend*," p. 6.

[100] Ibid.

[101] Patten, *Charles Dickens and His Publishers*, pp. 419, 432, 423.

Putting a Price upon a Man's Mind   93

Bradbury and Evans had spent the 1840s and 1850s turning such adjustments into a science. Even during the first week of May, days after the publication of No. 1, Dickens was reporting to Forster that orders for the novel were just *then* into their thirtieth thousand. If this was true—and while admitting that Dickens could be imperious with publishers who let his new work go out of print—it is hard to understand why Chapman and Hall ever let the print run begin at 40,000, let alone remain at 35,000 for No. 2. (By comparison, for *Little Dorrit* Bradbury and Evans printed 38,000 copies of No. 1 and only 35,000 copies of No. 2, even though that placed the print run for No. 2 *below* the 36,280 copies of No. 1 that were stitched.[102]) That they did so is misleading, inasmuch as it gives the impression that the novel lost more than half of its readers by the time it concluded, when it sold just 19,000 copies.[103] Really it probably lost more like one-third of its original readership—still more than usual for Dickens, but a figure that compares with *Copperfield* rather than tells a story of extraordinary failure in the literary market.

Ultimately, perhaps neither Dickens nor Chapman and Hall should have expected better than this from a novel published amid the complications of economy, format, and competition that surrounded *Our Mutual Friend*. Yet the novel did markedly better in the two-volume edition that appeared in January and October 1865. Whereas *Little Dorrit* outsold *Our Mutual Friend* dramatically in parts, in two volumes it sold just 2,400 sets at 6s per volume when it became part of the Library edition in 1859, compared against 2,700 sets at 11s per volume for *Our Mutual Friend* in 1865–66.[104] The two-volume *Our Mutual Friend* outsold the Library editions of *Bleak House* and *Dombey*, too, during their first year.[105] It did not outsell the three-volume *Great Expectations*, but Dickens had designed that novel from the beginning to suit the market for printed books rather than for serials, planning it as a triple-decker that would attract the leviathan Mudie and satisfy the circulating libraries' preference for novels in three volumes. Accordingly, Mudie took 1,400 copies of *Great Expectations* but only 832 copies of *Our Mutual Friend*.[106] Even so, the mere presence of so many copies of *Our Mutual Friend* at Mudie's, quite unusual for Dickens, may well have kept sales of the two-volume edition from going even higher.

Then again, it may well be that *Our Mutual Friend* was already as successful as the economic circumstances allowed. George Smith may have had plenty of money to throw at authors like Trollope, Collins, and Eliot to attract them to the *Cornhill*, but during the troubled economic years of the mid-1860s, none of these came so close to repaying the investment as *Our Mutual Friend* did for Chapman and Hall. From September 1862 to August 1863, *The Small House at Allington* and

---

[102] Ibid., p. 432.

[103] Ibid., p. 446.

[104] Ibid., pp. 393, 405.

[105] Patten's figures show sales of 2,118 for *Bleak House* during 1859 and 2,375 for *Dombey and Son*. See *Charles Dickens and His Publishers*, pp. 357, 384.

[106] Ibid., pp. 385, 405.

Romola appeared together in the *Cornhill* at a combined cost to Smith of £12,500. During these months the magazine shed around 20,000 readers, more than one-third of its circulation. Indeed, while Trollope had chosen to receive £2,500 from Smith for the rights to serialization and an 18-month lease on the copyright—instead, that is, of a larger figure of £3,500 for absolute copyright—*The Small House at Allington* sold so poorly in its first book edition in 1864 that Trollope did not bother to reissue the novel after the initial term expired.[107] Collins's *Armadale* was likewise a disappointment. Having drawn £5,000 from Smith, *Armadale* at first attracted a couple thousand new subscribers to the *Cornhill*, but by the end of its run in June 1866 the circulation had fallen from 41,000 to around 37,000, and *Armadale* had been demoted—beginning at No. 13—to a secondary position in the magazine.[108] Nor did things go better for the novel in volume form. Issued in two volumes at 26s, *Armadale* failed to exhaust its initial print run of 1,286, half of the two-volume sales for *Our Mutual Friend*, and it seems also to have failed to exhaust its one-volume edition at 6s, brought out in November 1866.[109] "In the long run," Sutherland remarks, "Smith probably got his money back," but only because he owned the absolute copyright and could work the title as much as he liked, and as long as he liked, to recoup his investment.[110]

Judging from appearances, very few books succeeded in the middle years of the decade, but it is very hard to credit the notion that, somehow and by sheer coincidence, virtually every major novelist going wrote his or her "worst" book during these years. Instead, when it comes to these novels and to *Our Mutual Friend*, we must consider the possibility that they were all hurt by the down publishing market, and that they ought not, perhaps, to be judged according to the commercial expectations raised by other books at other times. At the very least, we must reevaluate these things when it comes to *Our Mutual Friend*, for the market performance of Dickens's last finished novel looks very different against the backdrop of the mid-1860s than it does when compared with the much longer and more brilliant context of his extraordinary career. And amid all of this surprising and sometimes contradictory evidence, the biggest question remains: was *Our Mutual Friend* really a commercial failure? Chapman and Hall had reason to think so, and Dickens assuredly wanted the novel to have more readers. But despite a dismal economy, worn-out format, and fierce competition on several fronts, *Our Mutual Friend* sold 380,000 monthly parts and 2,700 two-volume editions, attracted £2,700 in advertising revenue, and made Dickens more money than he had earned from a single novel in his life. To Dickens, with his hard-won business acumen and longstanding determination to be paid what his intellectual work was worth, it all must have felt at least a lot like commercial success.

---

[107] Trollope, *Letters*, vol. 1, p. 156n.

[108] John Sutherland, "A Note on the Text," *Armadale* by Wilkie Collins (London, 1995), p. xxxi.

[109] Ibid., p. xxxii.

[110] Ibid.

Putting a Price upon a Man's Mind 95

III

Our Mutual Friend made three final appearances in print before Dickens died in 1870, and it may be that the novel's surprising commercial performance on one of these occasions, particularly, tells us much of what we need to know about its popularity with Victorian readers. Beginning in 1867 Chapman and Hall began publishing the Charles Dickens edition in 18 volumes, turning each novel into a single attractive volume bound in red cloth-covered boards and bearing Dickens's stamped signature in gold—to signify, according to the prospectus that appeared in the *Athenaeum*, "his present watchfulness over his own edition."[111] Dickens wrote new Prefaces and provided a descriptive header at the top of each page, and the pages were themselves reset in a single wide column to distinguish them from the two-column format of the Cheap and People's editions. As had been the case with *Our Mutual Friend*, Chapman and Hall marketed heavily, printing up nearly one and a half million prospectuses and spending, by December 1867, a total of £1,400 on advertising in England, America, and the colonies.[112] Priced at 3s for shorter works and 3s, 6d for longer ones like *Our Mutual Friend*, the Charles Dickens edition sold half a million volumes by the time of Dickens's death, netting £12,500 in profits.[113] Predictably, *The Pickwick Papers* was far and away the best-selling volume: it had always been Dickens's most popular novel, and during 1867–70 Chapman and Hall had to print it four times for a total of 76,000 copies.

Far less predictable was that, next to *Pickwick*, *Martin Chuzzlewit* and *David Copperfield* sold best, each of them running to a total of 45,000 copies printed even though neither had done well as a serial. Several of Dickens's other early works were also very popular: *Oliver Twist*, *The Old Curiosity Shop*, *Nicholas Nickleby*, and *Dombey and Son* each also passed through multiple printings totaling 40,000 copies. But the biggest surprise may have been *Our Mutual Friend*, for which Chapman and Hall seem to have expected only indifferent results. They may have done so because it was the most recently published of Dickens's works, or because they had so recently been through the fire with the novel and come away unpleasantly singed. It is also the case that Chapman and Hall introduced *Our Mutual Friend* into the third series of the Cheap edition in 1868, though this would presumably have reached a different audience. For the Charles Dickens edition they began by printing only 20,000 copies during the second half of 1868, fewer than for any volumes but *Hard Times* and the essays from *The Uncommercial Traveller*.[114] Yet within six months they had already ordered a further print run

---

[111] Quoted in Patten, *Charles Dickens and His Publishers*, p. 311. As Brattin points out, however, few if any of the 2,203 changes to *Our Mutual Friend* in the Charles Dickens edition were necessarily even made by Dickens himself. See Brattin, "'I will not have my words misconstrued': The Text of *Our Mutual Friend*," *Dickens Quarterly*, 15/3 (1998), pp. 167–76.

[112] Patten, *Charles Dickens and His Publishers*, p. 312.

[113] These were split evenly between Dickens and Chapman and Hall. See Patten, *Charles Dickens and His Publishers*, p. 312.

[114] Sutherland, *Victorian Novelists and Publishers*, p. 36.

of 5,000, and they repeated that order during the first half of 1870—even though, by then, *Our Mutual Friend* had also appeared (in 1869) in the Library edition of Dickens's novels. Despite both its recency and supposed unpopularity, in other words, by the time Dickens died the Charles Dickens edition of *Our Mutual Friend* had apparently outsold not just middling books like *Sketches by Boz*, *American Notes*, and *Hard Times* but also *Bleak House*, *Little Dorrit*, *A Tale of Two Cities*, and *Great Expectations*.[115] And this was so even though the novel had already sold better in volume form than almost all of these others when it was first collected in 1865. During 1867–70, in the Charles Dickens edition at least, *Our Mutual Friend* outsold every other Dickens novel written after *Copperfield*. Of course, in the meantime England's economy had recovered, and reviews like Dallas's may have persuaded readers that, unless they got past the first few numbers, they had no idea what they were missing.

More, *Our Mutual Friend* had clearly done nothing to diminish Dickens's immense popularity or dampen the sales of his next serial, *The Mystery of Edwin Drood*. Perhaps sensing that the 20-number novel had run its course, or perhaps doubting his failing health, when Dickens entered upon negotiations for one more novel with Chapman and Hall in October 1869, he proposed that the work should either appear weekly in *All the Year Round* or monthly in just 12 numbers. Given that, as Patten points out, "[w]eekly instalments in *All the Year Round* would shut him out entirely," Frederic Chapman wisely chose the latter.[116] Again Dickens was battling illness and coaching a new illustrator—this time Luke Fildes—and again his monthly-number format was working against the grain of the contemporary marketplace. Even so, and again, readers flocked to the new serial. "We have been doing wonders with No. 1 of Edwin Drood," a delighted Dickens wrote to his friend James Fields in April 1870, "*It has very, very far outstripped every one of its predecessors.*"[117] The novel may have been helped along by the knowledge of Dickens's poor health, and it certainly gained from the British economy's rebound after the end of the US Civil War. Before Dickens died in the middle of writing the sixth number, *Drood* was already selling 50,000 parts per month, a figure that he had not approached in 30 years.[118] In the wake of *Our Mutual Friend*, then, Dickens remained every bit as beloved by readers as he had been since the days of *Pickwick*, and every bit as ready to celebrate—and gloat over, at least a little bit—his unprecedented popularity and commercial success.

---

[115] Ibid.

[116] Patten, *Charles Dickens and His Publishers*, p. 316.

[117] *Letters*, vol. 12, p. 510.

[118] Forster, *Life*, p. 807n.

Chapter 4
A Dismal Swamp?
Our Mutual Friend and Victorian Critics

When Forster published the second volume of his *Life of Charles Dickens* in 1874, he issued a verdict on his dead friend's work that probably did, in its way, as much damage to *Our Mutual Friend*'s critical standing as any of the scorn James had heaped upon it in 1865. At the time the novel was published, Forster had extolled in a review for the *Examiner* its remarkable unity around the central argument "of the soul of life among the fictions of society," praising Lizzie and Bella as charming portraits of worthy women saved from the sordid realities of the riverside and the "Social Chorus."[1] But in the biography, writing at a distance from his lost friend rather than in the towering shadow the living man had cast, Forster responded differently. "[T]hough with fancy in it, descriptive power, and characters well designed," he wrote, *Our Mutual Friend*

> will never rank with his higher efforts ... the judgment of it on the whole must be, that it wants freshness and natural development. This indeed will be most freely admitted by those who feel most strongly that all the old cunning of the master hand is yet in the wayward loving Bella Wilfer, in the vulgar canting Podsnap, and in the dolls' dressmaker Jenny Wren.[2]

The novel, in Forster's view, simply "[had] not the creative power which crowded his earlier page, and transformed into popular realities the shadows of his fancy."[3] These remarks in the biography were the first major critical revaluation of the novel, and they cast *Our Mutual Friend* as an unmistakable signpost along the route of Dickens's sad decline. Coming from the pen of Dickens's longtime friend and literary executor, Forster's words had—and still have, probably—all the ring of a sober judgment of Dickens's last finished novel.

In the present day we are far more likely to read Forster's biography than his review in the *Examiner*, and more likely, too, to encounter James's contemptuous account of the novel than the admiring essays published in the *Athenaeum*, the *London Review*, and the *Times*. Because this is so, and also because of the serial's disappointing sales, we have now some vague impression that *Our Mutual Friend* was panned by Victorian critics—that the response in 1865 was indeed a dismal swamp. Worse, this impression is strengthened, even for serious critics, by the story of how the novel's manuscript came into Dallas's hands after he reviewed

---

[1]   [John Forster], "*Our Mutual Friend*," *Examiner*, October 28, 1865, p. 681.

[2]   Forster, *Life*, p. 743.

[3]   Ibid., p. 744.

the novel favorably for the *Times*. Two days after Dallas praised the book for "the immense amount of thought it contains" and called it one of Dickens's crowning achievements, Dickens wrote to thank him and to mention that, upon reading the review, he had been moved to a gesture that remains unique in his years as an author:

> As you could not write of my work of love in such a way, without thoroughly knowing what I would feel in reading your words I will say no more on that head here. But as you have divined what pains I bestowed upon the book, perhaps you might set some little value on the Manuscript, as your corroboration. At all events I have sent it to day to the Binder to put together substantially, and it will be very pleasant indeed to me if you will give it house-room as a token of my grateful regard.[4]

Forster's biography does not mention this gift to Dallas, perhaps because he was hurt that here, as with *Great Expectations*, Dickens gave the manuscript elsewhere instead of to him. During the Nelly years, though, Dickens and Forster drifted apart, partly because Dickens had moved on from needing or wanting Forster's stodgy advice—Forster did not approve of the public readings, of course, and beginning in the late 1850s Dickens had turned increasingly to Collins as a literary co-conspirator—and partly because Forster had married and entered upon a more exclusive social sphere that would have found Nelly scandalous, and that prompted Dickens to lampoon him as Podsnap in *Our Mutual Friend*.[5] Whatever his reasons, Dickens presented the manuscript of *Great Expectations* to old friend Chauncy Hare Townshend in 1861, then gave *Our Mutual Friend* to Dallas. Slater believes that the gift to Dallas was probably "motivated … simply by strong affection," but Ackroyd sees more in it.[6] For him, it underscores Dickens's perpetual "need for praise," his immense gratitude to Dallas for telling him "what he most wanted to hear: that he had never deteriorated, that he was still at the height of his powers, that his early popularity had not been succeeded by … 'permanent exhaustion.'"[7] In other words, Ackroyd reads the gift to Dallas as a hyperbolic thank you amid what was, implicitly, an otherwise dismal contemporary response.

Even had the critical reaction to *Our Mutual Friend* been thoroughly positive in other quarters, Dickens would undoubtedly have been grateful for Dallas's review. Dallas was influential, and any writer going in the 1860s would have been delighted to earn his praise in a publication so widely read as the *Times*. For more than a decade, Dallas had reviewed literature and prepared essays on art and politics for the *Times*, the *Daily News*, the *Cornhill*, *Blackwood's*, and the *Pall Mall Gazette*. By virtue of insightful reading, careful thought, and his own impeccable prose style—and by virtue, too, of holding himself mostly above the network of

---

[4]   [Dallas], "*Our Mutual Friend*," p. 6; *Letters*, vol. 11, pp. 117–8.

[5]   Johnson was perhaps the first to identify Forster with Podsnap. See vol. 2, pp. 1052–3.

[6]   Slater, *Charles Dickens*, p. 542.

[7]   Ackroyd, p. 968.

puffing, double-reviewing, and personal antagonisms that characterized much midcentury reviewing—Dallas had become one of the most respected critics of the day and embarked upon an ambitious project of elevating literary criticism to an objective enterprise founded upon clear aesthetic criteria. By the time he reviewed *Our Mutual Friend*, he had finished the first two volumes of his treatise on the subject, *The Gay Science* (1866), which he projected at four volumes but discontinued after two when the work sold poorly. Dickens's pleasure at being reviewed favorably by such a critic was genuine, perhaps the more so because Dallas's review complained about certain features of the novel. "That *Our Mutual Friend* has defects we not only allow," he wrote, "but shall ruthlessly point out."[8] He did point them out, focusing mainly, as we have seen, on the novel's slow beginning amid its "Social Chorus." But beyond these complaints Dallas made it clear that he admired the novel immensely, and moreover that he had no patience with those who would inevitably criticize Dickens for making the novel so dark and serious, and so persistent in its attacks on a myriad of social ills. "We hear people say, 'He has never surpassed *Pickwick*' ... " Dallas chided, "[but] we are not going to quarrel with tragedy because it is less mirthful than comedy. What if we allow that *Our Mutual Friend* is not nearly so funny as *Pickwick!* It is infinitely better than *Pickwick* in all the higher qualities of a novel."[9]

It is easy to see why Dickens would have responded gratefully, even hyperbolically, to such praise as this, particularly if he was as stung by slow sales and unflattering reviews as conventional wisdom suggests. But here as in most things Dickensian, the entire truth is more complex. By the summer of 1865 Dallas's credentials as a reader, reviewer, and essayist were such that he merited consideration for a vacant professorship in Rhetoric and Belles-Lettres at the University of Edinburgh, and in August he asked Dickens to recommend him for the position. Even as Dickens wrote himself into exhaustion and illness during his last weeks of work on *Our Mutual Friend*, then, he was working energetically to bring Dallas to the attention of Sir George Grey, the home secretary, and Lord John Russell, the once and future prime minister. On August 16 Dickens wrote to Wills of being "deep in [his] book, and proportionately neuralgic" and indicated that he was leaving London for a brief respite from heat and overwork.[10] But the same day he also wrote letters addressed to Grey and Russell, enclosing both to Dallas for his approval and also giving Dallas encouragement and advice. He told Dallas that he had spent the prior evening reading proof sheets of *The Gay Science* and admired it greatly, and in his letter to Russell he paved the way for Dallas to send him proof sheets, too, to demonstrate his qualifications for the position.[11] Dickens and Dallas were not exactly intimate friends, then, but each clearly had a healthy respect for the other's intellectual gifts. Despite Dickens's efforts, Dallas did not

---

[8]   [Dallas], "*Our Mutual Friend*," p. 6.

[9]   Ibid.

[10]   *Letters*, vol. 11, p. 83.

[11]   Ibid., p. 84.

win the professorship. It remains striking, though, that Dickens took such pains to help him at this critical moment in his composition of the novel.

We cannot possibly know what difference any of this made to Dallas's critical appraisal of *Our Mutual Friend*. As Slater points out, Dallas was not "wholly uncritical" of the novel, yet we might naturally speculate that he would have complained more loudly had he not felt indebted to Dickens for the aid and advice he had received.[12] In a broader sense, though, Dickens's entanglement with Dallas is merely part and parcel of the culture of Victorian reviewing: virtually every major contemporary review of *Our Mutual Friend*, positive and negative, was written by someone who knew Dickens at least in a small way and who came to the novel already loving or hating him and his work. Dallas reviewed it for the *Times* and Forster did so for the *Examiner*; H.F. Chorley, Dickens's friend and a staff writer for *All the Year Round*, wrote a positive review for the *Athenaeum*. Conversely, the *Westminster Review* attacked the novel ferociously, as did the *Saturday Review*, but both magazines had long bemoaned Dickens's writing, the *Westminster* most recently in Justin McCarthy's October 1864 essay "Modern Novelists: Charles Dickens," which effectively dismissed Dickens from any significant place in the pantheon of major nineteenth-century writers. In England, such attacks on Dickens were often motivated by political and class concerns, and increasingly, starting in the 1850s, by the desire of the younger generation of novelists and reviewers to topple the colossus. In the United States, James, too, wanted to escape from Dickens's enormous shadow, but he wanted also to devalue the English literary tradition in favor of one more distinctly American, realistic, and democratic. The negative reviews were not therefore dishonest, any more than the positive ones were. But it is worth remembering that reviews on both sides of the Atlantic were often driven by value judgments that extended beyond *Our Mutual Friend* to Dickens himself, to conceptions of what fiction did or ought to do, and to growing trans-Atlantic tensions as Americans—particularly northern intellectuals stung by England's sympathy for the South in the Civil War—attempted to articulate a distinct identity for their literature and culture.

The result of these literary, political, and personal contentions during 1864–66 is a fascinating array of responses to *Our Mutual Friend*. In his recent *The Dickens Industry* (2008), Laurence Mazzeno perpetuates the longstanding myth that "Dallas was in a distinct minority in [praising] Dickens's last completed novel"—a myth that has flourished largely because James's position as one of the great novelists of the period after Dickens's means that his opinion has dwarfed in memory the other reviews written at the time.[13] But the reviews of *Our Mutual Friend* were not uniformly negative, nor even predominantly so. Rather, they tended to be complimentary and even enthusiastic, very different from what we might expect. More to the point, however we interpret the motives of the critics who reviewed *Our Mutual Friend* when it first appeared, their assessments of the novel tell us

---

[12] Slater, *Charles Dickens*, p. 541.

[13] Laurence Mazzeno, *The Dickens Industry: Critical Perspectives 1836–2005* (Rochester, 2008), p. 23.

A Dismal Swamp?

a great deal about what Victorians found admirable or contemptible in the book, and they reveal the ways in which the contemporary reviews constructed enduring perceptions of *Our Mutual Friend*, principally by denying it, along with Dickens's other late novels, a place alongside "immortal" books like *Pickwick, The Old Curiosity Shop*, and *A Christmas Carol*. The Dickens of 1865—or even of 1852— was no longer the Dickens of *Pickwick*, and beginning with *Bleak House* some Victorian reviewers punished him for that with growing ferocity. After *Copperfield*, only *Great Expectations* enjoyed nearly universal critical acclaim, principally because reviewers seem to have missed the savage critique of capitalism lurking beneath the Christmas dinner, the good humor of Joe Gargery, and the hilarious circumnavigations of Trabb's boy. Partly, this chapter illustrates the workings of this critical trend, which saw Dickens fall out of favor with midcentury reviewers even as his popularity with middle-class readers soared. Subsequently, it tries to show the particular critical response to *Our Mutual Friend*, and—by situating it within the broader trajectory of Victorian reviews of Dickens—to demonstrate that this response was nearly 30 years in the making, and that it was certainly no dismal swamp.

I

The complexity of Dickens's relationship to contemporary reviews and reviewers as he fell from grace during the 1850s is perhaps clearest in two incidents from summer 1857, amid those emotionally charged months just before he met Nelly and long after he had concluded that his happiness with Catherine was over. In April, Dickens had invited Danish novelist Hans Christian Andersen to stay at Gad's Hill when he visited England that summer. The two had met in mutual admiration in 1847 during Andersen's first trip to England, and they had kept up an intermittent correspondence since. For his part, Andersen seems to have reverenced Dickens deeply, though the reverse was not equally true. Perhaps because Gad's Hill already bristled with impending disaster, the Dickenses received Andersen cordially but not enthusiastically on June 11, expecting him to stay two weeks. But two weeks stretched to five, and the family's patience wore thin. By June 29 Andersen was writing in his diary that he liked the gentle-natured Mrs. Dickens very much, but that neither Georgina nor the older children were kind.[14] Dickens himself remained the buoyant and eager spirit he always was in company, and even amid the exhausting preparations for the July performances of *The Frozen Deep* in London, he took time to give Andersen some much-needed artistic and emotional support.[15] Arriving from London to find Andersen upset—weeping and

---

[14]   Elias Bredsdorff, *Hans Andersen and Charles Dickens: A Friendship and Its Dissolution* (Copenhagen, 1956), p. 73.

[15]   That Dickens, too, was exhausted by Andersen's extended visit is apparent from an anecdote that Katey Dickens related years later to her friend Gladys Storey. After Andersen departed, Dickens stuck a card on the dressing-room mirror that read, "Hans Andersen slept in this room for five weeks—which seemed to the family AGES!" Storey, p. 22.

102   *Charles Dickens's* Our Mutual Friend

lying face down in the lawn, Ackroyd says—over an *Athenaeum* review of *To Be or Not to Be?*, his latest novel to be translated into English, Dickens told him, "You should never read the papers, except what you have yourself written. I have not for 24 years read criticism about myself!"[16] Then, predictably, Dickens insisted on a walk, where he continued catechizing by stopping and scratching a mark in the sand with his foot. "'That is criticism,' he said, and stroked over it with his foot: 'Gone!'"[17]

Dickens's advice to Andersen implies that he himself was immune to—or at least willfully insensible of—critical attack. But this was by no means true. Not long after his young sister-in-law Mary Hogarth died in 1837, when a distraught Dickens suspended both *Pickwick* and *Oliver Twist* for a month and so became the subject of fabulous rumors respecting his whereabouts, he had stopped reading, or at least he professed to have stopped reading, all accounts of himself that appeared in the press.[18] But he did not stop reading reviews of his work or caring what they said.[19] Just days after consoling Andersen, in fact, he was preparing a withering public rebuke for the young reviewer James Fitzjames Stephen, who had attacked him—and Reade and Gaskell besides—in an essay entitled "The License of Modern Novelists," printed in the July *Edinburgh Review*. In the unsigned review of *Little Dorrit*, Reade's *It is Never Too Late to Mend* (1856), and Gaskell's *Life of Charlotte Brontë* (1857), Stephen took all three writers to task, Dickens and Reade especially, for abusing their readers' trust by placing morbid exaggerations before them with the intent of instilling "into the minds of the young a blind admiration, or a blind contempt, of the institutions under which they live."[20] More particularly in *Little Dorrit*, he objected to Dickens's Circumlocution Office with its motto of "how not to do it," its shoal of Barnacles, and its array of pompous, self-interested, and incompetent hangers-on, members all of a mediocre English ruling class. Stephen belonged to that class—he was an Eton and Cambridge man and the son of an undersecretary of state—so he quite naturally despised Dickens's novel on political and personal grounds. He attacked it, however, in singularly unfortunate ways, first asserting that Dickens, in his perpetual zeal to capitalize on the scandal *du jour*, had "evidently borrowed" the collapse of the Clennam house "from the recent fall of houses in Tottenham Court Road," and then lodging two other, more substantial complaints.[21] Unlike Sir Walter Scott or even Bulwer-Lytton, Stephen opined, Dickens had never earned the right to be heard on political matters by first distinguishing himself in public life, and unlike Thackeray he had

---

[16]   Ackroyd, p. 779; Bredsdorff, p. 70.

[17]   Bredsdorff, p. 99.

[18]   Johnson, vol. 1, pp. 453–4; Ackroyd, p. 233.

[19]   Philip Collins makes this same point in his introduction to *Dickens: The Critical Heritage* (London, 1971), p. 9.

[20]   [James Fitzjames Stephen], "The License of Modern Novelists," *Edinburgh Review*, 106 (July 1857), p. 124.

[21]   Ibid., p. 127.

A Dismal Swamp?   103

neither the grace nor sense to confine his fictions to the social sphere he knew best. Moreover, the essay continued, Dickens was simply wrong about the government, as Stephen attempted to show by invoking Post Office reformer Rowland Hill as a perfect example of how the government *did* do it, vigorously and efficiently, when anything sensible was to be done. "It is not a little curious," Stephen quipped, "to consider what qualifications a man ought to possess before he could, with any propriety, hold the language Mr. Dickens sometimes holds about the various departments of social life."[22]

Of all the varieties of critical attack, this one always rankled Dickens most— this insinuation and reminder that he was no gentleman, that he did not have a gentleman's education or position, and that he ought therefore to submit to the opinions of his social betters. Despite his advice to Andersen, he dashed off almost immediately the essay "Curious Misprint in the *Edinburgh Review*," which he placed in *Household Words* on August 1. As he described it a few days later to Macready, he planned his response feverishly while on his way to give a public reading of *A Christmas Carol* at St. Martin's Hall, and once at his hotel he "[i]nstantly turned to, then and there, and wrote half the article. Flew out of bed early next morning and finished it by Noon ... broke up two numbers of Household Words to get it out directly."[23] Predictably, the essay both rebuts Stephen's specific charges against *Little Dorrit* and defends generally the novelist's right to address imaginative work to political concerns. It begins:

> The Edinburgh Review ... is angry with MR DICKENS and other modern novelists, for not confining themselves to the mere amusement of their readers, and for testifying in their works that they seriously feel the interest of true Englishmen in the welfare and honor of their country. To them should be left the making of easy occasional books, for idle young gentlemen and ladies to take up and lay down on sofas, drawing-room tables, and window-seats; to the Edinburgh Review should be reserved the settlement of all social and political questions, and the strangulation of all complainers. MR THACKERAY may write upon Snobs, but there must be none in the superior government departments. There is no positive objection to MR READE having to do, in a Platonic way, with a Scottish fishwoman or so; but he must by no means connect himself with Prison Discipline. That is the inalienable property of official personages; and, until Mr Reade can show that he has so much a-year, paid quarterly, for understanding (or not understanding) the subject, it is none of his, and it is impossible that he can be allowed to deal with it.[24]

After dispensing with Stephen's claim about the Clennam house's collapse— the monthly number was in proofs before the incident at Tottenham Court Road—Dickens goes on to identify what he facetiously assumes *must* be the

---

[22]   Ibid., p. 128.

[23]   *Letters*, vol. 8, pp. 399–400.

[24]   Dickens, "Curious Misprint in the *Edinburgh Review*," in *The Dent Uniform Edition of Dickens' Journalism*, vol. 3, p. 414.

104   *Charles Dickens's* Our Mutual Friend

"curious misprint": "the name of Mr. Rowland Hill," who, far from being a
shining illustration of the efficiency and adaptability of the government, must
have been "in toughness, a man of a hundred thousand" not to have had his heart
worn out by the unrelenting resistance to his recommendations for modernizing
the Post Office.[25] As Dickens gleefully points out, Hill had to wait 17 years from
his initial treatise on the subject in 1837 and endure multiple reassignments and
dismissals before he was finally named secretary of the Post Office in 1854 and
could implement his reforms fully.[26] For a variety of reasons, and though Stephen
probably thirsted after a chance to respond, Dickens's essay was the final word in
the dispute, or at least it was nearly so.[27] In a bland note in its October issue, the
Edinburgh retracted its obviously erroneous claim about the Clennam house and
Tottenham Court Road.

Although he expressed it in unusually aggressive and wildly inaccurate ways,
Stephen's disdain for *Little Dorrit* was characteristic of much critical response
to Dickens in the 1850s. But it had not always been so, nor had Dickens often
responded to critics with the stinging urgency of "Curious Misprint." In the heady
days of *Pickwick*, Dickens courted and was courted by many of the leading writers
and editors of the day, and reviews celebrated him routinely for the sympathy,
hilarity, inventiveness, and moral tone of his work. In 1835, around the time that
he first began attracting attention with his "Sketches," he became friendly with
the already well-established William Harrison Ainsworth, who introduced him
to Forster (then literary editor for the *Examiner*), Bulwer-Lytton, Macrone, and
the noted illustrator George Cruikshank.[28] Forster and Bulwer-Lytton influenced
Dickens for the rest of his life, and Macrone helped to launch his career by collecting
his early journalism into *Sketches by Boz*. Shortly after gaining this initial *entrée*,
Dickens met Macready through Forster, and the two men brought Dickens into
the Shakespeare Club, where he met the young Thackeray, Jerrold, and Thomas
Talfourd, among others.[29] Talfourd—to whom he dedicated *Pickwick*—introduced
him in turn to the Count D'Orsay, and Dickens became a regular visitor to Gore
House where he was befriended by Lady Blessington and the host of leading
literary figures gathered around her: Walter Savage Landor, William Jerdan,
Samuel Lover, Charles Whitehead, and probably Frederick Marryat, Benjamin
Disraeli, and Sydney Smith.[30]

---

[25]   Ibid., pp. 416–7.

[26]   Hill had *Post Office Reform: Its Importance and Practicability* published privately
and disseminated to government officials in 1837.

[27]   For a discussion of why Stephen remained silent despite this provocation, see
Christopher C. Dahl, "Fitzjames Stephen, Charles Dickens, and Double Reviewing,"
Victorian Periodicals Review, 14/2 (1981), pp. 51–8.

[28]   Johnson, vol. 1, pp. 103–4; Slater, *Charles Dickens*, pp. 53–4.

[29]   Tomalin, *Charles Dickens*, p. 90.

[30]   Johnson, vol. 1, p. 228. See also Dickens's letter to Richard Bentley on December
5, 1836, in *Letters*, vol. 1, pp. 206–8.

A Dismal Swamp?   105

In 1841 he also became intimate friends with perhaps the most important of his early literary allies, Lord Francis Jeffrey, who had co-founded the *Edinburgh Review* with Smith and served as its literary editor 1803–29. Though Jeffrey did not review Dickens for the *Edinburgh*, he fell in love with the early work, praised it freely in private letters, and eventually even dubbed himself Dickens's unofficial "Critic Laureate."[31] Many of Dickens's new friends did review his work in print, though, heaping praise on his early novels. Forster reviewed *Pickwick* favorably for the *Examiner* in 1837 and *Nickleby* for the *Sun* in 1839, and Jerdan—who edited the influential *Literary Gazette* and had urged him, during *Pickwick*, to develop Sam Weller as much as possible—wrote an enthusiastic notice of *Master Humphrey's Clock*'s first installment in June 1840.[32] In 1838, perhaps owing partly to Jeffrey's or Smith's influence, Dickens found an anonymous reviewer for the *Edinburgh* praising him as "the most popular writer of his day" and concluding that, despite his unhappy tendencies to exaggerate and imitate, "we know no writer who seems likely to attain a higher success in that rich and useful department of fiction which is founded on faithful representations of human character, as exemplified in the aspects of English life."[33] The review, a delighted Dickens told Forster, was "all even *I* could wish, and what more can I say!"[34]

This is not to suggest that the early critical response to Dickens was uniformly favorable. Despite the popularity of *Sketches by Boz*, Dickens was not in his very early days accorded the esteem given to novelists like Bulwer-Lytton and Disraeli, and the *Athenaeum* scoffed at *Pickwick*, remarking that Dickens "reminds you of the baying of several *deep dogs* who have gone before. The Pickwick Papers, in fact, are made up of two pounds of Smollett, three ounces of Sterne, a handful of Hook, a dash of a grammatical Pierce Egan—incidents at pleasure, served with an original *sauce piquante*."[35] As Ellen Miller Casey points out, the *Athenaeum* was unusual among Victorian periodicals in that it reviewed Dickens only tepidly during his early years but expressed increasing admiration as his fiction matured and social criticism deepened.[36] In October 1837, with *Sketches by Boz* still circulating and *Pickwick* and *Oliver Twist* appearing serially, the *Quarterly Review* complained of Dickens, too, remarking that he "writes too often and too fast" and warning, "If he persists much longer in this course, it requires no gift of prophecy

---

[31] Lord Henry Cockburn, *Life of Lord Jeffrey* (Philadelphia, 1857), vol. 2, p. 336.

[32] Slater, *Charles Dickens*, p. 74.

[33] [Thomas Henry Lister], [Unsigned review of *Sketches by Boz*, *The Pickwick Papers*, *Nicholas Nickleby*, and *Oliver Twist*], *Edinburgh Review*, 68 (October 1838), pp. 75, 97.

[34] *Letters*, vol. 1, p. 438.

[35] [Unsigned review of *The Pickwick Papers*], *Athenaeum*, December 3, 1836, p. 841.

[36] See Ellen Miller Casey, "'Boz has got the Town by the ear': Dickens and the *Athenaeum* Critics," *Dickens Studies Annual*, 33 (2003), pp. 159–90. As Charlotte Rotkin points out, the *Athenaeum* was also one of very few periodicals to review *Little Dorrit* favorably during Dickens's life, and it did so twice, in 1855 and 1870. See Rotkin's "The *Athenaeum* Reviews *Little Dorrit*," *Victorian Periodicals Review*, 23/1 (1990), pp. 25–8.

106   *Charles Dickens's* Our Mutual Friend

to foretell his fate—he has risen like a rocket, and he will come down like the stick."[37] And *Oliver Twist* was the subject of a new complaint after Ainsworth followed it in *Bentley's* with *Jack Sheppard* (1839–40), whereupon some reviewers, or "jolter-headed enemies" as Dickens called them, concluded that *Twist*, too, was a Newgate novel meant to romanticize criminal life, a charge that Dickens rejected explicitly in his Preface to the 1841 edition. Many critics were also lukewarm on *American Notes* and *Martin Chuzzlewit*, though these were bookended by two of Dickens's best received early works, *The Old Curiosity Shop* and *A Christmas Carol*, the latter of which Thackeray praised handsomely and called a "national benefit" in *Fraser's* in February 1844.[38] On balance, though the *Times* was often dismissive and individual books had each their detractors, Dickens was reviewed favorably throughout the 1840s, and never more so than with *Dombey and Son* and *David Copperfield*, both of which appeared to wide critical acclaim.

Through these years Dickens did more than read reviews of his work: he reveled in them, at least when they were positive, and he responded with effusive gratitude to those who thought well of his books and typically with disdain to those who did not. Often, this simply meant thanking friends, either for published reviews or for taking the trouble to look at his proofs or hear him read them aloud. But occasionally he even thanked reviewers he had never met, as in the case of Thomas Hood, whom Dickens wrote to in February 1841 to say how pleased he was by Hood's recent review of *Master Humphrey's Clock*, and how pleased he had been, too, by earlier notices that he had only just learned were also Hood's.[39] Seven years later, when he might understandably have been less attentive to or grateful for positive press, he sent a letter addressed to "the Editor of the *Sun*" saying:

> Have the goodness to convey to the writer of the [unsigned] notice of "Dombey and Son," in last evening's paper, Mr. Dickens' warmest acknowledgements and thanks. The sympathy expressed in it, is so very earnestly and unaffectedly stated, that it is particularly welcome and gratifying to Mr. Dickens; and he feels very desirous indeed, to convey that assurance to the writer of that frank and genial farewell.[40]

As it happened, the editor Charles Kent had also written the review, and the two struck up an acquaintance that was undoubtedly helped along by Kent's being a friend of Bulwer-Lytton. Dickens often responded to negative reviews, too—most often, as Philip Collins points out, by devoting the prefaces to his novels "to answering criticisms that had appeared during the novels' serialization."[41] Nothing else in his journalism resembles the aggressive public rejoinder he made in

---

[37]   [Abraham Hayward], [Unsigned review of *The Pickwick Papers, Sketches by Boz*, and *Sketches by Boz* (Second Series)], *Quarterly Review*, 59 (October 1837), p. 518.

[38]   See *Letters*, vol. 3, p. 71n.

[39]   Ibid., vol. 2, p. 220.

[40]   Ibid., vol. 5, p. 280.

[41]   Collins, *Dickens: The Critical Heritage*, p. 9.

A Dismal Swamp? 107

"Curious Misprint." Instead, he tended to complain to his friends or write private letters on occasions when he had been treated roughly, as he was by American reviewers after *American Notes* and *Chuzzlewit*, and as when he blamed the *Quarterly*'s rocket-and-stick analogy on his having, not long since, "declin[ed] the intimate acquaintance" of its author, Abraham Hayward.[42] Still, during the 1830s and 1840s Dickens was treated roughly far less often than he, or any writer so prominent, had a right to expect.

The turning point in Dickens's fortunes with reviewers was *Bleak House*, arguably his most powerful novel. With its remarkable conjunction of intensely personal narrative and massive social critique, *Bleak House* inaugurated a new artistic era for Dickens, for it is the first novel in which he really treats Victorian social ills as part of a vast and corrupt social system, a gross miasma of Parliamentary arrogance, Tom-All-Alone's squalor, Jo's wrenching pathos, and, standing over all, Chancery's senseless and insensible injustice at the heart of the mud and the fog. The novel sold spectacularly well. But it appeared at a time when the spirit of reform that it embraces had mostly died out, and when a rising generation of artists and critics—Stephen and his brother Leslie Stephen, George Henry Lewes, and Walter Bagehot among them—were prepared to attack Dickens, partly just to tear him down and make room for themselves, no doubt, but also because they objected to Dickens's sentimentality, his wild fancy, his politics, or all three. Certainly *Bleak House* gave these antagonists several avenues for attack. Those in the know recognized quickly that the airy and grossly selfish Harold Skimpole was a caricature of the ageing poet Leigh Hunt, a satire that became crystal clear in *Bleak House*'s No. 10, when Dickens mistakenly gave Skimpole's name as Leonard (his original plan) rather than Harold (which Forster and others had encouraged to mask the caricature, at least a little). The unprovoked attack on Hunt caused considerable indignation, particularly for Hunt's son Thornton and his intimate friend and literary associate Lewes, who had co-founded the weekly *Leader* in 1850.[43] The same number also contained Krook's spontaneous combustion, which Lewes objected to in the *Leader* as "a fault in Art, a fault in Literature, overstepping the limits of Fiction, and giving currency to a vulgar error."[44] The objection prompted a spirited and admittedly preposterous reply from Dickens, who wrote privately to Lewes to enumerate cases of death by combustion and then publicly in his Preface to *Bleak House* in September 1853, where he said that Lewes had found out, to his chagrin, that he was "quite mistaken ... in believing [spontaneous combustion] to have been abandoned by all authorities."[45]

---

[42] *Letters*, vol. 1, p. 316.

[43] For a time, Lewes and Hunt had also swapped wives. For an account of the quarrel that Dickens's caricature of Hunt provoked, see Brahma Chaudhuri, "Dickens and the Critic," *Victorian Periodicals Review*, 21/4 (1988), pp. 139–44. The controversy died down relatively quickly at the time, but it revived when Hunt died in 1859, prompting Dickens to publish "Leigh Hunt. A Remonstrance" in *All the Year Round* on December 24, 1859.

[44] George Henry Lewes, "Literature," *Leader*, December 11, 1852, p. 1189.

[45] Charles Dickens, *Bleak House* (London, 1996), p. 6.

108 *Charles Dickens's* Our Mutual Friend

The *Leader*'s rival paper, the fortnightly *Critic*, turned energetically on Lewes and Hunt in these skirmishes, but as Brahma Chaudhuri points out, this did not mean that it supported Dickens. On the contrary, the *Critic* was "hostile to both Dickens and *Bleak House*," despising Esther Summerson and most of the novel's other characters, pointing out that Dickens had come terribly late to the cause of Chancery reform, and criticizing his hypocrisy for championing the Guild of Literature and Art but refusing to allow his contributors to make names for themselves by signing contributions to *Household Words*.[46] Not all of this criticism was quite fair. But its ferocity shows the extent to which, in a single novel, Dickens had irritated the rising Hunt/Lewes circle, annoyed the realists, invited personal invective, and spelled out forcefully his thorough contempt for a government that ignored Jo while it sheltered the very Oxbridge men who, delivered from two decades of liberal reform, were preparing to take up pens and "educate" the masses about politics, literature, and everything between.

The vituperation against *Little Dorrit* in 1857 was, in other words, at least as much political as it was critical or aesthetic, and it was moreover characteristic of the charged environment for reviewing—and for journalism more generally—that succeeded England's misadventures during the Crimean War. As Dallas Liddle writes, the ability of journalists to expose British administrative incompetence during the war heightened "the political power of the newspapers, particularly the *Times*, whose discursive star continued to rise breathtakingly high as that of the government fell."[47] This power, Liddle contends, helps to explain the persistence of anonymity in journalism through the middle decades of the century, when "the British journalist's trademark pronoun 'We' … acquired the status of a nearly omnipresent Victorian rhetoric of authority."[48] The question of whether journalism generally, and reviews specifically, ought to remain anonymous was very much in the air—and in the press—during the 1850s, with men like the Stephens, Bagehot, and *Dublin University Magazine* editor Cheyne Brady taking the position that anonymity and the force of institutional authority and objectivity it implied were positively required, for "the public journalist of 1855 really was in the position of a teacher to a student."[49] Naturally, they also believed that the sort of person best suited to be such a journalist was a gentleman: a man of refined thought and taste who could not be tempted away from expressing ideas in the nation's best interest by any mean craving after money or fame. Hence Stephen's attack on *Little Dorrit* in July 1857, which mostly expanded upon ideas he had expressed six months earlier, also anonymously, in "Mr. Dickens as a Politician" in the *Saturday Review*. Gentleman journalists like Stephen and the *Saturday*'s Henry Sumner Maine could neither stomach Dickens's political meddling nor refrain from pointing out that he was vulgar, particularly when such members of the governing class

---

[46]   Chaudhuri, p. 142.

[47]   Dallas Liddle, "Salesmen, Sportsmen, Mentors: Anonymity and Mid-Victorian Theories of Journalism," *Victorian Studies*, 41/1 (1997), p. 38.

[48]   Ibid., p. 39.

[49]   Ibid., p. 40.

A Dismal Swamp?   109

relied implicitly upon their ability to use the periodical press to express, under the guise of institutional objectivity, a monolithic front for their personal views. Consequently, as Merle Mowbray Bevington writes in his history of the *Saturday Review*, the attacks on Dickens during the 1850s were "partly a result of an accident in time: Dickens happened to direct his sentimental attack upon the workings of the Court of Chancery"—and subsequently on factory production and education in *Hard Times* and on government inefficiency in *Little Dorrit*—"just when the *Saturday* appeared on the scene, staffed largely by barristers intensely proud of the traditions of their profession. To men like Maine and Fitzjames Stephen ... it was little less than blasphemy that Dickens should ridicule what he knew so little about."[50] To put it another way, "the question was not always whether the technique of his social criticism was clumsy or artful, but whether the criticism itself was palatable (as it was for many working-class readers) or infuriating (as it was for the contributors to the *Saturday Review*)."[51]

In this climate it was perhaps inevitable that many reviewers dismissed Dickens and his novels by reminding the public that he was no gentleman. But there were other complaints, too, about both Dickens and the middle-class readers who, undeterred by the *Edinburgh* and *Saturday*, flocked to his novels. Dickens's "immense popularity and commercial success," Kathleen Sell-Sandoval points out, posed a terrible dilemma for his critics.[52] They solved it, for the most part, by deriding his audience, too, and by resorting to a rhetoric of gender rather than the more publicly divisive rhetoric of class. The 1850s were a critical period of cultural debate in England, the years when public figures like Matthew Arnold and John Stuart Mill were working explicitly and aggressively to demarcate popular from high culture, Philistines from intellectuals, "writing based on an appeal to emotion from that which appeals to the intellect, [and] the masculine from the feminine."[53] Writing for *Blackwood's*, where Eliot's utterly un-Dickensian *Scenes of Clerical Life* was appearing—E.B. Hamley distinguished between the serious readers who deplored Dickens's recent work and the "thousands of silly mouths" who would repeat *Little Dorrit*'s "foolish joke about prunes and prism" until it became a household word.[54] In the *National Review* Bagehot complained about Dickens's exasperating and effeminate tendency to wrench tears from his readers through pathetic sufferers like Little Nell, Paul Dombey, and Jo.[55] Indeed, while

---

[50] Merle Mowbray Bevington, *The* Saturday Review *1855–1868: Representative Educated Opinion in Victorian England* (New York, 1966), p. 166.

[51] George Ford, *Dickens and His Readers: Aspects of Novel-Criticism since 1836* (Princeton, 1955), p. 82.

[52] Kathleen Sell-Sandoval, "In the Marketplace: Dickens, the Critics, and the Gendering of Authorship," *Dickens Quarterly*, 17/4 (2000), p. 230.

[53] Ibid., p. 234.

[54] [E.B. Hamley], "Remonstrance with Dickens," *Blackwood's Edinburgh Magazine*, 81 (April 1857), p. 503.

[55] See [Walter Bagehot], "Charles Dickens," *National Review*, 7 (October 1858), pp. 458–86.

110   *Charles Dickens's* Our Mutual Friend

gentleman journalists like Stephen attacked Dickens on political grounds, critics like Bagehot, Lewes, and Richard Hutton Holt used Dickens's tear-jerking as a grounds for chronic aesthetic complaint, writing of him in the language they used to write of "Lady novelists" and so punishing him for the very sentimentality that he had borrowed from eighteenth-century models and been praised for so often in his earlier works.[56] Underlying all of these complaints was the consistent message that Dickens's appropriate readers were silly girls and limp, maudlin fellows rather than the kind of serious-minded men who had gotten their gentleman's education and were destined to take up significant social roles. Self-taught geniuses, the critics discovered that Dickens was popular because he was irrelevant and unserious—a bit of light reading for the light-headed. Nothing durable could come of writing for such a public, though, or so the argument went.

There is a sense in which Dickens's entire professional course after 1850 was his enormous wager against that proposition. In *Bleak House, Hard Times*, and *Little Dorrit* he combined the vivacity of his earlier works with his darker social vision, hitting smartly at government neglect and genteel privilege in novels that were bought by tens—and read by hundreds—of thousands of people. As Juliet John has observed in her excellent *Dickens and Mass Culture* (2010), "It is easy to be cynical about Dickens's motivation for wanting what he envisaged as almost a direct line to the largest possible audience—a need to control, to be noticed, and indeed to feel loved, doubtless shaped this desire for mass visibility and influence. But," she continues, "Dickens's sense of the importance of mass journalism extended beyond the personal" and into matters of community and humanity, each of which he saw being eroded by the increasing mechanization and commercialism of mid-century England.[57] To be sure, in 1859 he abandoned *Household Words* partly to punish Bradbury and Evans for, as he thought, hindering his efforts to hush his domestic scandal, and he undertook his public readings at the same tumultuous time partly to reassure himself that he was still adored. But behind these more immediate provocations lay an artistic principle of much longer standing: his determination to be both immensely popular and critically acclaimed by writing enduring literature for the masses. He said as much at the close of *A Tale of Two Cities*, the last installment of which appeared in the same issue of *All the Year Round* that carried the beginning of *The Woman in White*. Between the two works of fiction, Dickens inserted a short notice describing his future intentions for the magazine:

> We purpose always reserving the first place in these pages for a continuous original work of fiction, occupying about the same amount of time in its serial publication, as that which is just completed. The second story of our series we now beg to introduce to the attention of our readers. It will pass, next week, into the station hitherto occupied by A Tale of Two Cities. And it is our hope and aim, while we work hard at every other department in our journal, to produce, in this one, some sustained works of imagination that may become a part of English Literature.[58]

---

[56]   See Sell-Sandoval, particularly pp. 226–9.

[57]   Juliet John, *Dickens and Mass Culture* (Oxford, 2010), p. 104.

[58]   Charles Dickens, [Untitled notice], *All the Year Round*, November 26, 1859, p. 95.

The brief note, with its capitalized "English Literature," indicates that Dickens envisioned his new magazine from the start as a vehicle for not just popular but also *literary* fiction, a genuinely radical notion for a weekly paper priced 2d and reaching a weekly audience of 100,000. He wanted, John writes, "to elevate and 'purify' the popular press," and so to "use his own work to supplant pernicious populist material"—like the fare of G.W.M. Reynolds's *Reynolds's Miscellany*—"which he saw as replacing a communal with a purely economic vision of art and society."[59] The extent to which he succeeded is perhaps most evident in the fact that, during the 11 years that Dickens edited *All the Year Round*, its serials included not just *A Tale of Two Cities*, *Great Expectations*, and *The Woman in White* but also Collins's *No Name* and *The Moonstone*, Reade's *Very Hard Cash*, and Gaskell's *A Dark Night's Work* (1863), all of them still read and studied in the present day. Dickens spent the 1850s venting his social outrage, separating from and publicly humiliating his wife, destroying *Household Words*, erecting and self-funding *All the Year Round* in its place, flouting social convention with Nelly, and turning himself into a traveling show. Yet every day he was more popular and more widely read. If anything, he was more dangerous and noxious to his exasperated critics after *Little Dorrit* than before, which may explain why James Fitzjames Stephen launched one final attack on Dickens in a review of *A Tale of Two Cities* in which he compared the novel to a dish of "puppy pie and stewed cat" and further remarked, amid other invective, that the novel at least had the one great "merit of being much shorter than its predecessors," which he surmised facetiously must have come as an enormous relief to its readers.[60] It was, Ford writes, "the most violently abusive [review] to appear in Dickens's lifetime" and caused the *Eclectic Review* two years later to recall that *A Tale of Two Cities* had "pleased nobody" and that the *Saturday*'s furious assault had sparked preposterous rumors that Dickens had taken to bed for some months in a "hopeless lethargy," attended by a dozen physicians, trying to recover from the attack.[61]

By the time Dickens began *Our Mutual Friend*, the greater—and shriller—part of this hostility had subsided. Critical response to *Great Expectations* had been mostly favorable, mainly because even Dickens's fiercest critics believed that at long last he had finally taken their hint and returned to his old humorous vein. And Dickens had intended the novel to be comic, at least in the early chapters, for he confided to Forster in October 1860 that he thought he had made the beginning "exceedingly droll. I have put a child and a good-natured foolish man, in relations that seem to me very funny."[62] In the *Times*, though he did not class himself among such readers, Dallas pointed out that those who longed for Dickens's "old *Pickwick* style" would find in *Great Expectations* "more of his earlier fancies

---

[59] John, p. 111.

[60] [James Fitzjames Stephen], "*A Tale of Two Cities*," *Saturday Review*, December 17, 1859, p. 741.

[61] Ford, *Dickens and His Readers*, p. 103; "Charles Dickens' *Great Expectations*," *Eclectic Review*, 1 (October 1861), pp. 458–9. Also, see Dahl, p. 51.

[62] *Letters*, vol. 9, p. 325.

112   *Charles Dickens's* Our Mutual Friend

than we have had for years."[63] Likewise, the anonymous reviewer for the *Dublin University Magazine*—though admitting that Dickens was sadly "already past his prime"—found an "artistic unity" in the novel that was "enhanced ... by the absence of much fine-drawn sentiment and the scarcity of surplus details."[64] "Even the *Saturday Review* began to relent," Philip Collins points out, its reviewer writing, "Mr. Dickens may be reasonably proud of these volumes. After a long series of his varied works—after passing under the cloud of *Little Dorrit* and *Bleak House*—he has written a story that is new, original, powerful, and very entertaining."[65] True, Margaret Oliphant was unimpressed, writing in *Blackwood's* that she found herself longing for Sam Wellers and Mark Tapleys as she read the "feeble, fatigued, and colourless" pages of *Great Expectations*.[66] But Dickens could hardly expect to please so discerning a critic as Mrs. Oliphant, so he contented himself with the novel's immense popularity and a great deal of other hard-won praise. If postmodern critics are correct about the novel's pervasive and nightmarish critique of Victorian capitalism, he may even have enjoyed a good laugh at having put one over on the contemporary reviewers who had complained incessantly about his political meddling but now welcomed *Great Expectations* as a gentle comedy from the old master. Such critics longed for Dickens—if they longed for him at all—only in the guise of a peerless humorist, entertainer, and co-conspirator in their domestic hilarities and holiday cheer. They did not take him seriously as an artist in that guise, of course, but they recognized these as the proper spheres for his particular brand of wild genius, and as the right groove for a popular writer who could aspire to nothing better.

In October 1864, the *Westminster Review*—inspired, no doubt, by the concurrent appearance of *Our Mutual Friend* in monthly numbers—published McCarthy's "Modern Novelists: Charles Dickens," which captures much of the essence of the lingering critical antagonism toward Dickens at the time of his last finished novel. In the essay McCarthy purports to review the 22-volume Library Edition of Dickens's work that Chapman and Hall published 1858–62. Really, he uses it to assess Dickens's place among nineteenth-century novelists and assert confidently that his literary legacy will never survive. McCarthy grants that Dickens is the most popular novelist in England and that he has altered British fiction in fundamental ways. "His genius is entirely original," McCarthy writes, "[*Pickwick*] has revolutionized comic writing and introduced a new standard of humour."[67] Too, according to McCarthy, Dickens had been the prime mover in

---

[63]   [E.S. Dallas], "*Great Expectations*," *Times*, October 17, 1861, p. 6.

[64]   "Mr. Dickens's Last Novel," *Dublin University Magazine*, 58 (December 1861), pp. 685, 693.

[65]   Philip Collins, *Dickens: The Critical Heritage*, p. 427; [Unsigned review of *Great Expectations*,], *Saturday Review*, July 20, 1861, p. 69.

[66]   [Margaret Oliphant], "Sensation Novels," *Blackwood's Edinburgh Magazine*, 91 (May 1862), p. 575.

[67]   [Justin McCarthy], "Modern Novelists: Charles Dickens," *Westminster Review*, 26 (October 1864), p. 415.

A Dismal Swamp?   113

two major developments, first by making the novelist into a "recognized public instructor" on matters of "social policy, law reform, the latest invention, [and] the most recent heresy," and second by using the novel to depict the lives of the middle and lower classes, who had no proper chronicler before Dickens arrived on the scene.[68] But these were only generous ways of saying what had often been said before: that Dickens was a humorist whose greatest achievements were a quarter-century old, that he was a political meddler, and that he was best suited to writing of and for the unwashed. More, even this equivocal praise is undercut in the essay by what McCarthy sees as wrong in Dickens, and what critics had seen as wrong in him since *Bleak House*.

Dickens might be popular, McCarthy reasons, but only because "[m]en immersed in active life have neither leisure nor inclination for fiction," which meant that novels were the province of only the young or those "grown-up women, [for whom] novels are the staple article of intellectual food."[69] Even Dickens's portraits of middle- and lower-class life are limited because he cannot create characters with "analytical depth"; rather, his characters are fit for the stage where they can appear solely through their externalities.[70] Consequently, McCarthy observes, Dickens is most adept at describing "the moral and intellectual peculiarities of animals" and "[m]ad, half-witted, weak, and simple people" with no identities beyond what is seen.[71] Incapable of understanding or narrating characters with complex motives for action, Dickens cannot even fashion a coherent plot. "His mind is in fragments," McCarthy writes. "To this strongly marked intellectual quality may be traced both his characteristic excellences and his characteristic defects."[72] In closing, McCarthy offers this severe verdict on Dickens's fate in the hands of posterity:

> We cannot think that he will live as an English classic. He deals too much in accidental manifestations and too little in universal principles. Before long his language will have passed away, and the manners he depicts will only be found in a Dictionary of Antiquities. And we do not at all anticipate that he will be rescued from oblivion either by his artistic powers or by his political sagacity.[73]

Ironically, in *Great Expectations'* extraordinary compressions and symbolic unity, Dickens had just published a novel of rare artistic power, and in *Our Mutual Friend* he was even then writing a novel with the political penetration to reveal with stunning clarity the processes of reification, displacement, and dehumanization that have characterized both Victorian and post-Victorian capitalism. Dickens has never quite needed rescuing from oblivion, it turns out. But in McCarthy's various

---

68   Ibid., pp. 416–17.
69   Ibid., p. 414.
70   Ibid., p. 426.
71   Ibid., pp. 427–8.
72   Ibid., pp. 437–8.
73   Ibid., p. 441.

arguments against Dickens's literary worth we see both a culmination of what reviewers had said since *Bleak House* and a laying of the groundwork for the critical judgments that would become standard for the first several decades after Dickens's death.

Even so, and the *Westminster*'s low estimate of him notwithstanding, Dickens returned to monthly numbers in *Our Mutual Friend* to wide critical acclaim, and reviews of the novel were mostly free from the kind of vitriol that had followed his work since the start of the decade before. Since then, his old rival Thackeray had died, and though Eliot and Trollope had succeeded to Thackeray's literary style, the more popular writers were the sensational ones: Collins, Wood, Reade, and Mary Elizabeth Braddon. In this new literary landscape, which the Leweses and Bagehots of the world abhorred, perhaps a new novel in 20 numbers by Dickens seemed at least like a return to normalcy, a striving after something more than moral effrontery, cheap thrills, and thinly veiled scandal. Or perhaps Dickens's long absence from monthly numbers, coupled with Thackeray's sad and sudden end, had created a suitable veneration for the master trying to reassert himself in the old way. Or perhaps, despite a new illustrator, struggles with installment lengths, illness, fatigue, scandal, Staplehurst, and the hundred and one things that one might, given the chance, banish utterly from *Our Mutual Friend*, Dickens really did write a novel well worth the praise that Dallas, Forster, Chorley, and others lavished upon it in 1865. Whatever the reason, and though James's review and Forster's biography have skewed our sense of the contemporary critical response, *Our Mutual Friend* was reviewed often by Dickens's contemporaries, and almost always favorably, with a great many critics even expressing some sense that the novel is one of Dickens's most powerful books. In these reviews, both positive and negative, we see what Victorians thought of *Our Mutual Friend*, and what, in many instances, we have not left off thinking since.

II

Our Mutual Friend was noticed 41 times in England and the United States during April 1864–April 1866 in forms ranging from long and full critical reviews to relatively short announcements of the novel's appearance to brief, monthly, mostly uncritical synopses of its action. Three prior volumes have reprinted one or more of these reviews, though rarely has any other than James's appeared in full. George Ford and Lauriat Lane's *The Dickens Critics* (1961) reprints James's complete review, and in *Dickens: The Critical Heritage* (1971) Philip Collins reprints excerpts from six of the most substantial reviews, including Dallas's and James's, and also alludes briefly to the long favorable reviews by Forster and Chorley and to a short positive notice of the novel that appeared in the *Annual Register* for 1865. Norman Page's 1979 casebook for *Hard Times*, *Great Expectations*, and *Our Mutual Friend* is slimmer and even a little misleading, inasmuch as it provides only brief excerpts from Chorley and Dallas but gives James's negative review in full. It also provides Forster's commentary from the biography—which Page subheads "A Lack of Freshness"—rather than from his favorable review in the *Examiner*.[74] These are the kinds of decisions and accounts that have contributed to our long sense that *Our Mutual Friend* was unsuccessful artistically, or at least that Victorian critics judged it to be so. Small wonder, then, that when he looks back Mazzeno sees principally James's review, as well as the predictably hostile ones from Dickens's old enemies at the *Saturday* and the *Westminster*, rather than the many positive ones that appeared alongside them.[75]

To be fair, neither Collins nor Page meant to be exhaustive in surveying the contemporary reviews of the novel, and Mazzeno—having probably expected to find that *Our Mutual Friend* was despised—simply reproduces, unexamined, the highbrow Victorian critical line. Thankfully, other recent studies have begun restoring the balance. Brattin and Hornback at least observe in their Introduction to Our Mutual Friend: *An Annotated Bibliography* (1984) that early reviews of the novel "were mixed; approximately equal numbers of reviewers praised and damned the plot, structure, and social criticism."[76] Litvack's web preview of materials related to the scholarly edition of *Our Mutual Friend*, now in preparation for Clarendon, is also even-handed in this respect, suggesting like Brattin and Hornback that the novel was loved and despised in roughly equal parts, but also quoting Forster's opinion from the biography instead of his review in the *Examiner*. This perennial historical misreading makes the facts even more surprising. Here and in Appendix 3, where I provide full transcriptions of all 41 reviews I have found, I attempt to be as complete as possible in providing information about those that appeared 1864–66.[77] Of the 41 reviews, 30 are British and 11 are American, 23 appeared during and 18 after serialization, and roughly one-third go beyond simply noticing or summarizing the work. The longest of them—a positive notice in the *Eclectic Review*—runs to more than 10,000 words. In our digital age, when so many documents that have long been lost for practical purposes are resurfacing in databases and reappearing *in toto* everywhere from Google Books to online scholarly projects, more reviews may yet resurface. For now, what we know of the contemporary critical response to Dickens's novel is contained in these 41 essays. Together, they tell us several things that revise significantly what we know, or think we know, about the novel.

For one thing, the reviews published during the early months of the novel's serialization tell a different story than Dallas does in his review for the *Times*. There, Dallas had remarked the novel's slow beginning and blamed readers'

---

[74] Norman Page (ed.), *Charles Dickens:* Hard Times, Great Expectations, *and* Our Mutual Friend (New York, 1979), p. 156.

[75] Mazzeno, pp. 23–4.

[76] Joel Brattin and Bert G. Hornback, Our Mutual Friend: *An Annotated Bibliography* (New York, 1984), pp. xiv–xv.

[77] In the cases of omnibus reviews and year-end reviews—i.e., those dealing with multiple works—I have given the full transcription *only* of those parts of the reviews that deal with *Our Mutual Friend*.

dislike of the Podsnap and Veneering set for *Our Mutual Friend*'s sluggish sales and relative scarcity in London's libraries. But the critics who reviewed the novel's early numbers made no such complaints. The *London Review* commented briefly on the novel each month in its "Short Notices" section—accounting for 19 of the 41 reviews—typically to provide synopses of the action but occasionally making small critical observations as well. It noticed No. 1 immediately, lauding the novel's beginning and noting the "mingled fidelity and poetic insight" that suffuse the opening portrait of the Hexams on the Thames.[78] The reviewer also quotes at length from Dickens's sketch of the Veneerings in Chapter 2, recommending the "admirable" account of "their pretentious dinner parties" to any reader who wants to see Dickens at his comic best.[79] "'Our Mutual Friend' opens well," the reviewer concludes, "and we are soon to know what the title means."[80] The *Athenaeum*—perhaps Chorley—also reviewed No. 1, comparing the "dark and impressive power" of the opening on the Thames to "a scene by Michael Angelo" and further remarking, "It is doubtful whether Mr. Dickens has produced a dinner-party in a style of more genuine comedy" than he manages with the Veneerings.[81] In the Wilfers, too, the critic found "a glimpse of character, a rollicksome gaiety, a tenderness of humour which no other living writer can approach"—almost as if, the critic observes, "[i]n returning to his old form of publication, Mr. Dickens ... [has] recovered the buoyancy and spirit of his youth."[82] When No. 2 appeared, the *London Review* again received the new installment enthusiastically, observing that Wegg and Boffin were done "in Mr. Dickens's well-known grotesque manner" and proclaiming Chapter 6, "Cut Adrift," "full of pathos and power."[83] The *Reader* also weighed in on No. 2 by declaring, "Mr. Dickens has never given to the public a conception more superbly comic in the richest style of grotesque invention than appears in the second part of *Our Mutual Friend*," by which the reviewer meant Boffin's decision to hire Wegg off the street, and Wegg's ludicrous errors reading Gibbon's *Decline and Fall of the Roman Empire*.[84]

What Dallas saw, in other words, these early reviewers did not. In almost all of its monthly notices, the *London Review* lauds the novel, whether by way of calling Dickens's account of the Children's Hospital "a picture of great power and beauty" or of watching carefully for signs and tokens amid the complications of Dickens's fascinating plot.[85] On the rare occasions when the reviewer is more

---

[78] "Mr. Dickens's New Story," *London Review*, 8 (April 30, 1864), p. 473.

[79] Ibid.

[80] Ibid., p. 474.

[81] "Our Weekly Gossip," *Athenaeum*, April 30, 1864, p. 613.

[82] Ibid.

[83] "Short Notices. *Our Mutual Friend* [No. 2]," *London Review*, 8 (June 11, 1864), p. 634.

[84] "Miscellanea," *Reader*, June 11, 1864, p. 745.

[85] "Short Notices. *Our Mutual Friend* [No. 8]," *London Review*, 9 (December 3, 1864), p. 622.

A Dismal Swamp?   117

critical of the novel, he is only gently so of Dickens, as when he complains of No. 14 that "[t]he story does not make much progress in the present number, which is hardly so interesting as some of those which have gone before."[86] In the hands of this same reviewer, though, Stone and his illustrations come in for heavy abuse. The illustrations to No. 1 were well enough, the reviewer writes in his review of No. 4, but since the first number "they have got worse and worse" to the point that they are now only "wretched abortions which Mr. Stone is giving under the designation of 'illustrations.'"[87] Subsequent notices find the reviewer shifting back and forth, occasionally finding Stone's illustrations much finer (as with those for Nos. 8 and 10) but then remarking his tumbles backward into something like artistic disgrace. None of this hostility is directed at Dickens's story, though. Considering the sales figures and the evident decline in the print run during the first few numbers, many of the novel's initial readers may have been minded like Dallas. But the early critical responses do not indicate any such dissatisfaction with *Our Mutual Friend*'s opening numbers, which may have been enormously encouraging to Dickens after the trouble he had had to write, rewrite, break, and rearrange the first four installments.

More important, and far more striking, the collected reviews tell us something that comes as a serious surprise: for all that James's place in the history of the novel—and, for that matter, in the history of criticism on the novel—has given his review of *Our Mutual Friend* a persistent significance for scholars, he was nearly alone in writing so negatively of the novel in 1865, and he was one of only two reviewers to do so in the absence of some longstanding antipathy to Dickens on the part of the magazine for which he wrote. Of the 41 reviews, only four are thoroughly negative, and these include James's and those published by Dickens's old enemies at the *Saturday* and *Westminster*. Otherwise, only the first critic to write on the novel for the *New York Times* offered a negative appraisal— which was mostly undone three weeks later by a much longer review in the same newspaper—remarking that while most readers might consider Dickens's new novel his best work, "a more matured judgment would place *Our Mutual Friend* much lower ... undoubtedly many degrees above (perhaps his worst work) *Little Dorritt* [*sic*], but also an equal number below *David Copperfield*, and the older stories to which he owes his fame."[88] Dickens probably never saw the review, but had he done so he might have considered thanking its author for placing him in select company, since the same "New Books" column that discussed *Our Mutual Friend* also offered, farther on, a repudiation of Walt Whitman's *Drum Taps*, which the reviewer declared was not poetry at all but rather prose characterized by a "poverty of thought, paraded forth with a hubbub of stray words."[89] Whitman,

---

[86]   "Short Notices. *Our Mutual Friend* [No. 14]," *London Review*, 10 (June 3, 1865), p. 595.

[87]   "Short Notices. *Our Mutual Friend* [No. 4]," *London Review*, 9 (August 6, 1864), p. 163.

[88]   "New Books," *New York Times*, November 22, 1865, p. 4.

[89]   Ibid.

118   *Charles Dickens's* Our Mutual Friend

the intrepid critic declared, would never be Winthrop Mackworth Praed—he was, it must be admitted, right on this point—so it was a good thing that Whitman had so sacrificed himself in the hospitals during the Civil War. That service, but never his poetry, might endear him to his nation. In Dickens's case, the *New York Times* reviewer allowed that *Our Mutual Friend* contained "many characters and scenes that could originate with no one else" but on the whole blamed Dickens for bringing in a "crowd of unnecessary persons" and constructing an elaborate plot without having "the skill to manage and unfold it."[90] Ranged against this and the few other negative reviews were the essays by Forster, Chorley, and Dallas, the long positive notices in the *London Review*, the *Eclectic*, and the *New York Times*, all of the shorter reviews, and even William Dean Howells's review in *The Round Table*, though he would later, and often, write disparagingly of Dickens through a quarter-century of commentary on British and American fiction.[91] Together, these reviews may well explain the robust sales of the two-volume *Our Mutual Friend* beginning in the fall of 1865.

Of all the reviews, the most balanced was probably the one that appeared in the *Reader* in December 1865, for its author acknowledges both that *Our Mutual Friend* has characteristically Dickensian flaws and that the novel is the work of a great writer—perhaps the greatest writer of the day. "The time has long gone by," he begins, "when criticism could do anything, for good or evil, for the works of Charles Dickens":

> No amount of literary censure or praise could lower or raise his estimation with the general public. Nor, on the other hand, do we believe that any criticism, however just, or fair, or thoughtful would lead him to alter his style, or tone, or mode of writing. We must make up our minds to take the author of "Pickwick" for better or for worse.[92]

He goes on to complain that, moreover, "no writer of eminence ... has shown less faculty of improvement—if we may use such a phrase—than Charles Dickens"; rather, his works are effusions of a peculiar kind of genius that takes its own distinctive form.[93] Like many of the critics of the 1850s (and many others of *Our Mutual Friend* besides), the *Reader*'s reviewer finds Dickens's determination to insert politics into his novel in the form of Betty Higden "undoubtedly wrong," considered from an artistic point of view.[94] But he writes, too, that no author has done more than Dickens to cause social progress, and he implies further that much of Dickens's political effectiveness owes to the precision with which he draws characters, making them far more vivid even than photographic likenesses. "And, in

---

[90] Ibid.

[91] See for instance Howells's *Criticism and Fiction* (New York, 1891), especially pp. 174–6.

[92] "Charles Dickens," *Reader*, 6 (December 9, 1865), p. 647.

[93] Ibid.

[94] Ibid.

our opinion," he continues, "it is this faculty of bringing his personages before us in flesh and blood which constitutes Mr. Dickens' extraordinary talent."[95] In the end, the reviewer offers no positive assessment of the "greatness" of the novel or its place among Dickens's immense oeuvre. But he does remark the "thousands of readers" who, if the accident at Staplehurst had killed Dickens, "would have grieved as for ... a friend, not mutual, but personal," and in place of a positive assessment he offers the following remark, "Whether [Dickens] has fallen off or not is a question of opinion, but it is certain that nobody has yet risen up to him. Let any candid reader try and picture to himself what a sensation 'Our Mutual Friend' would have produced if it had been written by a new and unknown author."[96]

Among the handful of negative reviews—surprisingly, given McCarthy's negative but carefully argued appraisal of Dickens there two years earlier—John Richard de Capel Wise's in the *Westminster* was the most hysterical. Beginning from the premise that Dickens falls very far short when considered against literature's other great humorists—Aristophanes, Molière, Jonathan Swift, Cervantes, and of course Shakespeare—Wise goes on to assert that all of Dickens's characters are mere "bundle[s] of deformities" and that "[h]is whole art ... is founded upon false principles."[97] In support of this thesis, Wise proposes to look solely at Chapter 11, "Podsnappery," since the novel is far too long to bother with the whole thing. "To do this in most cases would be as absurd as to exhibit a man's tooth as a specimen of his eloquence," he remarks, "But Mr. Dickens does not suffer by the process. He is seen to best advantage in detached pieces."[98] Though he sympathizes thoroughly, he writes, with Dickens's hatred of the principle of Podsnappery, Wise finds the chapter only "an explosion of dulness" rife with caricature, repetition, and "bad grammar," in support of which last he points to Dickens's observation that "the meek young man" engaged in conversation with Podsnap "eliminated Mr. Podsnap's flush and flourish by a highly unpolite remark."[99] As Adrian Poole observes in a footnote to this passage in the Penguin edition of the novel, Dickens presumably means "elicited," but the use of "eliminated" in the same context was common enough to be noted in the *Oxford English Dictionary*.[100] Even so, Wise seized gleefully on the "bad grammar" as a way of reminding readers that Dickens was uneducated and vulgar, writing, "Such a blunder implies that Mr. Dickens knows neither the meaning of the French *éliminer* nor the Latin *elimino*" and adding later that the objectionable "chapter ... may be taken as a very fair specimen of the whole work."[101] As Dickens had been living in France for longer and longer periods through most of the decade, he probably did know the difference, whether or not he miswrote it.

---

95   Ibid.

96   Ibid.

97   [John Richard de Capel Wise], "Belles Lettres," *Westminster Review*, 85 (April 1866), p. 582.

98   Ibid.

99   Ibid., p. 583; Dickens, *Our Mutual Friend* (London, 1997), p. 143.

100   Dickens, *Our Mutual Friend* (London, 1997), p. 812 and n.

101   [Wise], pp. 583–4.

The remainder of the review, some 500 more words, attacks Dickens's "Postscript" rather than the novel itself, finding fault point by point with its major contentions. Of Dickens's assertion that "an artist (of whatever denomination) may ... be trusted to know what he is about in his vocation," Wise retorts that it is "natural enough" that "a man who ... has never read a word of Aristotle" should think so.[102] He complains, too, of Dickens using his novel to cudgel the Poor Laws, misconstruing—either willfully or in a moment of extraordinary stupidity—Dickens's mention of the "leading incident" in the novel as a reference to the flight of Betty Higden. He even mocks Dickens's playful remarks concerning the accident at Staplehurst, ridiculing "the melodramatic way in which he speaks of his escape" and offering afterward this cutting and disingenuous disclaimer:

> We write this in no carping spirit, but because it so fully explains to us the cause of Mr. Dickens's failures, a want of sincerity, and a determination to raise either a laugh or a tear at the expense of the most sacred of things. After all that can be said, Art is still a flowering of man's moral nature.[103]

It is impossible to say for certain whether this reference to Dickens's "moral nature" was meant to remind readers of his old domestic troubles. Either way, the review actually says very little about *Our Mutual Friend*, but it says a great deal about Wise's and the *Westminster*'s antipathy to Dickens.

While the *Westminster*'s review of the novel consists mainly of personal invective, those by James and the *Saturday* offer more genuinely critical responses, and both center upon Dickens's same signal failing: his inability to write natural or fully drawn characters or to free those characters from subservience to the machinery of a labored plot. For James the entire problem is that the novel is so labored—"so intensely *written*, so little seen, known, or felt."[104] "It is hardly too much to say," he writes, "that every character here put before us is a mere bundle of eccentricities, animated by no principle of nature whatever."[105] In Jenny he sees only a "little monster"; in Rogue, the Boffins, the Lammles, and the Veneerings, he sees an array of bizarre and unlifelike props for whom the "word *humanity* [seems] ... strangely discordant."[106] Even in Headstone and Eugene, whom many reviewers have always felt to be *Our Mutual Friend*'s most finely drawn characters, he sees only a conflict that "is very insufficient":

> The friction of two *men*, of two characters, of two passions produces stronger sparks than Wrayburn's boyish repartees and Headstone's melodramatic commonplaces. Such scenes as this are useful in fixing the limits of Mr. Dickens's insight. Insight is, perhaps, too strong a word; for we are convinced that it is one

---

[102] Dickens, *Our Mutual Friend* (London, 1997), p. 798; [Wise], p. 584.

[103] [Wise], p. 585.

[104] [James], "*Our Mutual Friend*," p. 787.

[105] Ibid.

[106] Ibid.

A Dismal Swamp?   121

of the chief conditions of his genius not to see beneath the surface of things. If we might hazard a definition of his literary character, we should, accordingly, call him the greatest of superficial novelists … It were, in our opinion, an offence against humanity to place Mr. Dickens among the greatest novelists.[107]

The *Saturday* reviewer says much the same thing, charging Dickens with crowding "into his pages a parcel of puppets as uncommon as the business which they are made to transact."[108] Admitting Dickens's excellence as a caricaturist—and only as that, rather than as a creator of characters—he blames Dickens for giving here no honest caricatures of recognizable types and for "notic[ing] nothing which is not odd and surprising and absurd."[109] Worse, the reviewer suggests, *Our Mutual Friend*'s caricatures are "redolent of ill-temper and fractiousness," as in the portraits of the Podsnap and Veneering set; where they are not, they offer only Betty Higden "thoroughly sentimental and over-done," Mrs. Wilfer "ineffably grotesque and altogether inhuman," and John Harmon and Lizzie, "mere shadows."[110] Only in Headstone, the reviewer asserts, does Dickens nearly reach something finer, giving "the germ … of a very powerful creation" but unfortunately "no plot which might leave room for the working-out of the conception."[111]

Both reviews raise intelligent points about the novel's shortcomings, yet beneath the *Saturday*'s runs the magazine's old hostility to Dickens's politics and the polemical uses to which he puts his fiction. Like the *Westminster*, the *Saturday* objects to the novel's "Postscript" and Dickens's assertion that an artist ought to be trusted to know what he is about. (The *Reader* had objected mildly to this, too.) With some impatience for this "very doubtful doctrine," the reviewer cites it in order to defend the critic's role as a judge and guarantor of true art:

> If it were otherwise than doubtful, first, what is the function of criticism, or is there no such thing? and next, if every artist knows what he is about better than anybody or everybody else, who shall say that this or that is bad art, or is any bad art possible?[112]

Perfectly reasonable, so far as it goes. But as the review continues, the reviewer expresses more and more openly the distinctly political grounds of his irritation with Dickens and his novel. He finds Dickens's propensity to caricature in *Our Mutual Friend* ill-tempered and fractious, it turns out, mainly because it is directed at the Veneerings, "social impostors" who are far less loathsome, he contends, than earlier subjects like Chadband and Bumble, "whom [Dickens] had much more

---

[107] Ibid.

[108] "Reviews—*Our Mutual Friend*," *Saturday Review*, 11 (November 11, 1865), p. 612.

[109] Ibid.

[110] Ibid., pp. 612–3.

[111] Ibid., p. 613.

[112] Ibid., p. 612.

reason to detest."[113] Of the novel's final chapter, in which Twemlow and Mortimer come together over Eugene's marriage to Lizzie, the reviewer writes, "As a rule, it is not a good thing for a gentleman to marry beneath him. The Voice of Society is not so dreadfully wicked or corrupt for giving expression to the belief in the soundness of this view."[114] Predictably, too, the reviewer much prefers the good humor of *Pickwick*'s Eatanswill election to the "[a]ngry, screaming account" of Veneering's campaign in Pocket Breeches, and he finds Betty Higden's dread of the Poor Laws—though he professes to agree that these have been administered shamefully—"from the point of view of 'the interests of art,' thoroughly out of place in a novel."[115] In short, the review implies, had Dickens only stuck to lower-class caricatures, deferred entirely to social convention, and abandoned once for all his determination to write with a purpose, *Our Mutual Friend* would have been a much better novel.

Perhaps these political undertones explain why, in several of the favorable reviews, the very features of the novel that the negative reviews deplore become objects of especial praise. This is not always the case, of course. At times the novel's admirers agree with its detractors, as when the later, favorable reviewer for the *New York Times* finds Lammle "too intensely vulgar as an adventurer" and when Chorley complains that the demands of the plot tell upon the "personages of the story."[116] Like James, Chorley finds John Harmon "partially effaced" and Bella "hardly justifying the love she is described as inspiring"; like James, too, he finds Wegg and Jenny "a pair of eccentrics approaching that boundary-line of caricature towards which their creator is, by fits, tempted."[117] The *London Review* offers a similar opinion of Wegg and Venus, grotesque caricatures both, but remarks forgivingly:

> A certain extravagance in particular scenes and persons—a tendency to caricature and grotesqueness—and a something here and there which savours of the melodramatic, as if the author had been considering how the thing would "tell" on the stage—are to be found in "Our Mutual Friend," as in all this great novelist's productions. But when a writer of genius has fully settled his style ... it is the merest vanity on the part of the critic to dwell at any great length on general faults of manner. There they are, and there they will remain, say what we will.[118]

In his review for *The Round Table*, Howells writes nothing of caricatures, but he observes that Harmon "as a man, is utterly uninteresting" and also that "Headstone, as a study of murderous human nature, is not [even] so good as other

---

[113] Ibid., pp. 612–3.

[114] Ibid., p. 613.

[115] Ibid.

[116] "Literary. Charles Dickens' Last Novel," *New York Times*, December 14, 1865, p. 4; [Henry Chorley], "*Our Mutual Friend*," *Athenaeum*, October 28, 1865, p. 569.

[117] [Chorley], "*Our Mutual Friend*," p. 569.

[118] "Reviews of Books—*Our Mutual Friend*," *London Review*, 11 (October 28, 1865), p. 467.

like studies by the same author."[119] Both Chorley and Howells also complain about the resolution to the novel's plot in ways that echo those negative reviews that call Dickens's characters mere puppets. For Howells, *Our Mutual Friend*'s plot lacks even "secondary excellence ... for it appears to offer the different characters slight opportunity for consistent development ... The motives assigned to the personages are rarely sufficient to account for their actions, and they all act parts which have little or no coherence or propriety."[120] Likewise, Chorley finds Bella's conversion "too sudden," and he cannot quite believe in the simple Boffin's ability "to carry such a long-drawn piece of subtle comedy through"; consequently, he writes, "[t]ruth and nature are here strained, in subservience to the requirements of literary art."[121] Even the positive reviews, then, charge Dickens with writing unnatural characters, or with making characters behave in unnatural ways.

Far more often, though, the positive reviews celebrate the very features that the negative ones revile. Though Chorley is not satisfied with certain major characters or the wrenching resolution of the plot, he finds more finely wrought characters elsewhere in the novel and judges them more than adequate compensation. Headstone, he writes, "takes the foremost place among them as an original conception," and the scene in which Riderhood drags Headstone back to the lock "tortured by his rebuking consciousness" Chorley calls a "masterly ... display of blank, inevitable retribution and wretchedness."[122] He also pauses to admire "the comic parts of the tale": the pretentious Veneerings, the kindly Twemlow, "that old, mechanical harridan, Lady Tippins," Mortimer and Eugene, and even Boots and Brewer—all of them, he proclaims, "new people in print, whom every diner-out has met every week of his life in private."[123] Of all the happy scenes, though, he takes especial delight in the "incomparable dinner" at Greenwich after John and Bella's wedding, with the young man on liking and the older waiter presiding—as we have seen, one of Dickens's pure improvisations in the novel, written only when No. 16 came back short in proofs.[124] Considering its humor, its pathos, and its emotionally charged account of Headstone in his murderous and self-torturing despair, Chorley concluded that *Our Mutual Friend* was one of Dickens's "richest and most carefully-wrought books," adding:

> if, among his tales, we rank the highest 'David Copperfield,' which includes, so to say, neither plot nor surprise,—'Our Mutual Friend' must be signalized for an accumulation of fine, exact, characteristic detail, such as would suffice to set up in trade for life a score of the novel-spinners who give us situations without motives, scenes without characters, words without thoughts, and the dialogue, not of real life, but of melo-drama.[125]

---

[119] [William Dean Howells], "*Our Mutual Friend*," *The Round Table: A Saturday Review of Politics, Finance, Literature, Society*, December 2, 1865, p. 200.

[120] Ibid., p. 201.

[121] [Chorley], "*Our Mutual Friend*," p. 569.

[122] Ibid.

[123] Ibid., p. 570.

[124] Ibid.

[125] Ibid.

124   *Charles Dickens's* Our Mutual Friend

Small wonder that Dickens wrote to Chorley on the day that the review appeared to thank him "most heartily and earnestly" for his kind words.[126] Though he agreed in modest ways with the criticisms leveled by the novel's detractors, Chorley generally endorsed all those things that Dickens had tried hardest to achieve.

Likewise, the author of the favorable December review in the *New York Times* pointed out certain flaws in the novel mainly as a way of shrugging those off or remarking that, in effect, they were hardly flaws after all. Unlike Wise, the *New York Times* reviewer contends that the apparent "improbabilities as a story, the extravagance as a satire, and the grotesqueness in style, of certain elements" actually diminish "when the story is read, not in fragments as it appeared, but continuously as a whole," so that the "original features of the work in a great measure harmonize what is apparently incongruous."[127] He also argues that those who find Dickens's caricatures excessive or characters unnatural and unreal are fundamentally in the wrong. "At a superficial estimate," he writes, "the colloquies of Wrayburn and his friend, may seem quite unnatural," but this is only true for those who have never known university men in England or observed "their lazy confabulation among themselves."[128] Likewise, he writes, however much Dickens's portrait of the Veneering set depends upon caricature, it is a caricature born precisely of that "wearisome and utter artificiality as regards both intercourse and routine"; besides, he writes, in typical Yankee fashion, how otherwise than by thoroughly overdone caricature "can the truth involved therein be impressed on the obtuse English mind?"[129] Much of the rest of this second *New York Times* review is given over to a consideration of Dickens more generally, and a celebration of his salutary moral and social effects. But the reviewer first makes it clear that he admires *Our Mutual Friend*, and that "the spirit of the tale, its entire impression, its human significance, are alive with the author's peculiar genius."[130]

Also, while the *Westminster* and *Saturday* objected, entirely predictably, to Dickens taking up the Poor Laws, the *Eclectic* with its evangelical leanings made this a reason for praise. After first remarking, quite correctly, that *Our Mutual Friend* almost certainly had its origins partly in Horne's 1850 essay on dust-heaps in *Household Words*, the *Eclectic* reviewer calls attention to two laudable features of the novel: his satire on Podsnappery and the broader Veneering set, and his advocacy for the poor in the form of Betty Higden. Of the Veneerings' first dinner party, the reviewer observes, "We have got to deserve this satire ... Too unhappily, the Podsnaps and Veneerings constitute a very large proportion of our English population."[131] As for Betty Higden, the reviewer thanks Dickens for his

---

[126] *Letters*, vol. 11, p. 102.

[127] "Literary. Charles Dickens' Last Novel," p. 4.

[128] Ibid.

[129] Ibid.

[130] Ibid.

[131] "Mr. Dickens's Romance of a Dust-heap," *Eclectic and Congregational Review*, 9 (November 1865), p. 461.

A Dismal Swamp?   125

remarkable portrait and his "courage" in writing the exchange between "the meek man" and Podsnap on the subject of the Poor Laws, "for it needed some, to say all this, in setting the flagrant enormities of our most wicked, heartless, and national neglect before all his readers. He has, we know, been rather severely treated by sundry critics and circumlocutional champions."[132] But the review is not limited to cheers for what the reviewer calls Dickens's "religiousness of feeling"; on the contrary, it makes several perceptive observations about the novel.[133] The writer remarks Dickens's uncanny "power of imparting life to buildings, to dead things, things that never lived," arguing that "the abundant humanity of the man makes him see a human relationship in everything."[134] He also compares Dickens's elaborately detailed writing favorably against the Pre-Raphaelite painting of John Everett Millais. "His books are like himself," the reviewer writes, "illustrations of incessant mental activity, sympathy, and interest"—characterized, that is, by a mental agility that many critics fail to recognize as mental strength.[135] Like Chorley, the *Eclectic* reviewer closes by granting *Our Mutual Friend* "a place by the side of the two or three of the author's very best. Much higher and wider than *Great Expectations*, if without the peculiar soft English light of *David Copperfield*, if without the strong magic shadows of *Bleak House*, it should take its place as their equal."[136]

Forster, too, scoffed at the assertions that Dickens weakened his art by "'writing with a purpose;' as if any thing [*sic*] worth reading, anything worth seeing, anything worth hearing, were ever produced or uttered without a purpose to express distinct individual meaning of some sort."[137] Much of his review praises individual features of the novel—the pathos of Jenny, the grace and charm of Bella, and the "ingenious arrangement and skilful conduct of the story"—and he even goes some distance toward rehabilitating Boffin's unlikely masquerade as a miser.[138] So little do we suspect Boffin, Forster writes, that in the unfolding of this plot we "may have rashly supposed that there the master's hand had lost its cunning. In fact," he continues, "if we look back to those scenes in which Mr. Boffin enacted the part of the miser, we shall be surprised to see how skilfully and freely the novelist scattered what, with the key to it all in our possession, we see clearly enough to be indications of the true state of the case."[139] Like the favorable *New York Times* reviewer, Forster urges—somewhat unconvincingly—that apparent inconsistencies melt away when the novel is considered as a whole.

But Forster saves his highest praise for Dickens's ability to express the novel's central meaning in every character, scene, and twist of plot. "Every great English

---

[132] Ibid., p. 464.

[133] Ibid., p. 474.

[134] Ibid., p. 467.

[135] Ibid., p. 475.

[136] Ibid., pp. 475–6.

[137] [Forster], "*Our Mutual Friend*," p. 681.

[138] Ibid.

[139] Ibid., p. 682.

126   *Charles Dickens's* Our Mutual Friend

work of imagination, every good work of art, all the world over," he contends, "is, as it were, a crystallization of thought about some one central idea"—in this case, he writes, "the soul of life among the fictions of society."[140] More to the point, Forster situates this argument about *Our Mutual Friend* within a much larger context of English literature, ranging in his introduction from Shakespeare's plays to Henry Fielding's *Tom Jones* (1749). Each of these works expresses its "ideal unity," and Dickens, too, "invariably fulfils [*sic*] in his novels this condition of deep seated unity which has been always recognized in English art."[141] Forster's review does not just endorse the novel, then. It rejects the constant aspersions thrown on Dickens by magazines like the *Saturday* and the *Westminster* by affirming Dickens's characteristic Englishness and his place in the pantheon of England's greatest literary artists. It is even just possible, in fact, that Forster deliberately crafted it, at least in part, in response to McCarthy's assertions about Dickens's low place among "Modern Novelists" the prior October. Whether or no, it is the sort of argument advanced by a literary critic who is also a fast friend and literary executor—a steward of what Dickens would eventually leave to posterity, and a force in determining whether posterity would hold it dear—though the argument is not necessarily the less true for that.

Of the other major reviews of the novel published 1864–66, two in particular—Dallas's in the *Times* and the *London Review*'s—merit some further discussion, if only because each takes up *Our Mutual Friend* with less obvious partisanship and makes, at some length, cogent critical points. Two things in Dallas's review are worthy of particular note: first, that he is among the very few critics who found no fault with the novel's plot; and second, that unlike James he did not regard the obvious *labor* that Dickens poured into the novel as a mark against its artistic merit. Far from finding, with the *Westminster* and Chorley, that the plot's resolution was sudden or contrived, Dallas wrote that Dickens's "main story—the line of action in which he has thrown his whole heart ... is a masterpiece."[142] Nor did he dislike Bella, whom he calls "one of the prettiest pictures in fiction" and judges, compared especially against odd Dickensian women like Mrs. Gamp, "a higher reach of art."[143] As for Dickens's very hard work on the novel, Dallas writes:

> One thing is very remarkable about [*Our Mutual Friend*],—the immense amount of thought which it contains. We scarcely like to speak of the labour bestowed upon it, lest a careless reader should carry away a notion that the work is laboured. What labour Mr. Dickens has given to it is a labour of love, and the point which strikes us is that he, who of all our living novelists has the most extraordinary genius, is also of all our living novelists the most careful and painstaking in his work.[144]

---

[140] Ibid., p. 681.

[141] Ibid.

[142] [Dallas], "*Our Mutual Friend*," p. 6.

[143] Ibid.

[144] Ibid.

A Dismal Swamp?   127

The remark both precedes and flatly contradicts James, and it may be that this review with its discussion of *labor* provoked James to write as he did a few weeks later. Meanwhile, even with the "Social Chorus," Dallas faulted Dickens mainly for giving these "dull and dead" characters such a prominent place in the fiction, and he seems almost in spite of himself to have admired the "exceeding skill" with which Dickens exposes "the solemn twaddle of stiff dinner parties and the hollow friendships of which they are the religious rites."[145] On the whole, Dallas thought the novel a resounding success, with incident enough to please readers panting after sensation, humor enough for those who wanted comedy, and several exquisite studies of character for those who preferred quieter scenes. "Mr. Dickens's range is wide," he concludes, "and none of our living novelists can adapt himself, or herself, to so wide a circle of readers."[146]

The *London Review* did not mention Dickens's immense labor, nor was it terribly impressed with the complex machinery of the novel's plot. "Indeed," the reviewer confesses, "the whole story of old Harmon's bequest, and what arises out of it, strikes us as being faulty. This, we are aware, is to proclaim a serious defect in the novel, as such, since we have here the basis of the whole fiction."[147] Yet even this was not quite enough, in the reviewer's opinion, to mar seriously a novel of such rare power. The reviewer marvels at the persistent conflict between Headstone and Eugene, writing finally that the "murderous attack on [Eugene] in a lonely place up the river, is one of the finest things in fiction."[148] (He also asserts—with no hint of irony—that "the change that is afterwards wrought in Eugene's disposition is worked out without the smallest violence."[149]) Far more striking is the reviewer's remark, like the observation in the *Eclectic*, on Dickens's uncanny ability to make his novels teem and seethe with life, an excess that he describes as an unwelcome and uncomfortable obligation for readers:

> As in its author's previous fictions, we are almost oppressed by the fulness of life which pervades the pages of this novel. Mr. Dickens has one of the most mysterious attributes of genius—the power of creating characters which have, so to speak, an overplus of vitality, passing beyond the limits of the tale, and making itself felt like actual, external fact ... The creations of authors such as Mr. Dickens have a life of their own. We perceive them to be full of potential capacities—of undeveloped action ... The chief characters even of his earlier books still dwell in the mind with extraordinary tenacity, sometimes quite apart from the plot wherein they figure, which may be quite forgotten.[150]

---

[145] Ibid.

[146] Ibid.

[147] "Reviews of Books—*Our Mutual Friend*," p. 467.

[148] Ibid., p. 468.

[149] Ibid.

[150] Ibid., p. 467.

This, the critic suggests, is the highest sign of Dickens's genius, "[t]his imaginative fecundity [which] is seen in 'Our Mutual Friend' in undiminished strength" and without even "the slightest symptom of exhaustion or decline."[151]

This celebration of Dickens's genius entirely undiminished by time is ultimately the most significant refrain in the favorable reviews, and it is the one, too, that would have pleased and consoled him most—if anything could—for *Our Mutual Friend*'s sluggish sales. Even the *Westminster* had grudgingly granted that Dickens had "genius, not of the highest indeed, but still of a very rare order," and the earlier and unfavorable *New York Times* review, despite ranking *Our Mutual Friend* among Dickens's worst works, still concluded that it could "happily see no signs" of Dickens writing himself down.[152] This was also the opinion of the second *New York Times* reviewer, who wrote of his "grateful surprise" at finding in *Our Mutual Friend* "such striking evidence of unimpaired vigor, ingenuity, buoyant humor and genial sentiment."[153] Dickens's sins and failings, virtually all of the reviews agreed, were only the old ones, the characteristic traits of his artistic methods and intentions rather than the signs of any sad decline. And, more often than not, the positive reviews asserted that time had *deepened* Dickens's genius by granting him a mature control over his fancy that led him onward toward the highest attainments of literary art. In the *Examiner* Forster asserted that the "keen enjoyment of [Dickens's] genius" should supersede any narrow criticisms based upon "individual tastes and opinions," and Howells wrote, "We think [an] ideal critic would pronounce that he found this last romance as full of generous interest as any earlier one," before remarking finally that the style of this latest novel could not be "more luminous, flexible, felicitous."[154] Dallas, too, allowed that "[i]t would not be wonderful if so voluminous an author should now show some signs of exhaustion. On the contrary, here he is in greater force than ever, astonishing us with a fertility in which we trace no signs of repetition."[155] The *Eclectic*'s reviewer agreed, writing, "[i]t has been said for a long time his powers have been in their decay; we have never been able to perceive this … in the volumes through which we have just glanced, we have abundant evidence of the still imperial superiority of Mr. Dickens in his own old field of work."[156] And the *Eclectic*, the *London Review*, and the *Reader* all commented on Dickens's "Postscript," not to complain of it but rather to share in Dickens's obvious thankfulness that he had been spared at Staplehurst. As the *London Review* put it, almost elegiacally, "We cannot afford to lose such a writer as Mr. Dickens. A man of original, creative genius dying in the fulness of his strength, leaves a gap which nothing can fill, and a regret which the memory of his past triumphs only deepens and embitters."[157]

---

[151] Ibid.

[152] [Wise], p. 582; "New Books," p. 4.

[153] "Literary. Charles Dickens' Last Novel," p. 4.

[154] [Forster], "*Our Mutual Friend*," p. 682; [Howells], "*Our Mutual Friend*," p. 201.

[155] [Dallas], "*Our Mutual Friend*," p. 6.

[156] "Mr. Dickens's Romance of a Dust-heap," p. 474.

[157] "Reviews of Books—*Our Mutual Friend*," p. 468.

III

Five years later England did lose Dickens as he wrote the sixth number of *Edwin Drood*, and it mourned him as it had never mourned any other literary figure and as it has not mourned once since. Though Dickens had told his family that he wished to be buried in the small graveyard at Rochester Castle, public pressure—initiated mainly, Forster writes, by the *Times*—mounted to provide a greater recognition, and a greater chance for his enormous public to pay their respects.[158] After a one-column notice of Dickens's death on June 11, the *Times* ran a leader two days later, reminding readers of that "peculiar resting-place of English literary genius," Westminster Abbey, and saying that "among those whose sacred dust lies there ... very few are more worthy than Charles Dickens of such a home."[159] "If his friends prefer it," the writer continued,

> let them have as quiet a funeral as they please; their wishes will be religiously respected. But let him lie in the Abbey. Where Englishmen gather to review the memorials of the great masters and teachers of their nation, the ashes and the name of the greatest instructor of the nineteenth century should not be absent.[160]

Other obituaries and encomia of Dickens appeared, too, seemingly everywhere: by Chorley in the *Athenaeum*; by Blanchard Jerrold, Douglas's son, in *Gentleman's Magazine*; in occasional verse in *Punch*; and even in a poetical tribute by the young American Bret Harte, half a world away in California.[161] Eventually, having been assured that the strictest privacy and simplicity would be observed, the family consented to bury Dickens in Poet's Corner after a private funeral to which neither Nelly nor Catherine was invited.[162] For three days after, thousands of mourners from every rank of life filed past the grave to lay flowers there—so many flowers that they had to be removed time and again to make room for more; so many mourners for so many months that, long after the grave had closed, the Abbey floor around the stone bearing Dickens's name remained "a mound of fragrant color."[163] Three weeks after Dickens's death, Charley Dickens inserted into *All*

---

[158] For more on Dickens's funeral and will, see Forster, *Life*, pp. 855–61; and Slater, *Charles Dickens*, pp. 613–19. As Slater points out, Dickens did *not* express in his will this desire to be buried at Rochester, perhaps to leave the door open for receiving the honors of Westminster Abbey.

[159] [Unsigned leader on Dickens's death], *Times*, June 13, 1870, p. 11.

[160] Ibid.

[161] Henry Chorley, "Mr. Charles Dickens," *Athenaeum*, June 18, 1870, p. 804; Blanchard Jerrold, "Charles Dickens. In Memoriam," *Gentleman's Magazine*, 229 (July 1870), pp. 228–41; "Charles Dickens," *Punch*, June 18, 1870, p. 244; "The Grave of Charles Dickens," *Punch*, June 25, 1870, p. 253; Bret Harte, "Dickens in Camp," *Overland Monthly*, 5/1 (July 1870), p. 90.

[162] Claire Tomalin remarks that it is just possible, though unlikely, that Nelly made one of the mourners at the Abbey. See *Charles Dickens*, p. 399.

[163] Johnson, vol. 2, p. 1157.

the Year Round a front-page notice entitled "Personal"—repeating unconsciously his father's ill-fated "Personal" statement in *Household Words* a decade before—announcing that, according to his father's wishes, he was assuming control of the magazine, and that he hoped to suffuse it always with the "same spirit" as when his father was alive, the "same earnest desire to advocate what is right and true."[164] Not long after, Dickens's effects were sold by auction at Gad's Hill, and for the living everything began to return to normal, though perhaps two shades less vivid than they had been just a few weeks before.

As the dust settled and writers wrote and reviewers tried intermittently to assess Dickens's place in English letters, one principal implication of his death grew increasingly clear: by dying, Dickens had ceded the field once for all to the critics who had railed against him and his populist art for so long. For decades to come, the right to cement or cheapen his legacy would lay almost entirely in their hands. Some, at least, used the chance to say what they had said so often before. In 1872 in the *Fortnightly Review*, perhaps prompted by the appearance of Forster's first volume of biography the prior November, Lewes printed a new essay on Dickens that covered much of the old familiar ground, acknowledging Dickens's immense popularity but again denying him anything more than "merely an *animal* intelligence" and asserting that his grossest and most persistent failure was his inability to draw men and women in detail, as they really live and breathe and move and speak in the world.[165] In one sense, of course, this was nothing new. In another sense, with Dickens no longer present to defy them, it was the beginning of a critical and intellectual entrenchment that characterized highbrow response to Dickens for the next 70 years—that rejected his (and any) popularity, that ridiculed his earnestness about social injustice, that laughed at his sentimentality, that made him out a comedian and charlatan rather than an artist, that dismissed his post-*Copperfield* novels as "writing with a purpose," and that so demeaned his ability to draw characters that E.M. Forster was still essentially parroting Lewes a half century later in *Aspects of the Novel* (1927).[166] For 35 years Dickens had combined, as if by magic, the eighteenth century's rollicking humor and nearly unbearable sentimentality with Victorian England's sordid social realities, and he had juggled, too, the artistic demands for coherence of plot and symbolic unity, the rigors of serial publication, and the promptings of his own inimitable capacity for imaginative fancy and linguistic play. And in *Our Mutual Friend*, by almost all accounts, he had combined these things one last time in a triumphant, even culminating way. Then he died and his critics took over, and for more than half a century *Our Mutual Friend* went dark.

---

[164] Charles Dickens, Jr., "Personal," *All the Year Round*, July 2, 1870, p. 97.

[165] George Henry Lewes, "Dickens in Relation to Criticism," *Fortnightly Review*, 17 (February 1, 1872), p. 151.

[166] George Ford makes this same point in *Dickens and His Readers*, where he enumerates Lewes's seven major complaints against Dickens. See pp. 229–30.

Chapter 5
The Voice of Society:
Our Mutual Friend since 1870

In his excellent study *Other Dickens* (2000) published at the turn of the present century, John Bowen begins by explaining why he chose to devote an entire book to Dickens's first six novels. Most readers these days, he writes, "may well feel content with the familiar features of *Great Expectations*, *Bleak House*, *Hard Times*, *Little Dorrit*, and *Our Mutual Friend*," since these are now the most widely studied and read of Dickens's works.

> Common readers, though, have over the decades admired Dickens's earlier novels—*Pickwick Papers*, *Oliver Twist*, *Martin Chuzzlewit*—at least as much as their successors. ... we should be grateful that we have in his oeuvre not four or five major novels, but a dozen or more. To read all Dickens's works may be a long party, but the best bits are not all late in the evening.[1]

When Dickens died, and for a long time after, the need for such an argument on behalf of the early works would have been unthinkable. Very few reviewers in 1870 could have imagined a day when the comic novels that launched Dickens's career would go mostly unread and his reputation among critics would rest principally on the novels that came after *Dombey and Son*. Then again, those same reviewers—who would not recognize, either, the shape of today's academy or the tone and purpose of its literary criticism—would probably be stunned to find thinking people taking Dickens seriously at all. In the first edition of the *Dictionary of National Biography* begun in 1885, its editor Leslie Stephen prepared the entry on his old enemy Dickens himself, using it to remind readers that while 4 million volumes of his works had sold in the 15 years since his death, discriminating critics had long ago concluded "that his merits are such as suit the half-educated," and that future generations would hold Dickens cheap.[2] Writing mainly for a Lewesian audience, he was still towing the Lewesian line, as a great many critics would until World War II and even after. As late as 1955, according to Ford, Lewes's old objections to Dickens remained so current that some academic critics continued to repeat them "almost as if they were novelties."[3]

Highbrow disdain for Dickens took nearly a century to abate, and throughout this period the reputation of *Our Mutual Friend* and his other post-*Copperfield*

---

[1]   John Bowen, *Other Dickens* (Oxford, 2000), p. 1.

[2]   Leslie Stephen, "Dickens, Charles," in Sir Leslie Stephen and Sir Sidney Lee (eds), *The Dictionary of National Biography* (London, 1921), vol. 5, p. 935.

[3]   Ford, *Dickens and His Readers*, p. 230.

fiction tended to rise or fall as Dickens's did. His early books were esteemed for their humor, though not their art, and his later books went mostly disregarded. The ferocious attacks on his fiction during the 1850s turned out to have been nothing compared with the test his reputation faced between 1870 and the First World War. Despite much evidence to the contrary, highbrow writers and critics asserted often that Dickens was no longer read, or at least that he was read only by that childish and vulgar public that was incapable of appreciating anything better. Though he admitted that Dickens had sold incredibly well since his death, Mowbray Morris wrote in the *Fortnightly* in 1882 that he could not imagine posterity treating Dickens kindly, for "the true artist's touch ... we never, or hardly ever, find in Dickens."[4] Forty years later H.M. Tomlinson confessed that he was not at all surprised to hear from a young writer friend that Dickens "had gone the way of wax-fruit."[5] On the one side, realists from Lewes and Eliot to James complained of Dickens's romanticism, sensational plots, and impossible characters; on the other, aesthetes like George Meredith, Oscar Wilde, and eventually Virginia Woolf sneered at his cheery populism and middle-class conventionality.[6] Writers of both camps preferred the maturity and comprehensiveness of the Russian novelists—Ivan Turgenev, Fyodor Dostoevsky, Leo Tolstoy—who came into vogue in England toward the end of the nineteenth century. Compared against these, Dickens's mawkish sentimentality seemed childish and outmoded, especially in a Europe lurching inexorably toward war. As Wilson put it impatiently in "Dickens: The Two Scrooges" in 1941, "[t]he Bloomsbury that talked about Dostoevsky ignored Dostoevsky's master, Dickens."[7] In Russia, France, and Germany Dickens's reputation soared even as English critics reduced him, bit by bit, to the irrelevant humorist of a bygone time. Even Dickens admirer G.K. Chesterton, who reinvigorated appreciation for him in *Charles Dickens* in 1906, argued for Dickens's genius mostly in the conventional way: by praising Dickens's moral teaching and good cheer, finding *The Pickwick Papers* "something nobler than a novel," and scorning *Little Dorrit* and the other dark novels that came after.[8] Through it all, the so-called serious critics continued to deny Dickens seriousness, or at least to deny him artistic achievement even in his serious moods. Consequently, they also rejected out of hand the very novels—*Bleak House*, *Hard Times*, *Little Dorrit*, and *Our Mutual Friend*—that attempt the most in their social critique and artistic sophistication.

---

[4]   Mowbray Morris, "Charles Dickens," *Fortnightly Review*, 32 (December 1, 1882), p. 769.

[5]   John Middleton Murry, "Books of the Day: The Dickens Revival," *Times*, May 19, 1922, p. 16.

[6]   By the late 1930s, Woolf's antipathy to Dickens had apparently softened. She reread *Copperfield* for relaxation in 1936 and *Dorrit* in 1939. Yet even then she recorded in her diary that Dickens's work was "so abundant, so creative: yes: but not *highly* creative: not suggestive ... Thats [sic] why its [sic] so rapid & attractive: nothing to make one put the book down & think." See Woolf, *The Diary of Virginia Woolf* (London, 1984), vol. 5, p. 215.

[7]   Edmund Wilson, *The Wound and the Bow* (Cambridge, 1941), p. 1.

[8]   G.K. Chesterton, *Charles Dickens* (Ware, 2007), p. 41.

The Voice of Society 133

Still, it is not quite true, as I wrote at the end of the last chapter, that *Our Mutual Friend* simply went dark after Dickens's death. Whatever the critics thought, he was far too popular for that. As even the selected list of *Our Mutual Friend*'s editions in Appendix 4 shows, publishers in England and America never stopped printing and selling this or any other novel by Dickens, instead issuing edition after edition of both individual titles and the collected works. Long after his death, owing to the combined effects of population growth, rising literacy rates, and a higher standard of living, Dickens continued to sell better with each passing year. Through the last decades of the nineteenth century and first decade of the twentieth, Dickens's titles almost single-handedly kept Chapman and Hall afloat, the publishers working the copyrights cleverly and continuously until the last one for *Drood* finally expired in 1913. In 1872 they launched the "Household Edition" in bound volumes, monthly parts, and penny numbers, and during 1873–76 they issued the more costly "Second Illustrated Library Edition."[9] Then came the "De luxe Edition" of 1881, the 34-volume "Gadshill Edition" of 1897—which Waugh calls "the first really complete edition of Dickens" because it includes his speeches and journalism—with introductions to the novels by Andrew Lang, the "Authentic Edition" of 1900, the "National Edition" of 1906, and the "Centenary Edition" of 1910. Nor were these all. In 1906 Chapman and Hall had 14 editions of Dickens's collected works in print, even though most of the novels—*Our Mutual Friend* and *Edwin Drood* excepted—were out of copyright and under production by other publishers, as well.[10] When the copyright for *Drood* finally expired, Chapman and Hall flooded the market one final time with the economical 22-volume "Universal edition" of 1913, yet even this continuous reissue of Dickens's works was scarcely enough. During World War I, when most trade had slowed to a trickle, "Dickens sales were still enormous," according to Waugh. "The existing plates were used for one edition after another, and the profits were immediate and continuous."[11] Scribner's sold them in America and Waverley helped to do so in England, and dealers in retail goods from tea to embroidered silk to the *Encyclopedia Britannica* attracted buyers by promising free sets of Dickens's works.[12] Amid this relentless demand and despite continuous production, "the volumes could hardly be printed fast enough to keep pace."[13]

Since the copyright for Dickens's works expired title by title from 1878 on, it is very hard to know for sure how many copies of his books really sold. But Chapman and Hall's figures, inasmuch as they remained the principal publishers,

---

[9] For further information about these editions, see Arthur Waugh's *A Hundred Years of Publishing, Being the Story of Chapman & Hall, Ltd.* (London, 1930), pp. 175–6 and 192–3, and also "Part III" of Waugh and Hatton's *Retrospectus and Prospectus: The Nonesuch Dickens*, which gives particular information and even sample reprinted pages of selected editions of Dickens's works.

[10] James Milne, "How Dickens Sells," *The Book Monthly*, 3 (1906), p. 773.

[11] Waugh, *A Hundred Years*, p. 250.

[12] Patten, pp. 329–30; Waugh, *A Hundred Years*, p. 251.

[13] Waugh, *A Hundred Years*, p. 251.

at least give certain indications. According to these, in the first dozen years after his death Dickens's books sold 4,239,000 copies, and Waugh told *The Book Monthly* editor James Milne in 1906 that for the prior six years Dickens had sold an average of 330,000 volumes annually—four times what he had sold in 1869.[14] Moreover, Waugh reported, annual sales had been increasing at a rate of 30 percent each year, so while the average figure for 1900–1905 was around 330,000, in 1906 sales were running at more like half a million, not including sales in the United States.[15] Even in 1934 *David Copperfield* remained the best-selling book in J.M. Dent's 900-title "Everyman's Library," and nine other novels by Dickens were among the top 100.[16] Still, it is almost certain that Dickens's early works enjoyed the lion's share of the popular success. *Pickwick* and *Copperfield* were the perennial favorites, according to Waugh, while later titles like *Little Dorrit, Our Mutual Friend,* and even *Great Expectations* tended to languish. Nor does *Our Mutual Friend* seem to have been terribly popular with early filmmakers. In the first decades of the twentieth century, film turned often to Dickens: by 1912, he had a serious adapter in Thomas Bentley, who directed *Oliver Twist, David Copperfield, The Old Curiosity Shop, Hard Times,* and *Barnaby Rudge* in rapid succession between 1912 and 1915, and by 1920 Dickens's works had already been adapted in whole or in part more than 70 times. Only one of these early adaptations, the silent short "Eugene Wrayburn" (1911), came from *Our Mutual Friend.* By the time the BBC made *Our Mutual Friend* into a full-length feature for the first time in 1958—and then only for television—nearly 150 film and television adaptations of Dickens had appeared, including even for obscure titles like *The Chimes* (1844) and "The Magic Fishbone" (1867).[17] For nearly a century the voice of society had almost nothing to say about *Our Mutual Friend,* and precious little to say, either, about the Dickens novels most like it.

How times have changed. No novel in Dickens's oeuvre—not even the much-maligned *Little Dorrit*—has gained more than *Our Mutual Friend* from the critical revaluation of Dickens that began around 1940 and has continued to the present day. The time when *Our Mutual Friend* might have become one of Dickens's truly popular books is almost certainly long since gone, and it is unlikely now ever to be as familiar to an average reader as *Oliver Twist, A Christmas Carol,* or *Great Expectations.* But for scholars *Our Mutual Friend* has become a preferred title. It is taught more and more frequently in college, studied and published on with great regularity, and recognized increasingly as a crucial midcentury portrayal of the grim realities of the modern city and the horrors engendered by Victorian capitalism. Of course, this is somewhat true for all of Dickens's later titles, by which I mean the post-*Copperfield* novels that his contemporaries most deplored.

---

[14]   Morris, p. 762; Milne, p. 773.

[15]   Milne, p. 773.

[16]   Walter Dexter, "When Found—," *Dickensian,* 31 (Winter 1934), pp. 2–3.

[17]   Though it had not been done in England, a two-hour film adaptation of *Our Mutual Friend* (Dir. A.W. Sandberg) was made in Denmark in 1919.

The Voice of Society   135

Since the 1940s critics have seen the novels from *Bleak House* on, more and more commonly, as prescient accounts of class conflict and psychological rupture—as imaginative counterparts to Marx, and as precursors to Freud—with the result that Dickens is now, for all his comedy and sentimentality, regarded as intellectual and postmodern rather than childish, vulgar, or banal. In his Foreword to *Great Expectations* in 1937, George Bernard Shaw famously called *Little Dorrit* "a more seditious book than *Das Kapital*."[18] Critics since have mostly agreed, or at least they have treated *Little Dorrit*, *Our Mutual Friend*, and the other mature novels as the utterances of a piercing observer whose complex symbolism and wild fancy convey more Victorian (and post-Victorian) realities than all of the quieter realisms of Thackeray, Eliot, and Trollope combined. A review of the essays indexed by the *MLA International Bibliography* shows that four titles by Dickens—*Bleak House*, *Great Expectations*, *Little Dorrit*, and *Our Mutual Friend*—have been the subjects of almost half of all criticism on him since 1990, and the number is rising even as early titles like *Nickleby*, *Chuzzlewit*, and *Rudge* fall away into the dust.

Moreover, though *Bleak House* and *Great Expectations* have for decades been the two most studied Dickens novels, *Our Mutual Friend* draws critics like a lodestone, in a trend that grows more pronounced with each passing year. Even during the 1980s *Our Mutual Friend* was published on only about half as much as *Oliver Twist*, *Dombey and Son*, and *Hard Times*. But during the 10-year period 2000–2009, *Our Mutual Friend* surpassed all of these novels as well as *Little Dorrit* and *David Copperfield*, placing third on the list and serving as the subject of 50 percent more essays and chapters than had addressed it the decade before. Of course, published scholarship in every field of literary study has been increasing, and against even the proportional rise it might be argued that this publish-or-perish academic age has simply driven Dickens scholars to less exhausted materials. But this same culture has not driven critics away, necessarily, from novels like *Pickwick* and *Oliver Twist*, which have always been thought of kindly, nor has it driven them toward perennially neglected ones like *Nickleby* or *Rudge*. Instead, it has produced—with some help from poststructuralist theory—the phenomenon that Bowen noted in 2000: a heavy skewing of critical interest toward the later fiction, and toward very few Dickens novels more strongly than toward *Our Mutual Friend*. We critics have mostly left off worrying, as our ancestors did, about whether any particular novel or novelist is "great," and this as much as anything produced the interest in *Our Mutual Friend*, which may not be "great" in a purely technical sense but is almost impossibly rife with thematic tensions, symbolic resonances, self-conscious artistry, and ideological force. Between 1870 and 1940, as I will show, Dickens's reputation was at its nadir; only a very few of his novels were critically esteemed, and *Our Mutual Friend* was not one of them. Since 1940, Dickens's reputation has been on surer ground, and *Our Mutual Friend* has come increasingly to be regarded as a testament to Dickens's creative excellence rather than as the last gasp of a dying man. Perhaps the best way to

---

[18] George Bernard Shaw, *Shaw on Dickens* (New York, 1985), p. 51.

explain this change is to say that the novel's fierce interrogations of capitalism, the law, biology, and religion, among other things, have become more fascinating to us as Western culture has matured and as the very forces that darken the novel have threatened to pull that culture apart. In other words, the problem with *Our Mutual Friend*—if there ever was a problem at all—was in us all along. We have needed 150 years to catch up with a novel that was very far ahead of its time.

I

The story of *Our Mutual Friend* after 1870 is very much the story of Dickens himself: so long as he was disregarded by critics, his last finished novel mostly was, too. But for all that the critical current ran strongly against Dickens 1870–1940, he was never entirely without defenders. As George Saintsbury put it in 1895 in *Corrected Impressions*, where he records his own softening opinion of Dickens:

> There are few comparatively recent writers about whom it is more difficult to write at the present moment than it is to write about Dickens. Current public opinion seems to have got into a kind of tangle, and there are as many as four or five distinct views regarding him, all of which are held by considerable parties, each including some who deserve consideration quite independent of the numbers of their companions.[19]

If the realists and aesthetes loathed Dickens—and though *Corrected Impressions* suggests that its author sometimes did, too—Saintsbury confesses to experiencing undiminished joy in his frequent returns to *Pickwick*, and he admits that upon rereading Dickens's novels during his later years he found many of them far better and more literary than he had remembered. John Forster had also tried to champion Dickens, but the biography was hard on *Our Mutual Friend* and may, for several reasons, ultimately have injured Dickens's standing with critics. Many reviewers of the biography found it rather long on anecdotes of Forster's friendship with the great writer—the *Leeds Mercury* facetiously called it "The Autobiography of John Forster with Recollections of Charles Dickens"—but short on truly valuable commentary on his life and work.[20] Worse, the first volume's revelations about Dickens's childhood gave teeth to the old complaints that Dickens was uneducated and vulgar, and that he had no right to engage in social and political commentary as if he were a gentleman. Stephen could therefore remark with impunity on Dickens's "half-educated" audience in his entry for the *Dictionary of National Biography*, and Trollope, who had not been overtly hostile to Dickens during his life, could make similar insinuations in *An Autobiography* (1882), where he ranks Dickens below

---

[19] George Saintsbury, *Corrected Impressions: Essays on Victorian Writers* (London, 1895), p. 117.

[20] Quoted in Ford, *Dickens and His Readers*, p. 161.

Bulwer-Lytton, complains that his style is "jerky, ungrammatical, and created by himself in defiance of rules," and calls him "marvellously ignorant" of the political issues that Bulwer-Lytton and Thackeray wrote of with greater penetration.[21]

Other voices spoke up for Dickens. In 1888 in *Scribner's* Robert Louis Stevenson wrote approvingly of Dickens's ability to draw a gentleman—a power that many of the realists denied him—citing successful examples in the later fiction and reasoning that, if gentlemen did not appear elsewhere in Dickens, it was only because of his extraordinary ability to draw individuals. Dickens had the unusual power of making an individual "something more definite and more express than nature," Stevenson wrote, whereas it was the business of a gentleman to bow entirely to convention, leaving nothing of the individual about him.[22] Fourteen years later, in the same year that enthusiasts founded the Dickens Fellowship, two noted poets and essayists came out for Dickens, as well. On a lecture tour in America, Alice Meynell praised Dickens lavishly as a stylist and derided the men who "sav[e] their reputation as readers by disavowing [Dickens's] literature even while they confess the amplitude of its effects."[23] More unexpectedly, at least in retrospect, Algernon Swinburne came angrily to Dickens's defense. Dickens was, Swinburne wrote, "a genius of such inexhaustible force and such indisputable originality" that none of the highbrows could appreciate him—not Wordsworth imitator Matthew Arnold, not "the bisexual George Eliot," and certainly not that "consummate and pseudosophical ... quack" Lewes.[24] "It is just that they cannot see high enough," he continued. "And not even the tribute of equals or superiors is more precious and more significant than such disdain or such distaste as theirs."[25]

In later years other supporters chimed in, albeit with a little less rhetorical fire. American academic Walter Clarke Phillips made Dickens the subject of a full-length study in *Dickens, Reade and Collins: Sensation Novelists* (1919), and around the same time George Santayana, living in England during the First World War, composed a defense of Dickens that he later published in the *Dial*. Partly, Santayana reverted to the old praise of Dickens's early comic works, but he also credited Dickens for creating glorious characters who "differ from real people only in that they live in a literary medium."[26] By the 1920s Cambridge professor Arthur Quiller-Couch—"Q," as he was known—was revitalizing Dickens in his lectures, collected and published as *Charles Dickens and Other Victorians* in 1925.

---

[21]   Anthony Trollope, *An Autobiography* (Oxford, 1980), pp. 249–50.

[22]   Robert Louis Stevenson, "Some Gentlemen in Fiction," *Scribner's*, 3 (June 1888), p. 767.

[23]   Alice Meynell, "Charles Dickens as Man of Letters," *Atlantic Monthly*, 91 (January 1903), p. 52. In an interesting twist, Meynell's mother was the very Christiana Weller whom Dickens had developed the intense attachment to in 1844.

[24]   Algernon Swinburne, "Charles Dickens," *The Complete Works of Algernon Charles Swinburne* (London, 1926), vol. 14, pp. 85, 82, 77.

[25]   Swinburne, vol. 14, p. 86.

[26]   George Santayana, "Dickens," *Soliloquies in England and Later Soliloquies* (New York, 1922), p. 72.

Granting that Dickens had not yet had the opportunity to pass the test of time that measures all great writers, Quiller-Couch still argued for "the essential *greatness* of Dickens" and remarked, "if it come to the mere wonder-work of genius ... I do not see what English writer we can choose to put second to Shakespeare save Charles Dickens."[27]

Of those who championed Dickens during these contentious years, two men in particular stand out: George Gissing, who published *Charles Dickens: A Critical Study* in 1898, and Shaw, who wrote aggressive public and private defenses of Dickens—his later works, particularly—for nearly three decades. Each was a social radical, though in different ways, and each saw enormous merit in Dickens's biting social critiques and unstinting sympathy for the poor. Gissing's was the first book-length critical study of Dickens, or better, the first book-length critical defense. As he explains in his first chapter, he aimed principally to discuss Dickens's methods of characterization in order "to vindicate him against the familiar complaint that, however trustworthy his background, the figures designed upon it, in general, are mere forms of fantasy."[28] To that end, Gissing works through certain biographical details about Dickens's early life before moving on to a well-considered discussion of his abilities as a storyteller and drawer of character, calling particular attention to the humor and pathos with which Dickens depicts children, the enfeebled, and the poor. Readers who "exclaim at the 'unreality' of" his characters," he insists, "will generally be found unacquainted with the English lower classes of to-day"— likely true enough, and an obvious shot at the highbrows who were loudest in their disdain.[29] He also calls attention, a bit more troublingly to postmodern eyes, to Dickens's wonderful "gallery of foolish, ridiculous, or offensive women," describing them as "incontestable proof of Dickens's fidelity" and remarking that they alone "would establish his claim to greatness."[30] Besides these observations on Dickens's women, perhaps, Gissing's analysis is intelligent and far-reaching, and it has the especial merit of having restored maligned books like *Little Dorrit* and *Hard Times* to prominent places in Dickens's oeuvre. In fact, Gissing writes, "a competent judge" would be "tempted to call *Little Dorrit* the best book of all."[31] But Gissing's critical study also suffers from one major flaw, for he attempts to engage the highbrow critics on essentially their own terms. In an era when realists and aesthetes were articulating a rigid definition of the novel—its objectivity, its verisimilitude, its stodgy intellectualism—that no novel by Dickens could meet, Gissing spent his considerable critical powers trying to show that Dickens did meet their requirements, when really he should have expressed the much simpler truth: that Dickens's work was so profoundly original that such rules did not apply.

---

[27] Arthur Quiller-Couch, *Charles Dickens and Other Victorians* (Cambridge, 1925), pp. 23, 20.

[28] George Gissing, *Charles Dickens: A Critical Study* (New York, 1912), p. 12.

[29] Ibid., p. 13.

[30] Ibid., p. 172.

[31] Ibid., p. 109.

The Voice of Society 139

For this reason, the more powerful advocate was Shaw, who never offered a book-length defense of Dickens but who inaugurated, from his position inside the intellectual class, a very different sort of commentary on Dickens's work. Asked by *The Bookman* editor Sir William Nicoll in 1912 about his indebtedness to Dickens, Shaw replied:

> My works are all over Dickens; and nothing but the stupendous illiteracy of modern criticism could have missed this glaring feature of my methods ... It is not too much to say that Dickens could not only draw a character more accurately than any of the novelists of the XIX century, but could do it without ceasing for a single sentence to be not merely impossible but outrageous in his unrestrained fantasy and fertility of imagination ... Dickens was one of the greatest writers that ever lived—an astounding man, considering the barbarous ignorance of his period ... All his detractors were and are second-raters at heart.[32]

During the 1890s Shaw became friends with Dickens's daughter Katey, by then Mrs. Perugini, whom he met and charmed only after criticizing severely her paintings at the Royal Academy. Though they were never all that intimate, Shaw was even instrumental in saving from the fire 137 letters from Dickens to his wife, all of which Katey had thought to burn after inheriting them from Mamie in 1896.[33] Shaw had always admired Dickens, not only for his power to draw characters but also because of the prescience of his social criticism in *Hard Times* and the novels that followed. Such "slop work as *The Old Curiosity Shop* [was] indefensible" to Shaw, with his socialist leanings, but he judged that "the tremendous series of exposures of our English civilization which began in *Hard Times* in 1854 ... threw [Dickens's] earlier works, entertaining as they are, into the shade. *Little Dorrit* is the work of a prophet—and no minor prophet: it is in some respects the climax of his work."[34] He expanded on *Hard Times'* momentousness in the Introduction he wrote to the Waverley edition in 1913, and in a 1937 Foreword to *Great Expectations* he referred again to *Little Dorrit* as Dickens's "masterpiece among many masterpieces" and made his famous comparison of the novel to *Das Kapital*.[35] The merit in all of this from the standpoint of Dickens's critical reputation was the assertion, finally, that his work had both seriousness and political sophistication, and that these qualities far outweighed both his comic powers and any real or perceived shortcomings in "characterization" or "form." By the 1920s Woolf and E.M. Forster, among others, had largely succeeded to Lewes's objections to Dickens, but the nature of the critical conversation had finally begun to change.

Amid this fray, it is even possible sometimes to glimpse *Our Mutual Friend.* Gissing, though he esteemed *Little Dorrit*, clearly disliked the later novel.

---

[32] Shaw, p. 70.

[33] See Dan Laurence's "Introduction" to Shaw, p. xvii.

[34] Shaw, p. 72.

[35] Ibid., p. 51.

He objected that Dickens had overstepped realistic bounds by making Lizzie so very genteel, and he called Betty Higden "one of the least valuable of his pictures of poor life."[36] Forty years later, when Ernest Baker wrote his ambitious and voluminous *History of the English Novel*, he had only lukewarm regard for Dickens and liked *Our Mutual Friend* no better. It was, he wrote, "as far below his average as *Great Expectations* was above it"—"tired out, if not exhausted," and filled with characters who were only "second-rate editions of earlier ones."[37] But many others offered *Our Mutual Friend* at least qualified praise, for its parts if not for the whole. Saintsbury wrote that although he could not "believe that we lost much by the non-completion of 'Edwin Drood,' there is no doubt 'the true Dickens' in parts of 'Our Mutual Friend.'"[38] Likewise, Milne, in an effort to explain Dickens's continuous popularity, suggested smartly that *Our Mutual Friend* had been much underrated, and that one need only compare Little Johnny's muted, touching death to earlier tear-jerkers like Little Nell's or Paul Dombey's to see the development of Dickens's literary art.[39] Chesterton, too, though he much preferred Dickens's earlier works, recognized Eugene as an artistic advance in the presentation of "serious psychology," calling him "a marvellous realization" of "that singular empty obstinacy that drives the whims and pleasures of the leisured class."[40] Stevenson also admired Eugene, but he saved his highest praise for the portrait of Headstone, with its stunning emotional intensity. He calls the scene in which Headstone barks his fist against the church-yard wall "one of the most dramatic passages in fiction" and writes further that "[t]o handle Bradley (one of Dickens's superlative achievements) were a thing impossible to almost any man but his creator; and even to him, we may be sure, the effort was exhausting."[41] Swinburne preferred the scene in which Riderhood is pulled from the river and returns gradually to life, "one of the very greatest works of any creator who ever revealed himself as a master of fiction."[42] And for Shaw, *Our Mutual Friend* was neither more nor less than one of Dickens's several late masterpieces, all of them "mercilessly faithful and penetrating exposures of English social, industrial, and political life."[43]

Through these critical squabbles and reversals, Dickens's immense popularity continued unabated, and this was so much the case that it is hard even now to tell whether any but the stiffest intellectuals ever left him at all. Bloomsbury and Oxbridge might grumble, but in 1906 when Dickens's critical reputation was at its lowest ebb, Milne was already conjecturing that highbrow distaste for Dickens was fading: "the literary folk," Milne wrote, "are coming back to him."[44] Mazzeno

---

[36] Gissing, pp. 96, 270.
[37] Ernest Baker, *History of the English Novel* (New York, 1936), vol. 7, p. 314.
[38] Saintsbury, p. 123.
[39] Milne, p. 775.
[40] Chesterton, p. 119.
[41] Stevenson, p. 767.
[42] Swinburne, p. 81.
[43] Shaw, p. 30.
[44] Milne, p. 775.

The Voice of Society 141

dates the return to Dickens a little later, asserting that readers came back eagerly to his comforting high spirits and domestic cheer in the wake of World War I, as they would again during and after World War II.[45] Whatever the case, though critics were divided other readers were not. In 1920 a questionnaire circulated widely to England's public librarians found that Dickens's works were still "greatly in demand—of the 75 copies held in Newcastle libraries 53 were in use on the day when the City Librarian compiled his statistics. *Pickwick*, *Oliver Twist*, and *Copperfield* were most popular with London readers, *Barnaby Rudge* and *Bleak House* with Scottish ones."[46] *Great Expectations*, meanwhile, was least wanted everywhere. Two years later John Middleton Murry argued in the *Times* that a "Dickens Revival" had been underway since at least 1914, and he cited Santayana's appreciation of Dickens, then recently published in the *Dial*, as evidence that intellectuals, too, were returning to his work. All Dickensians, Murry wrote, could now "be content with the knowledge that the offence against art and intellect is no longer to know Dickens, but to be ignorant of him."[47] Much the same was true in America, where, as Slater points out, students voted Dickens their favorite author in both 1921 and 1922 and named *A Tale of Two Cities* their favorite book.[48] Nor had much changed by the 1940s, when American journalism expert Dean Mott conducted a study in honor of the centenary of *A Christmas Carol* and estimated that more than 2,000,000 copies of it had been sold in America since its first publication, that nine other Dickens novels had sold at least 1,000,000 copies, and that seven more had sold 500,000. All told, Mott concluded, Dickens was far and away "the best-selling author in the history of American publishing."[49]

It is impossible to know for certain how much *Our Mutual Friend* shared in this popular bonanza, either in England or the United States. In 1906, according to Waugh, it was Chapman and Hall's tenth best-selling title by Dickens, on a par with *Little Dorrit* and ahead of *Great Expectations* but considerably below Dickens's most popular works. At the time *A Tale of Two Cities* topped the list, but Waugh admitted that this was an anomaly fueled by the popularity of Martin Harvey's play *The Only Way*, which was based on *A Tale of Two Cities* and had recently been touring theaters in London and the provinces.[50] That sales of Dickens's novels could be driven by such an adaptation even in 1906 may give us some clue as to why *Our Mutual Friend*'s sales lagged in England and America for several decades compared with sales for many of Dickens's others novels. During the first half of the twentieth century, *Our Mutual Friend* never benefited, as several other Dickens titles did, from the exposure of a major film release on one or both sides of the Atlantic. Ford's ambitious study of British and American publishers of

---

[45] Mazzeno, p. 91.

[46] Michael Slater, "1920–1940 'Superior Folk' and Scandalmongers," *Dickensian*, 66 (May 1970), p. 125.

[47] Murry, p. 16.

[48] Slater, "1920–1940," pp. 125–7.

[49] Walter Dexter, "When Found—," *Dickensian*, 40 (March 1944), p. 56.

[50] Milne, p. 774.

142   *Charles Dickens's* Our Mutual Friend

Dickens, which attempted to estimate total sales of each novel for the single year 1968, concluded that by that time the top six sellers on both sides of the Atlantic included, in different orders, *Great Expectations*, *Oliver Twist*, *Hard Times*, and *David Copperfield*—most of them short, which may indicate principally their suitability for school reading, but most of them, too, having already been made into popular or even acclaimed adaptations: Stuart Walker's (Universal, 1934) and David Lean's (Cineguild, 1946) *Great Expectations*; William Cowen's (Monogram, 1933) and Lean's (Cineguild, 1948) *Oliver Twist*; and George Cukor's 1935 *David Copperfield* (Metro-Goldwyn-Mayer).[51] In the United States *A Tale of Two Cities* had been immensely popular since at least the 1920s and was undoubtedly helped thereafter by the 1935 Metro-Goldwyn-Mayer adaptation starring Ronald Colman; it remained the best-selling Dickens in America even in 1968, though it is perhaps worth pointing out that it remained only seventh on the list in England despite both a motion-picture release and BBC television serial during the prior decade. Meanwhile, *Our Mutual Friend* was still buried near the bottom, eleventh in England, tenth in America. At the time of its own centenary, in other words, *Our Mutual Friend* was no *Carol*. But by then the critics had long since changed their minds about both Dickens and his last finished novel.

The turning point came in 1940 when Wilson published "Dickens and the Marshalsea Prison" in the *Atlantic Monthly* and, a year later, revised and republished it as "Dickens: The Two Scrooges" in *The Wound and the Bow*. In one sense Wilson was only just arriving at the end of what had been a frenetic decade in Dickens studies, when the anti-Dickensians still held sway. During the mid-1930s two crucial works on Dickens had appeared, each damaging in its own way: Hugh Kingsmill's *The Sentimental Journey: A Life of Charles Dickens* (1934), which unapologetically made Dickens "into one of those Victorian scarecrows with ludicrous Freudian flaws," and Wright's *Life of Charles Dickens* with its explosive revelations about Dickens and Nelly.[52] Other, less antagonistic books appeared soon after. In 1937 Walter Dexter published the first volume of his Nonesuch edition of Dickens's letters, and in 1939 Gladys Storey published *Dickens and Daughter*, which largely vindicated Wright's slimly supported charges. The 1930s also produced the first recognizably modern critical study of Dickens, T.A. Jackson's *Charles Dickens: The Progress of a Radical* (1938), an often strained attempt to portray Dickens as a true believer in the socialist cause. Still, Slater is right to call it "some of the most intelligent and interesting criticism of Dickens published during this period," for it is among the first sustained studies to argue for not only Dickens's penetration as a social critic but also for his artistic care in constructing his novels.[53] Each of these books mattered in its way, but perhaps—ironically—none more than Wright's. In its salaciousness, and despite certain factual shortcomings, Wright's biography ushered in a new era in the study

---

[51]   George H. Ford, "Dickens in the 1960s," *Dickensian*, 66 (May 1970), pp. 163–82.

[52]   Wilson, pp. 2–3.

[53]   Slater, "1920–1940," p. 141.

of Dickens by revealing him as a tantalizingly flawed and complicated man rather than the cheery and conventional champion of the domestic hearth.

But Wilson's essay mattered more, for it was the first critical work to incorporate this new sense of Dickens into a penetrating analysis that does justice to Dickens's art by recognizing that it is characterized thoroughly by neither *Pickwick*'s optimism nor *Little Dorrit*'s bleakness but instead resides, often uncomfortably, in the unresolved tensions between the two. From the start, Wilson's essay challenges directly the received wisdom on Dickens, dismissing out of hand those "literary men from Oxford and Cambridge, who have lately been sifting fastidiously so much of the English heritage, [and] have rather snubbingly let him alone."[54] More, while he acknowledges the contributions of men like Gissing, Chesterton, Jackson, and Shaw, he argues that even they, in their praise for Dickens, have not done justice to the complexity of his work. Blending biographical details with insightful reading, Wilson describes a Dickens of remarkable psychological depth and argues that Dickens, whatever his methods of characterization, conveys that depth in his most compelling characters. Through close attention to *Bleak House*'s fog and mud, he also builds a case for a Dickens who understood symbolism perfectly, and who excelled at it long before the advent of the modern novel. As he puts it, "the people who talk about the symbols of Kafka and Mann and Joyce have been discouraged from looking for anything of the kind in Dickens, and usually have not read him, at least with mature minds."[55] He also accounts for much of the intellectual resistance to Dickens by turning the tables on the critics, pointing out that Dickens was one of the very few major artists who had the temerity to reject England's "governing class" when its stipendiaries and representatives offered to take him up.[56] Naturally Wilson's interests in psychological tensions and complex symbols led him to celebrate mainly *Little Dorrit* and the novels that followed, including *Our Mutual Friend*. Like Stevenson, he admires the intricacy of Headstone's compulsions and double life, and he asserts that the novels after *Hard Times* all have mounting psychological interest. *Our Mutual Friend* "compensates for its shortcomings," he writes, "by the display of an intellectual force which, though present in Dickens' work from the first, here appears in a phase of high tension and condition of fine muscular training"—the novel is his final judgment on "the whole Victorian exploit" and the most powerful example of "the serious exercise of his art."[57] By prizing the late novels, acknowledging Dickens's ability to draw complex psychologies, and treating Dickens as a self-conscious artist, Wilson laid the foundation for a pattern of criticism that characterizes Dickens studies to the present day.

This is not to say that critical change came entirely overnight. In the same year as *The Wound and the Bow*, George Orwell—finding Dickens only an indifferent

---

[54] Wilson, p. 1.

[55] Ibid., pp. 37–8.

[56] Ibid., p. 48.

[57] Ibid., pp. 74–5.

socialist—offered much more qualified praise, acknowledging Dickens's genius but returning all the same to the old arguments that he was a caricaturist and something of an ignoramus. "He has an infallible moral sense," he observed, "but very little intellectual curiosity. And here one comes upon something which really is an enormous deficiency in Dickens ... that he has no ideal of *work*."[58] Elsewhere he echoes McCarthy's old contention that Dickens's mind was "in fragments," writing, "Dickens is obviously a writer whose parts are greater than his wholes. He is all fragments, all details—rotten architecture, but wonderful gargoyles."[59] Nor were the Leavises, in all their majesty, quite ready to cede the field. In her 1932 book *Fiction and the Reading Public*, Q.D. Leavis was one of those still reciting the old saw about Dickens's half-educated reading public, and she made it clear that she blamed him for the startling rise of vulgar fiction in midcentury Victorian periodicals. Dickens himself, she wrote, was "not only uneducated but also immature"; only in *Copperfield* and *Great Expectations* did he rise high enough above his cruder impulses for his "novels to be called literature."[60] Throughout the 1930s and 1940s F.R. Leavis was expressing similar opinions, which he finally compiled into *The Great Tradition* in 1948. There, he identifies George Eliot, Henry James, and Joseph Conrad as the three great novelists of the nineteenth century and scorns the notion that Dickens was a painstaking or self-conscious artist:

> That Dickens was a great genius and is permanently among the classics is certain. But the genius was that of a great entertainer, and he had for the most part no profounder responsibility as a creative artist than this description suggests ... The adult mind doesn't as a rule find in Dickens a challenge to an unusual and sustained seriousness.[61]

Small wonder, then, that in spite of Wilson's notable essay Lionel Stevenson could still remark in 1943 that *Bleak House*, *Hard Times*, and *Little Dorrit* remained "the least read of [Dickens's] major works."[62]

But the tide had turned, and it continued to flow vigorously in Dickens's favor in the studies that appeared after 1940, from Stevenson's to Humphry House's intelligent and far-ranging *The Dickens World* (1941) to the several new biographies—Una Pope-Hennessey's *Charles Dickens* (1945), Jack Lindsay's *Charles Dickens: A Biographical and Critical Study* (1950), and Julian Symons's *Charles Dickens* (1951)—that used Wright, the Nonesuch letters, and Storey's memoir of Mrs. Perugini to recast Dickens as a far more fascinating figure than the

---

[58]   George Orwell, *Dickens, Dali and Others: Studies in Popular Culture* (New York, 1946), p. 51.

[59]   Ibid., p. 65.

[60]   Q.D. Leavis, *Fiction and the Reading Public* (London, 1965), pp. 157–8.

[61]   F.R. Leavis, *The Great Tradition: George Eliot, Henry James, Joseph Conrad* (New York, 1963), p. 19.

[62]   Lionel Stevenson, "Dickens's Dark Novels, 1851–1857," *Sewanee Review*, 51/3 (1943), p. 398.

The Voice of Society 145

moderns had dared to suspect. This reconstruction of Dickens's biography continued spectacularly in 1952 in *Dickens and Ellen Ternan*, when Ada Nisbet used infrared photography to recover passages about Nelly that had been purged from Dickens's letters, and when Johnson published his magisterial two-volume biography *Charles Dickens: His Tragedy and Triumph*. Together, the works on Dickens during these dozen years continued what Wilson had begun, for they gave a portrait of Dickens as not only a complex psychological figure but also an artist who quite deliberately produced books of greater aesthetic sophistication as his career advanced. They also, partly as a result of this new sense of Dickens's deliberate artistry, shifted the critical focus to the later novels, finding in his social critiques much more than the uninformed, sentimental clucking that his political opponents had often insisted they were. It was in the criticism of the 1940s and early 1950s, in other words, that Dickens first became by general acclaim the serious artist and perceptive observer that Lewes and the Stephens never saw. And it was these years, too, that gave the later novels artistic ascendancy—so much so, in fact, that when Steven Marcus published *Dickens, from Pickwick to Dombey* in 1965, the focus on the early novels already seemed strange. "Originally," Marcus explains in the opening chapter, "I had planned to encompass Dickens's entire life, and to place the strongest emphasis on the later novels."[63] Only too late did he realize that handling the earlier works, too, would take him well beyond the scope of a single volume.

By 1970 even the Leavises had given in, devoting an entire book to Dickens and declaring in their preface that their "purpose [was] to enforce as unanswerably as possible the conviction that Dickens was one of the greatest of creative writers; that with the intelligence inherent in creative genius, he developed a fully conscious devotion to his art ... and that, as such, he demands a critical attention he has not had."[64] Setting aside the fact that they were arguing partly against themselves, the fact is that the Leavises were arriving very late to an enormous party and still remained part of a dwindling minority that did not regard *Our Mutual Friend* as one of Dickens's most important books. They wanted, they said, to correct the "wrong-headed, ill-informed" critical trend that Wilson had begun, and to that end they proposed to study Dickens's six great novels: *Dombey, Copperfield, Bleak House, Hard Times, Dorrit*, and *Great Expectations*. But other critics were already moving on from *Dombey* and *Hard Times* and were instead extolling the virtues of Dickens's last—and darkest—novel. In 1949 Robert Morse insisted in the *Partisan Review* that Dickens was every bit as great an artist as Dostoevsky, Tolstoy, or Proust and called *Our Mutual Friend* "a sinister masterpiece," profoundly poetic in its symbolic suggestiveness.[65] Three years later, critics were praising the novel at every turn. In his 1952 Introduction to *Little Dorrit*, Lionel Trilling called *Our Mutual Friend*—along with *Dorrit* and *Bleak House*—"one of the three great novels of Dickens' great last period," and that same year E. Salter Davies introduced *Our*

---

[63] Steven Marcus, *Dickens, from Pickwick to Dombey* (New York, 1965), p. 9.

[64] F.R. Leavis and Q.D. Leavis, *Dickens the Novelist* (New York, 1970), p. ix.

[65] Robert Morse, "*Our Mutual Friend*," *Partisan Review*, 16/3 (1949), p. 277.

146   *Charles Dickens's* Our Mutual Friend

Mutual Friend for Oxford by declaring, "surely, none would deny it a place among his greatest works. In form it is, perhaps, the most artistic of all the novels, and in felicity of language it is surpassed by none."[66] But perhaps the greatest praise came from Johnson in the chapter of criticism he includes in his biography, where he asserts unequivocally that "*Our Mutual Friend* [is] among Dickens's crowning achievements. Intellectually and artistically it is one of the peaks of his stupendous creative power, the synthesis of his developing insight throughout a lifetime."[67] Even for great admirers like Gissing, Chesterton, and Shaw, Dickens's greatness in the late novels was always to be found elsewhere—in *Bleak House*, perhaps, or in *Dorrit* or *Great Expectations*. But Johnson made *Our Mutual Friend* for the first time a culmination, a glorious pinnacle rather than a plateau along Dickens's inevitable descent. Nearly a century after it was first published, educated opinion on *Our Mutual Friend* had finally come full circle, and the novel ascended for the first time to a preeminent place among Dickens's works.

II

There it has remained, gaining ground with scholars and readers with each passing year. In his 2011 Introduction to the Vintage edition of the novel, Nick Hornby, who calls Dickens "the greatest novelist to write in the English language," complains that *Our Mutual Friend* is unfortunately "far from his best" and that ultimately scholars alone have "saved the novel over the years, and given it a reputation that it perhaps doesn't deserve."[68] Whatever the novel "deserves," critical attention to it has certainly been persistent and extensive, and it has certainly been, too, the principal cause of its gains with a wider audience. Brattin and Hornback's comprehensive annotated bibliography describes everything related to *Our Mutual Friend* that appeared 1864–1984: editions, contemporary reviews, critical commentary and textual studies, biographies that address the novel, unpublished theses and dissertations, radio and film adaptations, and other lectures, performances, and creative or educational public displays related to the novel. Their tally runs to 683 items, and in 2003 Robert J. Heaman added 244 more in a "Supplement" published in *Dickens Studies Annual*, updating the record for items that appeared 1984–2000.[69] No further supplement has appeared, but one probably should since even a basic *MLA International Bibliography* search—which turns up only a subset of the kinds of items included in Brattin and Hornback and in Heaman—shows 125 new entries just for the period 2000–2012,

---

[66] Lionel Trilling, *The Opposing Self* (New York, 1955), p. 50; E. Salter Davies, "Introduction," in Charles Dickens, *Our Mutual Friend* (London, 1967), p. xvii.

[67] Johnson, vol. 2, p. 1041.

[68] Nick Hornby, "Introduction," in Charles Dickens, *Our Mutual Friend* (New York, 2011), pp. xi–xii.

[69] Robert J. Heaman, "*Our Mutual Friend*: An Annotated Bibliography, Supplement I—1984–2000," *Dickens Studies Annual*, 33 (2003): 425–506.

The Voice of Society   147

35 of which have appeared since the start of 2010. Considering that, at the time
of this writing, very little from the bicentenary year has yet been indexed in the
MLA International Biography, the figures suggest that scholarly output on *Our
Mutual Friend* continues to expand rapidly. All signs point to 2012 and, allowing
for inevitable publication delays, 2013 being extraordinary years for new studies
on Dickens.

Scholars wanting an exhaustive description of materials related to *Our Mutual
Friend* should consult Brattin and Hornback's work or Heaman's supplement.
Here, I attempt to provide only an accurate characterization of the trends in
scholarship on *Our Mutual Friend* since around 1970, when studies of the novel
began appearing with great regularity and unfolded an array of approaches to the
novel that remain, for the most part, cogent and common to the present day.[70] As
a further disclaimer, I will simply say that as with any generalization, this one
will probably omit much and—what is worse—much that is important. Too many
exceptional scholars have written on *Our Mutual Friend* to give each his or her
proper due. For the first 15 years or so after the remarkable eruption of praise
for the novel in 1952, criticism continued at a trickle that ranged across textual,
structural, and thematic issues. In 1957, near the start of his long and important
critical engagement with Dickens, Sylvère Monod published a French-language
essay on *Our Mutual Friend*, and the following year Stanley Weintraub published
a notable study of the novel's relation to Henrik Ibsen's *A Doll's House* (1879).
During these early years, the smattering of essays on the novel appeared most often
in the *Dickensian*, the *Victorian Newsletter*, and other relatively minor journals in
English studies. But by the late 1960s critical work on the novel was appearing
with much greater frequency and in prestigious journals like *Modern Philology*,
SEL: Studies in English Literature, *ELH*, and *Nineteenth-Century Fiction*. These
were also the years during which scholars who would become major late-century
voices on Dickens—Garrett Stewart and Stanley Friedman, for instance—first
published on *Our Mutual Friend*, and when Diane Sadoff, Wilfred Dvorak, and
James Marlowe were finishing dissertations on the novel and laying a groundwork
for its more prominent position in Dickens's oeuvre. Nor is it a coincidence that
this groundwork emerged simultaneously with the rise of poststructuralist theory.
Our Mutual Friend's unwieldy plot and multivalent Dust Mounds have never
been congenial to structural study; on the other hand, its mesmerizing tangle
of death, waste, sexuality, identity, and commodity culture has been irresistible
to scholars interested in psychoanalysis, gender, the old and new historicisms,
cultural materialism, Marxism, deconstruction, and any other theoretical approach
one might name. Consequently, by the late 1970s the critical revitalization of the

---

[70]   Brattin and Hornback also suggest that serious critical interest in *Our Mutual Friend*
began around 1940, and that 1970—the centenary of Dickens's death—saw a remarkable
surge in scholarship, a continued acceleration of interest in *Our Mutual Friend*, and "an
avalanche of doctoral dissertations on Dickens, many of which dealt with *Our Mutual
Friend*." See p. xvii.

148   *Charles Dickens's* Our Mutual Friend

novel was in full swing. Andrew Sanders, Barry Qualls, and Nancy Aycock Metz all published important essays on *Our Mutual Friend* during 1978–79, and the array of critical approaches to the novel continued to widen.

It is very hard even now to say what the most important approaches have been, or even what "most important" might mean in that context. Much depends upon the scholarly bent of the beholder. Besides, it is also the case that criticism passes through fashions and fads almost as quickly as the Veneerings—and often tends, one might add, to whatever still smells of varnish and is a trifle sticky. But this is not to say that critical approaches during the last 30 years have not been excellent or that they have not shed important light on the novel. In the Introduction to his "Supplement" Heaman characterizes the criticism 1984–2000 as falling into two camps: "those who are primarily concerned with Dickens's social analysis and those who are primarily concerned with artistic technique."[71] Some essays fit neither of these categories, really, from Brattin's several excellent textual studies to O'Hea's and Elizabeth Cayzer's articles on Stone's illustrations to Cotsell's 1984 essay "Mr. Venus Rises from the Counter," one of many to explore Dickens's sources for the novel. But even the essays that do fit Heaman's rough scheme deserve further nuancing here. During the last quarter-century, problems of psychology and identity—and increasingly of female identity—in the novel have led to excellent studies by Rosemarie Bodenheimer, Helena Michie, Goldie Morgentaler, Natalie Rose, Lisa Surridge, and Syd Thomas, and *Our Mutual Friend*'s heavy investment in the Hexams and Headstone has produced several fine essays on Dickens's interest in mid-Victorian education and education reform, as well as on literacy and the cultural and linguistic implications of reading. A smaller group of critics, from J. Hillis Miller in *Others* (2000) to Linda Lewis in *Dickens, His Parables, and His Reader* (2011), has investigated spiritual and biblical concerns in what many regard as Dickens's most explicitly sacramental novel. In very recent years, though, perhaps the most significant new approach to the novel has come via *Our Mutual Friend*'s rich intersections with Darwin and the ecology, the novel's simultaneous obsessions with the Thames and the detritus of modern industrial London functioning as complementary parts of a broader historical and cultural scene. Pamela Gilbert's work on this aspect of the novel stands out, but several other critics working in this area—among them Brattin, Litvack, Michelle Allen, Nicola Brown, and most recently Sally Ledger—have also produced very fine studies.

Of all the poststructuralist avenues of approach to *Our Mutual Friend*, though, the most frequent and in some ways most fruitful has been to interrogate the novel through its rich engagement with mid-Victorian capitalism, commodity culture, and the capitalist subject. In the Hexams' grim trade, in the Dust Mounds, in the "Social Chorus," and in a dozen other features besides, the novel suggests that Victorian capitalism pervades every part of its culture: death, ecology, the law, education, gender, race, psychological repression, and spiritual redemption. As a

---

[71]   Heaman, p. 432.

result, even critics who begin or end elsewhere are often drawn, like the characters themselves, into the complications of *Our Mutual Friend*'s economic investments. From Cotsell's 1984 essay "The Book of Insolvent Fates" to Deborah Epstein Nord's 2011 "Dickens's 'Jewish Question': Pariah Capitalism and the Way Out," dozens of critics have offered rich studies along these lines, finding in the novel's capitalism an interpretive key to everything from misogyny and homophobia to resurrection and the material corpse. Among the most provocative studies are those by Mary Poovey, Eve Kosofsky Sedgwick, Daniel Scoggin, John Kucich, and Catherine Gallagher, but many others are also outstanding. Moreover, only by reading them all can one get a comprehensive sense of the extent to which Dickens's portrayal of capitalism in *Our Mutual Friend* impinges upon and undergirds every other part of his social critique—a critique that takes its shape from capitalism's irresistible power, displayed so forcefully in the novel, to commodify the subject and transform the world into a vast funereal marketplace, a feast of corpses, what Scoggin calls a "Vampiric Economy."[72] In the criticism as in the story, the faintest touch on a distant thread seems to ripple and resonate back to the pitch-black center amid the money, bodies, and Dust Mounds that introduce the book.

Hornby is right to suggest that the outpouring of scholarship on *Our Mutual Friend* since 1970 has been a root cause of the novel's being pressed upon an ever-widening circle of readers. As university faculty have worked painstakingly at unpacking the novel's dense symbolism and ideological implications, they have quite predictably also introduced more and more students to the novel, at both the graduate and undergraduate levels. Besides appearing recently on many graduate-level course syllabi, *Our Mutual Friend* was a focal point of Robert Patten's Mellon Foundation Research Seminar "Dickens in the 1860s: Pollution, Violence, Empire, and Authorship" at Rice University during 2010–11. Faculty have also taken increasingly to including the novel in undergraduate classes—at least ones taken by English majors—and so introducing it to educated readers whose prior experience with Dickens may only have been through shorter works like *Hard Times* or *A Tale of Two Cities*. Gauging how frequently any book is taught is tricky, and I do not mean to propose any scientific means of measuring here. Victorian novels are not anthologized like poetry or nonfiction prose—there are no successive Norton or Longman or other editions to serve as signposts by which to trace what has entered or fallen away from the undergraduate "canon." Nor can we know with any certainty how often any novel was taught 5 or 20 or 50 years ago in the thousands of classes offered each year to the hundreds of thousands of college students on both sides of the Atlantic. But we do know that academic critics scarcely touched the novel until the 1960s, that in 1968 it sold far fewer copies than most other titles by Dickens—which probably means that it was not being assigned at the college level—and that in our present day it appears on a surprising number of syllabi at big public universities as well as small exclusive ones. Perhaps it is no surprise to

---

[72] See Daniel Scoggin, "A Speculative Resurrection: Death, Money, and the Vampiric Economy of *Our Mutual Friend*," *Victorian Literature and Culture*, 30/1 (2002), pp. 99–125.

see *Our Mutual Friend* included in a graduate seminar or as one of several books on a syllabus for a course on "Dickens," or "Dickens and Eliot," or "Dickens and Melville," and it now appears in such places routinely. But often, even in broader courses, it seems to have supplanted traditional choices like *Copperfield* and *Bleak House* as the semester's exemplary Dickens text. At Amherst College, the University of Idaho, the University of Iowa, and the University of California–Berkeley, according to just a modest perusal of syllabi and course descriptions posted online, *Our Mutual Friend* has recently served as *the* Dickens novel in several courses on Victorian and nineteenth-century fiction. And in our interdisciplinary, special-topics, subtitling pedagogical age, it has also been incorporated into recent courses like Jennifer Ruth's "Dickens and Popular Culture" at Portland State University and—in a move that would probably have appalled E.M. Forster—Mario Ortiz Robles's "Aspects of the Novel" class at the University of Wisconsin–Madison, where *Our Mutual Friend* sits alongside the realists and aesthetes from Jane Austen to Gustave Flaubert to Oscar Wilde. All of these courses are from the last decade, and most have been offered since 2008. Faculty who have found *Our Mutual Friend* so rewarding for their scholarly work are, in other words, creating gentle ripples in their classrooms that may eventually have far-reaching effects.

This does not mean that we should expect armadas of new readers to flock to the novel, hawk it in the streets, discuss its merits on Facebook, or download it eagerly to handheld devices for summer beach reading. But with faculty teaching the novel so much more frequently, and in the wake of so much excitement for all things Dickensian in 2012, it is no stretch to say that far more people have probably read *Our Mutual Friend* in the last five years than had done so since at least the time it was first published. In 1984 Brattin and Hornback lamented that "only a handful of inexpensive paperback editions of the novel [were then] in print, [despite] its ever-increasing popularity," and they were quite right.[73] According to *British Books in Print* and its American counterpart *Books in Print*, in 1977 there were only four English-language editions of *Our Mutual Friend* still in print, and Brattin and Hornback could find only five new editions total since 1960.[74] By 2006 the figure had tripled, and since 2007 10 new English-language print editions of the novel have appeared besides the eight audio editions and six electronic editions that have become available in formats as various as the free Project Gutenberg e-text and the downloadable Amazon Digital Edition published in 2009. More, while some publishers of *Our Mutual Friend* have remained constant for decades—Viking/Penguin with its academic paperback, Oxford University Press with its "Illustrated" and "World's Classics" editions, J.M. Dent's (now Random House's) "Everyman's Library" edition—newer entries to the market have come from Bantam, Wordsworth, Random House's Modern

---

[73] Brattin and Hornback, p. xiv.

[74] The figures for 1977–2006 are taken from *British Books in Print* and *Books in Print* for the abovementioned years. Those looking for more details, though, should be aware that *British Books in Print* has also been titled, during this period, *Whitaker's Books in Print* and, more recently, *Bowker's British Books in Print*.

The Voice of Society   151

Library and Vintage imprints, Sagebrush Educational, and Textbook Publishers. All of them specialize in relatively inexpensive paperbacks, and most publish implicitly or explicitly for an undergraduate academic market. We cannot know whether publishers are responding to or attempting to provoke heightened demand. Either way, by 2006 *Our Mutual Friend* was available in more printed editions than *Nickleby*, *Chuzzlewit*, or *Rudge*, and it had nearly caught up with *Pickwick*, which in 1977 was available in nearly three times as many print editions. If the perennial increase in scholarship on *Our Mutual Friend* continues to translate into the novel's more frequent presence in the classroom, and if those readers go on to become teachers, too, even the present ripples—modest as yet—may widen.

The persistent interest in the last decade or so of Dickens's life may also continue to inspire interest in *Our Mutual Friend*. The bicentenary has brought with it a new adaptation of *Great Expectations* directed by Mike Newell and starring Ralph Fiennes (Magwitch), Helena Bonham Carter (Miss Havisham), Holliday Grainger (Estella), and Jeremy Irvine (Pip), and Fiennes's other Dickensian project—a biopic based on Claire Tomalin's *The Invisible Woman*—is in postproduction and will be released late in 2013. *Our Mutual Friend* has not been, and somehow seems unlikely to be, appropriated in the wildly popular ways that so many of Dickens's other novels have been. It will likely never become an award-winning musical like *Oliver Twist*, a Disney hit like *A Christmas Carol*, or a flimsy Hollywood flop like the Ethan Hawke/Gwyneth Paltrow *Great Expectations* of 1998. It has been adapted to and rewritten for the stage, though, on dozens of occasions, almost all of them before the First World War and perhaps most intriguingly by American playwright Harriette R. Shattuck, who managed in 1872 to turn the novel into *Our Mutual Friend: A Comedy in Four Acts*. It has also been adapted three times as a radio serial, most recently in 20 parts for BBC Radio in 2009. As Brattin and Hornback show in their bibliography, too, before 1930 *Our Mutual Friend* was commonly adapted to other literary purposes, whether it was condensed into a children's version of the novel, excerpted into collections like Jesse Lyman Hurlbut's *Dickens' Stories about Children* (1909), or extended in works like Alice M. Holmes's short story "Ten Years Married: by Lizzie Wrayburn" (1938) or Sir Harry Johnstone's novel *The Veneerings* (1922). Very few literary appropriations have appeared in the last half-century, though. The best known, probably, is Frederick Busch's 1975 novel *The Mutual Friend*, but this is hardly an adaptation, for it draws almost nothing but its title from the novel. Instead, Busch offers a fictional, partly stream-of-consciousness narrative from George Dolby, who superintended Dickens's reading tour of the United States in 1867. A reviewer for the *Dickensian* panned the novel—a bit grumpily—but it does entertain with its imagined reminiscences about Dickens, Nelly, and the reading tour, however little these have to do with *Our Mutual Friend*.[75] On the other hand, Busch's novel does

---

[75]   See Brattin and Hornback's annotation for the novel (p. 19) for a summary of the *Dickensian*'s remarks. For the remarks themselves, see "When Found—," *Dickensian*, 75 (Fall 1979), p. 182.

not quite measure up to the wickedly fun literary appropriations of other Dickens works that have appeared in recent years—Louis Bayard's *Mr. Timothy* (2003), for instance, or Matthew Pearl's *The Last Dickens* (2009).

Apart from the silent short "Eugene Wrayburn" and the Danish feature film of 1919, *Our Mutual Friend* has been adapted to the screen three times, always by the BBC for broadcast as a television serial rather than by a major studio for cinema release. The first serial, directed by Eric Tayler and with screenplay by Freda Lingstrom, aired weekly in 30-minute installments from November 7, 1958, through January 23, 1959. For most readers of the novel, it is the least familiar adaptation, for it has not been reaired in recent memory or released by the BBC in any current format. In early 1959 the *Dickensian* observed blandly that the serial was "proceeding in fine style," but other information is in short supply.[76] That is certainly not the case, though, for the second television adaptation, which was unavailable for three decades but made a long-awaited return on DVD in 2008. Directed by Peter Hammond and written by Donald Churchill and Julia Jones, the second BBC adaptation aired weekly in seven 50-minute episodes from March 1 through April 12, 1976. Among its merits, it features excellent performances by Alfie Bass (Silas Wegg) and Nicholas Jones (Eugene Wrayburn) and also a noteworthy performance by Jane Seymour as a pretty and petulant Bella Wilfer. But the serial's true scene-stealer is 35-year-old actress Polly James, who gives a stunning rendition of Jenny Wren. These performances alone make the adaptation worth watching, though it is easy here, as with most adaptations of Dickens, to quibble with decisions about cuts and staging. For instance, through much of the film Warren Clarke plays Bradley Headstone as more sensitive and vulnerable than mechanical and self-suppressed, and John Collin's Rogue Riderhood is not exactly a sinister presence. Also, the characters of the "Social Chorus" are mostly conspicuous by their absence—no Fledgeby, no Lammles, no Podsnap, and no dinner party, even, to give us the "Voice of Society" at the story's close. Most of the serial also looks more theatrical than cinematic, its indoor scenes having been shot as if simply recording a play, while the few outdoor scenes provide much greater filmic authenticity. Mainly, the devil here is in the distracting inconsistency, which would be almost unthinkable with today's higher-budget, higher-quality productions.

The most recent BBC serial is such a production, and it is generally outstanding. Directed by Julian Farino and written by Sandy Welch, the serial aired in four 90-minute episodes from March 9–30, 1998, and it remains readily available on DVD both by itself and as part of the multi-DVD set *Charles Dickens Collection, Volume One*, which includes relatively recent BBC adaptations of *Oliver Twist*, *Martin Chuzzlewit*, *Bleak House*, *Hard Times*, and *Great Expectations*.[77] One of

---

[76] Leslie C. Staples, "When Found—," *Dickensian*, 55 (January 1959), p. 3. Also quoted in Brattin and Hornback, p. 18.

[77] Since the BBC has produced relatively new adaptations of *Bleak House* (2005) and *Great Expectations* (2011), it is worth pointing out that *Charles Dickens Collection, Volume*

Farino and Welch's most interesting decisions, in light of the 1976 adaptation, is that they restore much of the "Social Chorus," particularly the Lammles, and they also revert to Dickens's original plan for the narrative sequence by showing the Lammles marrying before John Rokesmith first comes to Mr. Boffin and before Venus enters the story at all. The 1998 film is also much darker than the 1976 one, owing partly to superior camera work but partly, too, to more sinister performances by David Morrissey as Headstone and David Bradley as Rogue Riderhood. The former, particularly, captures what the novel's admirers have always said about Headstone's intense self-suppression and psychological complexity. Timothy Spall, too, is excellent as Mr. Venus and earned a nomination for Best Actor in a television series from the British Academy of Film and Television Arts (BAFTA). Indeed, the 1998 *Our Mutual Friend* won four BAFTA awards and received several other nominations. On the other hand, this adaptation still gives us no Fledgeby, and very little of the Podsnaps or Veneerings. Obviously, here as in 1976, the decimation of the "Social Chorus" is a way of streamlining an enormous plot. But in both adaptations it also has the effect of stripping away some essential part of the novel's broader critique. For a big part of what the television serials miss is the novel's remarkable play with people and commodities—Veneering's bought election at Pocket-Breeches, Fledgeby's buying-up of the Lammles, Jenny's forcing the fine ladies to "try on," the narrative irruptions about "Shares" and the market in orphans—which unpacks and unfolds the implications of Gaffer's trade as if they are a set of Russian dolls. Admittedly, such a thing would be hard to put on the screen, and it is worth saying that the 1998 serial is surprisingly good at depicting the "pleasures of the chase." Still, for all its excellence, even the 1998 film cannot quite convey the symbolic and thematic unities at the heart of Dickens's novel.

Through it all, it is the novel itself that persists in all its weird, unwieldy, and unfilmable complexity and majesty, a final and ungovernable baggy monster that ended an era and quite nearly ended its author. And, strange to say, it may just be that *Our Mutual Friend*'s popular day is coming after all. The hoopla surrounding Dickens's bicentenary—itself an affirmation of Dickens's undiminished popularity—has produced during the last 12 months a great deal more evidence of *Our Mutual Friend*'s popular, rather than merely scholarly, presence. During 2011 the *Guardian* surveyed its readers on which Dickens novel was their favorite, and of course the overwhelming answer was *Great Expectations* followed somewhat distantly by *Bleak House* and *Copperfield*. *Our Mutual Friend* finished sixth, far ahead of its eleventh-place showing in Ford's 1968 study and significantly ahead of *Oliver Twist*, *The Old Curiosity Shop*, *Martin Chuzzlewit*, and *Little Dorrit*.[78] In her discussion of the results, columnist Alison Flood quotes Pulitzer Prize–winning novelist Jane Smiley, who participated in the survey and called *Our Mutual Friend* "one of my two or three favourite novels of all time," notable for its

---

One includes older versions of both films: *Bleak House* (Dir. Ross Devenish, 1985) and *Great Expectations* (Dir. Julian Amyes, 1981).

[78] Alison Flood, "*Great Expectations* Voted Readers' Favourite Dickens Novel," *Guardian*, October 3, 2011.

"magical" prose and "perfect blending of story and style."[79] Another, unidentified voter described the novel as "the great masterwork of Dickens's maturity."[80] The *Telegraph* got in on the Dickens fun, too, by inviting novelists Edmund White, Antonia Fraser, and David Lodge to choose their favorite passage from Dickens. Eschewing obvious possibilities like the beginning of *A Christmas Carol* or *A Tale of Two Cities*, White chose the passage from *Our Mutual Friend*'s Book 2, chapter 5, when Jenny Wren invites Fledgeby to "come up and be dead."[81] Columnist Martin Levin of the Canadian *Globe and Mail* wrote during early summer 2012 that his summer reading would include, among other things, his "favourite Dickens novel *Our Mutual Friend*," and in America *Time* magazine contributor Radhika Jones called the novel Dickens's fifth-best in her countdown of the Top Ten and suggested that it might have been higher except that, despite its brilliance, she cannot stomach the way that Dickens handles Bella's "education" at the hands of her husband and the Boffins.[82] Considering these accolades, it should almost go without saying that, in July 2012, when John Mullan compiled a list of the 10 greatest English novels to center upon a will, he gave *Our Mutual Friend* a place alongside *Sense and Sensibility* and *The Woman in White*.[83]

Impressed by so many recent mentions of *Our Mutual Friend* as one of Dickens's greatest novels, I decided as a final step in the research for this project to investigate—from a distance, at least—one last possible indicator of whether or not it has finally broken through into popular culture: the Dickens World theme park at Chatham in Kent, where, I conjectured, I might see for myself whether the park's creators had incorporated *Our Mutual Friend* into the single most obvious and bizarre attempt to popularize his work. Since opening in 2007 at a cost of £62 million, Dickens World has been both a minor tourist attract for Dickensians and something of a magnet for British primary and middle schoolers in need of an educational trip. It has also provoked fierce debate about whether it constitutes a "Disneyfication" that masks Dickens's very serious social concerns or rather a wildly postmodern opportunity to attract younger generations to his work.[84] The park had the misfortune to open its doors just as the global economy began to crash, so it has probably never attracted the 500,000 annual visitors its financers predicted during the planning. Unless things change soon, who knows how long it will survive—whether it will become a true fairyland like Boffin's Bower or

---

[79]   Ibid.

[80]   Ibid.

[81]   Edmund White, Antonia Fraser, and David Lodge, "Novelists Pick Their Favourite Dickens," *Telegraph*, January 7, 2012.

[82]   Martin Levin, "Cool Readings," *The Globe and Mail*, July 1, 2012; Radhika Jones, "Counting Down Dickens' Greatest Novels. Number 5: *Our Mutual Friend*," *Time*, February 1, 2012.

[83]   John Mullan, "John Mullan's 10 of the Best: Wills," *Guardian*, July 6, 2012.

[84]   John addresses this question intelligently and at length in her final chapter. See pp. 273–89.

The Voice of Society 155

rather a Tom-All-Alone's, left to the rankness and decay of a much-gilded and commodified age. Yet even in its current dismal grandeur, Dickens World provides some glimpse of how its owners hoped to market Dickens to the hobbyists and hobbledehoys of the twenty-first century. The park's website invites visitors to immerse themselves "in the sights, sounds and smells of nineteenth-century England"—I might pass on the smells—and experience a world made up of a "Great Expectations Log Flume," "Peggotty's Boathouse," a "Fagin's Den" play area, and even a scaled-down replica of the Marshalsea Prison. Excepting the last, these sites all come from the popular titles I expected to see represented, and in the case of the Marshalsea the implication really is that a park visitor should learn about its profound role in Dickens's childhood, not its significance to *Little Dorrit*.[85]

Then I noticed at the center of the park a reference that I had not really expected: a restaurant and pub called the Six Jolly Fellowship Porters—minus the shady waterside characters, I assume—where one can eat with friends, enjoy a drink and some good cheer, then wander across the way to a replica of the Britannia Theatre where, throughout the fall and winter, visitors to the park might enjoy a performance by George Michael, or the Maritime Jazz Festival, or even a tribute performance honoring late artists Luther Vandross and Whitney Houston. Though I have never been to Dickens World, it sounds almost Pickwickian, a carnival of stagey Victorianism and bizarre fun, consummate performers and devil-may-care charlatans delivering one-night-only shows against the backdrop of a grave and serious London that, as it happens, is never so serious after all. I wish we could know for sure how Dickens would have responded to such an impossibly funny thing as this park, with its unmistakable earnestness and almost unforgivable kitsch. Part of me wonders whether, overcome with horror, he would have crawled into an obscure corner of Peggotty's Boathouse to hide. He did this once, Forster tells us, at an appalling "serio-comic burletta" performance of *Oliver Twist* in 1838 "at the Surrey-theatre, when in the middle of the first scene he laid himself down upon the floor in a corner of the box and never rose from it until the drop-scene fell."[86] A much bigger part of me rather suspects that he would have been having too much fun not to laugh, that he would have been too delighted by the sheer madness of it all—the actors playing his characters, the Haunted House, the 4-D film about his life, the animatronix that "materialize Dickens's fascination with the animation of the inanimate world"—and by the fact, too, that the park is open on Sundays, clear evidence that he has finally won his long war against the Sabbatarians.[87] More than this, I think he would probably marvel at and be endlessly gratified by the enduring place he has earned, which is no more than the place he always intended to earn, in the histories of readership, social reform, and English letters, by writing books of serious intellectual content for the masses. He would be gratified, too, by the

---

[85] "Dickens World," Home page, *Dickens World*, 2012.

[86] *Letters* vol. 1, p. 388n; Forster, *Life*, p. 125.

[87] John, p. 282.

156   *Charles Dickens's* Our Mutual Friend

central place of *Our Mutual Friend* even in this strange park, at once the least and greatest emblem of the popular culture he helped to create.

III

This brings the story of *Our Mutual Friend* to the present day, which is both the bicentenary of Dickens's birth and very nearly the sesquicentennial of the novel. Readers generally admire the novel more than ever, but even Dickens fans are still not unanimous in singing its praises. Though he loves Dickens, Hornby asserts in his 2011 Introduction that what most separates *Our Mutual Friend* from Dickens's other novels is that, unlike the others, it has never "been able to shake free of its context and wander into our lives. There is no Micawber or Uriah Heep, no Scrooge, no Jarndyce versus Jarndyce or Gradgrind, no Miss Havisham, no Artful Dodger or Fagin or 'It was the best of times, it was the worst of times.'"[88] At first this seems right—it seems, that is, not just true but also explanatory of exactly what Dickens's readers missed in it during 1864–65 and for many a decade after. But there is another sense in which, however they may stay with us, the characters and incidents of *Pickwick* and *Nickleby*, of *A Christmas Carol* and even *Great Expectations*, are the ones that now seem so quaint and context bound: Mr. Pickwick skating at Dingley Dell, Joe Gargery hammering away at his forge. They were, as critics have often pointed out, anachronisms even when they were first published, retreats into the bygone England of Dickens's childhood, wrenched from his adult brain as extraordinary compounds of pathos, hilarity, and nostalgia. The measure of a great literary work, though, is its ability to endure. Many of Dickens's books do that because they make us laugh, because they contain an unforgettable character, or because they give us an unforgettable line. *Our Mutual Friend* may do none of these things, as Hornsby suggests. Yet it has done more than endure during the last 150 years. It has become better known, more critically esteemed, and more widely read decade by decade for the last half-century, and it seems to continue to do so with each passing year.

Shaw, who probably understood Dickens's work better than any other writer ever has, predicted it all a century ago. In a 1914 letter to the Sheffield Branch of the Dickens Fellowship, he wrote:

> If Dickens's day as a sentimental romancer is over, his day as a prophet and social critic is only dawning. Thackeray's England is gone, Trollope's England is gone; and even Thackeray and Trollope mixed with their truth a considerable alloy of what the governing classes like to imagine they were, and yet never quite succeeded in being. But Dickens's England, the England of Barnacle and Stiltstalking and Hamlet's Aunt, invaded and overwhelmed by Merdle and Veneering and Fledgeby,

---

[88]   Dickens, *Our Mutual Friend* (New York, 2011), p. xiii.

with Mr. Gradgrind theorizing, and Mr. Bounderby bullying in the provinces, is revealing itself in every day's news, as the real England we live in.[89]

As industrialism runs its course and capitalism matures and evolves, Dickens will become—has become—more and more relevant. And if this is so, it may be that *Our Mutual Friend*, in all the nightmarish glory of its indictment of Veneering and Podsnap, of public welfare that terrifies rather than raises up, of an economic system that depends upon and exults in the detritus of the human lives wrecked upon its shores, may yet supplant *Bleak House* and *Great Expectations* as the "best" book, the most important book, most read book that Dickens ever wrote. Of how many literary works, even among the most enduring, can we say with confidence that they resonate more strongly 150 years later than they did in their own day? We may be able to say this of *Our Mutual Friend* even now. And that, for Dickens, would assuredly have been enough.

---

[89]   Shaw, pp. 74–5.

Appendix 1
Dickens, Ellen Ternan, and Staplehurst

(A) "Mr Charles Dickens," from the Times, *June 7, 1858, p. 10*

We are requested to anticipate the publication of the following article:—
(From *Household Words* of Wednesday, June 9.)

Three and twenty years have passed since I entered on my present relations with the public. They began when I was so young that I find them to have existed for nearly a quarter of a century.

Through all that time I have tried to be as faithful to the public as they have been to me. It was my duty never to trifle with them or to deceive them, or presume upon their favour, or do anything with it but work hard to justify it. I have always endeavoured to discharge that duty.

My conspicuous position has often made me the subject of fabulous stories and unaccountable statements. Occasionally such things have chafed me, or even wounded me, but I have always accepted them as the shadows inseparable from the light of my notoriety and success. I have never obtruded any such personal uneasiness of mind upon the generous aggregate of my audience.

For the first time in my life, and I believe for the last, I now deviate from the principle I have so long observed, by presenting myself in my own journal in my own private character, and entreating all my brethren (as they deem that they have reason to think well of me, and to know that I am a man who has ever been unaffectedly true to our common calling) to lend their aid to the dissemination of my present words.

Some domestic trouble of mine of long standing, on which I will make no further remark than that it claims to be respected as being of a sacredly private nature, has lately been brought to an arrangement which involves no anger or ill-will of any kind, and the whole origin, progress, and surrounding circumstances of which have been, throughout, within the knowledge of my children. It is amicably composed, and its details have now but to be forgotten by those concerned in it.

By some means, arising out of wickedness, or out of folly, or out of inconceivable wild chance, or out of all three, this trouble has been made the occasion of misrepresentations, most grossly false, most monstrous, and most cruel—involving not only me, but innocent persons dear to my heart, and innocent persons of whom I have no knowledge if, indeed, they have any existence—and so widely spread that I doubt if one reader in a thousand will peruse these lines by whom some touch of the breath of these slanders will not have passed like an unwholesome air.

160   *Charles Dickens's* Our Mutual Friend

Those who know me and my nature need no assurance under my hand that such calumnies are as irreconcilable with me as they are, in their frantic incoherence, with one another. But there is a great multitude who know me through my writings, and who do not know otherwise; and I cannot bear that one of them should be left in doubt, or hazard of doubt, through my poorly shrinking from taking the unusual means to which I now resort of circulating the truth.

I most solemnly declare, then—and this I do, both in my own name and in my wife's—that all the lately whispered rumours touching the trouble at which I have glanced are abominably false, and that whosoever repeats one of them after this denial will lie as wilfully and as foully as it is possible for any false witness to lie before Heaven and earth.

CHARLES DICKENS.

(B) "Dreadful Railway Accident at Staplehurst," from the Times, *June 10, 1865, p. 9*

The two fatal accidents on the Great Western Railway have been followed by one even more startling on the South-Eastern line, and from the character of the train to which the disaster occurred the intelligence will be read with unusually painful interest. The fast tidal train, timed to leave Folkestone at 2 30 P.M. on the arrival of passengers from Boulogne, who quitted Paris yesterday morning at 7 o'clock, started, as usual, with almost 110 passengers, and proceeded nearly 30 miles on its journey, when, at a place called Staplehurst, the accident occurred which has been productive of such lamentable consequences. It appears that at this point the railway crosses a stream which in winter is of formidable dimensions and of considerable depth, but in summer shrinks to the proportions of a rivulet. On the bridge itself a plate had been loosened by the platelayers, and the engine running over this was thrown off the rails. Though displaced from its proper track the locomotive adhered to the permanent way, but the train broke into two parts, and seven or eight of the carriages plunged into or through the stream, a fall of several feet. These unhappy vehicles were so crushed and shattered to pieces that together they did not occupy the space of two whole carriages; cushions and luggage were thrown out, into, and upon the mud in all directions; and, as regards the occupants, the sad story was only too truthfully told in the telegram received in town shortly before 4 o'clock—"Several killed at Staplehurst; many more injured."

Mr. Eborall, the manager, and Mr. Knight, the traffic superintendent, on receipt of this information immediately left London-bridge, and proceeded to the spot in a special train, taking with them Mr. Sidney Jones, of St. Thomas's Hospital, Mr. Adams, of the London Hospital (surgeon to the company), Dr. Palfrey, Dr. Maule Sutton, and such other medical aid as could be procured at the moment. Assistance was also summoned from Ashford and Tunbridge, so that before very long 20 medical men, at least, were on the spot. There was but too much need for the services of one and all. A glance at the condition of the train and a hasty

Appendix 1: Dickens, Ellen Ternan, and Staplehurst

recognition of the class to which its occupants belonged showed that it was no ordinary accident which had occurred. The carriages that went down into the water were so twisted, flattened, and turned upon their sides that it was impossible to say whether the unfortunate travelers inside had been killed outright by the shock or suffocated as they lay in the water and mud. Those of the passengers who escaped injury in the first instance behaved nobly towards their fellows in distress; there was no standing irresolute on the bank; everything that willing hands could do was done, and done at once; but, in spite of every effort, ten lives had been lost beyond recall, and 20 is the lowest estimate that has been formed as to the wounded.

Mr. Hoare, a resident in the district, placed his carriage at the disposal of the medical staff, and valuable assistance was rendered by this agency in dealing with cases of the greatest emergency. In the confusion which prevailed, and owing to the manifest reluctance of most of the sufferers to alarm their friends by disclosing their names, the greatest difficulty was experienced in collecting anything like accurate information as to the casualties. Several of the dead remain still without identification, all that is known of one party being that they were persons of some position returning from India.

In the course of the evening successive trains brought to London those of the party whose condition fitted them to travel; but frequently it was evident that they themselves were scarcely conscious of the extent of the shock they had undergone. One gentleman had sustained serious injuries about the head. In two or three instances members of a party into which death had intruded came sadly and unaccompanied to town. One case of this kind was peculiarly affecting. A gentleman, evidently in acute pain, but in still greater distress of mind, carried, half unconsciously, the bonnet worn by his wife on the journey that was so lamentably and, in her case, fatally interrupted. Among those brought to London by their friends in the course of the evening were Mr. Graham, who proceeded to the St. James's Hotel, suffering from injuries to the leg and face; Madame Gouverneur, of York-house, Twickenham, contused and shaken; Mr. Blow, Tavistock Hotel, severely injured about the head; Mr. J. P. Lord, of Bolton, Lancashire, and Mrs. Lord, taken to the Castle and Falcon, Aldersgate street, Mrs. Lord having received severe injuries; and Mrs. Adams Hampson, who had received cuts on the head and face, this lady's husband being among the killed. Another lady, name unascertained, was taken to Guy's Hospital.

The friends of those known to have been in the train were scarcely less to be pitied than the sufferers themselves. Both at London-bridge and Charing-cross stations large numbers of eager inquirers gathered, the news of the accident having attained immediate and almost universal circulation, owing, doubtless, to the circumstance that the railway accidents occurring previously had prepared the public to watch for the next in the series of disasters that on these occasions follow each other with the fatal regularity of fires.

Mr. Charles Dickens had a narrow escape. He was in the train, but, fortunately for himself and for the interests of literature, received no injuries whatever. The disaster, it is thought, would have been even greater had it not been for the unusual amount of break-power [sic] incorporated with the train. In addition to the ordinary leverage power exerted in the three guards' vans, there were patent breaks [sic] as well, of the kind known as Cremer's, an American invention, supposed to possess properties of peculiar value in arresting the progress of a train. Taking into account the control exercised over the engine, there were no less than seven breaks in all regulating the speed of the train.

By the last of the special trains which reached town at or after 1 o'clock this morning two other gentlemen with injuries of a serious character reached town. These were Mr. Hunt, of Dalston, and a French gentleman, M. le Marchant, whose hip was fractured. The family and friends of Mr. Moss, partner in the firm of Messrs. Defries, chandelier manufacturers, of Houndsditch, were so uneasy on his account that, after the receipt of two or three telegrams from his medical attendants, they proceeded to Staplehurst by special train. It was understood, however, that in the case of this gentleman the injuries were principally confined to the foot.

The railway authorities appear to have recognized and admitted from the first the very severe character of the accident, and the necessity of affording full information to the public. Mr. Dyne, the superintendent of the London-bridge Terminus, in reply to eager and incessant inquiries, afforded all the information that was in his power; and his superiors added, on their return to town, such further details as the result of the inquiries enabled them to furnish. The provision made for the relief of the sufferers was, as already stated, prompt and ample. With the exception of one of the guards, who received contusions, and of the engineer and fireman, who were shaken but not otherwise hurt, the company's servants escaped miraculously, so that in this case there will be no difficulties in the way of a searching inquiry, such as are commonly encountered when death has withdrawn one of the witnesses whose evidence might be most material. The police have felt it right to take into custody the foreman of the gang of platelayers, responsible for the condition of the portion of the line at which the accident occurred. It will, of course, be matter for inquiry hereafter whether the plate was, in fact, improperly removed and the accident thereby occasioned; whether the flag protecting the operations of the platelayers was sent back to a sufficient distance, and there placed so that it could be seen by the engine-driver. But it would be plainly premature, as well as unjust towards the prisoner, to allude here to any of the rumours current on these points.

Suffice it to say the causes leading to the most lamentable interruption of what, though a tidal and therefore irregular service, has hitherto been a singularly safe one, will need probing to the very bottom, if public confidence in the present system of maintaining the permanent way is, after two recent accidents so very similar in their nature, to be restored.

The inquest upon the remains of the deceased will be opened formally this afternoon, but, pending complete identification, will probably be adjourned till Monday next.

Appendix 1: Dickens, Ellen Ternan, and Staplehurst 163

(C) "Charles Dickens Relieving the Sufferers at the Fatal Railway Accident, Near Staplehurst," from the Penny Illustrated Paper, *June 24, 1865, front page*

CHARLES DICKENS RELIEVING THE SUFFERERS AT THE FATAL RAILWAY ACCIDENT, NEAR STAPLEHURST.—SEE "GOSSIPER," PAGE 54.

Appendix 2
The Manuscript, the Proof Sheets, and the Berg Copy

The aim of this Appendix is to give complete particulars, as much as possible, respecting the conditions and locations of the three items I identify in Chapter 2 as the chief research resources available to scholars of the novel: the manuscript of *Our Mutual Friend*, the Proof sheets, and the Berg copy. Readers should consult Chapter 2, as well, since I try not to repeat here information I have already given.

The manuscript is owned by the Pierpont Morgan Library and Museum in New York and is described in their finding aid as items MA 1202 and MA 1203 in their Literary and Historical Manuscript collection. It was, the aid notes, "[f]ormerly bound in 2 vols. in ¾ brown morocco" but is now described as "(ca. 471 p.), unbound." In total, the manuscript as organized and held by the Morgan consists of the following materials, divided into two boxes. Box 1 (MA 1202) begins with certain letters and other documents related to the manuscript, including the date January 4, 1866 in Dickens's hand (perhaps from his inscription to Dallas), and contains thereafter Dickens's 10 monthly number plans for Volume 1 (fols 4–13) and 230 slips of the novel itself (fols 14–247), though the Morgan counts these as 234 slips for the reasons I describe in Chapter 2. Box 2 (MA 1203) contains 225 total slips, beginning with the nine monthly number plans for Volume 2 (Nos. 19/20 are planned together on one page) and continuing with 213 pages for the novel (fols 10–222) and 3 additional slips for the "Postscript" (fols 223–4), though the second of these is unnumbered as it only contains a single sentence to be inserted in another page. The last page of the Postscript, folio 224, rather than the last page of the novel itself bears on its verso in Dickens's hand "Our Mutual Friend / Nos. XIX and XX." Owing to recent conservation work, the chapters of the manuscript are now divided and each is protected by a Mylar sheath. Because of its fragility and uniqueness, the manuscript of *Our Mutual Friend* is available only to scholars working on projects for which study of the original is indispensable. Others may be asked to study the microfilm in lieu of the original, and determinations on this front are made case by case by the Morgan's curatorial staff. Provenance information does not indicate how the manuscript passed from its initial owner, Dallas, to Mr. George W. Childs of Philadelphia. But it does show that Childs bequeathed it subsequently to the Drexel Institute of Technology, and that the Morgan purchased it at the Drexel Institute Sale (as Catalog number 67) in New York on November 17, 1944.

The Proof sheets volume is owned by the New York Public Library and is part of the Henry W. and Albert A. Berg Collection of English and American literature. As Brattin and Hornback point out, though the Berg's catalogue describes the

166   *Charles Dickens's* Our Mutual Friend

volume "as a 'presentation copy, from the author to the illustrator, Marcus Stone,' the proofs are not inscribed by Dickens, and there is no accompanying letter."[1] Instead, the only real identifying information comes from Dickens's occasional revisions, and from the verso of page 309 in the volume—the last page of the Postscript—which bears the typeset designation "London: / Printed by William Clowes and Sons, Stamford Street / and Charing Cross."[2] Brattin and Hornback also point out, as I have in Chapter 2, that the proofs seem to have come from both corrected and uncorrected sets gathered at different times. The volume remains worth noting, but its utility to scholars is very much compromised by its uncertain origins and uneven contents, as well as by the fact that no single part of the proofs appears necessarily to be a definitive or final set of corrections to the novel.

The Berg copy of *Our Mutual Friend* is another issue altogether, for it far surpasses the Proof sheets in the interest it may have for scholars of the novel. As I indicate in Chapter 2, the Berg copy is, at its core, a two-volume first edition from Chapman and Hall that was at some point unbound, heavily grangerized, then rebound in two volumes. It now stands as a stunning repository of materials related to *Our Mutual Friend*—one that might be of considerable use to scholars, but that seems mostly to have been left alone. Its key elements are the monthly wrappers and advertisers collected at the back of each volume and the manuscript illustrations by Stone. In the case of the former, it is perhaps worth saying that although a wrapper and "Advertiser" appears for each month of serialization, library stickers and other identifiers on the wrappers show that the collected materials did not all come from a single source or location, and the card catalog entry (see below) makes it clear that some advertisements are missing. Too, the wrappers are collected in sequence first, and the advertisers are collected in sequence thereafter, so it is harder work than it first appears to be sure of the publication date of any particular "Advertiser" or to discern where one ends and the next begins. In the case of Stone's manuscript illustrations, I have tried in Chapter 2 to discuss their most noteworthy features and particularly how they differ, sometimes substantially, from those published. Another pair of eyes might see other items of significance.

Those seeking the Berg copy should be advised that the Berg Collection's card catalogue simply calls it "Copy 4" and describes it as follows:

> 4. 2 v. Rebound by Riviere & son as 22 1/2 cm. Covers and advertisements bound in at end of volumes. Back cover of no.1 wanting. Some advertisements wanting; a few additional advertisements inserted. Extra illustrated with 2 proof engravings of portraits of Dickens; the 40 original drawings of the illustrations (12 with captions in Dickens' hand), also the proofs on India paper; the original sketch and proof on India paper of the wrapper of the parts; 5 small sketches of details or figures for the completed drawings; 15 proofs on India paper of the illustrations for a later edition of the work. M. C. D. Borden bookplate.

---

[1]   Brattin and Hornback, p. 6.

[2]   Proof sheets, vol. 2, p. 309.

Appendix 2: The Manuscript, the Proof Sheets, and the Berg Copy 167

The two volumes are bound in attractive green boards with black spines and gold lettering, and the pages are gilt-edged at the top. As for provenance, at least with respect to Stone's illustrations, the card catalogue in the Berg Collection offers none, but in *Dickens and His Illustrators* (1899) Frederic G. Kitton observes that "[t]he original sketches of 'Our Mutual Friend' were disposed of by the artist, many years ago, to the late Mr. F. W. Cosens," a collector of Dickensiana.[3] From Cosens in 1890 Stone's sketches went to auction at Sotheby's, where the series of 40 illustrations sold for £66 to a purchaser acting on behalf of a "well-known firm of American publishers."[4] At the time when Kitton was writing, he could only say that "the treasured volume now reposes in the library of a New York Collector"—quite possibly this was in the private library of Albert Berg, who, of the brothers, was the great Dickens *aficionado*, and who along with Henry accumulated a massive collection in Victorian literature over several decades late in the nineteenth and early in the twentieth century in the brothers' town house on East 73rd Street in New York.[5]

---

[3]   Kitton, p. 201.

[4]   Ibid.

[5]   Ibid.

Appendix 3
Contemporary Reviews of
Our Mutual Friend

The following items are complete transcriptions of 41 reviews and notices of *Our Mutual Friend* that appeared during and just after its serial run and first publication in two volumes. They include reviews from England and the United States, since the novel was published simultaneously on both sides of the Atlantic. Six appeared abridged in *Dickens: The Critical Heritage* (ed. Philip Collins) in 1971; two appeared abridged and James's appeared in full in *Charles Dickens:* Hard Times, Great Expectations, *and* Our Mutual Friend, *A Casebook* (ed. Norman Page) in 1979; and James's appeared in full in *The Dickens Critics* (eds George Ford and Lauriat Lane) in 1961. Additionally, in 1984 Brattin and Hornback's Our Mutual Friend: *An Annotated Bibliography* identified and annotated, but did not reproduce, 33 of the 41 reviews and notices included here. In other words, eight of the reviews that follow are entirely new, and very few have been collected or reprinted fully in prior volumes. Here they are complete except in those instances when *Our Mutual Friend* was reviewed in a longer essay dealing with multiple works. In such cases, all portions of the essay dealing with *Our Mutual Friend* appear here in full. No reviews were signed, as was typical during the 1860s, but earlier scholars have identified authors for eight of them, and I identify another here.

The reviews are therefore arranged into two categories: "Identified," for the nine cases in which the identity of the reviewer is known, and "Unidentified" for the 32 cases in which the author remains anonymous. Within each group, I have further arranged the reviews in order of publication date, which means that both the "Identified" and "Unidentified" groups begin with reviews that appeared during, not after, serialization.

A few further notes on the "Identified" reviews are worth mentioning. The authorship of items C and F, which I give as reviews by Chorley for the *Athenaeum* and Dallas for the *Times*, respectively, is confirmed by Dickens's own letters to both men in 1865.[1] Brattin and Hornback give Alfred Hudson Guernsey, editor of *Harper's New Monthly Magazine* during the period of *Our Mutual Friend*'s serial run, as the author of Items A, B, and E and John Richard de Capel Wise as the author of Item I, "Belles Lettres" from the *Westminster Review*, though I have here corrected their dating of that essay to April 1866 (Volume 85) rather than April 1868, which they give in their bibliography.[2] Item D, which I describe as a review by John Forster for the *Examiner*, was unsigned when published,

---

[1] See *Letters*, vol. 11, pp. 102, 117.

[2] Brattin and Hornback, p. 41.

170   *Charles Dickens's* Our Mutual Friend

but Philip Collins has demonstrated that Forster contributed the review.[3] Item H, Henry James's review in *The Nation*, has been known as James's work since at least 1908, when it was reprinted as "The Limitations of Dickens" in *Views and Reviews*.[4] Of all the "Identified" reviews, item G may be of especial interest, for it is a review of *Our Mutual Friend* almost certainly written by William Dean Howells, then 28 years old and writing for several magazines including *The Round Table*, where this review of *Our Mutual Friend* appeared. Major biographies of Howells mention that he read and admired Dickens's novel in 1865, but not that he composed and published a review. Signed "W. D. H." and making a distinction between the "novelist" and the "romancer" that would become characteristic of his essays, however, the *The Round Table* review is certainly his work.

Page numbers given in the heading to each review indicate the page(s) on which material about Dickens and *Our Mutual Friend* appears. For full bibliographic citations, including comprehensive page ranges for those reviews that include works other than *Our Mutual Friend*, consult the "Contemporary Reviews of *Our Mutual Friend*" section in the Bibliography.

Finally, for the sake of clarity, I offer the following note on the texts of these reviews. Except in two ways—and apart from the observation above that I have, in the cases of essays reviewing multiple books, included only the material related to *Our Mutual Friend*—I have not in any way corrected, amended, or abridged the essays that follow. Ellipses, misspellings, errors in punctuation, and the like should all be understood as *original to the review*, even though in many cases the errors are obvious. I have transcribed rather than edited, except with respect to two matters. First, in the cases of reviews that include extended quotations from *Our Mutual Friend*, I have reformatted those quotations to show an indented left margin and slightly smaller font, since Victorian periodicals had rather inconsistent ways of using punctuation to indicate the beginnings and endings of quotations—or worse, of hardly indicating these things at all. I have, therefore, deleted the original indications of such quotations and used indenting and modernized quotation marks consistently throughout all of the essays to show quotes from the novel. Second, in three cases when printer error has made a word indecipherable or where the content is such that it might create confusion, I have provided a footnote for clarification.

Identified Reviews

(A) [Alfred Hudson Guernsey], from "Editor's Easy Chair," Harper's New Monthly Magazine, June 1864, p. 135

It is no more necessary to invite our friends to read Dickens's new story than to exhort them to eat the fresh strawberries. They will be very sure to do both; and in both cases they will find the old flavor unimpaired. Dickens begins "Our

---

[3] Philip Collins, "Dickens's Self-estimate: Some New Evidence," in Robert B. Partlow (ed.), *Dickens the Craftsman: Strategies of Presentation* (Carbondale, 1970), pp. 21–43.

[4] See Henry James, *Views and Reviews* (Boston, 1908), pp. 153–61.

Appendix 3: Contemporary Reviews of Our Mutual Friend   171

Mutual Friend" with a buoyancy which shows all the vitality and opulence of his genius—just as Thackeray's "Denis Duval" reveals the unshaken and riper power of Thackeray. Had the latter only lived we should have renewed the old delightful days of Pendennis and Bleak House, when the two great athletes contended, and every generous reader wished each combatant to win. Only one remains, but the other still speaks to us. In the pages of our next Number will be found both Thackeray's "Denis Duval" and Dickens's "Our Mutual Friend;" and rich as all other Magazines may be, we are modestly content with our own.

(B) [Alfred Hudson Guernsey], from "Editor's Easy Chair," Harper's New Monthly Magazine, August 1864, p. 407

We hope that no reader omits the new novel of Dickens, "Our Mutual Friend," in the vain expectation of reading it when it is finished and published collectively. If he does, he loses a great deal of pleasure every month, and declines to prolong his delight. The sale of the first number, separately, in London, was forty thousand copies within the first few days. Nor is that surprising, for the work is as gushing and exuberant as any of his long list. The humor is more rollicking than in any tale he has written for many a year, while its curious and various revelations of the lower strata of London life are as much contributions to history as the extraordinary pictures of Paris in "A Tale of Two Cities."

The fertility of Dickens's power is amazing. There is a general resemblance of manner in his stories, but there is very little repetition of character. His profusion is Shakespearian. But that which Shakespeare could do perfectly, and beyond comparison in literature, Dickens can not do at all. He can not draw a gentleman. Noble men and transcendently heroic women he delineates with love and skill. Common and uncommon people he pictures as few have ever done. But a figure like Hamlet, like Mercutio, like Sir Philip Sidney, like the Master of Ravenswood, does not move across his page. Of course, the absence is noted only because the company is so rich and various. Upon the Rialto we look to see representatives of all the world.

Never forget that every number of the tale has a certain completeness, and that serial reading in these days is a most desirable and economical habit.

(C) [Henry Chorley], "Our Mutual Friend," Athenaeum, October 28, 1865, pp. 569–70

A new novel by the greatest novelist living is not to be dismissed with a few jaunty phrases of rapture, or of qualification; for a simple yet serious reason. Those who, with understanding, as distinct from that wonderment which belongs to the foolish face of praise, have followed Mr. Dickens throughout his career of authorship cannot fail to have perceived that time and success have not made him careless,—whether as concerns his art, his public, or himself. As little have they spoilt, or dimmed, or turned aside his quick sympathies, his power of minute observation, his keen desire to advocate what he deems right, his wondrous force of hand and colour as a painter in words. Every true and conscientious man becomes increasingly solicitous on these points with time and success. The boy may dash off a brilliant sketch as a matter of course: the ripe artist will ponder over his coming picture. But may he not ponder too long and over-solicitously? This question, we fancy, may be asked with respect to 'Our Mutual Friend.' Only the other day its author gave us that French story of 'Little Bebelle,' one of the most exquisite pieces of pathos in fiction, the value of which will be best tested by comparing it with Sterne's Shandy-isms. Only yesterday, out of a dingy street in the Strand, from no more promising place than a lodging-house, the artist by a touch brought to light a homely, loving fellow-creature, worthy to "sit above the salt" among the best of the best; *Mrs. Lirriper*—as real "a being of the mind" as *Mr. Pickwick*, as *Mrs. Gamp*, as the *Micawbers*,—as any of the long line of living creatures called up by the novelist, whom we know intimately, in all their strength and weakness, and whose deeds and sayings have passed into household words.

If, therefore, we say that, during the course of fragmentary publication, 'Our Mutual Friend' has raised more question than certain of its predecessors, the circumstance arises from the nature of the story, and not because the fountain of variety shows signs of exhaustion. None of the series is so intricate in plot as this tale. It would be wasted labour to detail or analyze a chain of events which every one has already handled. Enough to state our conviction, that the closest attention is required to hold certain of its connecting links. From the first number it was evident to us that the murdered John Harmon was not murdered, but had set himself down in the household of the wife allotted to him by the fantastic will, for the purpose of testing her real nature. The circumstances of the deed, which led to his shipmate Radfoot being mistaken for, and murdered with, himself, are mistily revealed in the long soliloquy during which he determines on the renunciation of his identity. Some incompleteness, referable to partial recollection, may have been an intentional stroke of art on the novelist's part—may belong to the nature of the catastrophe, but it produces an impression of uncertainty. Then, again, the complications of the story may have necessitated sharp turns and surprises, which bear unfavourably on some of the characters. We fancy the conversion of Bella Wilfer, the capricious beauty longing for wealth and emancipation from her portentous mother and shrewish sister, to be somewhat too sudden,—even though it did grow out of her dismal experience of the simulated avarice overgrowing Mr. Boffin. This avarice, again, however adroitly devised and minutely wrought out as a piece of masquerade, leading to a final surprise for which no one can have been prepared, has, of necessity, implied the introduction of some elements discordant with those of the character so forcibly conceived and broadly sketched. The honest, truthful Boffin of the Mounds, whose simple right-mindedness virtually overruled his wretched old miser-master who had the fortune to leave, might have been led by his desire to right what was wrong and to regenerate what was defective, to connive in the scheme of amending the coquetries of Bella, the oddly-designated bride of the great fortune; but his inability to carry such a long-drawn piece of

Appendix 3: Contemporary Reviews of Our Mutual Friend   173

subtle comedy through, we beg (respectfully to our great novelist) to question. And we are satisfied that so great-hearted a man should not on any excuse of plot or plan whatsoever, or any desire to "lead on" a miserable knave to the full display of his greed and knavery, have been submitted to the degradation of the scene with Wegg, after the discovery of old Harmon's second will, in the house of the anatomical curiosity-monger. That which belongs and befits a detective policeman, apt at disguises as *Mr. Bucket* of never-to-be-forgotten memory, sits ill on an honest, ignorant, affectionate creature, such as he is. And though we love Mrs. Boffin, the comfortable and instinctively-delicate woman (one of Mr. Dickens's most genial creations), with all our hearts, we cannot but feel as if we owed her a grudge for her connivance. Truth and nature are here strained, in subservience to the requirements of literary art.

We fancy that the necessity of conducting an unusually large crowd of characters through a maze of unusual intricacy has told on other of the personages of the story. Harmon, its hero, is, by his position, betwixt light and dark, inevitably partially effaced. Bella, the coquettish daughter of Mrs. Wilfer the stupendous, is capitally touched in the cameleon hues of her character, and royally righted at last; but during a large part of the tale she keeps us in a state of perpetual uneasiness, hardly justifying the love she is described as inspiring. Then Lizzie Hexam, though not precisely a sketch, has not substance enough for the place she is expected to fill in the reader's interest. Lastly, we cannot conceive the possibility of a man so holy, humble, affectionate and beneficent as Riah the Hebrew on any grounds of compact, obligation or sophistry, lending himself, one hour after it was known, to the hypocritical wickedness of such a tyrant as Fledgeby, the usurer, the meanest creature (this is saying much) as yet created by the hand that painted the money-lenders in 'Nickleby'; and *Brass*, and *Krook*, and *Fagin*, and *Uriah Heep*. The explanation made by him at last to the little weird doll's dressmaker shows us that Mr. Dickens has felt the necessity of some explanation, which is insufficient to convince us. We cannot but be reminded by it of an awkwardness, somewhat similar, in Miss Edgeworth's 'Ormond,'—a tale expressly undertaken by her in atonement for what had been represented to her as too wholesale a depreciation of a people against whom "every man has his hand."

Thus much by way of qualification,—or call it speculation rather,—concerning a novel which gains immensely by being perused without "stop, let, or hindrance." On returning to the characters, that of Bradley Headstone, the schoolmaster, dogged, sensual, unready;—his tremendous passions compressed by the responsibilities and respectabilities of his position, takes the foremost place among them as an original conception. Frightfully though he suffers, even though when he confronts Wrayburn, his *poco-curante* rival, there is a show of reason and of championship on his side, there is no possibility of any one's feeling a moment's pity on his behalf, so utterly is the master-desire of his life rendered unlovable by the forms in which it is clad. There have been many murders, and many pictures of remorse in novels;—and none more powerful than the pages in which we were shown the wanderings of *Bill Sykes*, and the slinking home of *Jonas Chuzzlewit*, after his bloody deed in the wood; but Mr. Dickens has exceeded even those in the scene where the wretched criminal, tortured by the rebuking consciousness of his having failed in his diabolical design, is dogged and dragged back to the fatal spot by his hideous confidant. Nothing can be more masterly as a display of blank, inevitable retribution and wretchedness. Redeeming touch there is none about Bradley Headstone; even the concealed love for him of the soft-hearted, prim little schoolmistress, delicately indicated as it is, fails to furnish it.

To change the fancy,—the author of 'Pickwick' never revelled among richer whimsies than are to be found in the comic parts of this tale;—in the Veneering household, and the guests assembled by it. The mistress of the mansion and of the camels on the dinner-table, with her readiness to weep, her stupid sentimentalities about "Baby," her inane admiration of the prancing gossip of that old mechanical harridan, Lady Tippins, because the same passes with her as a fashionable pearl of great price,—the portentous Podsnap, who knocks down argument by British sentiments and laconic, insolent dogmatism,—the civil, misty, nobly-connected old Twemlow (who would be a true gentleman, every inch of him, were he not a little too promiscuously willing to sit at anybody's feast),—the pair of lawyers, Mortimer and Eugene (whose sincerity of attachment one for the other is not the worst point in the book),—the *supers* (as they say on the stage) Boots and Brewer,— are all new people in print, whom every diner-out has met every week of his life in private. The vivacity and variety of this division of the novel are admirable. But when talking of dinners in 'Our Mutual Friend,' we must not forget the most incomparable dinner of all, that of the newly-married couple, Bella and John, at Greenwich, for the sake of the sentimental waiter, "the young man on liking," so ignominiously thrust aside by the arch-potentate in waiting, who conceived that he had alone a right to the solemn monopoly of the secret of the day.

We must stop,—though touches and traits rise on us by the hundred, justifying what has been said, that 'Our Mutual Friend' is one of Mr. Dickens's richest and most carefully-wrought books. If we demur to Wegg and to Miss Jenny Wren as to a pair of eccentrics approaching that boundary-line of caricature towards which their creator is, by fits, tempted, we cannot recall anything more real, more cheering, than the sketch of the Milveys,—clergyman and clergyman's wife, both so unconscious in their self-sacrificing virtue and goodness, yet the two so capitally discriminated by the extra touch of zeal and briskness (and suspicion of the Jews) on the woman's part. It might be suggested that too much space is given to the impostor-couple, the Lammles, and their designs on Podsnap's poor, foolish little daughter; but, again, how capitally thrown in to the woman's part is its scrap of shame and of remorseful feeling! Her figure, ere she quits the scene, unconsciously sketching on the table-cloth with her parasol, is not to be forgotten, as marked by that attitude and occupation.

Enough, then, has been said to indicate in what point of view we conceive this novel may be regarded, and to prove that, on its being read and read again, every lover of types of human character, every student of Art in fiction, every man who has "humour" in his soul, will find, each and all, enjoyment. If, as regards broad

Appendix 3: Contemporary Reviews of Our Mutual Friend 175

outline, there are former stories by Mr. Dickens which we prefer,—if, among his tales, we rank the highest 'David Copperfield,' which includes, so to say, neither plot nor surprise,—'Our Mutual Friend' must be signalized for an accumulation of fine, exact, characteristic detail, such as would suffice to set up in trade for life a score of the novel-spinners who give us situations without motives, scenes without characters, words without thoughts, and the dialogue, not of real life, but of melo-drama.

(D) [John Forster], "Our Mutual Friend*," Examiner, October 28, 1865, pp. 681–2*

Latinized races accuse English writers of a disregard of unity in works of art, and yet there is no great English work of imagination that does not recognize it in a far higher degree than is involved in acceptance of the classic formula for securing an external unity in respect of time and place and action. We rightly hold the imagination capable of passing with ease over intervals of space and time, and although we recognize even more thoroughly than our neighbours the demand for unity and action, what we mean by that is not outward simplicity and singleness of plot, but a well-harmonized relation of all parts to one central thought; ideal unity that lies far deeper than any of those considerations on which the old triad of classic unities is based. Every great English work of imagination, every good work of art, all the world over, is, as it were, a crystallization of thought about some one central idea. Nowhere, perhaps, is the sense of this true unity so perfectly shown as in the literature of England. In Shakesepare, grave or gay, it is distinctly seen. Every turn of the light trifling in *Love's Labour's Lost*, every character of the play, blends with the rest in a poet's graceful jest over the taste of his day for idle ornament. In the plot nothing is done. All the ingenious rhyming of the courtiers agrees with the state of Don Armado with the brave outside, who, being called upon to strip to his shirt and fight, owns that he has not a shirt to his back under all his bravery. In the *Merchant of Venice* the play crystallizes round the central thought of the relation between justice and mercy, law and gospel. In *King Lear* earthly sovereignty breaks like a bubble on the wind as it flies through the stir of the grand forces of Nature. In *Julius Cæsar* the central thought is the problem of government. The supreme sovereignty of Cæsar, the philosophical republicanism of Brutus, the self-seeking republicanism of Cassius, and all other parts of the play, show, as it were, the different faces of the crystal of which all parts have their harmonious relation to the single point of thought. If we turn from Shakespeare to Fielding, in *Tom Jones*, broad as the canvas is on which that work is painted, and crowded as it is with various incident, there also we find every detail tending to one centre, the idea of the relation of man to society. Jones and Blifil are types of the two opposite halves of the social world: Jones faulty but honest, his faults open and incurring blame; Blifil keeping the faults of a worse nature secret, giving a fair show to the worst acts and escaping blame. In the relation of man with society open truth is contrasted with false seeming; and the episode of the Old Man of the Hill is contrived to provide for the middle case of the man who cuts the knot of the social problem by avoiding conversation with his fellows.

Mr Dickens invariably fulfils in his novels this condition of deep seated unity which has been always recognized in English art. All readers can feel that he does so, and some readers who have paid little attention to good literature have raised thereupon arguments upon the propriety or impropriety of 'writing with a purpose;' as if any thing worth reading, anything worth seeing, anything worth hearing, were ever produced or uttered without a purpose to express a distinct individual meaning of some sort. There must be in every good novel, play, or poem one true thought for the mainspring that keeps all its wheels in action; and we must start from the mainspring if we would trace properly the movement of the works.

In this novel of *Our Mutual Friend* the argument is of the soul of life among the fictions of society. We are shown in the first chapter Lizzie Hexam, a true-hearted girl in a position as degraded as imagination can conceive without stain to her inner purity. She is bringing a pure heart to a revolting way of life; her father supports a wretched home among scum of the riverside by fishing for drowned men. In this girl chiefly, but not in her only, we are, as the story grows, to see the radiance of the soul of life. We turn from her and the deep social degradation of her outward life, at once, in the second chapter, to the other side of the book's argument, the fictions of society. These are typified throughout by the friends, collected round the dinner-table of the Veneerings. The Veneerings themselves have their root in nothing, being social Jonah's gourds under whose leaves (leaves of a dinner-table) prophets of society extend their legs as long as the gourd flourishes. There is Podsnap, the pompous, unimaginative oracle, who sweeps behind him what he does not choose to see. There is the great speculator, who adds up the right and wrong of life in three parallel columns of figures. There are Boots and Brewer, types of the throng of people in society whose thoughts are but faint echoes of other men's opinions. There is the incarnation of the whole company, the genius of the heartless, frivolous, vain, and exceedingly ill-favoured Society consisting of the knot of empty folks who are most apt to call themselves the World, in Lady Tippins. Yet even conventional society, thus uttering its censures around Mr Veneering's table, is not in every member selfish. There belongs to it, even in this its heartless form, faint representation of a subdued generosity and honour, and we have that in the timid Mr Twemlow. The book ends with Society's discussion of affairs under Mr Veneering's presidency; he is president for the last time, since the worm has its teeth already at the root of his gourd, but he will not want a successor. Of two friends, careless, thoughtless, and therefore half heartless, who had joined listlessly the circle of the Veneerings, endured the flirtations of Lady Tippins, and by the foremost of whom—Eugene Wrayburn—evil was wrought for want of thought, that Eugene receives slowly the warmth of a true life into his heart from Lizzie Hexam, and at last makes her his wife. Eugene's comrade hears, as the book closes, the verdict of Society upon the deserter, and he gets it from each member of the typical group about the Veneerings' dinner-table. But the last voice taken,—they had almost forgotten to ask his opinion,—was Twemlow's, and it put the rest to silence; for among the mean and shallow fictions of society Twemlow brought, boldly for once, as a true gentleman, his sense of the reality of the great soul of life.

Appendix 3: Contemporary Reviews of Our Mutual Friend   177

Within the bounds thus marked for the elaboration of the main idea, there is everywhere the same essential unity with the liveliest variety of detail. There is a great heap of money in the centre of the story, made out of dust by a dustman, and treated as a dust-heap in comparison with human truth and tender graces of the mind. There is a Bella Wilfer, whose character, at every period full of light and shade, is shown also in process of development,—our literature does not contain a happier study of light girlish grace advancing, with no loss of charms, into a pure womanly earnestness. Bella, when young, believes that she is sordid. She has come out of a mean home into the daily relish of what wealth can buy; is guest and friend of Mr and Mrs Boffin, social nobodies, who happen, for a time, to sit on the gold heap with homely honest hearts that love of gold can never spoil. Then the Boffins join with Bella's lover, to whom really all the gold belongs, in plot for the girl's education and the fetching out of the true soul of life known to be in her. Boffin covers himself with glory,—and much mystifies the reader of the novel,—by appearing in the character of a man spoilt by wealth and turned into a greedy miser. Everybody knows how the story runs, and so we need not describe at length or quote any of its passages. We would only show that in this central plot also of *Our Mutual Friend,* as in the outlying incidents connected with it, the inner thought of the book is still the same; is of the soul of life greater than all the fictions of society. To this design belongs the sharp contrasting of such characters as Mr and Mrs Boffin and Mr and Mrs Lammle; the story of the strong heart of Betty Higden, who showed qualities of heroism in avoidance of the workhouse; the weak intellect with malice and greedy cunning in Fledgeby; the weaker intellect with love and the tender spirit of self-sacrifice in Sloppy. How full of a quaint generous humour again is the sketch of the doll's dressmaker, little Miss Wren, with her broken back and feeble frame, her precocious wit sharpened by trouble, in which the spirit of childhood casts its golden threads across the dull woof of her life of care, and whose kindliness is at times touched with a malice as of childish playfulness familiar with bitter years of trouble.

Nobody who reads this book as a whole can fail to be struck with the ingenious arrangement and skilful conduct of the story. Read piecemeal, it was satisfactory only to those who had faith in their author. The secret of Mr Boffin's little plot is so well kept, that while it was in action they who believed their old friend to be shown to them as really spoilt by wealth, believed unwillingly, and sometimes may have rashly supposed that there the master's hand had lost its cunning. In fact, if we look back to those scenes in which Mr Boffin enacted the part of a miser, we shall be surprised to see how skilfully and freely the novelist scattered what, with the key to it all in our possession, we see clearly enough to be indications of the true state of the case.

The wealth of wit poured over all the pages of this book would be an intellectual Harmon's estate, large enough to set on horseback every Wegg of a literary gentleman with a wooden head. We may say, if we will, that here we like and there we don't like any character or passage, but far above desire to criticize by the small way of personal comparison between our individual tastes and opinions

178   *Charles Dickens's* Our Mutual Friend

and those of our author is the keen enjoyment of his genius. And, after all, there is the strictest justice in the heartiest appreciation of a liveliness of fancy that spends all its gaiety in quickening the honest sympathies of life, of a pathos that derives its strength from a firm hold on the realities of life, a perception of character that seizes accurately types of men, presents vividly their distinctive characters, and all tinged with the observer's humour, that is to say, with his own character contained in the suggestions of them; with ridicule only for that which is meanly false, scorn for all that is basely false, and innumerable touches of respect and fellow-feeling for every form of life that is, or honestly endeavours to be, frank and true.

(E) [Alfred Hudson Guernsey], from "Editor's Easy Chair," Harper's New Monthly Magazine, *November 1865, p. 809*

We hope that no habitual reader of this magazine has omitted "Our Mutual Friend." It is one of the most charming of Dickens's stories. The wonderful fertility, the frolicsome humor, the power of picturesque description, the skill in construction of his genius were never more illustrated than in "Our Mutual Friend." It is purely characteristic. His great excellences and obvious faults are all in it. It is perfect in its own key, but its key is strange. It deals with every variety of human passion. There are multitudes of human figures intermingling in the tale. But there is a glamour over all. There is a grotesque exaggeration which is delightful and fascinating, but unlike the world we know. The passions, the play of character, the incidents are such as we encounter every day; but the persons are quaint beyond experience. Meanwhile the suggestions are so subtle, the range of sympathy so wide and deep, the psychological analysis often so vivid and accurate, the panoramic effect of the whole so astonishing, that the superiority of this great master is constantly manifest.

Tried by certain details Dickens is not so successful as some other novelists. Parts of his stories always have an unpleasant unreality. Many of his persons could never be matched in actual life. Even the humor sometimes creaks as in Mr. Wegg, in "Our Mutual Friend." Mrs. Wilfer is a lady whom it would be very hard to encounter in any part of London or any where in the world. But nothing can be more droll and delightful than Mrs. Wilfer issuing proclamations from her corner and forever posing upon her pedestal as a domestic Mrs. Simeon Stylites. "The cherub," who preserves your affection and even respect, despite his amiable inefficiency, could clearly have had no other wife, and the impossible Wilfer household is yet a luminous hint of a thousand actual homes in the world.

It is always remarkable, however, in Dickens's stories, that even those parts which are masterly transcripts from fact—such as the life by the river in the opening chapter of "Our Mutual Friend" and elsewhere, and the scene of the murder in the October Number—unite themselves without a break with the airier and fairier portions. You go from the first fearfully graphic incident in the book—the towing of the body of the murdered man along the Thames, which has all the veracity of common experience—to the absurdities of Boffin's Bower without a single stumble by the way. You dine with the Podsnaps, and watch the

Appendix 3: Contemporary Reviews of Our Mutual Friend   179

Lammles, conscious that they are abstractions, and descend to the usurer's or ascent to the Jew's housetop among human beings, without a jar. Kind Miss Jenny Wren compels the haughty ladies of the kingdom to furnish patterns for her dolls' dresses, and rogue Riderhood plots for more blood money, with equal probability. Then comes a truly great chapter, like that of Bradley Headstone's crime, and its effect upon him, and, recalling Bulwer's treatment of Eugene Aram, another schoolmaster and murderer, you are conscious of the essential different between genius and the most adroit talent.

What a power it is, and how nobly it is used! For a generation Dickens has held the ear and heart of the world, and he has not betrayed his trust. He has always told the truth. He has always shown the essential dignity of honesty and noble effort, however humble the circumstance. Every tale of his is a plea for what is most manly in man, and a protest against the prejudice, the convention, the insidious power of caste. Rank, ease, refinement, luxury, wealth, are never suffered by him to dazzle or bewilder the mind of his audience. He attacks the Molochs of tradition, the organized forms of injustice and selfishness. He exposes the chafing and tainting of apparent prosperity, and the pure content of mutual affection. A true democrat, he asserts the equal rights of men, and compels us to measure every man by his manhood.

How pleasant to know that such a writer is the most popular author in the world; that of all men who write the English language he is the most universally known and beloved.

*(F) [E.S. Dallas], "*Our Mutual Friend,*" Times, November 29, 1865, p. 6*

Novels published in parts have the advantage and disadvantage that their fortunes are often made or marred by the first few numbers; and this last novel of Mr. Charles Dickens, really one of his finest works, and one in which on occasion he even surpasses himself, labours under the disadvantage of a beginning that drags. Any one reading the earlier numbers of the new tale might see that the author meant to put forth all his strength and do his very best; and those who have an eye for literary workmanship could discover that never before had Mr. Dickens's workmanship been so elaborate. On the whole, however, at that early stage the reader was more perplexed than pleased. There was an appearance of great effort without corresponding result. We were introduced to a set of people in whom it is impossible to take an interest, and were made familiar with transactions that suggested horror. The great master of fiction exhibited all his skill, performed the most wonderful feats of language, loaded his page with wit and many a fine touch peculiar to himself. The agility of his pen was amazing, but still at first we were not much amused. We were more impressed with the exceeding cleverness of the author's manner than with the charm of his story; and when one thinks more of an artist's manner than of his matter woe to the artist. Very soon, however, Mr. Dickens got into his story; the interest of it grew; the reader, busied with the facts of the tale, learned to forget all about the skilfulness of the artist, and found himself rushing on eagerly through number after number of one of the best of even Dickens's tales. Still, upon some minds the first impression prevails, and Mr. Dickens's publishers have been obliged to announce that complaints are made of the difficulty of procuring his work at some of the London libraries, and that this difficulty is caused entirely by the librarians who have contented themselves with a short supply. We are reminded of *Waverley*, and begin to speculate as to its fate, and as to the fate of all its successors, if it had originally been published in shilling numbers. The first few chapters of that tale are very heavy and give no promise of the originality, the vigour, and the interest of the story as a whole. Perhaps if *Waverley* had been published in shilling numbers Scott, who had been accustomed to great hits, might have been so disheartened by the want or by the slowness of success as to have abandoned all further attempt at prose fiction.

That *Our Mutual Friend* has defects we not only allow, but shall ruthlessly point out. The weak part of the work is to be found in what may be called "The Social Chorus." This is the title which Mr. Dickens gives one of the chapters; but it is the proper name not only for that chapter, but also for every chapter in which the same personages figure. We can divide the tale distinctly into two parts, like a Greek drama—one part truly dramatic and given to the evolution of the story which Mr. Dickens has to tell; the other, a sort of social chorus, having no real connexion with the tale in which we are interested, and of importance only as representing the views of society on the incidents of the story as it comes before them. Now, the idea here is a great one, but it has not been worked out with details of sufficient interest. Of Mr. Dickens's main story—the line of action into which he has thrown his whole heart, we cannot speak too highly; it is a masterpiece. We see life in all its strength and seriousness and tenderness; the fierce passion that drives it into action, and the gentle passion that stirs it into play. But in contrast to this fine story Mr. Dickens has thought fit to present to us in a parallel line of action—the spectator—the chorus of the Greek play. Let us imagine to ourselves one of the most frigid dinner parties in London—any little party that arrogates to itself the name of society, and the members of which lead lives either inane or frivolous. They fill up their empty lives by meeting at each others' houses, by sitting in state round a dinner table and discoursing on the events of lives that move with greater speed than their own. Into this little circle come stray rumours of what is going on without; and we may listen to the remarks of this society on the stirring life which it does not share. It is a good idea, we say, to bring the chorus of idle spectators into the story; to contrast them with the living agents, to let some of the incidents of the story come to our knowledge filtered through their gossip, and to show life at once in two views—namely, in its terrible reality, and in the paltry reflection of it which passes current in the gabble of a careless, heartless, brainless knot of gadabouts.

But it is no easy task to work out such an idea; and this for two reasons. In the first place, a reader likes the story to go on, and does not like to be interrupted as he follows the plot by the talk and the movements of people who have no distinct connexion but a *quasi*-connexion with its incidents. As if that of itself were not a sufficient difficulty to be overcome, the novelist has this further difficulty in

Appendix 3: Contemporary Reviews of Our Mutual Friend   181

story: he has to make us care to read about people who are remarkable only for their nothingness, he has to make us interested in people who, by the hypothesis, are uninteresting. Now, it is in dealing with this cruel problem that Mr. Dickens falls short of the success which in the other parts of his tale he not only reaches, but reaches triumphantly. The social chorus of the present story has for its leader a mighty giver of dinners—Mr. Veneering, and the Veneering set of people are so poor of wit and so dull of feeling that Mr. Dickens has hard work to galvanize them into something like vitality. But in so doing he has in the earlier portions of his narrative seemed to give them a greater importance than they deserve or than he intends. We read the opening chapters of *Our Mutual Friend* under the impression that its chief interest would centre in the Veneering group, and that the very title of the story was one of the common-place phrases of that soulless tribe. This latter supposition is, indeed, quite correct, or we fancy that it is correct; for Mr. Dickens again and again lays great stress on the facility of friendship that prevails in the Veneering order of society. Thus—to quote from his first number:—

Mr. and Mrs. Veneering were brand-new people in a brand-new house in a brand-new quarter of London. Everything about the Veneerings was spick and span new. All their furniture was new, all their friends were new, all their servants were new, their plate was new, their carriage was new, their harness was new, their horses were new, their pictures were new, they themselves were quite new, they were as newly married as was lawfully compatible with their having a brand-new baby, and if they had set up a great-grandfather he would have come home in matting from the Pantechnicon, without a scratch upon him, French polished to the crown of his head. For in the Veneering establishment, from the hall chairs with the new coat of arms, to the grand pianoforte with the new action, and upstairs again to the new fire-escape,—all things were in a state of high varnish and polish. And what was observable in the furniture was observable in the Veneerings—the surface smelt a little too much of the workshop and was a trifle stickey. There was an innocent piece of dinner-furniture that went upon easy castors, and was kept over a livery stable-yard in Duke Street, St. James's, when not in use, to whom the Veneerings were a source of blind confusion. The name of this article was Twemlow. Being first cousin to Lord Snigsworth, he was in frequent requisition, and at many houses might be said to represent the dining-table in its normal state. Mr. and Mrs. Veneering, for example, arranging a dinner, habitually started with Twemlow, and then put leaves in him, or added guests to him. Sometimes the table consisted of Twemlow and half a dozen leaves, sometimes of Twemlow and a dozen leaves, sometimes Twemlow was pulled out to this utmost extent of 20 leaves. Mr. and Mrs. Veneering on occasions of ceremony faced each other in the centre of the board, and thus the parallel still held, for it always happened that the more Twemlow was pulled out the further he found himself from the centre, and the nearer to the sideboard at one end of the room or the window curtains at the other. But it was not this which steeped the feeble soul of Twemlow in confusion. This he was used to, and could take soundings of. The abyss to which he could find no bottom, and from which started forth the engrossing and ever-swelling difficulty of his life, was the insoluble question whether he was Veneering's oldest friend or newest friend. To the excogitation of this problem the harmless gentleman had devoted many anxious hours, both in his lodgings over the livery stable-yard and in the cold gloom, favorable to meditation, of St. James's-square. Thus. Twemlow had first known Veneering at his club, where Veneering then new nobody but the man who made them known to one another, who seemed to be the most intimate friend he had in the world, and whom he had known for two days—the bond of union between their souls, the nefarious conduct of the committee respecting the cookery of a fillet of veal, having been accidentally cemented at that date. Immediately upon this, Twemlow received an invitation to dine with Veneering, and dined, the man being of the party. Immediately upon that, Twemlow received an invitation to dine with the man, and dined, Veneering being of the party. At the man's were a Member, an Engineer, a Payer-off of the National Debt, a Poem on Shakespeare, a Grievance, and a Public Office, who all seem to be utter strangers to Veneering. And yet, immediately after that, Twemlow received an invitation to dine at Veneering's, expressly to meet the Member, the Engineer, the Payer-off of the National Debt, the Poem on Shakespeare, the Grievance, and the Public-office; and dining, discovered that all of them were the most intimate friends Veneering had in the world, and that the wives of all of them (who were all there) were the objects of Mrs. Veneering's most devoted affection and tender confidence. Then it had come about that Twemlow had said to himself in his lodgings, with his hand to his forehead, 'I must not think of this. This is enough to soften any man's brain,' and yet was always thinking of it, and could never form a conclusion.

In this shallow society everybody is everybody's friend. One man meets another casually at the house of a casual acquaintance, forthwith asks him to dinner, addresses him as his dear friend, and speaks of him as "our mutual friend." But need we wonder that, when the novel takes its title from the little society in which such a phrase is honoured, readers should suppose that "Our Mutual Friend" is mainly concerned with the doings of that society? People read superficially and hurriedly nowadays—do not, indeed, read books, but skim them; and they may easily carry away this first impression, that *Our Mutual Friend* cannot be a good novel, because it has to do chiefly with people in whom it is impossible to feel any interest.

Here is a great mistake—the mistake of the author in naming his work from the least interesting portion of it, the mistake of the too superficial reader not finding out the author's mistake. The Social Chorus who do the "mutual friendship" business first of all provide the story with a false name, and then to the world of the readers they give it a bad name. The reader is not happy in their company, and, looking for the story in their movements, he finds none. The story is elsewhere. We cannot, however, dismiss "The Social Chorus" from further notice without remarking on the cleverness with which they are delineated by Mr. Dickens. It must be remembered that if they somewhat bore the reader, it is because they are bores by nature. Several times lately our novelists have attempted to make us live with people very dull and dead. George Eliot made the attempt in *The Mill on the Floss*; Mr. Anthony Trollope tried it in *Miss Mackenzie*; and now Mr. Dickens is

Appendix 3: Contemporary Reviews of Our Mutual Friend   183

bent on the same task in "The Social Chorus" of his new novel. In each of these attempts it is impossible not to admire the exceeding skill of the author; but we doubt if readers feel that the author has in any of these instances contributed much to their amusement. The people to whom Mr. Dickens introduces us in "The Social Chorus" are, properly speaking, not people at all, but sticks; and his business is to show as well as he can the wooden character of their minds. In the passage above quoted, in which Mr. Dickens introduces them to our notice, Twemlow is described as a piece of furniture that went upon easy castors; and all through the novel we have to think of him and his associates not as men with the hearts of men, but as a species of knick-knacks. The carefulness of the writing, however, in that passage contains sufficient evidence that Mr. Dickens has spared no pains in the exhibition of such knick-knacks. With great zest he exposes the solemn twaddle of stiff dinner parties and the hollow friendships of which they are the religious rites. Some of his portraits, too, of the Veneering lot are, with a few swift touches, given with great effect, as that of Lady Tippins, the aged flirt, and again those of the Lammles, who married each other for money, and discovered amid the joys of the honeymoon that they were deceived.

So far we have dealt with the mere onlookers of the story, not with the story itself; and we say deliberately that we have read nothing of Mr. Dickens's which has given us a higher idea of his power than this last tale. It would not be wonderful if so voluminous an author should now show some signs of exhaustion. On the contrary, here he is in greater force than ever, astonishing us with a fertility in which we can trace no signs of repetition. We hear people say, "He has never surpassed *Pickwick.*" They talk of *Pickwick* as if it were his masterpiece. We do not yield to any one in our enjoyment of that extraordinary work. We never tire of it. We are of those people who can read it again and again, and can take it up at any page with the certainty of finding in it the most merry-making humour. But we refuse to measure a work of art by the amount of risible effect which it produces; and we are not going to quarrel with tragedy because it is less mirthful than comedy. What if we allow that *Our Mutual Friend* is not nearly so funny as *Pickwick!* It is infinitely better than *Pickwick* in all the higher qualities of a novel, and, in spite of the dead weight of "The Social Chorus," we class it with Mr. Dickens's best works.

One thing is very remarkable about it,—the immense amount of thought which it contains. We scarcely like to speak of the labour bestowed upon it, lest a careless reader should carry away a notion that the work is laboured. What labour Mr. Dickens has given to it is a labour of love, and the point which strikes us is that he, who of all our living novelists has the most extraordinary genius, is also of all our living novelists the most careful and painstaking in his work. In all these 600 pages there is not a careless line. There are lines and pages we object to as wrong in execution, or not quite happy in idea; but there is not a page nor a line which is not the product of a full mind bursting with what it has to say, and determined to say it well. Right or wrong, the work is always thoroughgoing and conscientious. There is nothing slurred over—no negligence, no working up to what are called in stage language "points"—to the detriment of the more level passages. And then see what a mass of matter he lays before his readers. There is a gallery of portraits in the present novel which might set up half a dozen novelists for life: Bella Wilfer, the most charming of all, her father, her mother, her sister; then Boffin and Mrs. Boffin, and Silas Wegg, and Venus, the practical anatomist; then, again, Riderhood, and Lizzie Hexam, and Bradley Headstone; once more, Mortimer Lightwood, Wrayburn, the doll's dressmaker, and her father. There are many more, and among these we must not forget poor old Betty Higden, because without such a character as hers Mr. Dickens's tales would be unlike themselves. Mr. Dickens cannot write a tale without in some way bringing it to bear upon a social grievance, with regard to which he has a strong feeling. He has a strong feeling as to the manner in which the Poor Law is administered in this country, and he devotes one of his most powerful chapters to showing with what horror poor Betty Higden shrinks from parochial charity:—

> The train of carts and horses came and went all day from dawn to nightfall, making little or no daily impression on the heap of ashes, though, as the days passed on, the heap was seen to be slowly melting. My lords and gentlemen and honourable boards, when you in the course of your dust-shovelling and cinder-raking have piled up a mountain of pretentious failure, you must off with your honourable coats for the removal of it, and fall to the work with the power of all the queen's horses and all the queen's men, or it will come rushing down and bury us alive. Yes, verily, my lords and gentlemen and honourable boards, adapting your Catechism to the occasion, and by God's help so you must. For when we have got things to that pass that with an enormous treasure at disposal to relieve the poor, the best of the poor detest our mercies, hide their heads from us, and shame us by starving to death in the midst of us, it is a pass impossible of prosperity, impossible of continuance. It may not be so written in the Gospel according to Podsnappery; you may not 'find these words' for the text of a sermon in the returns of the Board of Trade, but they have been the truth since the foundations of the universe were laid, and they will be the truth until the foundations of the universe are shaken by the Builder. This boastful handiwork of ours, which fails in its terrors for the professional pauper, the sturdy breaker of windows and the rampant tearer of clothes, strikes with a cruel and wicked stab at the stricken sufferer, and is a horror to the deserving and unfortunate. We must mend it, lords and gentlemen and honourable boards, or in its own evil hour it will mar every one of us. Old Betty Higden fared upon her pilgrimage as many ruggedly honest creatures, women and men, fare on their toiling way along the roads of life. Patiently to earn a spare bare living, and quietly to die, untouched by workhouse hands—this was her highest sublunary hope ... But, the old abhorrence grew stronger on her as she grew weaker, and it found more sustaining food than she did in her wanderings. Now she would light upon the shameful spectacle of some desolate creature—or some wretched ragged groups of either sex, or of both sexes, with children among them, huddled together like the smaller vermin for a little warmth—lingering and lingering on a doorstep, while the appointed evader of the public trust did his dirty office of trying to weary them out and so get rid of them. Now she would light upon some poor

Appendix 3: Contemporary Reviews of Our Mutual Friend   185

decent person, like herself, going afoot on a pilgrimage of many weary miles
to see some worn-out relative or friend who had been charitably clutched off to
a great blank barren union-house, as far from old home as the county gaol (the
remoteness of which is always its worst punishment for small rural offenders),
and in its dietary, and in its lodging, and in its tending of the sick a much more
penal establishment. Sometimes she would hear a newspaper read out, and
would learn how the Registrar-General cast up the units that had within the last
week died of want and exposure to the weather: for which that Recording Angel
seemed to have a regular fixed place in his sum, as if they were its halfpence.
All such things she would hear discussed, as we, my lords and gentlemen and
honourable boards, in our unapproachable magnificence never hear them, and
from all such things she would fly with the wings of raging Despair. This is not
to be received as a figure of speech. Old Betty Higden however tired, however
footsore, would start up and be driven away by her awakened horror of falling
into the hands of Charity. It is a remarkable Christian improvement to have made
a pursuing Fury of the Good Samaritan; but it was so in this case, and it is a type
of many, many, many. Two incidents united to intensity the old unreasoning
abhorrence—granted in a previous place to be unreasoning, because the people
always are unreasoning, and invariably make a point of producing all their
smoke without fire. One day she was sitting in a market-place on a bench outside
an inn, with her little wares for sale, when the deadness that she strove against
came over her so heavily that the scene departed from before her eyes; when it
returned, she found herself on the ground, her head supported by some good-
natured market-woman, and a little crowd about her.

'Are you better now, mother?' asked one of the women. 'Do you think you
can do nicely now?'

'Have I been ill, then?' asked old Betty.

'You have had a faint like,' was the answer, 'or a fit. It ain't that you've
been a-struggling, mother but you've been stiff and numbed.'

'Ah!' said Betty, recovering her memory. 'It's the numbness. Yes. It comes
over me at times.'

Was it gone? The women asked her.

'It's gone now,' said Betty. 'I shall be stronger than I was afore. Many
thanks to ye, my dears, and when ye come to be as old as I am, may others do
as much for you!'

They assisted her to rise, but she could not stand yet, and they supported
her when she sat down again upon the bench.

'My head's a bit light and my feet are a bit heavy,' said old Betty, leaning
her face drowsily on the breast of the woman who had spoken before. 'They'll
both come nat'ral in a minute. There's nothing more the matter.'

'Ask her,' said some farmers standing by, who had come out from their
market-dinner, 'who belongs to her.'

'Are there any folks belonging to you, mother?' said the woman.

'Yes, sure,' answered Betty. 'I heerd the gentleman say it, but I couldn't
answer quick enough. There's plenty belonging to me. Don't ye fear for me, my
dear.'

'But are any of 'em near here?' said the men's voices; the women's voices
chiming in when it was said, and prolonging the strain.

'Quite near enough,' said Betty, rousing herself. 'Don't ye be afeard for me, neighbours.'

'But you are not fit to travel. Where are you going?' was the next compassionate chorus she heard.

'I'm a going to London when I've sold out all,' said Betty, rising with difficulty. 'I've right good friends in London. I want for nothing. I shall come to no harm. Thankye. Don't ye be afeard for me.'

A well-meaning bystander, yellow-leggined and purple-faced, said hoarsely over his red comforter as she rose to her feet that she 'oughtn't to be let to go.'

'For the Lord's love, don't meddle with me!" cried old Betty, all her fears crowding on her. 'I am quite well now, and I must go this minute.'

She caught up her basket as she spoke and was making an unsteady rush away from them, when the same bystander checked her with his hand on her sleeve, and urged her to come with him and see the parish doctor. Strengthening herself by the utmost exercise of her resolution, the poor trembling creature shook him off, almost fiercely, and took to flight. Nor did she feel safe until she had set a mile or two of by-road between herself and the market-place, and had crept into a copse, like a hunted animal, to hide and recover breath. Not until then for the first time did she venture to recall how she had looked over her shoulder before turning out of town, and had seen the sign of the White Lion hanging across the road, and the fluttering market-booths, and the old gray church, and the little crowd gazing after her but not attempting to follow her.

We quote that passage, because when such a man as Mr. Dickens has a practical object in view, it is more in his mind than all the triumphs of his art. It would please him more to do good to the thousands of poor people who never read novels than to entertain all the novel readers in the world. Still, it is not with these practical questions that we are now concerned, but with the question of the writer's art, and we return to the point on which we were insisting, as to the fulness of matter that appears in the pages of *Our Mutual Friend*. We have referred to one of Mr. Dickens's peculiarities, that he generally makes his novels bear on some practical grievance to which he desires to call attention. Another of his characteristics is, that he likes to introduce us to people engaged in some special business. In one little tale he will tell us all about the man who draws the picture of salmon on the pavement; in another story we shall have the man-milliner; in yet another, Mrs. Gamp and her congeners. Here we are introduced to two great curiosities—the dolls' dressmaker, and the man who makes it his business to find dead bodies in the Thames. In the occupation of the latter there is something too horrible to permit of our being thoroughly entertained by Mr. Dickens's revelations of the secrets that belong to such a calling; but the dolls' dressmaker is one of his most charming pictures, and Mr. Dickens tells her strange story with a mixture of humour and pathos which it is impossible to resist. The picture is one of those in which he delights, in which he can give the reins to his fancy; and as he displays all the sorrow and all the pleasantry of the little dressmaker we are driven to the dilemma of not knowing whether to laugh or to be sad.

Appendix 3: Contemporary Reviews of Our Mutual Friend   187

But the finest picture in the novel is that of Bella Wilfer. Mr. Dickens has never done anything in the portraiture of women so pretty and so perfect. We have more than once in these columns had to remark upon Thackeray's *dictum* that a novelist at 50 cannot write of love with success. Mr. Dickens is an example to the contrary. At the same time it must be observed that the love which he has set forth so gracefully is the love not of a man but of a woman. The man whose love he describes is not one in whom we can feel a strong interest. But for that matter, we men have little sympathy with love-sick men. When love in a man gets to the point of sickness or extravagance it becomes rather ridiculous. A man may love a woman as much as he likes, but he must have his love well in hand or men do not sympathize with it. He may break his heart for a woman, but he must not show it. And so it need excite no surprise if we have to report that Mr. Dickens's love-sick hero is no more interesting than love-sick heroes are in general. But this love-sick woman is without exception the prettiest picture of the kind he has drawn—one of the prettiest pictures in prose fiction. The little dialogues in which Mr. Dickens has exhibited first her love for her father, then her love for her lover, and then the two combined, are full of a liveliness and a grace and a humour that seem to us to surpass any attempt of the same description which he has ever before made. There is an enchanting airiness and a winning charm about the lady which mark her out as one of his most brilliant portraits—and that, too, in a species of portraiture peculiarly difficult of attainment. Everybody knows and admires the odd sort of characters for which Mr. Dickens is famous, such as Mrs. Gamp; but to paint Bella Wilfer seems to be a higher reach of art. The strong hard lines of Mrs. Gamp's character it is comparatively easy to draw. In drawing Bella Wilfer, Mr. Dickens has to touch most delicately a beautiful woman, and render with the utmost tenderness the soft contour of her character. He has perfectly succeeded, and we shall be greatly surprised if the portraiture of this wayward girl does not rank among his highest performances.

The story, of course, we are not going to tell. It is very ingenious, and the plot is put together with an elaboration which we scarcely expect to find in a novel published in parts. All we shall say of it is, that those readers who pant for what is called "sensation" may feast in it to their heart's content on sensation; and that those who care more for quiet pictures and studies of character will also find that the author has provided for them. Mr. Dickens's range is wide, and none of our living novelists can adapt himself, or herself, to so wide a circle of readers.

(G) W.[illiam] D.[ean] H.[owells], "Our Mutual Friend," The Round Table: A Saturday Review of Politics, Finance, Literature, Society, December 2, 1865, pp. 200–201

Dividing prose fictions into the two classes of novel and romance, with the theory that the novel is a portraiture of individuals and affairs, and the romance a picture of events and human characteristics in their subtler and more ideal relations, we believe we are right in saying that Mr. Dickens is not at all a novelist but altogether a romancer. The novelist deals with personages, the romancer with types. Thackeray, the greatest of novelists, has given us characters which have such absolute and perfect personality that we know them as we know Smith and Jones. Dickens, the first of living romancers, gives us types by which we can characterize all the qualities of our acquaintance. Pendennis, Clive Newcome, Blanche Amory, Becky Sharp, are faultless likenesses of individual life in the world; Micawber, Mr. Pecksniff, Harold Skimpole, Mrs. Nickleby, are images of cheerful haplessness, hypocrisy, amiable, irresponsible selfishness and folly, which exist at large in human nature. We are far from thinking the novelist's art less than the romancer's; only we do not think it more. You do homage to the exquisite, reproachless fidelity of Thackeray, while you marvel at the creative power of Dickens. You know that Micawber and Pecksniff are individually impossibilities, but you constantly find men who remind you of them. When you go to London you feel it not unlikely you may meet Fred Bayham; but who ever expected to encounter Dick Swiveller in any particular locality? Mr. Dickens's people are essentially types, not persons; and though they have, by the sovereign laws of art, a right to individual existence in the books where we find them, yet if we attempt to translate them into real life, as we do Becky Sharpe and Arthur Pendennis, they lose all organic propriety, and dissolve into traits and resemblances.

Believing in romance's office to produce images of universal truth and value, we have slight patience, and less sympathy, with the criticism which accuses Mr. Dickens of exaggeration; and we have no blame for his last books because most of its people are improbable. So long as they are not moral impossibilities, we cannot think them exaggerations except in the sense that Lear and Othello are exaggerations; and we are rather surprised that critics who have observed the Shakespearian universality of Mr. Dickens's feeling, have not been struck with the Shakespearian universality of his art. We find that it will be useless to condemn Mr. Dickens for Wegg and Podsnap, unless we condemn Shakespeare for Falstaff and Pistol, and Cervantes for Sancho Panza. It is even idler to object that Mr. Dickens places his physically impossible characters among us in our own day; for they certainly represent present longings, interests, and delusions, though nobody has seen their whole likeness in life. Cervantes made his knight to live in his own day; it was impossible that he should exist then in geographical and political Spain, but nevertheless he did exist then in the spirit of most Spaniards.

Whether Mr. Dickens has given us new types in his new work, is to us the most interesting question in regard to it, for we count the management of plot as comparatively unimportant in his fictions, and only value it as it develops his characters. If the plot is one in which a fitting part falls to each character, we think it successful, no matter what gross improbabilities it may involve as a scheme of action; it has to preserve in the characters consistency and harmony, and nothing more.

Some of the people in "Our Mutual Friend" must inevitably remind the reader of former creations by the same master. In Mr. Podsnap we have Mr. Bounderby, of Coketown, removed to London, and greatly enlarged and improved. Bounderby

Appendix 3: Contemporary Reviews of Our Mutual Friend   189

was exceptional in his former career; and, though we might meet his like at rare intervals, he was not of great use to epithet; but, as Podsnap, he becomes of universal acceptance. Podsnap is a word to be used for ever to name an otherwise unspeakably odious order of human creature, and the world will receive gratefully the author's suggestion of Podsnappery as a fit term for the thinking and doing of this kind of human creatures. Still, however, Podsnap is scarcely more than a more practicable Bounderby, and we cannot salute him as a novel type. In like manner, we have had earlier acquaintance with Lady Tippins, and knew that gray enchantress in "Dombey and Son" as Cleopatra. Lady Tippins, indeed, is less vulgar, and less a fool than Cleopatra; but she has much of her manner, and, with Major Bagstock for company instead of the young men Wrayburn and Lightwood, we suspect would do and say the same things that Cleopatra did. Rogue Riderhood, again, who gets his living by the sweat of his brow, is too nearly related to the honest tradesman in "The Tale of Two Cities" to be of great original value, and his daughter Pleasant, slightly as she is sketched, is more admirable as a creation. As for Lizzie Hexam, though her part is dwelt on a great deal, she fails to interest us, and we think her selfish, mean-souled brother an infinitely better work of art. One of the least natural characters in the book is one which was quite possibly copied from life, and one on which the author has unmistakably bestowed great pains—that of the doll's dress-maker, Miss Jenny Wren. The other women are all admirable in their way. Bella Wilfer is delicious; but it would be hard for any reader to say where he left off disliking her for a pert and selfish little wretch and began liking her for the sweetest and best of lovely women; for long before her furious outburst against Mr. Boffin, the most bewitching goodness had been visible in her most bewitching badness. Her mother is almost as great a fool, pure and simple, as Mrs. Nickleby, which is the highest praise we can pronounce, unless we add that her folly is of quite a different sort—a serious and stately idiotcy perfectly unique. Miss Podsnap is the very soul of bashful, nervous sincerity and artlessness, with only enough of the common mother of our race to make her frantically vindictive under the torture of polite attentions at her birth-day party. Mrs. Lammle would have been better managed by Thackeray, as, indeed, would the whole episode of the Lammles have been. But who besides Mr. Dickens could have so perfectly presented Mrs. Milvey and all her good, energetic little life by merely the virtue of that emphasis, recurrent and capricious, she bestows on her words?

The hero of the romance, if John Harmon be its hero, is a mere hinge on which the plot works, and, as a man, is utterly uninteresting. Neither does Mr. Boffin convey the impression of consistent character, and we cannot believe him fitted to play the part assigned him in Harmon's prolonged and clumsy *ruse*.

Eugene Wrayburn has a slight but genuine value in representing the sort of purposeless, graceful *ennui* which, no doubt, largely exists among well-educated and well-bred young men in England, but which our late war has terribly abolished among them here—for ever, let us hope. The author cures Wrayburn by that attempted murder, which the reader knows, and afterwards we find him so full of true and noble stuff that we are sorry not to have seen more of him. Bradley

Headstone, as a study of murderous human nature, is not so good as other like studies by the same author; but he is excellent as showing how barren and stony the mere culture of the mind leaves the soul; especially when this culture is not wide and deep enough to make the mental principle distrust its own infallibility. Mr. Alfred Lammle is not successful, it seems to us, though the author has taken pains to mark his devilishness with white dints in the nose, so that it may be recognized at all times; but Fascination Fledgeby is finely done, and admirably punished at last with the sort of retribution which the reader had instinctively longed for. It is curious with what skill Mr. Dickens manages beatings so as to lift them out of the province of farce and pantomime, and make them felicitous points of the drama, on which ladies and children may look "with cheerfulness and refreshment." There is an exquisite enjoyment to the reader in the thrashing which Nicholas Nickleby gives Squeers the schoolmaster, which we find also in the caning of Mr. Fledgeby under quite different circumstances; while we look with just as keen a relish on Sloppy dropping Mr. Wegg into the slush and garbage of the scavenger's cart. Not but that we have a high opinion of Mr. Wegg as a character. Indeed, we think him, altogether, the most original and successful character in the book; that mean and doggish sagacity which leads him to suspect a secret value in himself because some one seems to need him, and his wretched, groveling purpose not to let himself go cheap, though he could not say why he should be worth anything, are traits of human nature embodied in him with faultless art. His different bargains with Mr. Boffin are evidence of a marvellous subtlety and keenness in the author's study of men; while Wegg's envy of Mr. Boffin's wealth, his sense of deadly injury received through the benefits bestowed on him, and his resolution to ruin his benefactor in return for them, are consequences resulting so naturally from existing tempers and relations that the reader may be slower than he should to discern the unique art with which they are made to appear. In fine, Wegg seems to have been not only born, but to have lost his leg, in order to be fitted perfectly for the part he plays in this book.

Mr. Dickens, in the postscript to his romance, says when he devised the story he foresaw the likelihood that a class of readers and commentators would suppose that he wished to conceal what he really tried to suggest—that is, the common identity of John Harmon and John Rokesmith. Impression of this sort, it must be confessed, was more creditable to Mr. Dickens's prophetic qualities than complimentary to his readers, among whom such a mistake was presumably possible. We think that, to people of very ordinary perspicacity and very moderate acquaintance with fiction, this part of the plot was visible from the beginning, though it does not seem to us very ingenious. Indeed, we find the plot scarcely to have even the secondary excellence which we would have demanded, for it appears to offer the different characters slight opportunity for consistent development, and it ends like a Christmas pantomime, with a most boisterous distribution of poetical justice. The motives assigned to the personages are rarely sufficient to account for their actions, and they all act parts which have little or no coherence or propriety. Indeed, the reader, after passing through the painful scenes of John Rokesmith's

Appendix 3: Contemporary Reviews of Our Mutual Friend   191

dismissal and year-long enmity with the Boffins, angrily resents the explanation
offered him that John Rokesmith and Mr. Boffin were only making believe in order
to prove Bella's devotion to the utmost—resents the explanation as a weak refuge
from the events invented after their occurrence. In a young writer the device would
be pronounced a puerile invention, and it has not even the justification of Mr.
Boffin's long delusion of Mr. Wegg, for that brings out all the despotic baseness of
Wegg's character; while John Harmon's *ruse* leaves us no better acquainted with
him than we were before, but rather disposed to like him less than before. The
main plot of the book scarcely seems to concern the other characters who figure
in different episodes of slender coherence; and one vainly asks himself at the end
what any of them has done to help the story forward, though he would be loth to
lose any one of them from the book.

Whether the reader will think that Mr. Dickens has improved upon his former
works in the present one, or has fallen below them in excellence, will greatly
depend upon whether he can read him now with that eager sympathy which he
gave to the perusal of his romances in other days. Men are prone to think (even
when they are not very old men) that the pleasure and excellence of these days are
not at all comparable to the pleasure and excellence of other days; and though "Our
Mutual Friend" may be intrinsically as good as "David Copperfield," it is scarcely
possible that any old-established admirer of "David Copperfield" should allow it.
To him who read of the courtship in the latter book when he was himself first in
love, and who reads of the courtship in the former book after having lived through
the champagne of life, Dora must be infinitely more bewitching and lovable than
Bella. So, if you please, the present writer would rather have the opinion of some
intelligent person newly experienced in Mr. Dickens's former romances—if that
person exists; and he would care more for the judgment of eighteen or twenty
years than thirty or forty, in the matter. We think this ideal critic would pronounce
that he found this last romance as full of generous interest as any earlier one; that
he found in its pages the same intimate friendship with the nature of fields and
woods and the nature of docks and streets; the same warm-blooded sympathy with
poverty and lowliness; the same scorn of solemn and respectable selfishness, and
of mean and disreputable cunning; the same subtle analysis of the motives and
feelings and facts of crime; the same exuberant happiness in love and lovers; the
same comprehension of what Carlyle calls "inarticulate natures"; the same gay,
fantastic humor; the same capricious pathos. As to the manner, it should scarcely
seem the old manner, though the critic could not tell where it departed from it; and
for the style, could that ever have been more luminous, flexible, felicitous?

*(H) [Henry James], "Our Mutual Friend," The Nation, December 21, 1865,
pp. 786–7*

"Our Mutual Friend" is, to our perception, the poorest of Mr. Dickens's works.
And it is poor with the poverty not of momentary embarrassment, but of permanent
exhaustion. It is wanting in inspiration. For the last ten years it has seemed to

us that Mr. Dickens has been unmistakably forcing himself. "Bleak House" was forced; "Little Dorritt" was labored; the present work is dug out as with a spade and pickaxe. Of course—to anticipate the usual argument—who but Dickens could have written it? Who, indeed? Who else would have established a lady in business in a novel on the admirably solid basis of her always putting on gloves and tieing a handkerchief round her head in moments of grief, and of her habitually addressing her family with "Peace! hold!" It is needless to say that Mrs. Reginald Wilfer is first and last the occasion of considerable true humor. When, after conducting her daughter to Mrs. Boffin's carriage, in sight of all the envious neighbors, she is described as enjoying her triumph during the next quarter of an hour by airing herself on the door-step "in a kind of splendidly serene trance," we laugh with as uncritical a laugh as could be desired of us. We pay the same tribute to her assertions, as she narrates the glories of the society she enjoyed at her father's table, that she has known as many as three copper-plate engravers exchanging the most exquisite sallies and retorts there at one time. But when to these we have added a dozen more happy examples of the humor which was exhaled from every line of Mr. Dickens's earlier writings, we shall have closed the list of the merits of the work before us. To say that the conduct of the story, with all its complications, betrays a long-practised hand, is to pay no compliment worthy the author. If this were, indeed, a compliment, we should be inclined to carry it further, and congratulate him on his success in what we should call the manufacture of fiction; for in so doing we should express a feeling that has attended us throughout the book. Seldom, we reflected, had we read a book so intensely *written*, so little seen, known, or felt.

In all Mr. Dickens's works the fantastic has been his great resource; and while his fancy was lively and vigorous it accomplished great things. But the fantastic, when the fancy is dead, is a very poor business. The movement of Mr. Dickens's fancy in Mrs. Wilfer and Mr. Boffin and Lady Tippins, and the Lammles and Miss Wren, and even in Eugene Wrayburn, is, to our mind, lifeless, forced, mechanical. It is the letter of his old humor without the spirit. It is hardly too much to say that every character here put before us is a mere bundle of eccentricities, animated by no principle of nature whatever. In former days there reigned in Mr. Dickens's extravagances a comparative consistency; they were exaggerated statements of types that really existed. We had, perhaps, never known a Newman Noggs, nor a Pecksniff, nor a Micawber; but we had known persons of whom these figures were but the strictly logical consummation. But among the grotesque creatures who occupy the pages before us, there is not one whom we can refer to as an existing type. In all Mr. Dickens's stories, indeed, the reader has been called upon, and has willingly consented, to accept a certain number of figures or creatures of pure fancy, for this was the author's poetry. He was, moreover, always repaid for his concession by a peculiar beauty or power in these exceptional characters. But he is now expected to make the same concession with a very inadequate reward. What do we get in return for accepting Miss Jenny Wren as a possible person? This young lady is the type of a certain class of characters of which Mr. Dickens

Appendix 3: Contemporary Reviews of Our Mutual Friend   193

has made a specialty, and with which he has been accustomed to draw alternate smiles and tears, according as he pressed one spring or another. But this is a very cheap merriment and very cheap pathos. Miss Jenny Wren is a poor little dwarf, afflicted, as she constantly reiterates, with a "bad back" and "queer legs," who makes doll's dresses, and is for ever pricking at those with whom she converses, in the air, with her needle, and assuring them that she knows their "tricks and their manners." Like all Mr. Dickens's pathetic characters, she is a little monster; she is deformed, unhealthy, unnatural; she belongs to the troop of hunchbacks, imbeciles, and precocious children who have carried on the sentimental business in all Mr. Dickens's novels; the little Nells, the Smikes, the Paul Dombeys.

Mr. Dickens goes as far out of the way for his wicked people as he does for his good ones. Rogue Riderhood, indeed, in the present story, is villanous with a sufficiently natural villany; he belongs to that quarter of society in which the author is most at his ease. But was there ever such wickedness as that of the Lammles and Mr. Fledgeby? Not that people have not been as mischievous as they; but was any one ever mischievous in that singular fashion? Did a couple of elegant swindlers ever take such particular pains to be aggressively inhuman?—for we can find no other word for the gratuitous distortions to which they are subjected. The word *humanity* strikes us as strangely discordant, in the midst of these pages; for, let us boldly declare it, there is no humanity here. Humanity is nearer home than the Boffins, and the Lammles, and the Wilfers, and the Veneerings. It is in what men have in common with each other, except the fact that they have nothing in common with mankind at large. What a world were this world if the world of "Our Mutual Friend" were an honest reflection of it! But a community of eccentrics is impossible. Rules alone are consistent with each other; exceptions are inconsistent. Society is maintained by natural sense and natural feeling. We cannot conceive a society in which these principles are not in some manner represented. Where in these pages are the depositaries of that intelligence without which the movement of life would cease? Who represents nature? Accepting half of Mr. Dickens's persons as intentionally grotesque, where are those exemplars of sound humanity who should afford us the proper measure of their companions' variations? We ought not, in justice to the author, to seek them among his weaker—that is, his mere conventional—characters; in John Harmon, Lizzie Hexam, or Mortimer Lightwood; but we assuredly cannot find them among his stronger—that is, his artificial creations. Suppose we take Eugene Wrayburn and Bradley Headstone. They occupy a halfway position between the habitual probable of nature and the habitual impossible of Mr. Dickens. A large portion of the story rests upon the enmity borne by Headstone to Wrayburn, both being in love with the same woman. Wrayburn is a gentleman, and Headstone is one of the people. Wrayburn is well-bred, careless, elegant, sceptical, and idle; Headstone is a high-tempered, hard-working, ambitious young schoolmaster. There lay in the opposition of these two characters a very good story. But the prime requisite was that they should *be* characters: Mr. Dickens, according to his usual plan, has made them simply figures, and between them the story that was to be, the story that should have been, has evaporated. Wrayburn lounges about with his hands in his pockets, smoking a cigar, and talking nonsense. Headstone strides about, clenching his fists and biting his lips and grasping his stick. There is one scene in which Wrayburn chaffs the schoolmaster with easy insolence, while the latter writhes impotently under his well-bred sarcasm. This scene is very clever, but it is very insufficient. If the majority of readers were not so very timid in the use of words we should call it vulgar. By this we do not mean to indicate the conventional impropriety of two gentlemen exchanging lively personalities; we mean to emphasize the essentially small character of these personalities. In other words, the moment, dramatically, is great, while the author's conception is weak. The friction of two *men*, of two characters, of two passions, produces stronger sparks than Wrayburn's boyish repartees and Headstone's melodramatic commonplaces. Such scenes as this are useful in fixing the limits of Mr. Dickens's insight. Insight is, perhaps, too strong a word; for we are convinced that it is one of the chief conditions of his genius not to see beneath the surface of things. If we might hazard a definition of his literary character, we should, accordingly, call him the greatest of superficial novelists. We are aware that this definition confines him to an inferior rank in the department of letters which he adorns; but we accept this consequence of our proposition. It were, in our opinion, an offence against humanity to place Mr. Dickens among the greatest novelists. For, to repeat what we have already intimated, he has created nothing but figure. He has added nothing to our understanding of human character. He is master of but two alternatives: he reconciles us to what is commonplace, and he reconciles us to what is odd. The value of the former service is questionable; and the manner in which Mr. Dickens performs it sometimes conveys a certain impression of charlatanism. The value of the latter service is incontestable, and here Mr. Dickens is an honest, an admirable artist. But what is the condition of the truly great novelist? For him there are no alternatives, for him there are no oddities, for him there is nothing outside of humanity. He cannot shirk it; it imposes itself upon him. For him alone, therefore, there is a true and a false; for him alone it is possible to be right, because it is possible to be wrong. Mr. Dickens is a great observer and a great humorist, but he is nothing of a philosopher. Some people may hereupon say, so much the better; we say, so much the worse. For a novelist very soon has need of a little philosophy. In treating of Micawber, and Boffin, and Pickwick, *et hoc genus omne*, he can, indeed, dispense with it, for this—we say it with all deference—is not serious writing. But when he comes to tell the story of a passion, a story like that of Headstone and Wrayburn, he becomes a moralist as well as an artist. He must know *man* as well as *men*, and to know man is to be a philosopher. The writer who knows men alone, if he have Mr. Dickens's humor and fancy, will give us figures and pictures for which we cannot be too grateful, for he will enlarge our knowledge of the world. But when he introduces men and women whose interest is preconceived to lie not in the poverty, the weakness, the drollery of their natures, but in their complete and unconscious subjection to ordinary and healthy human emotions, all his humor, all his fancy, will avail him nothing if, out of the fulness of his sympathy, he is unable to prosecute those

Appendix 3: Contemporary Reviews of Our Mutual Friend 195

generalizations in which alone consists the real greatness of a work of art. This may sound like very subtle talk about a very simple matter; it is rather very simple talk about a very subtle matter. A story based upon those elementary passions in which alone we seek the true and final manifestation of character must be told in a spirit of intellectual superiority to those passions. That is, the author must understand what he is talking about. The perusal of a story so told is one of the most elevating experiences within the reach of the human mind. The perusal of a story which is not so told is infinitely depressing and unprofitable.

(I) [John Richard de Capel Wise], from "Belles Lettres," Westminster Review, *April 1866, pp. 582–5*

His severest critics, we suppose, will not deny Mr. Dickens genius, not of the highest indeed, but still of a very rare order. When we look back at his long gallery of portraits, Sam Weller, Chadband, Pecksniff, Pickwick, and Mrs. Gamp; when we consider how much we should lose if deprived of all these, and all their whims and fancies, we must confess that their creator does not belong to the common roll of authors. But on the other hand, when we compare Mr. Dickens to the world's greatest humorists, Aristophanes, Molière, Swift, Cervantes, and Shakespeare, then we see how far short he comes of the highest rank of genius. Pecksniff weighs as chaff in the balance against Tartuffe, and Pickwick is a mere monster beside the Don of Spain. The more we study Falstaff, Gulliver, and Sancho Panza, the more we perceive the art of the artist and thinker, but the closer we look at Mr. Dickens's characters, the more we detect the trickery of an artificer. The more we analyse Mr. Dickens, the more we perceive that his humour runs into riotous extravagance, whilst his pathos degenerates into sentimentality. His characters, in fact, are a bundle of deformities. And he appears, too, to value them because they are deformed, as some minds value a crooked sixpence more than a sound coin. He has made the fatal mistake against which Goethe warned the artist. Everything with him is not *supra naturam*, but *extra naturam*. His whole art, as we shall presently show, is founded upon false principles. When we put down a work of his, we are tempted to ask, *Quid hinc abest nisi res et veritas?* And if this criticism may be pronounced upon his master-pieces, what can be said of his later works? Our answer must be found in our remarks upon "Our Mutual Friend." As it is impossible for us here to analyse the whole work, we must content ourselves with a chapter. To do this in most cases would be as absurd as to exhibit a man's tooth as a specimen of his eloquence. But Mr. Dickens does not suffer by the process. He is seen to the best advantage in detached pieces. And we shall take the chapter on Podsnappery, both because it has been so much praised by Mr. Dickens's admirers, and because, too, we think it is most characteristic of his mind. A more suitable character than Podsnap could not have fallen into Mr. Dickens's hands. We fully sympathize with him in his hatred of Podsnappery. For Podsnap, be it known, is the incarnation of Grocerdom, that stolid British Grocerdom, which deems that only coronets and titles make heroes, only silks and jewels heroines, that the feast of reason comes only with venison, and the flow of wit only with Sneyd's claret—that Grocerdom where riches instead of elevating only enervate their possessors, instead of refining only brutalize each passion, and instead of broadening only swathe the mind in intolerance. In a crusade against this Mr. Dickens has our warmest wishes. And Podsnap, if well conceived and well carried out, might have been the pendant to Pecksniff. But when we open the chapter, we find it an explosion of dulness. A number of automatons are moving about, who are all, so to speak, tattooed with various characteristics. There is the great automaton Podsnap, who is tattooed with a flourish of the right arm and a flush of the face, and the minor automaton Mr. Lammle, who is tattooed with ginger eyebrows. Dancers are called "bathers," and one of them is distinguished by his ambling. In fact Mr. Dickens here seems to regard his characters as Du Fresne says the English did their dogs, *quanto deformiores eo meliores æstimant.* The conversation is still more wonderful. Mr. Dickens here alternates between melodrama and burlesque. If he is not upon stilts, he goes upon crutches. For instance, take the following—

> Said Mr. Podsnap to Mrs. Podsnap, 'Georgiana is almost eighteen.'
> Said Mrs. Podsnap to Mr. Podsnap, assenting, 'Almost eighteen.'
> Said Mr. Podsnap then to Mrs. Podsnap, 'Really I think we should have some people on Georgiana's birthday.'
> Said Mrs. Podsnap then to Mr. Podsnap, 'which will enable us to clear off all those people who are due.' (Vol. i., p. 98.)

The only thing we can compare with this wonderful passage is "Peter Piper picking pepper." Let us now turn to the satire. Here are Mr. Podsnap's views upon art—

> Literature; large print, respectfully descriptive of getting up at eight; shaving close at a quarter past, breakfasting at nine, going to the City at ten, coming home at half-past five, and dining at seven. (p. 97.)

Now as these exact words are repeated under Painting and Music and again under Dancing (p. 104), we must conclude that Mr. Dickens thinks he has written something very effective. Our comment is that sham wit, like a sham diamond, can cut nothing. But then whilst some jokes are dull, others are old. Thus we read of an epergne "blotched all over as if it had broken out in an eruption" (p. 99.) This poor old joke has broken out year after year amongst Mr. Dickens's followers ever since Leech's woodcut of the page "who had broken out into buttons and stripes." The chapter also contains a specimen of Mr. Dickens's bad grammar. We are told that a certain meek young man "eliminated Mr. Podsnap's flush and flourish" (p. 106), whereas the context shows that he produced them. Such a blunder implies that Mr. Dickens knows neither the meaning of the French *éliminer* nor the Latin *elimino.* He appears to confuse "eliminate" with "elicit." The chapter, however, may be taken as a very fair specimen of the whole work. *Tota Natura in minimis.* Much of the caricature in the second volume is simply like trying to frighten a man by making faces at him; whilst in the chapter on "The Voice of Society," Mr.

Appendix 3: Contemporary Reviews of Our Mutual Friend   197

Dickens becomes as angry as a woman, and as inconsistent as the *Times*. But more extraordinary than any chapter is the preface, or postscript, or apology, for we don't know what to call it, which closes the work. It is divided into five sections, and each section contains a separate fallacy, except one, which contains two. In the first, Mr. Dickens lays down the proposition "that an artist (of whatever denomination) may, perhaps, be trusted to know what he is about in his vocation." Mr. Dickens's later works are the best refutation of his own words. He attempts to be a satirist when he is only a caricaturist, and a philosopher when he is only a humorist. That a man who, as far as can be gathered from his works, has never read a word of Aristotle, should hold such a doctrine, is natural enough. The second contains the old rock on which Mr. Dickens has so often been shipwrecked. His object in "The Mutual Friend," he says, is to "turn a leading incident to a pleasant and useful account," that is to say, if we rightly understand him, to set forth the wrongs of Betty Higden and the Poor Law. Now, true art has nothing to do with such ephemeral and local affairs as Poor Laws and Poor Law Boards; and whenever art tries to serve such a double purpose, it is like an egg with two yolks, neither is ever hatched. This clause also contains the further fallacy that a work of art is best produced in a serial form. As Mr. Dickens gives no reasons whatever for this opinion, we cannot possibly examine them. In the third clause Mr. Dickens defends the plot of his story by the fact that it is founded on reality. But how does that affect the matter? Truth is not always probable. And it is probability which is required in a novel. When honest Wilars de Honecort, in the thirteenth century, wrote under his carved animals, "et saciez bien quil fu contrefais al vif," he only showed how far he still was from a true conception of art. Further, Mr. Dickens's conduct of the plot makes the story still less probable. In Greene's play of "Tu Quoque" occur the following stage directions: "Here they two talke and rayle what they list," "Here they all talk." This may be taken as a short summary of the personages in "The Mutual Friend." In the fourth section Mr. Dickens explains his views about Betty Higden and the Poor Law. Our reply is that a novel is not the place for discussions on the Poor Law. If Mr. Dickens has anything to say about the Poor Law, let him say it in a pamphlet, or go into Parliament. Who is to separate in a novel fiction from fact, romance from reality? If Mr. Dickens knows anything of human nature, he must know that the practical English mind is, as a rule, repelled by any advocacy in the shape of fiction. And to attempt to alter the Poor Law by a novel is about as absurd as it would be to call out the militia to stop the cattle disease. The fifth and last section is entirely personal. We believe that all England would have been deeply shocked had Mr. Dickens been killed in the Staplehurst accident. But many minds will be equally shocked by the melodramatic way in which he speaks of his escape. Those who are curious to understand the tricks of his style should analyse the last section. He first endeavours to raise a joke about Mr. and Mrs. Lammle, "in their manuscript dress," and his other fictitious characters being rescued from the railway carriage, and then turns off to moralize and improve upon his own escape, concluding the whole with a theatrical tag about "The End," which refers both to the conclusion of his book and his life. We write this in no carping spirit, but because it so fully explains to us the cause of Mr. Dickens's failures, a want of sincerity, and a determination to raise either a laugh or a tear at the expense of the most sacred of things. After all that can be said, Art is still the flowering of man's moral nature.

[The final two paragraphs of the review essay move on to two other books, Alfred Austin's *Won by a Head. A Novel* and Winwood Reade's *See-Saw. A Novel.*]

Unidentified Reviews

(A) "Mr. Dickens's New Story," London Review, *April 30, 1864, pp. 473–4*

Few literary pleasures are greater than that which we derive from opening the first number of one of Mr. Dickens's stories. The chief of modern novelists, or at any rate among the chief, he has now, by the intimate knowledge of many years, become a cherished and familiar friend. We associate his "Pickwick" with our younger days, and thence, down a long array of wonderful creations, track his course in pleasant memories and abiding impressions. It is so long since we have had a new novel from him in the old form of monthly numbers that we welcome the present return of that mode of issue with all the greater zest. The small morsels of "Great Expectations" which he used to give us from week to week in *All the Year Round* were only sufficient to provoke, not to satisfy, our appetites, and we always felt that nothing could permanently supplant the monthly parts. Here, then, we have them again. Here is the pleasant green cover, with its pictorial foreshadowing of the story; here are the well-known thirty-two pages demy octavo; here are the two illustrations—not, however, steel etchings by Mr. Hablot K. Browne, but woodcuts by Mr. Marcus Stone. This is an alteration which, we confess, we regret; for, although Mr. Stone's drawings are striking and artistic, we cannot readily give up the old companionship.

The story opens with a scene on the river at sunset, at which time a dirty and disreputable looking boat, with two figures in it (a man and a girl) is floating between Southwark and London-bridge. The man is looking out for waifs and strays in the current; the girl is rowing, with "a touch of dread or horror" in her face. We do not see or hear much of these characters (father and daughter, as the reader may suppose) in the first chapter; but they come in again in the third, where we find that the 'longshore man had discovered a dead body in the river, in which a gentleman named Mortimer Lightwood has some species of interest. In the intermediate chapter, Mortimer Lightwood has related at the dinner-table of a friend a strange story of this man, whose death he is not then aware of, from which it appears that he is the son of an eccentric old dust-contractor, deceased, who has left him the bulk of his property, on condition of his marrying a certain girl. The son has been at the Cape, and is on his return to England, after his father's death, where he meets with his own, seemingly by foul play. The future course of the story is very obscurely intimated in this first instalment, and the tale is evidently intended to be one of mystery and gloom; but enough is foreshadowed to make us all eager for the next number. A lurid glare invests the scene on the river and

Appendix 3: Contemporary Reviews of Our Mutual Friend   199

in the river-side colony of Rotherhithe; and all the component parts of the picture are painted with the mingled fidelity and poetic insight for which Mr. Dickens is remarkable. The comic, however, is not overlooked. The sketch of the Veneerings, and of their pretentious dinner parties, is admirable. Here is what the looking-glass reflects on one of those grand occasions:—

> The great looking-glass above the sideboard reflects the table and the company. Reflects the new Veneering crest, in gold and eke in silver, frosted and also thawed, a camel of all work. The Heralds' College found out a Crusading ancestor for Veneering who bore a camel on his shield (or might have done it if he had thought of it), and a caravan of camels take charge of the fruits and flowers and candles, and kneel down to be loaded with the salt. Reflects Veneering; forty, wavy-haired, dark, tending to corpulence, sly, mysterious, filmy—a kind of sufficiently well-looking veiled-prophet, not prophesying. Reflects Mrs. Veneering; fair, aquiline-nosed and fingered, not so much light hair as she might have, gorgeous in raiment and jewels, enthusiastic, propitiatory, conscious that a corner of her husband's veil is over herself. Reflects Podsnap; prosperously feeding, two little light-coloured wiry wings, one on either side of his else bald head, looking as like his hairbrushes as his hair, dissolving view of red beads on his forehead, large allowance of crumpled shirt-collar up behind. Reflects Mrs. Podsnap; fine woman for Professor Owen, quantity of bone, neck and nostrils like a rocking-horse, hard features, majestic head-dress in which Podsnap has hung golden offerings. Reflects Twemlow; grey, dry, polite, susceptible to east wind, First-Gentleman-in-Europe collar and cravat, cheeks drawn in as if he had made a great effort to retire into himself some years ago, and had got so far and had never got any farther. Reflects mature young lady; raven locks, and complexion that lights up well when well powdered—as it is—carrying on considerably in the captivation of mature young gentleman; with too much nose in his face, too much ginger in his whiskers, too much torso in his waistcoat, too much sparkle in his studs, his eyes, his buttons, his talk, and his teeth. Reflects charming old Lady Tippins on Veneering's right; with an immense obtuse drab oblong face, like a face in a tablespoon, and a dyed Long Walk up the top of her head, as a convenient public approach to the bunch of false hair behind, pleased to patronize Mrs. Veneering opposite, who is pleased to be patronized.

"Our Mutual Friend" opens well, and we are soon to know what the title means.

(B) From "Our Weekly Gossip," Athenaeum, *April 30, 1864, p. 613*

In a fly note to the first number of 'Our Mutual Friend,'—a little green book, which, to the delight of thousands of readers, has made its appearance—Mr. Dickens explains that on arriving at the ninth chapters of his story the public will understand the use of the popular phrase "Our Mutual Friend" as the title of his new book. This ninth chapter will appear in July, in the third number; but we dare say the reader will guess, and will be satisfied with the guess, that the popular phrase has been chosen by our great novelist as expressive of the humour of one

200   *Charles Dickens's* Our Mutual Friend

of his characters, just as the phrase "Something will turn up" might have been used as a title for the fabulous history of Mr. Micawber. The story, about the name of which the critics are finding so much easy and needless fault, opens in a tragic vein—with a powerful scene (suggestive as the heath and witches in 'Macbeth') on the Thames, between Southwark and London Bridges. That some persons live on the great river, and by the great river—mudlarks and others—we know;—but that people make a profession of boating for dead bodies, rifling the clothes and selling the corpses, is a horrible fact, of which few have any suspicion. Gaffer and his daughter Lizzie follow this trade, with such rough sensibilities and chivalries as belong to their class. The picture of their doings is lightly touched; but for dark and impressive power the sketch is like a scene by Michael Angelo. Not less good, though in a bright and humorous style, is the account of Mrs. Veneering's house, with the new furniture, the new friends, the new baby, the new plate, and everything else that is gay and fresh to match. It is doubtful whether Mr. Dickens has produced a dinner-party in a style of more genuine comedy than the one in this new place and family. The table is succeeded by a gallery of portraits. In the Wilfer Family, again, we have a glimpse of character, a rollicksome gaiety, a tenderness of humour, which no other living writer can approach. In returning to his old form of publication, Mr. Dickens seems to have recovered the buoyancy and spirit of his youth.

[Remainder takes up topics of contemporary interest.]

(C) From "Short Notices. Our Mutual Friend *[No. 2],"* London Review, *June 11, 1864, p. 634*

Several fresh characters are introduced into the second number of Mr. Dickens's work—Silas Wegg, an old fellow who keeps a stall at a dusty, east-windy corner near Cavendish-square; Mr. Boffin, a fat, well-to-do, ignorant man, who engages Mr. Wegg to come to him in the evening, and read Gibbon's "Decline and Fall;" Mr. Venus, a stuffer of dead beasts and birds, who has had transactions with Harmon, the deceased dust-contractor; and some others. The two first of these characters are in Mr. Dickens's well-known grotesque manner; and Mr. Venus is also somewhat of an oddity. The gem of the number is the chapter in which the girl, Lizzie Hexam, her brother, and her father, are re-introduced, and which is full of pathos and power. We still see but little of the future course of the story, but it promises to be curiously involved.

[Remainder consists of reviews and notices of other recently published books.]

(D) From "Miscellanea," Reader, *June 11, 1864, p. 745*

Mr. Dickens has never given to the public a conception more superbly comic in the richest style of grotesque invention than appears in the second part of *Our Mutual Friend.* It ought to be taken note of at once as positively an event or feat. We refer to the notice of Nicodemus Boffin, the retired labourer, who, having come into a

Appendix 3: Contemporary Reviews of Our Mutual Friend   201

little property in his old age, and never having learnt to read, takes his exclusion from the world of print so much to heart that he resolves to break into it in a way of his own. He hires a stall-keeper whom he picks up at a street-corner to come and read to him in the evenings for five shillings a-week—having ascertained that the stall-keeper can read anything in print right off by hearing him read a ballad to a butcher-boy. When the stall-keeper goes for his first reading, he finds that Boffin has laid in for the purpose a book in eight volumes, purchased at hazard for its bulk and binding. This is Gibbon's "Decline and Fall of the Roman Empire," and the confusion of head into which Boffin gets into after his first dose of the Roman emperors is something magnificent.

[Remainder consists of miscellaneous notices of recent public and social events.]

(E) From "Short Notices. Our Mutual Friend *[No. 3],"* London Review, *July 2, 1864, p. 25*

In the new number, Mr. Boffin, "of the Bower," in accordance with the terms of old Harmon's will, comes into the possession of £100,000, and consults Mr. Lightwood, as his legal adviser, upon drawing up a will, leaving the whole of it to Mrs. Boffin. He is very explicit on this point:—"Make it as short as you can, but make it tight." On his road home, he meets Rokesmith, who wishes to become his secretary. This Rokesmith gives the title to the story. He is the "Mutual Friend" of Boffin and the Wilfers, and, during his residence with the family of the latter, has enjoyed several opportunities of ingratiating himself with Bella. Boffin holds a consultation with his wife, and those excellent persons agree to adopt an orphan, to remind them of young Harmon. We are again introduced to the Veneerings—in this instance at a wedding-breakfast, the description of which is written in Mr. Dickens's most peculiar and humorous style. As the eye glances over the green cover, we are enabled from the first three numbers to account for the several groups, with the single exception of the bottom one representing two young men, *exactly alike*, meeting apparently for the first time. Is one of these John Harmon (not murdered, after all), and the other an impostor attempting to pass off as the son of old Harmon? and is either of them Rokesmith? Time will answer these questions; but we cannot help thinking Rokesmith knows more of John Harmon than either Boffin or Bella dream of.

[Remainder consists of reviews and notices of other recently published books.]

(F) From "Short Notices. Our Mutual Friend *[No. 4],"* London Review, *August 6, 1864, pp. 162–3*

Mr. Podsnap, one of Mr. Veneering's bran-new bosom friends, appears this month to great advantage. He is the personification of what Mr. Dickens is pleased to call "Podsnappery." One of the characteristics of "Podsnappery" is the "young person," an institution which is carefully guarded from the outside world, yet so insecurely as not to prevent Mr. and Mrs. Lammle ("most loving of husbands and wives") from forming a connection with it. This promises to be of considerable importance to Miss Georgiana Podsnap, who is the sole representative of "the institution." Of Boffin we hear incidentally that his neighbours have named him "the golden dustman." Lightwood and Wrayburn, while discussing their arrangements for the long vacation, are waited upon by Rogue Riderhood, some time "pardner of Gaffer Hexam," whom he accuses of the murder of Harmon in order to obtain the large reward offered. This necessitates a visit to Mr. Inspector and the "Six Jolly Fellowship Porters," and the Gaffer is sought for, but only his boat found. Mr. Marcus Stone depicts Podsnappery and the interior of Hexam's hovel as seen by Eugene while on the watch for the accused murderer. The girl is waiting for her father, but we fail to see any character in her face. We must, indeed, protest against the wretched abortions which Mr. Stone is giving under the designation of "illustrations." The two in the first number led us to expect better things; but since then they have got worse and worse. In changing his old companion, Mr. Hablot K. Browne, Mr. Dickens has made, we think, an unfortunate mistake.

[Remainder consists of reviews and notices of other recently published books.]

(G) From "Short Notices. Our Mutual Friend *[No. 5],"* London Review, *September 3, 1864, pp. 273–4*

The disappearance of Gaffer Hexam, with which the August number of *Our Mutual Friend* concluded, is sufficiently accounted for in the opening chapter for this month by the discovery of his body by Riderhood. The impressions of "Mr. Inspector" lead to the conclusion that the miserable man died by his own hand—not indeed intentionally, but by accident, and in a way rather too singular and elaborate for us to describe in a brief paragraph. We are treated to a much longer interview with our Mutual Friend this time than we have hitherto been permitted to enjoy. Rokesmith waits upon Boffin, yclept the Golden Dustman at the Bower, and, catching that worthy in the act of muddling his papers and brains at the same time, judiciously takes the task out of his hands, indites a letter to himself offering the secretaryship which he had previously solicited when he first attained the position which gives the title to the story, and accepts it to the satisfaction of Boffin and wife. As a highflyer at Fashion, the amiable Mrs. B. has succeeded in the contest against her husband's predilections for "Comfort," and it has been decided that they shall "go neck and crop for Fashion." The first step taken, with Rokesmith's assistance in furtherance of this design, is the purchase of "the eminently aristocratic mansion," near to which Wegg keeps his stall, soon to be given up for the guardianship of the Bower, with "coals and candles, and a pound a-week," and his salary as reader of the "Decline and Fall" going on, not forgetting the special arrangement, "that the dropping into poetry is friendly." Bella Wilfer is invited to the big house, at which the Veneerings, Twemlow, and Podsnap, *et hoc genus omne*, feel it incumbent upon them to leave "copper plates,"

Appendix 3: Contemporary Reviews of Our Mutual Friend   203

either "requesting the honour of Mr. and Mrs. Boffin's company to dinner with the utmost analytical solemnities," or "Mrs. Tapkins at home Wednesdays. Music, Portland Place." This new state of things, in the midst of which the Boffins find themselves, is styled "A Dismal Swamp," and in its description we have several of the shams of society exposed with a master hand. In a private interview which Rokesmith has with Miss Wilfer, and at which he falls deeper in love with her, to be treated, however, only with contemptuous pride, a little light is thrown upon each of their characters which, though it gives the reader a clearer knowledge of the lady, only deepens the mystery which surrounds "Our Mutual Friend." We leave Wegg poking about the dust-mounds in "Boffin's Bower," peering under the bedsteads and surveying the tops of presses and cupboards in a way that seems to suggest the probability that he expects to find something. The story is getting very complicated and curious. With this, the fifth number, the first book of Mr. Dickens's romance is brought to a close.

[Remainder consists of reviews and notices of other recently published books.]

(H) From "Short Notices. Our Mutual Friend *[No. 6], "* London Review, *October 1, 1864, p. 386*

The October part of this tale commences Book II., which is entitled "Birds of a Feather." The first two chapters are "Of an Educational Character," and in them we once more meet Charley Hexam, who by this time (six months after the death of Gaffer) is a pupil-teacher in the school of which Mr. Bradley Headstone is the master. The master and pupil pay a visit to Lizzie, who supports herself with work at a wholesale clothier's, and lives in a house kept by a drunken vagabond, named Cleaver. This Cleaver has a daughter, Fanny, a poor little cripple, who works at dressing dolls. As "the person of the house," this little thing takes upon herself to lecture her father for his bad habits. Eugene Wrayburn is a frequent visitor at Lizzie's lodgings, and, though he has lost none of his characteristic carelessness, his admiration for the pure-minded girl rapidly increases. After some time, he urges her to allow him to provide a teacher for her, and she consents. While Headstone and Charley are returning home, they meet Wrayburn on the road to Lizzie's. This greatly annoys the brother, who consults with his master upon the very question then occupying the mind of the seemingly thoughtless barrister. The third chapter—"A Piece of Work"—relates to the Veneerings. Britannia finds she wants Veneering in Parliament, and accordingly applies to him through a legal gentleman. Veneering, in his turn, applies to Twemlow, Podsnap, and the rest, and, by their united efforts, not to forget the herculean labours of Lady Tippins, the worthy gentleman is returned for Pocket-Breeches, after a fine address to the free and independent electors. We cannot conclude our notice of this last part without again referring to the wretched character of the illustrations, which would be disgraceful even to a small provincial town.

[Remainder consists of reviews and notices of other recently published books.]

204   *Charles Dickens's* Our Mutual Friend

(I) From "Short Notices. Our Mutual Friend *[No. 7],"* London Review, *November 5, 1864, p. 518*

In the new number of Mr. Dickens's tale, the friendship which Podsnap the Great allows the Young Person to form with the happy Lammles is in a very fair way to produce results quite remote from the usual course things take in connection with Podsnappery. We are admitted to a closer inspection of the private life of Mrs. Lammles and her dear Alfred, and meet strange company at their house. Mr. Fascination Fledgeby, "a young gentleman living on his means, but known secretly to be a kind of outlaw in the bill-broking line, and to put money out at high interest in various ways," is, through the disinterested kindness of the worthy pair, introduced to Georgiana, after he has carefully ascertained beforehand that the Young Person has money in her own right. "Cupid Prompted"—the opening chapter of the present number—gives the details of the conspiracy to get the unsuspecting child firmly into the grasp of these wretches. Young Hexam, accompanied by his schoolmaster, pays a visit to Eugene Wrayburn, who receives them with the most irritating politeness. The young barrister's visitors have to complain of his marked attentions to Lizzie, and young Hexam delivers himself of a very violent speech, characterized by utter selfishness. Wrayburn requests the schoolmaster to look more carefully to the manners of his pupil, and thus brings upon himself the wrath of that worthy. After he has pursued the same line as the boy had taken, both quit the Temple, and Wrayburn immediately relapses into his ordinary manner. The scene is most effectively worked out, and helps to unfold the complicated and not very pleasing disposition of Wrayburn in a natural and striking way. Though the story does not make much progress in the present number, the exhibition of character will make amends for the absence of exciting incidents. Of the illustrations we can only say what we have said before, that they appear to us slovenly and feeble.

[Remainder consists of reviews and notices of other recently published books.]

(J) From "Short Notices. Our Mutual Friend *[No. 8],"* London Review, *December 3, 1864, p. 622*

In the present number we return to Silas Wegg, whose residence at the Bower affords him opportunities of prying about, his mind being haunted with the belief that under one of the gigantic dust-mounds something lies hidden, the discovery of which may prove of great advantage to himself, and bring ruin upon his benefactor, the good-natured and simple-minded Boffin, against whom he cherishes a bitter hatred, though at present he has the cunning to conceal it. Having found by personal experience that his wooden leg is not conducive to dispatch in "prodding and scraping" after lost papers and jewellery buried under enormous dust-heaps, he invites Mr. Venus, of Clerkenwell, to "rum-and-water and pipes," and the interesting couple arrange terms of partnership on which to carry on the business. During their *tête-à-tête*, Rokesmith, the secretary, somewhat unexpectedly makes

Appendix 3: Contemporary Reviews of Our Mutual Friend   205

his appearance at the window of the room in which the two scamps are enjoying themselves. But he quietly gives Wegg a kind message from Mr. Boffin, and then unconcernedly leaves, without affording either of them or the reader an idea as to whether he has overheard the conversation. The origin of Wegg's ingratitude is to be traced in a great measure to his jealousy of the influence Rokesmith exercises over their common employer. Miss Wilfer has left her parents, and gone to live with Mr. and Mrs. Boffin at their large mansion "at the corner," where she enters upon all the ceremonials incident to her changed position with becoming grace, growing lovelier day by day, and causing Rokesmith many a heartache. Mr. Rokesmith is as indefinite as ever—very indefatigable in all that relates to the Golden Dustman's business, still residing with the Wilfers, never on any account meeting any of the visitors at the corner house, and more especially avoiding Lawyer Lightwood. The only thing about him that at all approaches to certainty is his love for Bella. This young lady visits her home, quarrels with her mamma and sister, and then goes into the city for her papa, with whom she "elopes" to Greenwich for the day, after having made him purchase a very superior suit of clothes, with boots, hat, and gloves to match, out of a purse which Mr. Boffin has given her. Bella is gradually being spoilt with her good fortune; but her love for her father is a redeeming feature. She tells him she is "very mercenary, and has made up her mind to marry money." It would appear from this that Mr. Secretary's chance is but slight. "Our Johnny," whom Mrs. Boffin had intended to adopt as John Harmon, is suddenly taken ill, and, when too late, admitted to the Children's Hospital to die. This gives Mr. Dickens an opportunity to describe the sick ward, which he does in words which present a picture of great power and beauty. A successor to "Our Johnny" is found in "Sloppy," who turns the mangle for old Mrs. Higden. We are glad to be able to note an improvement this month in Mr. Marcus Stone's illustrations, which exhibit more character and power.

[Remainder consists of reviews and notices of other recently published books.]

(K) From "Short Notices. Our Mutual Friend *[No. 9]," London Review, January 7, 1865, p. 22*

Mr. Dickens has in this number removed the mystery surrounding Mr. Boffin's Secretary. A man, disguised as a sailor, visits Rogue Riderhood, and, working upon his fears, extorts from that worthy a promise to sign a paper declaring Gaffer Hexam to be innocent of the charges laid against him. This person is none other than John Harmon, the son of the late owner of the Bower, and heir to the fortune now in possession of the Golden Dustman. Upon his arrival in England, he changed clothes with a sailor, Radfoot, very much like him in appearance, by whom he was drugged, and thrown for dead into the river. Escaping from these perils, he assumed the name of Julius Handford, but was soon after horrified at sight of the body of the murdered sailor, supposed by the public to be Harmon. Wishing to learn something of Bella Wilfer before proving his identity, he kept the secret to himself, and as John Rokesmith took lodgings at the Wilfers.' Hearing

206   *Charles Dickens's* Our Mutual Friend

that Riderhood had accused an innocent man of the murder, he visits him, dressed in Radfoot's clothes; and the Rogue, conscious of his own villainy in the attempt at a double murder, readily promises to clear the memory of Hexam for the sake of his family. The reader being now fully aware of the reality of John Harmon in the person of Rokesmith, much additional interest is centred in the "mercenary" Bella. The Secretary takes an opportunity to declare his affection for her, and is somewhat harshly repulsed. His proposal is treated with disdain, and he resolves to "bury" John Harmon—to "cover him, crush him, keep him down" for ever. Harmon is not the only one disappointed in love. Poor little plump Miss Peecher, the certificated school-mistress, is rendered very miserable because Mr. Bradley Headstone thinks more of Lizzie Hexam than of her; though, had she known the result of an awkward visit which he made to his pupil teacher's sister, she might have taken comfort to herself. There is no doubt that poor Lizzie is devotedly attached to Eugene Wrayburn; but whether under the carelessness which that young barrister affects there lies hidden a regard for Lizzie, the future pages of this interesting story will unfold.

[Remainder consists of reviews and notices of other recently published books.]

(L) From "Short Notices. Our Mutual Friend *[No. 10]," London Review, February 4, 1865, p. 156*

The last number of "Our Mutual Friend" brings the first volume to a conclusion; for, contrary to Mr. Dickens's usual custom, the work is to be so divided. In the present part, John Harmon is still determined to bury himself from his friends, and, as a preliminary, makes arrangements for leaving the Boffins, and with them Miss Bella Wilfer. The Golden Dustman is still engaged in doing good. Betty Higden is furnished with a well-filled pedlar's basket, with which she intends to try her fortunes in the country, but with the primary object of running away from Sloppy. Poor devoted Sloppy thinks he "can do right by the Boffins and Betty both together;" while Betty is of opinion that, "to give himself up to being put in the way of arning a good living and getting on, he must give her up;" and she accordingly takes this step to assist his advancement. The Boffins decide upon the cabinet-making business for Sloppy, and the Secretary arranges with Mr. Bradley Headstone for giving instruction to this youth, whose unselfish nature contrasts so strongly with the worldly character of Charles Hexam. From the schoolmaster Rokesmith gets some information concerning Lizzie, to whom he sends the document which Riderhood signs, declaring Gaffer Hexam innocent of the crime of murder. Bradley, in pursuance of his promise, seeks another interview with Lizzie, who gently but firmly rejects his proposals. The interview is a terrible one, and is told with more than ordinary force. Bradley rushes away in fury, threatening the life of Wrayburn, and leaving Lizzie with her brother, who adds to her distress by his selfish conduct. She is found in this extremity by Mr. Riah, who conducts her home. On the way they are met by Eugene, whose assumed carelessness scarcely hides his anxiety for her welfare. The next we hear of her is related at

Appendix 3: Contemporary Reviews of Our Mutual Friend   207

Mr. Lammle's anniversary of his wedding breakfast, where Lightwood informs the guests, by way of a sequel to the story of the "man from somewhere," that Lizzie has "disappeared, nobody knows how; nobody knows when; nobody knows where." Mrs. Lammle has experienced a year of married life, and inaugurates the new one by betraying to Twemlow her husband's designs upon Georgiana Podsnap, after extorting a promise from that nervous gentleman not to betray her, but to put himself into immediate communication with the fountain-head of Podsnappery, in order to warn him of the danger to which the "young person" is exposed by her intimacy with the "happy couple." Mrs. Lammle proves herself to be a very clever woman when she relates all this to Twemlow in her husband's immediate presence, and with his suspicious eye upon her. —We cannot, in justice to Mr. Marcus Stone, whose illustrations we have had occasion, in previous parts, to decry for their slovenliness, conclude this brief notice without giving very high praise to the two sketches in the present number. The one called "A Friend in Need" is most admirable for its character, picturesqueness, and effective management of light and shade.

[Remainder consists of reviews and notices of other recently published books.]

(M) From "Short Notices. Our Mutual Friend *[No. 11]," London Review, March 4, 1865, p. 258*

Book the Third—"A Long Lane"—opens with an account of "the lodgers in Queer-street," among whom are included the Lammles, whose designs upon Georgiana Podsnap have been nipped in the bud, the august head of Podsnappery having addressed a characteristic note to Alfred Lammle, Esq., to "communicate his final desire that the two families may become entire strangers." Lammle seeks his friend Fledgeby in this extremity, and receives advice from that worthy to avoid Pubsey & Co., whose representative, Riah, he finds closeted with young "Fascination." The bill-discounter orders his humble Jewish auxiliary to buy up a parcel of "queer bills," in order that he may get the run of Queer-street, and play some games with his "knowing friends," who little dream of his connection with the firm of Pubsey & Co. Fledgeby has found out that Lizzie Hexam is secreted in the country by Riah, but what interest he has in this discovery does not yet appear. Lizzie has given Rogue Riderhood's declaration of her father's innocent to Riah, who, accompanied by Jenny Wren, pays a visit to the Six Jolly Fellowship Porters, to show it to Miss Abbey, the landlady. While the old Jew is copying it at the request of the latter, Riderhood is brought in, apparently lifeless, having been run into in a fog by a steamer. The restoration, effected by the doctor's care, is told with peculiar force. The Wilfer family keep the anniversary of the Cherub's wedding day, and Bella graces the ceremony, making her *début* as cook. On her way home, she tells her father, under a promise of strict silence, four secrets. The first two are that Mr. Rokesmith has proposed to her, and that Mr. Lightfoot wishes to do the same; the third is that the Boffins intend to portion her off handsomely if she marry with their consent; while the last is that Mr. Boffin is being spoilt

208   *Charles Dickens's* Our Mutual Friend

by prosperity, and is changing every day, growing suspicious, capricious, hard, tyrannical, and unjust. We are now more than half through Mr. Dickens's story; but the final development of its complicated plot is as yet only dimly visible.

[Remainder consists of reviews and notices of other recently published books.]

(N) From "Literary Notices," Godey's Lady's Book and Magazine, *April 1865, p. 373*

We have received the first half of Dickens's last, and, we are convinced, his best story. Dickens is in the zenith of his power. Every person who figures in this book is either a character or a caricature. Silas Megg and Mr. Boffin are destined to earthly immortality, and Mr. Veneering will be the standard example of English "shoddydom;" while "Podsnappery" is a word with a significance too pointed and apt to be overlooked. We shall anxiously await the second part of the story.

[Remainder consists of reviews and notices of other recently published books.]

(O) From "Short Notices. Our Mutual Friend *[No. 12],"* London Review, *April 8, 1865, p. 389*

The readers of "Our Mutual Friend" had in the two previous numbers received no tidings of "the Golden Dustman." In the present part, however, Mr. Boffin occupies a large share of attention. He is represented as having fallen into bad company, and growing every day fonder of money. He is seized with a mania for story-books of misers and other eccentric characters, and from time to time conveys whole cab-loads of such volumes to "the Bower" for Wegg to exercise his elocutionary powers upon. On one occasion, after hearing the lives of several extraordinary misers, he visits the mounds, and extracts a bottle from one of them, being watched, however, by Wegg, and his friend and partner, Mr. Venus. The gentleman with the wooden leg is represented as the evil genius of the house of Boffin, and, as matters at present stand, there is little doubt that he consistently sustains the character. During his researches at "the Bower," he accidentally finds in the pump a cash-box containing a paper labeled "My Will, John Harmon, temporarily deposited here." When Venus hears of this discovery, he cunningly gets the document from Wegg into his own keeping; and the two arrange to offer it to Boffin for half his fortune. The will, as to which there is at present no evidence of forgery, is of later date than the one bequeathing the whole of the property to Boffin, is duly witnessed, very short, and runs thus: —"Inasmuch as he has never made friends, and has ever had a rebellious family, he, John Harmon, gives to Nicodemus Boffin the little mound, and gives the whole rest and residue of his property to the Crown." Boffin is, of course, quite unconscious of the existence of this will; and his penurious habits are the source of great anxiety to his wife, and to Rokesmith, his secretary, whom he begins to treat as a menial. Bella, though assured of his attachment to her, views this change in the old man with alarm. Mrs. Lammle, having given up her designs upon Georgiana Podsnap, has, by her husband's directions, directed them towards

Appendix 3: Contemporary Reviews of Our Mutual Friend   209

Bella; and that young lady has already told two secrets to her false friend. The plot begins to thicken, and the interest of the story increases with its progress.

[Remainder consists of reviews and notices of other recently published books.]

(P) From "Short Notices. Our Mutual Friend *[No. 13]," London Review, May 6, 1865, p. 492*

Old Betty Higden, who was supplied with a well-filled pedlar's basked by Mr. Boffin before that gentleman had turned his attention to the absorbing histories of celebrated misers and other eccentric persons, reaches in the present number the end of her long journey. She dies on the roadside, her head supported in the lap of Lizzie Hexam. Betty's repugnance to "the parish" affords Mr. Dickens an opportunity of addressing "my lords and gentlemen, and honourable boards," on the shortcomings of the Poor-law system, which he sums up in these words: —"This boastful handiwork of ours, which fails in its terror for the professional pauper, the sturdy breaker of windows, and the rampant tearer of clothes, strikes with a cruel and wicked stab at the stricken sufferer, and is a horror to the deserving and unfortunate." Betty, twice narrowly escaping from its tender mercies, finds at last repose in a quiet village churchyard in Oxfordshire. Lizzie, at the dying woman's request, transmits the paper which Boffin had given her to the address written on it, and the secretary, Miss Wilfer, and the heart-broken Sloppy, accompanied by the Rev. Frank Milvey and his wife, attend the funeral. Bella has a commission to execute for Mrs. Boffin, and, as Lizzie is the subject of it, the two girls are closeted together for some time. Poor Lizzie opens the whole of her heart to the young lady, and the surmises of the reader are now confirmed. Her love for Eugene is gaining strength from her forced separation from him. "His eyes," she says, "may never look at me again. But I would not have the light of them taken out of my life for anything my life can give me." Bella's prejudices in favour of money receive a mortal wound from the brief intercourse with her new friend, and Mr. Rokesmith gains materially by the change which immediately results. Lizzie Hexam's fears lest the schoolmaster should do Eugene Wrayburn some injury are, it would appear, well-grounded. He never misses an opportunity of following the footsteps of the young barrister, to endeavour to find the whereabouts of his pupil's sister. Wrayburn is as ignorant in this respect as Bradley Headstone, but is equally determined to discover the fact, and for this purpose accepts the proffered services of the drunkard Wren, the "troublesome child" of the doll's dressmaker. Hedstone unceasingly pursues Wrayburn, and on one occasion is observed by Lightwood, "looking like the hunted and not the hunter, baffled, worn, with the exhaustion of deferred hope and consuming hate and anger in his face, white-lipped, wild-eyed, draggle-haired, seamed with jealousy and anger, and torturing himself with the conviction that he showed it all, and they exulted in it." The horrible apparition of this man haunts the mind of Lightwood, but makes no visible change in the cool, careless Eugene; and with the latter's expression of his unconcern the number concludes.

[Remainder consists of reviews and notices of other recently published books.]

210   *Charles Dickens's* Our Mutual Friend

(Q) From "Short Notices. Our Mutual Friend *[No. 14]," London Review, June 3, 1865, p. 595*

Mr. Bradley Headstone, continuing to follow the footsteps of the Templars, makes the acquaintance of Rogue Riderhood, who has obtained honest employment as deputy lock-keeper at Plashwater Weir Lock. Bradley, in the hands of Riderhood, soon betrays his hatred of Wrayburn, and the acquaintance seems likely to lead to serious consequences for more than one of the characters in the story. The Lammles are in pecuniary difficulties, as is also poor little harmless Twemlow, which affords Fledgeby an opportunity to distress his "friend," which he accomplishes through the firm of Pubsey & Co., by the agent, Mr. Riah. Miss Wren is witness of Mr. Riah's apparent harshness, and, from what Mr. Fledgeby tells her, she loses all confidence in the protector of Lizzie Hexam. Boffin hears from Mr. Venus of the existence of the will found by Wegg, but appears to take the information rather coolly, though he is somewhat disturbed when he finds he was watched while removing the bottle from the dust-mound. He overhears Wegg's spiteful intentions, and, while cogitating how to act under the circumstances, he is caught by Mrs. Lammle in a trap she has laid with the connivance of her husband to upset Rokesmith's waning influence, and to get Mr. Lammle the control of the Golden Dustman's property. The story does not make much progress in the present number, which is hardly so interesting as some of those which have gone before. The illustrations, moreover, are inferior to some in the last few parts, and are even worse than what we objected to in the earlier instalments of the work. Mr. Stone's achievements this month are discreditable to the art of the present day, and are certainly nothing like so good as the woodcuts of the penny periodicals.

[Remainder consists of reviews and notices of other recently published books.]

(R) From "Short Notices. Our Mutual Friend *[No. 15]," London Review, July 8, 1865, p. 49*

That Mrs. Lammle is a very clever woman there can be no doubt. Her designs, shared by her husband, upon the property of the Golden Dustman, already begin to bear fruit. The information she gave to the too suspicious Boffin during her last ride in the hired brougham produces a remarkable change in the domestic arrangements at the Corner House. John Rokesmith is insultingly dismissed, in the presence of Bella, from his situation as secretary, and, after he has taken his departure, Bella gives Mr. Boffin a bit of her mind, and leaves the house for ever, thereby renouncing the fortune promised to her. Fearing to go home, she calls at Veneering's office in Mincing-lane, and there takes tea with her cherubic father. Father and daughter are unexpectedly joined by Rokesmith, and, after a very brief explanation, Bella "seemed to shrink to next to nothing in the clasp of his arms, partly because it was such a strong one on his part, and partly because there was such a yielding to it on hers." The great part of the evening, moreover,

Appendix 3: Contemporary Reviews of Our Mutual Friend   211

is spent in a succession of similar "mysterious disappearances." A glimpse at the Cherub's house shows matters to be unaltered, except that Lavvy has accepted the addresses of Mr. George Simpson, and is as irrepressible as ever. Lammle has the pleasure of seeing his things sold by auction under a bill of sale, and his wife is made to perceive Fledgeby's true conduct in the matter. Veneering gives a dinner-party on the inauspicious occasion, to which the usual people are invited, and from which Eugene Wrayburn is summoned by "Old Dolls," who has procured Lizzie Hexam's address, and parts with it for fifteen shillings Altogether, the number for this month takes a considerable step towards the *dénouement*, and is consequently of greater interest than one or two previous issues.

[Remainder consists of reviews and notices of other recently published books.]

(S) From "Short Notices. Our Mutual Friend *[No. 16],"* London Review, *August 5, 1865, p. 153*

With the current number of this story commences the Fourth Book, entitled "A Turning." The reader is introduced to Rogue Riderhood in his new situation as deputy lock-keeper at Plashwater Weir-Mill, where he has to open the creaking lock-gates to permit "T'other governor," Mr. Eugene Wrayburn, to pass through on his visit to Lizzie. Of course, Bradley Headstone has not lost sight of the lawyer-lover, and, taking advantage of his holidays, he is enabled to follow him, dressed in a suit of clothes corresponding in every particular to those usually worn by Riderhood. In spite of his disguise, he is discovered by the Rogue, who is rather perplexed at the schoolmaster's appearance. However, he "sets a trap" for him, and Bradley unconsciously falls into it, which sets the Rogue "a thinking." Affairs are rapidly approaching a crisis. Mr. Boffin rises a step in the moral scale by the way in which he gets rid of the Lammles—husband and wife—and by the protection he affords Georgiana Podsnap; but he soon sinks even lower than the level he occupied when dismissing Rokesmith. Wegg applies the "grindstone," and Boffin, without a struggle, submits to the humiliating operation. Mr. Venus does not treat the Golden Dustman to Wegg's satisfaction, and so that worthy takes upon himself to deal with "the minion of fortune and worm of the hour;" and right savagely does he set about his task. Boffin is obliged to consent to a division of his property, being allowed to retain only one-third of it for his own use. It was not to be expected that Miss Wilfer could endure for any length of time the monotony of her parental dwelling. She therefore very readily falls into Rokesmith's plans, and, with her father as a consenting party, starts for Greenwich, where, at the parish church, she is married to her dear John. The trio adjourn to an hotel, and partake of the wedding breakfast; after, which, the Cherub is hastily packed off to town to change his white waistcoat, and present himself in the evening to his wife, to hear the unexpected tidings which are sent to "Ma" in a very brief note.

[Remainder consists of reviews and notices of other recently published books.]

212   *Charles Dickens's* Our Mutual Friend

(T) From "Short Notices. Our Mutual Friend *[No. 17]," London Review, September 2, 1865, p. 261*

When the Cherub comes home after the intelligence of the wedding has reached Mr. Wilfer he does not find his position more pleasant: but after the irrepressible Lavinia has had a fit of hysterics, "Ma" relents, and the "happy couple" are invited to tea. Bella soon puts things upon their accustomed footing, and we are treated to a very pretty sketch of her domestic arrangements, and the gradual growth of her affection for her husband. Rokesmith finds it a difficult matter to keep the secret of his identity from his dear little wife, but he has at present not betrayed it. From the cheerful home of Bella the scene changes to the village where poor Lizzie Hexam resides and where Eugene Wrayburn is staying. By appointment she meets him by the river-side, and the lovers are watched by Bradley Headstone, in the disguise of a bargeman dressed to represent Riderhood. After drawing from Lizzie a confession of her attachment to him, Eugene leaves her, and immediately afterwards is attacked by Headstone. Stunned by the blows, he is thrown into the river, and Headstone makes with all haste to Plashwater Weir Mill Lock-house. As Eugene's body floats down the stream, it is recognised by Lizzie, who, with great difficulty, contrives to secure it, but the surgeons pronounce life extinct. When the murderer makes his appearance at Plashwater, the Rogue judges from his manner, and torn and soiled dress, what has transpired. While dining together, Bradley contrives to cut his hand, and sprinkle the blood over the Rogue. This apparent accident confirms Riderhood's suspicions that the schoolmaster is desirous that the murder should be ascribed to him. He therefore resolves to follow him; and, while doing so, he sees him bathe in the river and dress in his proper clothes, which had been secreted under some timber. Bradley makes a bundle of the bargee's clothes, and throws them into the river, but Riderhood fishes for, and finally secures them. As soon as the report of the outrage upon Wrayburn reaches town, Charley Hexam, who is by this time an assistant master in another school, and, if possible, more selfish than ever, visits his old master, and upbraids him with his conduct, hinting that he is of opinion that the murdered man owes his death to him.

[Remainder consists of reviews and notices of other recently published books.]

(U) From "Short Notices. Our Mutual Friend *[No. 18]," London Review, October 7, 1865, p. 395*

Though we are now approaching the end of Mr. Dickens's story, there is no diminution of our interest in the characters. Last month we were left in doubt whether Eugene Wrayburn was killed or not; the present number removes that source of anxiety, but leaves us in still greater suspense as regards his future life, for, as he has become the husband of the true-hearted Lizzie, his welfare is all the more a subject of moment. Over his bed watches the tender child Jenny Wren, who has been still further refined by the horrible death of her father in the streets. Lightwood is also there, a splendid type of college friendship. Mr.

Appendix 3: Contemporary Reviews of Our Mutual Friend 213

and Mrs. Rokesmith are invited to the solemn service which makes Lizzie the wife of Eugene; but, as John does not care to meet Lightwood, Bella is, much against her will, obliged to go alone. At the station she is joined by the Rev. Milvey and his lady, and, just before the train starts, that reverend gentleman, in a casual conversation with Headstone, whom he accidentally meets, tells him of Lizzie's contemplated marriage. This intelligence throws the unhappy man into a fit, and the train starts off, leaving Bradley under the care of the railway porters. We thought the Lammles had taken their departure for the Continent immediately after their attempt upon Boffin; but it appears they had one reckoning to pay before quitting England. This was an account due from Lammle to Fledgeby, and right honestly does he pay it, compelling the young man to receive a very heavy amount of interest. Pubsey & Co. dismiss Riah, who sets himself straight with the Dolls' Dressmaker, and assists her under the trying circumstance of her father's death; and so we are left, to bear our impatience for the final development of the story as well as we can.

[Remainder consists of reviews and notices of other recently published books.]

*(V) "Reviews of Books—*Our Mutual Friend*," London Review, October 28, 1865, pp. 467–8*

Mr. Dickens has now been so long before the public, and his name is associated with so many triumphs, some of which were achieved before the present generation of young men and women was born, that he has already obtained the position of a classic, and we judge him by the standard of names consecrated by time. He has exhibited a degree of productiveness rarely seen except in combination with a marked and melancholy falling off from the freshness and power of early manhood. The collected editions of his works now spread over many volumes; the characters he has invented would almost people a town; and we might well excuse an author who has done so much, if we found in him some slackening of the creative force which has been at work for such a length of time. But Mr. Dickens stands in need of no allowance on the score of having out-written himself. His fancy, his pathos, his humour, his wonderful powers of observation, his picturesqueness, and his versatility, are as remarkable now as they were twenty years ago. In some respects, they are seen to still greater advantage. The energy of youth yet remains, but it is united with the deeper insight of maturer years. Not that we mean to say Mr. Dickens has outgrown his faults. They are as obvious as ever—sometimes even trying our patience rather hard. A certain extravagance in particular scenes and persons—a tendency to caricature and grotesqueness—and a something here and there which savours of the melodramatic, as if the author had been considering how the thing would "tell" on the stage—are to be found in "Our Mutual Friend," as in all this great novelist's productions. But when a writer of genius has fully settled his style, and maintained it through a course of many years—when his mind has passed beyond the period of pliability and growth, and can only deepen without essentially changing—it is the merest vanity on the part of a critic to dwell at any great length on general faults of manner. There they are, and there they will remain, say what we will. The tender rind wherein they were cut in youth has become hard bark long since, and the incisions are fixed for ever. To rail at them is simple waste of time, besides implying a great deal of ingratitude on the part of the railer. We shall therefore make but brief allusion here to the characters of Wegg and Venus, who appear to us in the highest degree unnatural—the one being a mere phantasm, and the other a nonentity—and shall pass on to a consideration of the more solid parts of the book, in which Mr. Dickens's old mastery over human nature is once more made splendidly apparent.

As in its author's previous fictions, we are almost oppressed by the fulness of life which pervades the pages of this novel. Mr. Dickens has one of the most mysterious attributes of genius—the power of creating characters which have, so to speak, an overplus of vitality, passing beyond the limits of the tale, and making itself felt like an actual, external fact. In the stories of inferior writers the characters seem to possess just sufficient personality and presence to carry on the purpose of the narrative; one never thinks of them as enjoying any existence at all outside the little tissue of events that has been woven for them. They are ghosts whom the author has evoked out of night and vacuity to perform certain definite offices within the charmed circle of the fiction to which they are attached; and when we step out of that circle at the conclusion of the ceremonies, they vanish again into nothingness, and we think no more of them. Such is not the case with the conceptions of larger geniuses. These do not seem to belong wholly to the one set of events with which they are associated, any more than the men and women we actually know present themselves to our thoughts as the puppets of a definite train of circumstances. The creations of authors such as Mr. Dickens have a life of their own. We perceive them to be full of potential capacities—of undeveloped action. They have the substance and the freedom of actual existences; we think of what they would do under our conditions; they are possessed of a principle of growth. Certainly, the most amazing manifestation of this amazing gift is that which is to be found in the plays of Shakespeare; but all men of genius have it in a greater or less degree, and that strange and even awful power is, perhaps, the surest test for distinguishing between genius and talent. That Mr. Dickens possesses it to a remarkable extent, we believe few will be found to dispute. The chief characters even of his earlier books dwell in the mind with extraordinary tenacity, sometimes quite apart from the plot wherein they figure, which may be utterly forgotten; and no writer of our time has furnished contemporary literature and conversation with so many illustrative allusions. This imaginative fecundity is seen in "Our Mutual Friend" in undiminished strength. The book teems with characters, and throbs with action; but it may perhaps be objected that there is a want of some one conspicuous figure, dominating over the rest, and affording a fixed centre to all this moving wealth of life. John Rokesmith must, we suppose, be regarded as the hero; but he is certainly not the chief character, nor the most interesting. Though in many respects well-drawn, he does not greatly enlist our sympathies—perhaps because his motives of action are strange and improbable. Indeed, the whole story of old Harmon's bequest, and what arises out of it, strikes

Appendix 3: Contemporary Reviews of Our Mutual Friend   215

us as being faulty. This, we are aware, is to proclaim a serious defect in the novel, as such, since we have here the basis of the whole fiction. But Mr. Dickens's collateral conceptions are often better than his main purpose. We must confess that in reading "Our Mutual Friend" from month to month, we cared very little as to what became of old Harmon's property, excepting in as far as the ultimate disposal of that sordid aggregation of wealth affected the development of two or three of the chief characters. The final explanation is a disappointment. The whole plot in which the deceased Harmon, Boffin, Wegg, and John Rokesmith, are concerned, is wild and fantastic, wanting in reality, and leading to a degree of confusion which is not compensated by any additional interest in the story. Mr. Dickens seems to be aware that his tale is liable to this objection, for in the very interesting "Postscript, in Lieu of Preface," which he has appended to the second volume, he says:— "There is sometimes an odd disposition in this country to dispute as improbable in fiction what are the commonest experiences in fact. Therefore I note here, though it may not be at all necessary, that there are hundreds of Will Cases (as they are called) far more remarkable than that fancied in this book; and that the stores of the Prerogative Office teem with instances of testators who have made, changed, contradicted, hidden, forgotten, left cancelled, and left uncancelled, each many more wills than were ever made by the elder Mr. Harmon of Harmony Jail." We do not for a moment doubt this is the fact, and it is not to the terms of Mr. Harmon's will that we object, but to the circumstances flowing from that source. That the son, John Harmon, known through the greater part of the book as John Rokesmith, should come back to England under the circumstances related, should disappear as related, should live for months at the house of his childhood's friends, the Boffins, without being discovered, and should then be suddenly found out without any sufficient explanation; that Mr. Boffin should get entangled with a man like Wegg; that, granting the entanglement, Wegg, with all his cunning, should make his calculations with such transparent stupidity—taking no account of the Dutch bottle which he has seen dug up by Boffin from the dust-heap, and which contains, as the reader all along foresees, the later will which nullifies the will relied on by Wegg for forcing Boffin to give up half his property; that the coarse and insolent treatment of Rokesmith by Boffin, and the growing miserliness of the latter, maintained at all times, and before all people, should be a mere trick, concocted between the two, to turn the regards of proud little Bella Wilfer towards John, and to cure the young lady of her sordid aspirations; and that all this, when the right moment arrives, should be verbally set forth, as in those explanations which we find at the end of plays, when the characters range themselves before the footlights, make their confessions, and unravel the imbroglio; these are features in Mr. Dickens's story which we cannot but regard as in the highest degree improbable, and as detracting from the merit of the book as a whole. The explanation, given towards the close, of the miserly ways and speeches of Mr. Boffin, is particularly unsatisfactory, for it has the effect of making what would otherwise have been a very masterly development of character comparatively poor, forced, and artificial. Mr. Boffin is introduced to the reader as a man of a fine, open, genial, though rough and uncultivated, nature; but, under the influence of the wealth he inherits from old

216   *Charles Dickens's* Our Mutual Friend

Harmon, in consequence of the strange will made by the deceased dust-contractor, he (apparently) becomes hard, miserly, suspicious, and insolent. Assuming this to be a real change, as the reader is led to suppose up until the last chapter but four, nothing can be more natural; and the gradual narrowing of the cheerful, pleasant character of Mr. Boffin, the stealthy creeping of that sordid shadow over heart, and mind, and character, is subtly represented. But when we are told that the whole is a piece of acting, the conception takes a far lower standing artistically, though Mr. Boffin himself takes a higher standing morally. We should be strongly inclined to believe that Mr. Dickens altered his design in the course of publication, were it not for a passage in the Postscript in which, if we rightly understand it, allusion is made to this very part of the story. We there read:—

> "To keep for a long time unsuspected, yet always working itself out, another purpose" [he has just been mentioning the mystery connected with John Rokesmith's double personality], "originating in that leading incident, and turning it to a pleasant and useful account at last, was at once the most interesting and most difficult part of my design. Its difficulty was much enhanced by the mode of publication; for it would be very unreasonable to expect that many readers, pursuing a story in portions from month to month through nineteen months, will, until they have it before them complete, perceive the relations of its finer threads to the whole pattern, which is always before the eyes of the story-weaver at his loom. Yet, that I hold the advantages of the mode of publication to outweigh its disadvantages, may be easily believed of one who revived it in the 'Pickwick Papers' after long disuse, and has pursued it ever since."[5]

If the foregoing passage be really, as we suppose, a reference to the surprise prepared for the reader in connection with Mr. Boffin's miserly manners, it is of course conclusive as to there having been no divergence from the author's original intention. Yet this only renders the whole conduct of the business more violent and arbitrary. Mr. Boffin is described in several places as changing his whole nature, and as even altering in his face, which becomes lined and puckered with the carking thoughts that possess his soul, and which is constantly assuming a cunning look on trivial occasions, when his pocket seems to be touched. His very wife, though concerned in the plot, exhibits grief and surprise at what we are afterwards told she all along knows to be a generous device. Bella has observed this, and, when the explanation is made, she not unnaturally refers to it. Mr. Boffin replies:—"It was a weakness in the old lady; and yet, to tell you the whole truth and nothing but the truth, I'm rather proud of it. My dear, the old lady thinks so high of me that she couldn't abear to see and hear me coming out a reg'lar brown one" (Mr. Boffin's designation for a bear). "Couldn't abear to make believe as I meant it! In consequence of which, we was everlastingly in danger with her." We venture to think that most readers will feel that the story loses in verisimilitude and interest by such a mode of winding it up.

---

⁵ Quotation marks, square brackets, and enclosed phrase appear in the original as shown.

Appendix 3: Contemporary Reviews of Our Mutual Friend   217

The termination of Mr. Dickens's novels is often hurried, and such is the case in the present instance. The complication of events does not work itself clear by a slow and natural process, but is, so to speak, roughly torn open. And, even before we are half through the book, the mystery concerning John Rokesmith is explained in an equally objectionable manner. Young Rokesmith, or Harmon, *tells himself* his own previous history, in a sort of mental soliloquy (in which a long series of events is minutely narrated), evidently for no other purpose than to inform the reader. It is surprising that so experienced a romance-writer as Mr. Dickens could not have devised some more artful means of revealing that portion of his design. Yet, notwithstanding these defects (which we have pointed out with the greater freedom, because such a writer demands the utmost candour from his critic), the story of "Our Mutual Friend" is interesting for its own sake, even apart from the treatment; which, we need not say, is that of a master, if we except those points already objected to. We repeat what we said at the commencement—that, in conception and evolution of character, and in power of writing, this latest work of the pen that has so often delighted and astonished us shows not the slightest symptom of exhaustion or decline. Perhaps the most admirable of the *dramatis personæ*, considered on artistic grounds, are Eugene Wrayburn, Lizzie Hexam, Bradley Headstone, and Bella Wilfer. The first of these characters is a consummate representation of a nature, originally noble, degenerating, under the effects of a bad education and of subsequent idleness, into a laughing indifference to all things worthy—into a gay and sportive disbelief in itself, in manhood, in womanhood, and in the world. From first to last, the conception is wonderfully developed, and the change that is afterwards wrought in Eugene's disposition is worked out without the smallest violence. In strong contrast with the good-natured levity of Wrayburn is the stern, self-contained, narrow, yet (within its contracted and mechanical limits) earnest, nature of Bradley Headstone, the self-educated schoolmaster. Lizzie Hexam is the cause of bringing these two men into dangerous contact. She is the daughter of a man who drags the river for anything he can get—dead bodies among the rest—and who is sometimes suspected of having more to do with the dead bodies than he would like to confess. The girl, however, is a fine sensitive being, handsome, and of a deep, tender nature; and when Eugene Wrayburn sees her after the death of her father on the river, he takes an interest in her fate, and has her educated. His interest deepens into love, yet he cannot bring himself to make an honest offer of marriage to one who comes of such humble and even questionable parentage. Bradley Headstone also is in love with Lizzie; and the way in which his impassive, artificially-restrained nature breaks up into raging fury under the combined influences of hopeless love, jealousy, and some pungent taunts which Wrayburn gaily flings at him, is exhibited by Mr. Dickens with marvellous power and truthfulness. The transformation of this pattern of all the decencies into a dark, haggard, self-tormenting evil genius, perpetually dogging the steps of Eugene Wrayburn, and at length making a murderous attack on him in a lonely place up the river, is one of the finest things in fiction. Bradley Headstone is a psychological study of the deepest interest, and, we are persuaded, of the profoundest truth.

Natures like his, originally cold, and still further repressed by the routine of a dry and formal education, are no doubt especially liable to outbreaks of ungovernable passion when some great emotion at length sweeps away the old habits of self-control. Mr. Dickens has traced this with a singularly close and analytical eye, and nothing can be more tragic and impressive than the culmination of Bradley Headstone's wrath in the attempted murder of Eugene. All the preparations for that act, and all the accessories in the way of scenery and atmospherical conditions, are managed in Mr. Dickens's highest style; and the mental state of a man about to commit the greatest of crimes has seldom been depicted with such elaboration and apparent truthfulness. We are prepared to hear from a certain class of critics who can tolerate nothing beyond the civilities of everyday life, and who seem to think that great passions are among those vulgar mistakes of nature to which novelists should be superior, that this character is "sensational;" but the genius that could conceive it has nothing to fear from such objectors. Very touching and beautiful is the character of Lizzie Hexam; but probably the greatest favourite in the book will be—or rather is already—Bella Wilfer. She is evidently a pet of the author's, and she will long remain the darling of half the households of England and America. Perverse, petulant, wilful, wrong-headed, not a little inclined at first to be selfish and money-loving, she is yet a bewitching little creature, and it is no surprise to find that in the end all the good in her impulsive nature bursts into efflorescence beneath the sunshine of a happy love. Of the less important characters of the book it is impossible to speak, they are so numerous; but reference should be made to the pathetic sketch of Betty Higden and little Johnny, her great-grandchild. That the poor old creature's proud defiance of workhouse charity is true to a large number of our English lower class, is but too certain from cases with which we are familiar; and the sketch is more especially interesting as having drawn from Mr. Dickens, in the final words from which we have already quoted, a declaration of his views on the present administration of the Poor Laws:—

In my social experiences since Mrs. Betty Higden came upon the scene and left it, I have found Circumlocutional champions disposed to be warm with me on the subject of my view of the Poor Law. My friend Mr. Bounderby could never see any difference between leaving the Coketown 'hands' exactly as they were, and requiring them to be fed with turtle soup and venison out of gold spoons. Idiotic propositions of a parallel nature have been freely offered for my acceptance, and I have been called upon to admit that I would give Poor Law relief to anybody, anywhere, anyhow. Putting this nonsense aside, I have observed a suspicious tendency in the champions to divide into two parties; the one contending that there are no deserving poor who prefer death by slow starvation and bitter weather to the mercies of some relieving officers and some Union houses; the other, admitting that there are such poor, but denying that they have any cause or reason for what they do. The records in our newspapers, the late exposure by the *Lancet*, and the common senses of common people, furnish too abundant evidence against both defences. But, that my view of the Poor Law may not be mistaken or misrepresented, I will state it. I believe there has been in England, since the days of the Stuarts, no law so often infamously administered, no law so

Appendix 3: Contemporary Reviews of Our Mutual Friend   219

often openly violated, no law habitually so ill-supervised. In the majority of the shameful cases of disease and death from destitution that shock the public and disgrace the country, the illegality is quite equal to the inhumanity—and known language could say no more of their lawlessness.

We must also instance among the creations of this book the little deformed dolls' dressmaker (fantastic and semi-poetical, yet with a deep instinct of truth); her drunken father—a sketch in which tragedy and comedy are mingled in a way wherein Mr. Dickens is quite unrivalled; Bella's father, a beautiful specimen of a truly loveable nature; the Podsnaps and Veneerings, and the crew of rapscallions and adventurers, male and female, by whom they are surrounded—portraits admirable for the social satire they embody; Rogue Riderhood, and some of the other hangers-on about the river. We might almost mention the river itself as a character. It plays a most important part in the story, and always with great picturesqueness.

We cannot refrain, ere we conclude, from referring once more to the Postscript, for the sake of its allusion to an event in which at the time we were all deeply interested:—

> On Friday, the 9th of June in the present year, Mr. and Mrs. Boffin (in their manuscript dress of receiving Mr. and Mrs. Lammle at breakfast) were on the South-Eastern Railway with me, in a terribly destructive accident. When I had done what I could to help others, I climbed back into my carriage—nearly turned over a viaduct, and caught a-slant upon the turn—to extricate the worthy couple. They were much soiled, but otherwise unhurt. The same happy result attended Miss Bella Wilfer on her wedding day, and Mr. Riderhood inspecting Bradley Headstone's red neckerchief as he lay asleep. I remember with devout thankfulness that I can never be much nearer parting company with my readers for ever than I was then, until there shall be written against my life the two words with which I have this day closed this book:—THE END.

In that "devout thankfulness" the whole English-speaking race will share. We cannot afford to lose such a writer as Mr. Dickens. A man of original, creative genius dying in the fulness of his strength, leaves a gap which nothing can fill, and a regret which the memory of his past triumphs only deepens and embitters.

(W) "Mr. Dickens's Romance of a Dust-heap," Eclectic and Congregational Review, *November 1865, pp. 455–76*

After a lapse of nearly ten years, Mr. Dickens has returned to his old, and apparently still much beloved method of developing his various impressions of social life, and entertaining his multitude of readers. We do not wonder that for him this method has strong fascination, so that he says he holds the advantages of the mode of publication during which the plot and persons of a story are two years in the course of unfolding their relations to each other, to outweigh the disadvantages. Undoubtedly, for writers of Mr. Dickens's character, this method has its advantages. We have always thought that with him to tell a story was the least part of his design; his characters affect him far more than his plot; he writes, as we shall see, much more for the purpose of holding up sketches of society, home life, and individual idiosyncrasy, than for the purpose of telling a tale. This is not so thoroughly remarkable in any of his other works as in the *Pickwick Papers*, but it does characterize them all. Hence, while, of course, you want to get at the secret—and every story must have its secret—you are even well satisfied with every number, because it not only carries you forward in the story, but is a portfolio of sketches in Mr. Dickens's own manner, of the graphic, the quaint, and the queer, of the London life of our times; added to which, as a grateful and affectionate man, Mr. Dickens can never be insensible to that strange fame in which he suddenly found himself encircled nearly thirty years since, when, in every nook and corner of England, and of our empire, in every London coffee-house, in every tolerably intelligent household room, there was going on, all England over, from month to month, a succession of shocks of laughter. Mr. Dickens has done many better things, we believe, than the *Pickwick Papers*; but they were so new, and he was so fresh and young, that we do not wonder at his affection for that mode of publication, which must be to him such a pleasant memory in the history of his fame.

But Mr. Dickens has now, to our knowledge, for sixteen years been haunted by a great Dust-heap. In the *Household Words* for 1850 first appeared the account of that amazing mound. All his life long, at any rate in all that portion of it with which the public is acquainted, our writer has been industriously engaged in attempting to ferret out the bright things in dirty places; he has been like a very Parisian chiffonnier, industriously searching, with intense eye, among the sweepings, the odds and ends, and puddles of society, if haply some overlooked and undiscovered loveliness might not be found there. In the sixteenth number of the *Household Words* for 1850, he surprised many of his readers by a description of some of those huge, suburban heaps and mounds, more common and conspicuous, we fancy, then than now. We should think that our readers have not forgotten the paper. A Dust-heap, he told his readers, was very frequently worth thousands of pounds. Here is the paragraph out of which, we suppose, has grown, to its huge dimensions, the present story:—

> The principal ingredient of all these Dust-heaps is fine cinders and ashes; but as they are accumulated from the contents of all the dust-holes and bins of the vicinity, and as many more as possible, the fresh arrivals in their original state present very heterogeneous materials. We cannot better describe them, than by presenting a brief sketch of the different departments of the Searchers and Sorters, who are assembled below to busy themselves upon the mass of original matters which are shot out from the carts of the dustmen.
>
> The bits of coal, the pretty numerous results of accident and servants' carelessness, are picked out, to be sold forthwith; the largest and best of the cinders are also selected, by another party, who sell them to laundresses, or to braziers (for whose purposes coke would not do so well); and the next sort of

Appendix 3: Contemporary Reviews of Our Mutual Friend   221

cinders, called the *breeze*, because it is left after the wind has blown the finer cinders through an upright sieve, is sold to the brickmakers.

Two other departments, called the "soft-ware" and the "hard-ware," are very important. The former includes all vegetable and animal matters—everything that will decompose. These are selected and bagged at once, and carried off as soon as possible, to be sold as manure for ploughed land, wheat, barley, &c. Under this head, also, the dead cats are comprised. They are, generally, the perquisites of the women searchers. Dealers come to the wharf, or dust-field, every evening; they give sixpence for a white cat, fourpence for a coloured cat, and for a black one according to her quality. The "hard-ware" includes all broken pottery,—pans, crockery, earthenware, oyster-shells, &c., which are sold to make new roads.

"The bones" are selected with care, and sold to the soap-boiler. He boils out the fat and marrow first, for special use, and the bones are then crushed and sold for manure.

Of "rags," the woollen rags are bagged and sent off for hop-manure; the white linen rags are washed, and sold to make paper, &c.

The "tin things" are collected and put into an oven with a grating at the bottom, so that the solder which unites the parts melts, and runs through into a receiver. This is sold separately; the detached pieces of tin are then sold to be melted up with old iron, &c.

Bits of old brass, lead, &c., are sold to be melted up separately, or in the mixture of ores.

All broken glass vessels, as cruets, mustard-pots, tumblers, wine-glasses, bottles, &c., are sold to the old-glass shops.

As for any articles of jewellery,—silver spoons, forks, thimbles, or other plate and valuables, they are pocketed off-hand by the first finder. Coins of gold and silver are often found, and many "coppers."

Meantime, everybody is hard at work near the base of the great Dust-heap. A certain number of cart-loads having been raked and searched for all the different things just described, the whole of it now undergoes the process of sifting.

Since the publication of this paragraph, of course many of these heaps have been compelled to yield to that great Macadamizing spirit of change and progress, the railway line and station. The North London line now probably cuts right through that very region where stood Mr. Boffin's Bower, and the vast heap of miserly old John Harmon. Thus, it is only like Mr. Dickens to attempt to construct his fairy palace upon such an unsightly mound. A romance from a Dust-heap is so far from impossible that it is not even improbable. Following Mr. Dickens's observant eye and rapid foot, other visitors have traversed and circumambulated these extraordinary mounds. In that excellent and arousing little book, *The Missing Link*, there is a chapter entitled "The Bible Woman among the Dust-heaps;" and many facts recited in that interesting little chapter go to confirm the more romantic and imaginative settings of the great social novelist. All sorts of things are found in the Dust-heaps; inferior things which poverty, necessity, or science knows how to turn to account; or rings, brooches, silver spoons, forks, and golden sovereigns occasionally get carted away, while, among Dust-heaps, there are places like stables, in which the much-enduring and ravenous poor live. These find in the Dust-heap other things than brooches or sovereigns, as appears in a story like the following, told by the authoress of *The Missing Link*:—"The kind city missionary of the district once went in to visit an old man, who, being bed-ridden, asked him to stir the saucepan on his fire; the missionary observed, in doing so, 'that it was a savoury mess.' The reply was, 'Well, mayhap, you mightn't like to eat it, sir; it's some bones well washed, and some potatoes, and onions, my wife picked off the heap; it's very well for me.'" So much for the place on which Mr. Dickens picked up his story. Somewhere, we gather about a spot, very well known to ourselves, upon which, when we lived in the neighbourhood, we often thought a fiction of another kind might have been reared, a district between King's Cross and Holloway, turning out of Maiden Lane, known to the inhabitants and the neighbours as *Belle Isle*, a name derived from an old French refugee, who lived there for many years, brought as much of the manners and the blasphemy of his country as he could with him, and, when he died, left them as a legacy behind him. The spot, however, was very likely twenty-five years since a pleasant little bit of rural suburbanness, and still, until the recent railway changes, retained, to an eye able to see it, something of its old character in the little detached cottages, with the little patches of garden before most of them. Gradually accumulated the Dust-heaps; the more respectable labouring class, or London-clerk-like character of the houses faded away, and we only saw Mr. Boffins Bower in its decline, just before it made way for the traffic and goods department of the immense station.

Needless work, we presume, it would be to attempt to tell the outline of Mr. Dickens's story. Most of our readers have either read, or will read it; those who have not read will, perhaps, not thank us for attempting to tell it. We have already said, however, that, as in all Mr. Dickens's books, so in this, the story is only a part of the work. Yet, perhaps, as a story, it is quite equal to any Mr. Dickens has told; it is sustained throughout; there is nothing in the plot too strained or unnatural. Mr. Dickens has not always been thought happy in this, for a writer with so much of nature; he has sometimes and often devised most unnatural positions and situations. He has been fond always, and he has continued his old trick in this book, of giving to the very virtues of some of his characters an unnatural and unvirtuous aspect, as in *The Battle of Life*, *The Cricket on the Hearth*, &c. There can be no justification for John Harmon's marrying under an assumed name; it was a poor way either to test or to reward the faithfulness and affection of his very bright and delightful little wife, Bella Wilfer, who certainly, if ever a woman deserved confidence, complete and full, deserved it. If the secret had to be maintained for a time, surely a right conception of every kind of duty, legal not less than emotional, would have commanded the revelation, at any rate to the wife, before marriage. We have called this an old vice of Mr. Dickens, and it is so; he is fond of putting goodness into false positions, so that a solemn reader, sometimes, shakes his head, and says, "I don't know whether to call that goodness or the

Appendix 3: Contemporary Reviews of Our Mutual Friend   223

contrary," and feels as Mr. Inspector felt when he became possessed of the secret, "a disposition to break at intervals into such soliloquies as that 'he never did know such a move, that he never had been so gravelled, and that what a game this was to try the sort of stuff a man's opinion of himself was made of.'" Yet there is less that offends in this way than in many other works of the writer, as even in *Great Expectations*, where the reader is startled by the half grotesque and half horrible episodical thread of Miss Haversham. Perhaps the first thing which will strike the reader in the work will be its severe, although good-natured satire upon, we will not say our social foibles, but our great social sins; the Veneerings, Podsnaps, the Lady Tippinses, the invisible Lord Snigsworth, the Brewers, Boots,' and Buffers, expressing in their persons the voice of "society." It is to be supposed that we have all been victims in some dinner party as the following:—

Mr. and Mrs. Veneering were bran-new people in a bran-new house in a bran-new quarter of London. Everything about the Veneerings was spick and span new. All their furniture was new, all their friends were new, all their servants were new, their plate was new, their carriage was new, their harness was new, their horses were new, their pictures were new, they themselves were new, they were as newly married as was lawfully compatible with their having a bran-new baby, and if they had set up a great-grandfather, he would have come home in matting from the Pantechnicon, without a scratch upon him, French polished to the crown of his head.

For, in the Veneering establishment, from the hall-chairs with the new coat of arms, to the grand pianoforte with the new action, and upstairs again to the new fire-escape, all things were in a state of high varnish and polish. And what was observable in the furniture, was observable in the Veneerings—the surface smelt a little too much of the workshop and was a trifle stickey.

There was an innocent piece of dinner furniture that went upon easy castors and was kept over a livery stable-yard in Duke Street, Saint James's, when not in use, to whom the Veneerings were a source of blind confusion. The name of this article was Twemlow. Being first cousin to Lord Snigsworth, he was in frequent requisition, and at many houses might be said to represent the dining-table in its normal state. Mr. and Mrs. Veneering, for example, arranging a dinner, habitually started with Twemlow, and then put leaves in him, or added guests to him. Sometimes, the table consisted of Twemlow and half a dozen leaves; sometimes, of Twemlow, and a dozen leaves; sometimes, Twemlow was pulled out to his utmost extent of twenty leaves. Mr. and Mrs. Veneering on occasions of ceremony faced each other in the centre of the board, and thus the parallel still held; for, it always happened that the more Twemlow was pulled out, the further be found himself from the centre, and the nearer to the sideboard at one end of the room, or the window-curtains at the other.

But, it was not this which steeped the feeble soul of Twemlow in confusion. This he was used to, and could take soundings of. The abyss to which he could find no bottom, and from which started forth the engrossing and ever-swelling difficulty of his life, was the insoluble question whether he was Veneering's oldest friend, or newest friend. To the excogitation of this problem, the harmless gentleman had devoted many anxious hours, both in his lodgings over the livery stable-yard, and in the cold gloom, favourable to meditation, of St. James's Square. Thus. Twemlow had first known Veneering at his club, where Veneering then knew nobody but the man who made them known to one another, who seemed to be the most intimate friend he had in the world, and whom he had known two days—the bond of union between their souls, the nefarious conduct of the committee respecting the cookery of a fillet of veal, having been accidentally cemented at that date. Immediately upon this, Twemlow received an invitation to dine with Veneering, and dined; the man being of the party. Immediately upon that, Twemlow received an invitation to dine with the man, and dined; Veneering being of the party. At the man's were a Member, an Engineer, a Payer-off of the National Debt, a Poem on Shakespeare, a Grievance, and a Public Office, who all seemed to be utter strangers to Veneering. And yet immediately after that, Twemlow received an invitation to dine at Veneerings, expressly to meet the Member, the Engineer, the Payer-off of the National Debt, the Poem on Shakespeare, the Grievance, and the Public Office, and, dining, discovered that all of them were the most intimate friends Veneering had in the world, and that the wives of all of them (who were all there) were the objects of Mrs. Veneering's most devoted affection and tender confidence.

This evening the Veneerings give a banquet. Eleven leaves in the Twemlow; fourteen in company all told. Four pigeon-breasted retainers in plain clothes stand in line in the hall. A fifth retainer, proceeding up the staircase with a mournful air—as who should say, "Here is another wretched creature come to dinner; such is life!"—announces, "Mis-ter Twemlow!"

Mrs. Veneering welcomes her sweet Mr. Twemlow. Mr. Veneering welcomes his dear Twemlow. Mrs. Veneering does not expect that Mr. Twemlow can in nature care for such insipid things as babies, but so old a friend must please to look at baby. "Ah! You will know the friend of your family better, Tootleums," says Mr. Veneering, nodding emotionally at that new article, "when you begin to take notice." He then begs to make his dear Twemlow known to his two friends, Mr. Boots and Mr. Brewer—and clearly has no distinct idea which is which.

We have quite got to deserve this satire to which all people—we suppose Mr. Dickens among the rest—yield themselves, and which everybody votes an infinite annoyance and bore. A more empty, wretched thing than a modern dining-out, or a modern evening party, society has never invented. Too unhappily, the Podsnaps and Veneerings constitute a very large proportion of our English population; the amazing transmutations of wealth, the rapid series of metempsychoses and transmigrations by which a Whitechapel costermonger may now become a stupendous West-end parvenu, are so frequent; and, of course, the standard of modern society is the house, the carriage, the dinners, which make it impossible for those who desire to struggle into a kind of social importance to be other than subject to frequent jostlings against the Veneerings and the Podsnaps.

Mr. Dickens does not think very highly of the modern mode of making money; rather type-people in that way are Alfred Lammle, Esq., and Mr. Fledgeby. Mr. Lammle is reputed to be a gentleman of property—is really a mere share-gambler:—

Appendix 3: Contemporary Reviews of Our Mutual Friend   225

He invests his property. He goes, in a condescending amateurish way into the City, attends meetings of Directors, and has to do with traffic in Shares. As is well known to the wise in their generation, traffic in Shares is the one thing to have to do with in this world, Have no antecedents, no established character, no cultivation, no ideas, no manners; have Shares. Have Shares enough to be on Boards of Direction in capital letters, oscillate on mysterious business between London and Paris, and be great. Where does he come from? Shares. Where is he going to? Shares. What are his tastes? Shares. Has he any principles? Shares. What squeezes him into Parliament? Shares. Perhaps he never of himself achieved success in anything, never originated anything, never produced anything? Sufficient answer to all; Shares. O mighty Shares! To set those blaring images so high, and to cause us smaller vermin, as under the influence of henbane or opium, to cry out, night and day, "Relieve us of our money, scatter it for us, buy us and sell us, ruin us, only we beseech ye take rank among the powers of the earth, and fatten on us!"

Glorious old Mr. Boffin's money came out of dust. His immense fortune raised him instantly to be a man of mark, his patronage and support coveted by men who, from their scale of rank, would have looked with overwhelming scorn upon Mr. Boffin's "antecedents." Mr. Podsnap, like Mr. Veneering, suggests what he was in his name—one of these gamblers with which society abounds. He had put his original property by a good inheritance from a wife, with lucky speculations in the Marine Insurance way. "He was an eminently respectable man, and being such, Mr. Podsnap was sensible of its being required of him to take Providence under his protection; consequently, he always knew exactly what Providence meant. Inferior and less respectable men might fall short of that mark; but Mr. Podsnap was always up to it, and it was very remarkable, and must have been very comfortable, that what Providence meant, was invariably what Mr. Podsnap meant." Mr. Podsnap it is, principally, who has got his biographer into hot water about the Poor Law. In Mr. Podsnap's palatial halls, at one of his dinner parties, a certain discussion took place referring to the existing Poor Law. Some meek man holding, it would seem, some of Mr. Dickens's heresies, had referred to some half-dozen people who had lately died in the streets, of starvation. "I don't believe it," says Mr. Podsnap; the meek man was afraid we must take it as proved from the inquests and the registrar's returns.

> The man of meek demeanor intimated that truly it would seem from the facts, as if starvation had been forced upon the culprits in question—as if, in their wretched manner, they had made their weak protests against it—as if they would have taken the liberty of staving it off if they could—as if they would rather not have been starved upon the whole, if perfectly agreeable to all parties.
>
> "There is not," said Mr. Podsnap, flushing angrily, "there is not a country in the world, sir, where so noble a provision is made for the poor as in this country."

The meek man was quite willing to concede that, but perhaps it rendered the matter even worse, as showing that there must be something appallingly wrong somewhere.

"Where?" said Mr. Podsnap.

The meek man hinted Wouldn't it be well to try, very seriously, to find out where?

"Ah!" said Mr. Podsnap. "Easy to say somewhere; not so easy to say where! But I see what you are driving at. I knew it from the first. Centralization. No. Never with my consent. Not English."

An approving murmur arose from the heads of tribes; as saying, "There you have him! Hold him!"

He was not aware (the meek man submitted of himself) that he was driving at any ization. He had no favourite ization that he knew of. But he certainly was more staggered by these terrible occurrences than he was by names, of howsoever many syllables. Might he ask, was dying of destitution and neglect necessarily English?

"You know what the population of London is, I suppose," said Mr. Podsnap.

The meek man supposed he did, but supposed that had absolutely nothing to do with it, if its laws were well administered.

"And you know; at least I hope you know;" said Mr. Podsnap, with severity, "that Providence has declared that you shall have the poor always with you?"

The meek man also hoped he knew that.

"I am glad to hear it," said Mr. Podsnap with a portentous air. "I am glad to hear it. It will render you cautious how you fly in the face of Providence."

In reference to that absurd and irreverent conventional phrase, the meek man said, for which Mr. Podsnap was not responsible, he the meek man had no fear of doing anything so impossible; but—

But Mr. Podsnap felt that the time had come for flushing and flourishing this meek man down for good. So he said:

> "I must decline to pursue this painful discussion. It is it not pleasant to my feelings; it is repugnant to my feelings. I have said that I do not admit these things. I have also said that if they do occur (not that I admit it), the fault lies with the sufferers themselves. It is not for me"—Mr. Podsnap pointed "me" forcibly, as adding by implication thought it may be all very well for you—"it is not for me to impugn the workings of Providence. I know better than that, I trust, and I have mentioned what the intentions of Providence are. Besides," said Mr. Podsnap, flushing high up among his hair-brushes, with a strong consciousness of personal affront, "the subject is a very disagreeable one. I will go so far as to say it is an odious one. It is not one to be introduced among our wives and young persons, and I—" He finished with that flourish of his arm which added more expressively than any words, And I remove it from the face of the earth.

We are very thankful to Mr. Dickens for his courage, for it needed some, to say all this, in setting the flagrant enormities of our most wicked, heartless, and national neglect before all his readers. He has, we know, been rather severely treated by sundry critics and circumlocutional champions. He has very greatly

Appendix 3: Contemporary Reviews of Our Mutual Friend 227

anticipated his present line of remarks many years since; so long since as the publication of *The Chimes* and *Hard Times*, Mr. Dickens has been no friend to the present Poor Law and its administration. Mr. Bounderby could never see any difference between leaving the Coketown hands just exactly as they were, and requiring them to be fed with turtle soup and venison out of gold spoons. Mr. Dickens tells us, what we can well believe, that he has had idiotic propositions of parallel nature offered for his acceptance, calling upon him to admit that he would give Poor-Law relief to anybody, anywhere, and anyhow. He contemptuously puts aside such nonsense; in his postscript he says:—

> That my view of the Poor Law may not be mistaken or misrepresented, I will state it. I believe there has been in England, since the days of the Stuarts, no law so often infamously administered, no law so often openly violated, no law habitually so ill-supervised. In the majority of the shameful cases of disease and death from destitution, that shock the public and disgrace the country, the illegality is quite equal to the inhumanity—and known language could say no more of their lawlessness.

For ourselves, we also take the opportunity of expressing our profound sense of the great inhumanity and general inefficiency, in all large towns and districts, and especially in London, of the existing Poor Law. We attempted to state our impressions strongly at the commencement of the present year. We know that the administration of such matters is very greatly in the hands of the Veneerings and Podsnaps, the Brewers and Buffers, and we therefore scarcely know how to expect or hope for satisfactory change; but those thick strata of destitute and wretched poor may well excite our gravest fears; and that in the practical administration of the law no difference should be drawn between Rogue Riderhood and Betsy Higden, may well fill every humane heart with indignation. One thing it would be impertinent and ignorant to attempt to deny, people with hard hearts, thick heads, and good digestions—the three great qualities which command success—may attempt to make out a case for the Poor Law; but there is no possibility of resisting or overcoming Mr. Dickens's facts. We have plenty in our own memory of a like nature. We trust this subject will soon receive searching revision and improvement.

But such portions of the book as those to which we have referred form only its side-scenes and characters. We are glad to get away from the halls of Veneering and Podsnap, and the whole of the unpleasant lot. Once again we have to say, fresh as if he had never written upon London before, the book is quite in Mr. Dickens's old, well-known vein. One feels that he loves London, and he knows all its nooks and corners, courts and alleys, high streets and bye streets well. In every work he interests us by some new, well-drawn, and sharply-defined London-life character. Sometimes one makes his appearance reminding us that Mr. Dickens has produced a character somewhat like it before, as in the case of Mr. Inspector, who reminds us very much of our old friend, Buckett, in *Bleak House*; yet this remark, it may be, is not quite just, for the one circumstance most indisputable about Mr. Dickens's immense procession of characters, next to their remarkable variety, is their distinctness and individuality; certainly, in some things, he is almost unexampled. It has been truly said that he could not see a blind beggar with a dog on the curb, or a pump in a London court, or any character of society, high or low, without instinctively, at a glance, fetching out of it the especial grotesqueness or ridiculousness, the queer, human suggestion, let us also add as true, the touching and pathetic. It is in this mingled vein of the queer, quaint, grotesque, and pathetic that the undertaker and his men, blossom-faced, pompously striding before and by the side of the corpse, seem, in their affected and stately walk, like policemen of the D(eath) division.

It is in his later works he has more especially trailed through his pages the sombre garments of tragedy; perhaps the tragic does not strike and startle so impressively in *Our Mutual Friend* as in *Bleak House*, but the reader feels at the commencement that he is near to a tragic suggestion, and something of the shadow is frequently thrown across the book, if not arising from the main circumstance, then from the other characters, the occupations of their lives and their incidents. The picture of the bird of prey, Gaffer Hexam, slowly creeping in his boat down the Thames, with his daughter Lizzie, dragging for the dead body, will, we think, impress most readers as a striking piece of London-life painting. On the Thames and along its shores, some of the most vivid of the scenery is sketched. The night scenes, if we may call them such, on the river, and in the neighbourhood of the river, are given with painful strength, and when the bird of prey is brought down, that shivering night, while Lizzie is waiting for her father, and all the careless life goes on in the six jolly fellowship porters, and the poor girl hears borne in to her, through the rain and the mist, the strange mystical cry of her father, the reader will, we think, feel himself out in that rain, along that shore, among those ships, and be unable to escape from the weary, miserable fascination by which it compels him. Fond of conducting some character through a hunt or a flight, Mr. Dickens often tells some such story: our readers recollect the wanderings of the old man with little Nell, the terrible and pitiful tragedy of Lady Dedlock's long rushing from place to place, and night to night; the reader feels the same impression of interest through those chapters to which we have referred, in which the bird of prey is brought down; but Betty Higden and her flight is in our author's sweetest style of sympathy with the proud but holy poor. Critics of the hard-headed school will call this mere sentiment. Such critics have been fond of charging upon Mr. Dickens the spreading upon his palate certain colours, and sketching out upon his canvas certain patchwork forms intended to produce the mingled effects of the grotesque and the pathetic; but very different is our impression. There are many things in the writings of Mr. Dickens, perhaps in these volumes, which we regret, and from which we are free to dissent; but, true in these, his last essays, to the spirit of his earliest works, the poor—the poor, lowly, unknown outcasts and offcasts, seem to be the objects of intensest interest to him. "Mr. Dickens," say many of his critics, "always fails when he attempts to draw the habits of good society; then he becomes a mere caricaturist." But is not a good deal of what we call

Appendix 3: Contemporary Reviews of Our Mutual Friend   229

"good society" itself mere caricature?—a caricature upon living, not life itself? These critics surely would not intend to imply that Mr. Dickens does not know "good society," as it is called, as well as he knows the haunt of Gaffer Hexam, the cottage of Betty Higden, the home of Mr. Wilfer, or the factory and lodgings where Lizzie found both labour and rest? But we could very well conceive Mr. Dickens replying were he to condescend to reply, to such critics, "Well, I know what you call 'good society,' but it is not so interesting to me; it is monotonous; it wants variety, it wants earnestness. Even Rogue Riderhood, the villain, is a more entertaining character to me than your Podsnaps. There is a character all alive, no make-up there; neither whitewash, veneer, nor lacquer; an utter rascal, but a most interesting one, always up to dodges, which are not merely a shuffling of shares about, but dodges having all the interesting intensity of a real rascal in them;" and that Rogue Riderhood is one of Mr. Dickens's most sustained and thorough portraits; every rag, every syllable, every accent, everything about the ill-looking dog, is as complete as a bull-dog would be if Landseer painted him. A fascination for low life beckons Mr. Dickens into and through all out-of-the-way places; he is perpetually attempting to show the bright lights which gleam round the walls of poorest cottages, the rays of holy effort and hope which lighten up the humblest hearts and lowliest lots. We are not concerned to put in any very long defence for Lizzie, who must, we suppose, be regarded as the heroine. The character, in its origin and growth, is far away from impossible. We think we ourselves have known some such. But the love of our author for the poor is not shown in selecting a heroine from their lowliest ranks, and giving to her the attributes and the instincts of highest womanhood—this any novelist might do;—his affection for the poor is like that of Wordsworth for nature; it is a compelling instinct, and it is shown in the distinct eye he has for all the humblest pieces of furniture which mark the poor and scantily furnished dwelling, and the tenderness and strength with which he touches the meanest lives and their destinies. He has a power of imparting life to buildings, to dead things, things that never lived; the abundant humanity of the man makes him see a human relationship in everything; and just as satirists have been fond of tracing animals in human faces, the kinder humorist, on the contrary, gives to mute and to material things some touch of kindred nature, making the thing, or the place, or the house alive with human feeling. Thus the old Dustman's Bower, and the room in which he died:—

> A gloomy house the Bower, with sordid signs on it of having been, through its long existence as Harmony Jail, in miserly holding. Bare of paint, bare of paper on the walls, bare of furniture, bare of experience of human life. Whatever is built by man for man's occupation, must, like natural creations, fulfil the intention of its existence, or soon perish. This old house had wasted more from desuetude than it would have wasted from use, twenty years for one.
>
> A certain leanness falls upon houses not sufficiently imbued with life (as if they were nourished upon it), which was very noticeable here. The staircase, balustrades, and rails, had a spare look—an air of being denuded to the bone— which the panels of the walls and the jambs of the doors and windows also bore.

The scanty moveables partook of it; save for the cleanliness of the place, the dust into which they were all resolving would have lain thick on the floors; and those, both in colour and in grain, were worn like old faces that had kept much alone.

The bedroom where the clutching old man had lost his grip on life, was left as he had left it. There was the old grisly four-post bedstead, without hangings, and with a jail-like upper rim of iron and spikes; and there was the old patchwork counterpane. There was the tight-clenched old bureau, receding atop like a bad and secret forehead; there was the cumbersome old table with twisted legs, at the bedside; and there was the box upon it, in which the will had lain. A few old chairs with patch-work covers, under which the more precious stuff to be preserved had slowly lost its quality of colour without imparting pleasure to any eye, stood against the wall. A hard family likeness was on all these things.

Betty Higden is one of his most touching, we think truthful, paintings of this order. The death of "our Johnny" is one of these pathetic lights from the homes of the poor. The little creature, the grandchild of Betty Higden, and the adopted of Mr. and Mrs. Boffin, died in some child's hospital. The "boofer lady" referred to was Bella Wilfer, who had once seen him with her bright radiant face, and had given him kisses from among her cloud of curls. But with his Noah's ark, and other toys, he had been transferred to the hospital to die, old Betty wailing and weeping with him. Is not this in Mr. Dickens's best manner?—

Johnny's powers of sustaining conversation were as yet so very imperfectly developed, even in a state of health, that in sickness they were little more than monosyllabic. But, he had to be washed and tended, and remedies were applied, and though these offices were far, far more skilfully and lightly done than ever anything had been done for him in his little life, so rough and short, they would have hurt and tired him but for an amazing circumstance which laid hold of his attention. This was no less than the appearance on his own little platform, in pairs, of All Creation, on the way into his own particular ark: the elephant leading, and the fly, with a diffident sense of his size, politely bringing up the rear. A very little brother lying in the next bed with a broken leg, was so enchanted by this spectacle that his delight exalted its enthralling interest; and so came rest and sleep.

"I see you are not afraid to leave the dear child here, Betty," whispered Mrs. Boffin.

"No, ma'am. Most willingly, most thankfully, with all my heart and soul."

So they kissed him, and left him there, and old Betty was to come back early in the morning, and nobody but Rokesmith knew for certain how that the doctor had said, "This should have been days ago. Too late!"

But, Rokesmith knowing it, and knowing that his bearing it in mind would be acceptable thereafter to that good woman who had been the only light in the childhood of desolate John Harmon dead and gone, resolved that late at night he would go back to the bedside of John Harmon's namesake, and see how it fared with him.

The family whom God had brought together were not all asleep, but were all quiet. From bed to bed, a light womanly tread and a pleasant fresh face passed

Appendix 3: Contemporary Reviews of Our Mutual Friend

in the silence of the night. A little head would lift itself up into the softened light here and there, to be kissed as the face went by—for these little patients are very loving—and would then submit itself to be composed to rest again. The mite with the broken leg was restless, and moaned; but after a while turned his face towards Johnny's bed, to fortify himself with a view of the ark, and fell asleep. Over most of the beds, the toys were yet grouped as the children had left them when they last laid themselves down, and, in their innocent grotesqueness and incongruity, they might have stood for the children's dreams.

The doctor came in too, to see how it fared with Johnny. And he and Rokesmith stood together, looking down with compassion on him.

"What is it, Johnny?" Rokesmith was the questioner, and put an arm round the poor baby as he made a struggle.

"Him!" said the little fellow. "Those!"

The doctor was quick to understand children, and, taking the horse, the ark, the yellow bird, and the man in the Guards, from Johnny's bed, softly placed them on that of his next neighbour, the mite with the broken leg.

With a weary and yet a pleased smile, and with an action as if he stretched his little figure out to rest, the child heaved his body on the sustaining arm, and seeking Rokesmith's face with his lips, said:

"A kiss for the boofer lady."

Having now bequeathed all he had to dispose of, and arranged his affairs in this world, Johnny, thus speaking, left it.

Betty's flight from the Poor Law guardians, and scarcely less from her friends, is drawn with great pathos:—

Old Betty Higden fared upon her pilgrimage as many ruggedly honest creatures, women and men, fare on their toiling way along the roads of life. Patiently to earn a spare, bare living, and quietly to die, untouched by workhouse hands— this was her highest sublunary hope.

Nothing had been heard of her at Mr. Boffin's house since she trudged off. The weather had been hard and the roads had been bad, and her spirit was up. A less stanch spirit might have been subdued by such adverse influences; but the loan for her little outfit was in no part repaid, and it had gone worse with her than she had foreseen, and she was put upon proving her case and maintaining her independence.

Faithful soul! When she had spoken to the Secretary of that "deadness that steals over me at times," her fortitude had made too little of it. Oftener and ever oftener, it came stealing over her; darker and ever darker, like the shadow of advancing death. That the shadow should be deep as it came on, like the shadow of an actual presence, was in accordance with the laws of the physical world, for all the light that shone on Betty Higden lay beyond death.

The poor old creature had taken the upward course of the river Thames as her general track; it was the track in which her last home lay, and of which she had last had local love and knowledge. She had hovered for a little while in the near neighbourhood of her abandoned dwelling, and had sold, and knitted and sold, and gone on. In the pleasant towns of Chertsey, Walton, Kingston, and

Staines, her figure came to be quite well known for some short weeks, and then again passed on.

She would take her stand in market-places, where there were such things on market days; at other times, in the busiest (that was seldom very busy) portion of the little quiet High-street; at still other times she would explore the outlying roads for great houses, and would ask leave at the lodge to pass in with her basket, and would not often get it. But ladies in carriages would frequently make purchases from her trifling stock, and were usually pleased with her bright eyes and her hopeful speech. In these and her clean dress originated a fable that she was well to do in the world: one might say, for her station, rich. As making a comfortable provision for its subject which costs nobody anything, this class of fable has long been popular.

In those pleasant little towns on Thames, you may hear the fall of the water over the weirs, or even, in still weather, the rustle of the rushes; and from the bridge you may see the young river, dimpled like a young child, playfully gliding away among the trees, unpolluted by the defilements that lie in wait for it on its course, and as yet out of hearing of the deep summons of the sea. It were too much to pretend that Betty Higden made out such thoughts; no; but she heard the tender river whispering to many like herself, "Come to me, come to me! When the cruel shame and terror you have so long fled from, must beset you, come to me! I am the Relieving Officer appointed by eternal ordinance to do my work; I am not held in estimation according as I shirk it. My breast is softer than the pauper-nurse's; death in my arms is peacefuller than among the pauper-wards. Come to me!"

Still, as she went on, she became insane in her flight from the dreadful poor-house, and in lines of very distinct and sustained feeling, our writer follows her upon her way. She falls into fits and drops down on the road, but as soon as she is restored, she is up again on her way:—

The morning found her afoot again, but fast declining as to the clearness of her thoughts, though not as to the steadiness of her purpose. Comprehending that her strength was quitting her, and that the struggle of her life was almost ended, she could neither reason out the means of getting back to her protectors, nor even form the idea. The overmastering dread, and the proud stubborn resolution it engendered in her to die undegraded, were the two distinct impressions left in her failing mind. Supported only by a sense that she was bent on conquering in her life-long fight, she went on.

The time was come, now, when the wants of this little life were passing away from her. She could not have swallowed food, though a table had been spread for her in the next field. The day was cold and wet, but she scarcely knew it. She crept on, poor soul, like a criminal afraid of being taken, and felt little beyond the terror of falling down while it was yet daylight, and being found alive. She had not fear that she would live through another night.

Sewn in the breast of her gown, the money to pay for her burial was still intact. If she could wear through the day, and then lie down to die under the cover of the darkness, she would die independent. If she were captured previously, the money would be taken from her as a pauper who had no right to it, and she would be carried to the accursed workhouse. Gaining her end, the letter would be found in her breast along with the money, and the gentlefolks would say

Appendix 3: Contemporary Reviews of Our Mutual Friend   233

when it was given back to them, "She prized it, did old Betty Higden; she was true to it; and while she lived, she would never let it be disgraced by falling into the hands of those that she held in horror." Most illogical, inconsequential, and light-headed, this; but travellers in the valley of the shadow of death are apt to be light-headed; and worn-out old people of low estate have a trick of reasoning as indifferently as they live, and doubtless would appreciate our Poor Law more philosophically on an income of ten thousand a year.

So keeping to byways, and shunning human approach, this troublesome old woman hid herself, and fared on all through the dreary day. Yet so unlike was she to vagrant hiders in general, that sometimes, as the day advanced, there was a bright fire in her eyes, and a quicker beating at her feeble heart, as though she said exultingly, "The Lord will see me through it!"

By what visionary hands she was led along upon that journey of escape from the Samaritan; by what voices, hushed in the grave, she seemed to be addressed; how she fancied the dead child in her arms again, and times innumerable adjusted her shawl to keep it warm, what infinite variety of forms of tower and roof and steeple the trees took; how many furious horsemen rode at her, crying, "There she goes! Stop! Stop, Betty Higden!" and melted away as they came close; be these things left untold. Faring on and hiding, hiding and faring on, the poor harmless creature, as though she were a Murderess and the whole country were up after her, wore out the day, and gained the night.

"Water-meadows, or such like," she had sometimes murmured, on the day's pilgrimage, when she had raised her head and taken any note of the real objects around her. There now arose in the darkness, a great building, full of lighted windows. Smoke was issuing from a high chimney in the rear of it, and there was a sound of a water-wheel at the side. Between her and the building, lay a piece of water, in which the lighted windows were reflected, and on its nearest margin was a plantation of trees. "I humbly thank the Power and the Glory," said Betty Higden, holding up her withered hands, "that I have come to my journey's end!"

She crept among the trees to the trunk of a tree whence she could see, beyond some intervening trees and branches, the lighted windows, both in their reality and their reflection on the water. She placed her orderly little basket at her side, and sank upon the ground, supporting herself against the tree. It brought to her mind the foot of the Cross, and she committed herself to Him who died upon it. Her strength held out to enable her to arrange the letter in her breast, so as that it could be seen that she had a paper there. It had held out for this, and it departed when this was done.

"I am safe here," was her last benumbed thought. "When I am found dead at the foot of the Cross, it will be by some of my own sort; some of the working-people who work among the lights yonder. I cannot see the lighted windows now, but they are there. I am thankful for all!"

        *   *   *   *   *   *

The darkness gone, and a face bending down.

"It cannot be the boofer lady?"

"I don't understand what you say. Let me wet your lips again with this brandy. I have been away to fetch it. Did you think that I was long gone?"

It is as the face of a woman, shaded by a quantity of rich dark hair. It is the earnest face of a woman who is young and handsome. But all is over with me on earth, and this must be an Angel.

"Have I been long dead?"

"I don't understand what you say. Let me wet your lips again. I hurried all I could, and brought no one back with me lest you should die of the shock of strangers."

"Am I not dead?"

"I cannot understand what you say. Your voice is so low and broken that I cannot hear you. Do you hear me?"

"Yes."

"Do you mean Yes?"

"Yes."

"I was coming from my work just now, along the path outside (I was up with the night-hands last night), and I heard a groan, and found you lying here."

"What work, deary?"

"Did you ask what work? At the paper-mill."

"Where is it?"

"Your face is turned up to the sky, and you can't see it. It is close by. You can see my face, here, between you and the sky?"

"Yes."

"Dare I lift you?"

"Not yet."

"Not even lift your head to get it on my arm? I will do it by very gentle degrees. You shall hardly feel it."

"Not yet. Paper. Letter."

"This paper in your breast?"

"Bless ye!"

"Let me wet your lips again. Am I to open it? To read it?"

"Bless ye!"

She reads it with surprise, and looks down with a new expression and an added interest on the motionless face she kneels beside.

"I know these names. I have heard them often."

"Will you send it, my dear?"

"I cannot understand you. Let me wet your lips again, and your forehead. There. O poor thing, poor thing!" These words through her fast-dropping tears. "What was it that you asked me? Wait till I bring my ear quite close."

"Will you send it, my dear?"

"Will I send it to the writers? Is that your wish? Yes, certainly."

"You'll not give it up to any one but them?"

"No."

"As you must grow old in time, and come to your dying hour, my dear, you'll not give it up to any one but them?"

"No. Most solemnly."

"Never to the Parish!" with a convulsed struggle.

"No. Most solemnly."

"Nor let the Parish touch me, nor yet so much as look at me!" with another struggle.

Appendix 3: Contemporary Reviews of Our Mutual Friend　　　235

"No. Faithfully."

A look of thankfulness and triumph lights the worn old face. The eyes, which have been darkly fixed upon the sky, turn with meaning in them towards the compassionate face from which the tears are dropping, and a smile is on the aged lips as they ask:

"What is your name, my dear?"

"My name is Lizzie Hexam."

"I must be sore disfigured. Are you afraid to kiss me?"

The answer is, the ready pressure of her lips upon the cold but smiling mouth.

"Bless ye! *Now* lift me, my love."

Lizzie Hexam very softly raised the weather-stained grey head, and lifted her as high as Heaven.

    *　　　*　　　*　　　*　　　*　　　*

"'WE GIVE THEE HEARTY THANKS FOR THAT IT HATH PLEASED THEE TO DELIVER THIS OUR SISTER OUT OF THE MISERIES OF THIS SINFUL WORLD.'" So read the Reverend Frank Milvey in a not untroubled voice, for his heart misgave him that all was not quite right between us and our sister—or say our sister in Law—Poor Law—and that we sometimes read these words in an awful manner, over our Sister and our Brother too.

We cannot quote anything from Mr. Dickens with the hope of indicating any new or hitherto unmarked characteristics of style—only for the sake of imparting pleasure, and showing that those same lines of interest with which all his previous works have abounded, continue still: the same variety of inferior characters too— inferior we mean to the general plot and scheme of the story—some of whom we would have liked, like casual fellow passengers in a railway carriage with whom we have spent a little time, to know more, like the Rev. Frank Milvey and his wife, of whom our author in a sentence of singular beauty we think, says, "They were representatives of hundreds of other good Christian pairs, as conscientious and as useful, who merge the smallness of their work in its greatness, and feel in no danger of losing dignity when they adapt themselves to incomprehensible humbugs." And throughout the whole volumes, let the critics call it sentiment or by what name soever they will, there is a geniality and kindliness, even a religiousness of feeling which pervades, like an influence, the whole—as the author says in one of his noblest aphorisms and truest strokes, "This is the eternal law. Evil often stops short at itself and dies with the doer of it, but good never does."

What relation does the work bear to the long range of the author's previous works? Have his admirers cause to grieve over the evident decadence of his genius and powers? It has been said for a long time his powers have been in their decay; we have never been able to perceive this. It must be remembered that Mr. Dickens has created a style of social painting and writing; he has hosts of imitators now who attempt to write about, and look at men and things in the same manner; he has, to a great extent, as we have already said, created or quickened that feeling in which man is dear to man. But in the volumes through which we have just glanced, we have abundant evidence of the still imperial superiority of Mr. Dickens in his own field of work. The critic again will remark upon, and quarrel with, his diffuseness; it is so, but it is his style. He is not a Pre-Raphaelite in painting; or if he be, he is not content merely to give the cold, hard, and unrelieved, and Millais-like expression. It must be understood that Mr. Dickens, like the great Sir Walter, takes a personal love and interest in filling in the details of an impression. His details, though they look diffuse, will, we believe, generally be found to add something to the picture he desires to convey to the mind, like that variety of placards, with the ominous inscription, *Found Drowned*, round the rude room of Gaffer Hexam; they seem to bring themselves into a Pre-Raphaelite distinctness—the occupation of the man, and the whole furniture of the place, and perhaps the agility of Mr. Dickens's eye is greater than the weight of his brain. His books are like streets; he does not exact from his readers so much thought as rapid observation and feeling; his books are like himself, illustrations of incessant mental activity, sympathy, and interest. He carries his reader along with him from place to place, and does not aim to tighten his sentences into cords. He has very little of that which, in the general use of language, is called wit; he does not seek to make his sentences bite, hence, to, many readers they seem wanting in the proper proportion of mental strength. To many persons agility never can indicate strength; the tenacity and spring of the tiger is held as contemptible by the slow stride of the elephant; the strengths are different. Mr. Dickens we will not suppose to be much acquainted with books in general, or the reading life through bibliopolic spectacles; we take him to be thoroughly up in newspapers, thoroughly up in the use of his own eyes, and not the less reflective because he is not the more homiletic, though occasionally, as we have seen, he preaches, and preaches severely too. Our admiration, therefore, of him is not unconsciousness of other qualities possessed by other writers, and which he does not possess; but in the feeling of the infinite ease with which he manipulates his own material—the rapid spring and dart of his social sympathies, and of that overflowing kindness of heart, which his wide knowledge of man in all his relations, that shrewd glance into social foibles, and appalling sins, are unable to impair or prevent. But, for the reasons we have mentioned, it perhaps follows that Mr. Dickens has not the finished and symmetrical power of the artist in the proportion of some two or three of his contemporaries; perhaps in that particular, even the present work may be found to fall short. What became of Potterson and Kibble after Mr. Inspector hand-cuffed them away? Had John Harmon any difficulty in getting through a stiff cross-examination? What became of that utterly ungrateful young vagabond, whom we think we dislike as much as any hypocritical scamp we ever met with in fiction, Charley Hexam? Did he repent? Why will not novelists look a little at the finish of their stories? These things seem to indicate haste in winding-up. But from the course of our criticism, it will be gathered that we, at any rate, do not think that this work indicates any declension in our writer's powers; on the contrary, it seems to deserve a place by the side of the two or three of the author's very best. Much higher and wider than *Great Expectations*, if without the peculiar soft English light of *David Copperfield*, if

Appendix 3: Contemporary Reviews of Our Mutual Friend   237

without the strong magic shadows of *Bleak House*, it should take its place as their equal, still the more, because doing no injustice to the story or the painting as a whole. It is one of the clearest pieces of the author's great London scenes and social paintings; it ought to be a great sermon to those able to hear it. We close the volumes, and put them by with gratitude for much pleasure, and more especially with thankfulness, that Mr. Dickens, being where he is, and what he is, is able so courageously to speak and preach to, and reprove some of our great social sins; and with thankfulness, too, for the hope that he may yet be spared for many years to do the work of a man and a brother, in the work of an artist. We are glad to close as he closes, and give him our hearty congratulations that he is able to write for himself and for his readers that cheerful little note:—

> On Friday the Ninth of June in the present year, Mr. and Mrs. Boffin (in their manuscript dress of receiving Mr. and Mrs. Lammle at breakfast) were on the South Eastern Railway with me, in a terribly destructive accident. When I had done what I could to help others, I climbed back into my carriage—nearly turned over a viaduct, and caught aslant upon the turn—to extricate the worthy couple. They were much soiled, but otherwise unhurt. The same happy result attended Miss Bella Wilfer on her wedding day, and Mr. Riderhood inspecting Bradley Headstone's red neckerchief as he lay asleep. I remember with devout thankfulness that I can never be much nearer parting company with my readers for ever, than I was then, until there shall be written against my life, the two words with which I have this day closed this book:—THE END.

(X) "Dickens and Depravity," New York Evangelist, November 9, 1865, p. 6

While the Spencer and Draper school of materialists are preaching the doctrine that man is the creature of circumstances, and is controlled by physical and social laws, Mr. Dickens, the greatest of living novelists, who has made character the study of his life, proclaims the old-fashioned Bible doctrine of the sinfulness of sin, and the wilful perverseness of the sinner. His latest story, "Our Mutual Friend," now running its monthly career in *Harper's Magazine*, contains some touches in the analysis of character, which may well give lessons to the pulpit itself.

Take this picture of the love-smitten school-master, who nurses his jealousy of his rival up to the verge of murder. "The state of the man was murderous, and he knew it. More: he irritated it with a kind of perverse pleasure akin to that which a sick man sometimes has in irritating a wound upon his body." Few men are as familiar as Mr. Dickens with the pathology of crime. He has studied it under the most favorable circumstances, and with a *penchant* for morbid phases of human character. He has, moreover, a masterly penetration of character under all possible subtleties and disguises. And now, in the maturity of his powers, after many years of observation and reflection upon this, his favorite theme, so far from giving countenance to the theory that society engenders criminals, and that temptations create the disposition to crime, he finds the propensity to evil in the man himself, and fastens the responsibility upon the sinning soul:

If great criminals told the truth—which, being great criminals, they do not—they would very rarely tell of their struggles against their crime. Their struggles are toward it. They buffet with opposing waves to gain the bloody shore, not to recede from it. This man perfectly comprehended that he hated his rival with his strongest and worst forces, and that if he tracked them to Lizzie Hexam, his doing so would never serve himself with her, or serve her. All his pains were taken to the end that he might incense himself with the sight of the detested figure in her company and favor in her place of concealment. And he knew as well what act of his would follow if he did, as he knew that his mother had borne him.

Granted, that he may not have held it necessary to make express mention to himself of the one familiar truth any more than of the other. He knew equally well that he fed his wrath and hatred, and that he accumulated provocation and self-justification by being made the nightly sport of the reckless and insolent Eugene. Knowing all this, and still always going on with infinite endurance, pains, and perseverance, could his dark soul doubt whither he went.

All will agree that this is a marvellous unveiling of the innermost workings of a soul that is yielding itself steadily, deliberately, to some great sin. But what is it that is here unveiled? The victim of circumstances? the creature of fate? the automatic subject of temptation, or the product of a vicious constitution of society? No; none of these; but simply a man who is bent upon doing what he knows to be wrong, and who dallies with his own evil passions till these overmaster him. The actor in all this scene is a man of intelligence, of education, of good position, the head master of a school; but he is led on by jealousy in a case where he *knows* his own pretensions to be hopeless. What a commentary is this upon that saying of the apostle that "every man sinneth when he is drawn away of his own lust and enticed." Let those who quarrel with the orthodox doctrine of depravity, try their criticisms upon Mr. Dickens's picture of human nature. —*Congregationalist.*

(Y) "Reviews—Our Mutual Friend," Saturday Review, November 11, 1865, pp. 612–3

In his postscript, Mr. Dickens tells those of the public who had in some way complained of what they took for a certain fault in his story, that "an artist, of whatever denomination, may perhaps be trusted to know what he is about in his vocation." In itself this is surely very doubtful doctrine. If it were otherwise than doubtful, first, what is the function of criticism, or is there no such thing? and next, if every artist knows what he is about better than anybody or everybody else, who shall say that this or that is bad art, or is any bad art possible? A writer who has given more delight to his generation than any other living man may, perhaps reasonably, think himself at liberty to snub his audience by a preposterous paradox. But this is only by the way.

We at least shall not presume to question that an author ought to know his own trade best, if Mr. Dickens thinks a hint to this effect useful "in the interests of art." It cannot, however, be hostile to these interests to consider the denomination of art

Appendix 3: Contemporary Reviews of Our Mutual Friend   239

which the most popular author of his day professes or practices. From this point of view, it is a circumstance peculiarly worthy of remark that, in nearly all his novels, there is some leading incident which to the plain man seems extravagant, or amazingly exceptional, or quite impossible, and yet which Mr. Dickens is ready to vindicate, with somewhat of a swagger, in his preface or his postscript, as quite ordinary, and warranted by abundant facts and evidence. Spontaneous combustion, or an incredible Chancery suit, or a school in Yorkshire of the nature of a horribly metamorphosed château in Spain, or a wild kind of Will Case, or something equally out of the common range of observation, seems absolutely indispensable to Mr. Dickens's mental comfort. He cannot feel that his story is sufficiently realistic, or properly based on fact, unless it rests on something which scarcely comes within the experience or the notice of one person out of a hundred thousand. There is no harm in this. That is a starved conception of art which would limit the name to the reproduction of what lies within the experience or observation of each and all of us. In the kingdom of art there are many mansions, and the representation of the commonplace is certainly not exclusively entitled to the whole of them. There is such a gift as the artistic delineation of what is in itself grotesque and improbable, or even downright impossible. Painting and music and poetry perhaps supply more abundant and undoubted instances of the gift than fiction, but there is nothing in the nature of fiction which absolutely unfits it to be the medium of this kind of treatment. It is not the improbability of a leading incident which takes such a book as *Our Mutual Friend* out of the region of what is usually considered art. That a man should pretend to be dead, and refrain from claiming a large fortune, for no reason in particular except that he does not wish "sordidly to buy a beautiful creature whom he loves," is improbable and extraordinary enough. But this is only the key to what has always been Mr. Dickens's principle of composition, and it is more conspicuous in his last novel than in any which went before, just because the colouring is so much weaker, and the tone so much less pleasing, that one has more attention left for the fashion in which the artist likes to select and group his figures.

After securing a central incident sufficiently extraordinary, the author crowds into his pages a parcel of puppets as uncommon as the business which they are made to transact. Nobody is admitted to the distinction of a place in *Our Mutual Friend* who is at all like the beings who have a place in the universe. The characters may be divided into two sets of people—those whom the author intended to be faithful copies of ordinary persons or classes of persons, and those whom even the author must in his inner consciousness know to be immeasurably remote from the common experience of human life. But, in one set of people as much as in the other, the writer seems to notice nothing which is not odd and surprising and absurd. The people whom he does, equally with those whom he does not, intend to be curious and abnormal, are caricatured in the most reckless way. Mr. Venus, who is meant for an oddity, is in reality not a bit more odd, and does not act or talk more inconsistently with the common modes of men, than does Mr. Eugene Wrayburn, who is not meant for an oddity at all. Silas Wegg, the sort of man whom Mr. Dickens does not expect us to be familiar with, and Lady Tippins, the sort of woman with whom he does expect us to be familiar, are strange and unknown just in the same degree. The majestic Mrs. Wilfer, avowedly an exceptional person, does not strike one as being at all more exaggerated and uncommon than Betty Higden, expressly designed to exemplify the feelings of a very common class. In this respect *Our Mutual Friend* is like all the novels that have come from the same mint. Mr. Dickens has always been, and always will be, essentially a caricaturist. He always either discovers people who are grotesque enough in themselves and their surroundings to bear reproducing without caricature, or else he takes plain people and brings them into harmony with the rest of his picture by investing them in caricature. And it is just to notice two things. First, as a caricaturist, Mr. Dickens, in humour, in inexhaustible fertility of fancy, in quickness of eye for detecting the right points, when he is at his best, stands altogether unrivalled. And, in the next place, as is the case in all good caricature, Mr. Dickens, in those books in which he has been most himself, is substantially truthful. He exaggerates, but he adheres to the original outline, and conveys a virtually correct impression. Chadband, Jefferson Brick, Elijah Pogram, Gradgrind, and a long gallery of others, the very recollection of whom makes one look into *Our Mutual Friend* with blank amazement, are all caricatures, many of them broad caricatures; still they do not convey a single untrue impression of the originals, and they do convey the truth which is most striking about the people caricatured. In *Our Mutual Friend* we still find only caricatures, but they are caricatures without either of Mr. Dickens's characteristic excellences. They are not very witty or humorous, and we are unable to recognise their truth and purpose. Nothing, for instance, can be more dismal in the way or parody or satire than the episode of the Veneerings and their friends. Where is either the humour or the truth of the caricature? The execution is coarse and clumsy, and the whole picture is redolent of ill-temper and fractiousness. This spoils it. A good caricaturist enjoys his work, however angry he may be against the object of it. Mr. Dickens, in this case, seems to screech with ill-will and bitterness. Yet he could caricature Chadband and Bumble, whom he had much more reason to detest, without raising his voice into a scream of anger. Surely bitterness is the last feeling with which such harmless social impostors as the Veneerings are meant to represent ought to be regarded by a man who talks about being an artist. The extravagance, the ill-humour, and the utter want of truthfulness reach a climax in the last chapter of all, entitled "The Voice of Society." Society is sometimes unjust, and generally contents itself with quick and surface judgments. But then, from its very composition, this could not be otherwise. Society has never all the facts, and therefore cannot always be just, or profound either. And its judgments can go only upon general grounds. As a rule, it is not a good thing for a gentleman to marry beneath him. The Voice of Society was not so dreadfully wicked and corrupt for giving expression to the belief in the soundness of this view. The odious vulgarity and malevolence which Mr. Dickens has put into the mouth of Society are mere moonshine, and not creditable to the author's insight or shrewdness. We do not venture to deny that Mr. Dickens knows "what is best in his vocation." Only, "in the interests of art," as he would say, we cannot but think the vocation of

Appendix 3: Contemporary Reviews of Our Mutual Friend   241

making spiteful and clumsy attacks on Society is an uncommonly poor one. And, unfortunately, we cannot help wondering whether the artist would consider equally good in its way the genial and witty picture of the Eatanswill Election for instance, and what strikes us as the sour and pithless account of the election of Mr. Veneering for the ancient borough of Pocket Breeches. Angry, screaming caricature such as this is not caricature at all, and we frankly confess ourselves ignorant of the "denomination of art" to which it may be considered to belong. It was not always Mr. Dickens's vocation.

In the character of Mr. Podsnap, blunt as is a good deal of what is designed for cutting humour, there is still, it must be admitted, a large amount of underlying truthfulness. Most of Mr. Dickens's readers were quick to recognize what he means by Podsnappery. After all, Podsnap is only a very roughly executed representation of what the Germans call a Philistine and the French a grocer. Many persons who would perhaps have failed either to create from their own observation this ogre of society, or to acquire from the light touches of a more refined and a deeper satirist a proper idea of the hateful traits of the ogre, may have their minds opened by the telling, if broad and coarse, sketch in the present story. And this is connected with one of Mr. Dickens's conspicuous merits. In spite of the lurid and melodramatic air which he loves to throw over parts at least of nearly all his novels, in spite of his exaggeration and frequent affectations of all sorts, he has always shown a sincere hatred of that form of cant which implies that all English habits and institutions are the highest product of which civilization is capable. He has a most wholesome conviction that the abuses of the world are more or less improveable, and were not ordained and permanently fixed by the Almighty. This is patent enough, no doubt, but it is the most patent truths which are most habitually overlooked. Mr. Dickens has always been more or less in earnest about things, and has not contented himself with looking out on the world from the dilettante point. For example, in *Our Mutual Friend*, the character of Betty Higden, the old woman to whom the prospect of coming on the parish is the most appalling thought of her life, and whose only wish is that she may die in a ditch—this character is to our minds thoroughly sentimental and over-done. The reflections to which her terror gives rise are, from the point of view of "the interests of art," thoroughly out of place in a novel. But, for all this, one cannot help feeling that Mr. Dickens is both sincere and justified in his abhorrence of much in the administration of the Poor Law. We demur altogether to an "artist" writing a story to show or prove a position of this sort. But it is impossible for those who watch the subject not to feel that Mr. Dickens is not wrong in his emphatic assertion that "there has been in England, since the days of the Stuarts, no law so often infamously administered, no law so often openly violated, no law habitually so ill supervised." His outspoken disgust at cant and red-tape and Bumbledom has perhaps won him almost as many admirers as his fancy and wit. Admirers of this sort will certainly not be diminished by Mr. Podsnap. Of the other characters, those which are not outrageous caricatures are mere shadows. What do we know, after all, of Lizzie Hexam or John Harmon? And even Bella Wilfer, for all her willfulness and impatience and hatred of poverty, is

242   *Charles Dickens's* Our Mutual Friend

sadly wanting in vitality. Her tender conversations, first with her half-idiotic father, and then with her mysterious and exceedingly dull husband, may rank among the most wearisome dialogues in modern fiction. Her majestic mother we take to be one of the best of those ineffably grotesque and altogether inhuman creations in which the author's fancy has always revelled. Bradley Headstone, the schoolmaster with dull plodding intellect, and full of overwhelming and irrepressible passion, is, in a different way, another of the characters in which Mr. Dickens has generally delighted. Such a character throws the required luridness over the story. Perhaps there is the germ in Bradley Headstone of a very powerful creation. But the author had provided no plot which might leave room for the working-out of the conception. Even Mr. Dickens has seldom written a book in which there is so little uniformity of plot, so few signs of any care to make the parts fit in with one another in some kind of proportion. The characters all come on the stage anyhow; one or two of them look somber and dull, and do nothing; most of them merely perform grotesque antics, and make quaint grimaces at the public and one another, and then retire. On the whole, this makes a very tedious performance, and the general verdict will probably be that *Our Mutual Friend* is rather hard reading.

    Some of the minor affectations in which the author, as usual, thinks fit to indulge, do not at all make the reading more cheerful. There is a gloomy butler, whom Mr. Dickens thinks it rather humorous to liken to an analytical chemist, "always seeming to say, after 'Chablis, Sir?' 'You wouldn't if you knew what it's made of.'" Well, this is not a very bad joke as jokes go, but it is quite another thing when we find the butler brought in as often as possible, and always under the name of the Analytical. Then there is Fledgeby, who is invariably introduced as "feeling for his whiskers"; and what is the humour of again and again repeating minutely the statement that Fledgeby's friends always talked about "the Bourse and Greek and Spanish and India and Mexican and par and premium and discount and three-quarters and seven-eighths"? This and a hundred other weak reiterative tricks of the same sort show that Mr. Dickens is utterly deaf to the advice of those who admire his genius sufficiently to believe that he can dispense with such artificial silliness. The admirable freshness and fancy of the Doll's Dressmaker do something to console us for having to bear with these, "his tricks and his manners," as she would say. Whether the consolation is quite adequate and satisfactory must depend on the reader's temperament.

(Z) From "New Books," New York Times, November 22, 1865, p. 4

By most readers—fresh from the influence exercised over them by the spell of the author's genius—the last work by Dickens will be considered his best. We fancy, however, that a more matured judgment would place *Our Mutual Friend* much lower in the long list of Dickens's books, if they were ranked according to merit. It would stand undoubtedly many degrees above (perhaps his worst work) *Little Dorritt*, but also an equal number below *David Copperfield*, and the older stories to which he owes his fame. The partiality for an involved plot,

Appendix 3: Contemporary Reviews of Our Mutual Friend   243

combined with an entire absence of the skill to manage and unfold it, though characteristic of Dickens generally, was perhaps never so conspicuous as in his latest work. The crowd of unnecessary persons brought in, and described with singular elaborateness and detail, and then dismissed or forgotten, was never so much in the reader's way before, and yet, curiously enough, the author speaks in his Preface of the pains employed in devising the story, and the ingenuity shown in conducting it. Of course, in every book that Dickens writes, there must be many characters and scenes that could originate with no one else—much rich and fanciful appropriate detail founded on the close observation of nature that no one else could give us, and a hearty sympathy with the right, and hatred and cruelty of oppression. These will all be found in *Our Mutual Friend.* The portrait gallery that we owe to Dickens is enlarged by the never-to-be-forgotten pair, Mr. and Mrs. Boffin, although the simplicity that distinguishes them is strangely at variance by the author's device, by which they assume fictitious characters and language in a plot, even though its object is a good one. There is no occasion to discuss at length a book now in every one's hands. Were it a total failure, its sale would scarcely be diminished, for it takes a long time for an author like Dickens to write himself down, and of this we happily see no signs.

[Remainder consists of reviews and notices of other recently published books, including Walt Whitman's *Drum Taps.*]

(AA) "Charles Dickens," Reader, December 9, 1865, p. 647

The time has long gone by when criticism could do anything, for good or evil, for the works of Charles Dickens. No amount of literary censure or praise could lower or raise his estimation with the general public. Nor, on the other hand, do we believe that any criticism, however just, or fair, or thoughtful, would lead him to alter his style, or tone, or mode of writing. We must make up our minds to take the author of "Pickwick" for better or for worse. We do not, indeed, agree with the opinion expressed in the postscript to "Our Mutual Friend," that an author must always understand what he is about better than a critic. If this were so, a painter, writer, sculptor, or artist of any kind, would be the only competent judge of the merit of his own work—an argument which refutes itself. But we do hold, that with every artist a time comes when the function of criticism ceases, as far as he himself is concerned. A very young husband may think it worth while to try and improve the mind and elevate the character of a youthful bride, though the task generally ends in disappointment. But no sane elderly married man ever dreams of trying to correct the faults of the mother of grown-up children. Now, Mr. Dickens and the public have been, so to speak, wedded too long together, and, on the whole, love each other too dearly, to dream of any possible improvement of their marital relations.

Moreover, there is probably no writer of eminence who has shown less faculty of improvement—if we may use such a phrase—than Charles Dickens. By the force of an almost unequalled genius, he placed himself, on his first appearance, in the foremost rank of English authors; and from that rank he has never receded or advanced. In the novels of Thackeray or Bulwer you can trace a marked improvement in the art of writing and story-telling, as the author gained skill by experience. You can trace nothing of the kind in those of Dickens. "Great Expectations" is as perfect or imperfect as a novel as "The Old Curiosity Shop," and in the same manner. As a veteran novelist, Mr. Dickens evinces the same inability to compose a story which he showed as a mere literary tyro. With the exception, perhaps, of "Barnaby Rudge"—the least popular of all his novels—there is not one in which the story, as story, is not unsatisfactory, in which the plot is not confused, the explanation inadequate, and in which there is not an absence of proportion between the foundation of the superstructure and the superstructure itself. In his latest novel, the "Mutual Friend" himself, the Veneerings, the Podsnaps, and the Lammles, have absolutely nothing to do with the development of the story, which they introduce, as it were, to the reader. The murder of John Harmon, the supposed keynote of the novel, is almost lost sight of throughout the bulk of the novel; and the main interest centres, not about the chief actors, but about Eugene Wrayburn, and Lizzie Hexam, and Bradley Headstone, mere supernumeraries in the drama of "Our Mutual Friend," whose presence might be dispensed with without injury to the main plot. In trying to unravel one of Mr. Dickens' plots, we are always reminded of the Maze at Hampton Court; the clues which appear the most promising end in nothing, and we make a dozen false starts before we catch hold of the correct path. We fancy, for instance, that the adoption of Johnny and Sloppy is to lead to something important in the solution of the Boffin mystery, but Johnny dies before he can be brought home, and Sloppy only reappears in the last chapter, to aid in administering due castigation to Silas Wegg. Then, too, the hero and heroine of the "Mutual Friend" are of the usual cast-iron, or rather cast-wax, stamp we are used to in all Mr. Dickens' novels. M. Henri Taine, in his able critique on English novelists, says that he always feels inclined to address the excellent young men and amiable young women who play the lovers in Mr. Dickens' works as good little boys and girls. "Soyez sages, mes bons petits enfans," is the valedictory benediction he would bestow upon them. Ruth Pinch, Ada Jarndyce, Florence Dombey, Kate Nickleby, Little Dorrit, and the rest, are all twin sisters. Every now and then we have a heroine who begins by being a little wilful and proud, like Bella Wilfer, but she always ends by toning down into a perfect woman. So, in like manner, the heroes are always well-conducted, excellent young men, with the highest principles, and all the domestic virtues. And, somehow, Mr. Dickens himself seems aware of their essentially prosaic nature. He has created scores of characters which will live as long as the English literature of our time is read; but he has never thrown the whole power of his matchless genius on the delineation of a hero or heroine. "Vanity Fair" was called a novel without a hero; but Dickens' novels might, we think, be more truly called novels without heroes and without plots.

Then, also, since we are picking out faults, we may say that the artistic merit of Mr. Dickens' pictures is strangely injured by his passion for irrelevant discussions—a passion which has grown upon him in later years. When Thackeray

Appendix 3: Contemporary Reviews of Our Mutual Friend   245

stopped in the middle of his narrative to enter on some topic which took his fancy, we were almost sorry when the topic was dropped and the narrative resumed. But with Dickens the case is different. We may or may not agree with Mr. Dickens' views about Chancery suits and administrative reform; but, agreeing or disagreeing, we do not wish to have them forced upon us in the middle of a novel, like a dose of medicine or a spoonful of honey. Thus in "Our Mutual Friend" one of the most fanciful and brilliant passages is the protest against the modern Poor-law system, given through the narrative of old Betty, but it has no more to do with the story than with Captain Cook's voyages. Mr. Dickens would, perhaps, urge in reply, that a great moral lesson can be enforced better through the medium of a novel than of an elaborate Blue-book. We are quite willing to admit the plea in the interests of social progress, but not in those of art. As an earnest reformer, Mr. Dickens may be right in interlarding his novels with political and social discussions; as an artist, he is undoubtedly wrong.

In "Our Mutual Friend," all the peculiar merits and defects of the writer we all admire so much may be found in their full force and development. It is the fashion, amongst the class of critics in whose eyes popularity is the heaviest sin that can be laid to a writer's door, to say that Dickens has fallen off. Whether he has fallen off or not is a question of opinion, but it is certain that nobody has yet risen up to him. Let any candid reader try and picture to himself what a sensation "Our Mutual Friend" would have produced if it had been written by a new and unknown author. It is only because we are so used to the marvellous creative power of the great English novelist that we have almost ceased to wonder at his creations. We have plenty of clever novel-writers at the present day, and Anthony Trollope, Bulwer, Miss Evans, Charles Reade, and a dozen others, might be named as novelists whose works will live after them; but what single writer is there amongst the lot would have written the account of the Pool below the bridges, of little Johnny's death, of Bradley Headstone's death agony, or of the doll-dressmaker's "bad boy?" It is getting the fashion, now-a-days, for novelists to photograph the features, habits, tricks of voice and manner of their friends and acquaintance, and so to produce a life-like portraiture. But yet, even to those who know the originals, the impression produced by those photographic likenesses is not half so vivid as that which Mr. Dickens creates out of his own genius. Nobody can give a name to Mr. Podsnap, or Fascination Fledgeby, or Mr. Twemlow, or Alfred Lammle, but yet everybody feels that he knows them personally, the moment he has read "Our Mutual Friend." Just as no critic can ever discern the art by which a great painter produces a resemblance by a few touches, so no disquisition can explain how it is that Mr. Dickens throws off his likenesses. We know far more of the real nature of Becky Sharpe and Colonel Newcome than we do of any personage in Mr. Dickens' novels; but if the latter writer had painted them—a thing he could not have done— we should have seen them before us as they lived and moved; we should have known them if we had met them in the street.

And, in our opinion, it is this faculty of bringing his personages before us in flesh and blood which constitutes Mr. Dickens' extraordinary talent. In spite of

246   *Charles Dickens's* Our Mutual Friend

the extravagance of his plots, the men and women of his pages are living beings. When once seen they come home with us, as persons we have known in life. Mr. Pickwick and Sam Weller, Mark Tapley and Jonas Chuzzlewit, Pecksniff and Harold Skimpole, Little Nell and Paul Dombey, and a hundred others, are personages whose names you may recall in writing or conversation with a far greater certainty that those you address will understand the reference, than if you mentioned the most famous names in modern science, or art, or politics. To this great Dickens portrait gallery "Our Mutual Friend" will add not a few pictures. Bella, the "boofer lady," Mrs. Wilfer, Silas Wegg, old Betty, Rogue Riderhood, and Mr. Veneering, are henceforth recognized public characters. Nor is there any failing in this, the latest of the series, in that wonderful power of seeing what everybody feels he ought to have seen himself, but did not see—which distinguishes all Mr. Dickens' works. When the tavern waiter in the Christmas story complained about the hardship of his having to profess an interest in the prospects of the moors, we all felt quite astonished that this observation had never struck us before. So the mere phrase about the Lammle household, that their servants were not quite like any other people's servants, gives us an idea of the Lammle interior which pages of minute description would not produce. Mr. Dickens tells us in his preface how "Our Mutual Friend" was nearly being abruptly removed from the world by the dreadful Staplehurst accident. Had it so been, there is no living author for whose death so many thousands of readers, to whom his face is unknown, would have grieved as for that of a friend, not mutual, but personal.

(BB) "Literary. Charles Dickens' Last Novel," New York Times, December 14, 1865, pp. 4–5

Fresh from the *consecutive* perusal of this somewhat complicated, but remarkably vivid and characteristic tale, and on the edge of Christmas, whose cheery kindliness and holy trust its author has embodied and embalmed wherever the English language is spoken—we are not disposed for a rigid performance of the critic's task, but rather inclined to express the grateful surprise with which we recognize in our and the public's *Mutual Friend*, such striking evidences of unimpaired vigor, ingenuity, buoyant humor and genial sentiment. In deference to the strict canons of artistic law in fiction, we cannot, indeed, but confess the improbabilities as a story, the extravagance as a satire, and the grotesqueness in style, of certain elements in the plot and details of the execution; they are too obvious for indication; but when the story is read, not in fragments as it appeared, but continuously as a whole, these perversities become sensibly diminished, and the true, graphic, original features of the work in a great measure harmonize what is apparently incongruous. As a verbal artist DICKENS herein exhibits often all his own peculiar grace and picturesqueness: the interior and the landscape are not seldom of Flemish accuracy; many of the scenes are richly dramatic, and some of the characters veritable additions to his own unrivaled gallery. Jenny Wren is a consistent and fresh creation, admirably suggestive of the compensatory influence,

Appendix 3: Contemporary Reviews of Our Mutual Friend   247

so often seen in real life, of wit and temperament in atoning for physical defect. Wegg and Venus are curious instances of the effect of coarse conceit and "a little learning;" and the former a remarkable embodiment of vulgar selfishness worked out with skill; R. W. is well drawn—another of the author's inimitable incarnations of triumphant good nature; his wife is, indeed, an exaggeration, but, as such, gives dramatic significance to the domestic dialogue. At a superficial estimate, the colloquies of Wrayburn and his friend, may seem quite unnatural; but whoever has known young university-men in England, with a competence and no ambition, and heard their lazy confabulation among themselves, will find a basis at least for this kind of talk, in real life. Lammle is too intensely vulgar an adventurer, and the virtues of Lizzie Hexam seem miraculous, considering her birth and breeding. Very broad and course is the caricature of "society;" but whoever has gone home from a London conventional dinner-party given by an egotistic materialist, and thought of its social barrenness and its wearisome and utter artificiality as regards both intercourse and routine, has perchance put his hand to his aching head like Twemlow, and wondered in his soul at the fatuity of the exhibition. The Veneering episode is a caricature; but how otherwise can the truth involved therein be impressed on the obtuse English mind? Such rough and rude pictures of a certain class of men and a certain phase of life are, doubtless, repulsive to the Tory mind; but, objectionable as they are in an artistic view, we doubt if more refined and strictly accurate delineations would make the perversities of social life, now and there, palpable and patent. As usual, the children of the story are genuine; poor little Johnny and the "inextinguishable baby" are worthy of the wonderful nursery CHARLES DICKENS has peopled. Had he, at the outset, made Boffin—besides having a good soul—a natural actor, his transformation would be more plausible; as it is, so far as the story goes, it is a bold stroke of narrative art, and has all the zest of surprise. But, after all, and above all, the spirit of the tale, its entire impression, its human significance, are alive with the author's peculiar genius. To open the eyes of a spirited and, at heart, affectionate girl, to the moral deformity of avarice, by a near and dear example, is a thought and a purpose which cannot be too highly praised: and it is carried out most effectively, however improbably. Indeed, the old problem which, in so many forms, this prolific writer has genially solved— the antagonism between *Self* and *Soul*, and the moral and human necessity of the latter's triumph—is here freshly and forcibly, often delectably, and with infinite relish and humor, made manifest.

It is now a little more than thirty years since the *Pickwick Papers* opened a new vista to that love of and capacity for humorous observation of life and delineation thereof which is the most distinctive feature of Anglo-Saxon literary genius, culminating in SHAKESPEARE and quaintly or genially scintillating from STERNE, GOLDSMITH and LAMB. The individuality of the humor of DICKENS was instantly recognized. It was a new vein, and yet full of nature and truth, exuberant with vital sympathy, ludicrous, zestful and characteristic. Pickwick and Weller immediately and henceforth became household words—new and domesticated portraits in the long array of ideal and representative men and women, created by the British novelist from FIELDING to SCOTT, and from

STERNE to THACKERAY. Heroes of the middle and lower classes—those, and a score of others that succeeded them—were all the more attractive because identified with the scenes of average experience, the life of the mass. Herein began the great work of DICKENS as a delineator of human nature; that his studies were elaborated from no exceptional sphere—far away and comparatively inaccessible to the multitude—but were drawn from the haunts of lowly toil, the dens of indigence and crime in the heart of the English metropolis, and the scenes of every-day business and pastimes. Thus to illustrate and emphasize the familiar and common-place, and elicit therefrom the picturesque, the dramatic, and, above all, the human, in elemental significance, has been and is the peculiar and the perpetual triumph of CHARLES DICKENS—the combined result of very keen and sympathetic observation, and a sense of the ludicrous and the loving at once *naïve* and profound. And just in proportion that he has been true to this idiosyncracy he has been successful; as a direct social critic, an interpreter of the past in Italy and the present in America, there was a lack of comprehensiveness and insight that made his books on both subjects, except in descriptive passages, inadequate and superficial; for in each case the requisite knowledge and sympathy were wanting; but when he deals with the reality and romance of a sphere of life, every phase, phenomenon and detail of which is familiar to his vision and his thought—especially that region where the struggle and the stress of humanity is most constant and obvious, among the poor, the working and the trading classes—he is thoroughly at home with his materials, and has only to vitalize them by the magnetic humor and graphic delineation of his own mind and heart, to make a fascinating or impressive story, When we come to examine the qualities of this creative humor, we find, first of all, a glow of feeling which incarnates itself in a character and overflows therefrom; goodness of heart, honesty of purpose, tender faith, disinterested love—these and such as these redeeming traits of our nature, are made to freshen and purify scenes of toil and misery, made to compensate for sterile fortunes, to elevate humble creatures, to glorify narrow and lowly lives. And, as we have said, these characteristics, as embodied by DICKENS, are *magnetic*, not mechanical; they are heart-born, the cheeriness of the Brothers Cheeryble and their old clerk, the dauntless self-devotion of Little Dorrit and Jarndyce, the angelic patience of Paul Dombey and Little Nell, the magnanimous simplicity of Captain Cuttle, and so many other genial creations, are so genuine as to infect the reader and thereby expand and soften if not his heart at least his mood; they put him in relation with instead of on his guard against mankind; revive his faith in humanity—renew his primal trust and tenderness. Herein is the great good of DICKENS as a popular writer. It is objected by the fastidious that he excels in depicting the vulgar side and scenes of life; that there is a gross relish of the comfortable and convivial in his pictures; that he exalts mere *disposition* above heroism, and makes *good-nature* a sublime virtue. In these very objections we find the evidence of his superior claims and his benign mission. What we need in this age is to be won back to the primitive and normal sources of happiness—to recognize homely and available joys—to realize that in the native sympathies of the soul, independent of outward conditions, exist the legitimate sources of human pleasure, progress and peace; and, of all

Appendix 3: Contemporary Reviews of Our Mutual Friend

249

living writers, in the English tongue, no one has so effectually brought home this vital truth to the average consciousness of the age as CHARLES DICKENS. In an epoch of extravagance and conventionalism, of rivalry and restlessness, of factitious luxury and artificial habitudes, it is a singular blessing that the most popular writer of fiction, instead of pandering to the vapid materialism and social vanities of his day, persistently exhibits winsome triumphs of human virtue, genuine love, noble independence, genial and gentle ideals, unindebted for their inspiration to any other source than the gifts of nature—the endowments, the discipline, and the compensations bestowed on our common humanity by the fatherhood of God! The atmosphere of such a genius is wholesome, the smile it awakens is kindly, the sympathies it fosters are humane, the amusement it affords not only innocent but cheering and suggestive. It is, therefore, as a moral artist that DICKENS is peerless. He reconciles, harmonizes, warms those feelings and fancies which worldliness and egotism warp and harden; hence we regard him as a great personal benefactor, and, looking back over the long list of books he has given us, and remembering how often they have beguiled us of the thing we are, cheered, charmed, consoled, tickled our fancy, kindled our imagination, put us on the track of curious observation and into the mood of forbearance, compassion or favor, we have no other word but gratitude, no other criticism but admiration. Such, in a broad view, and as a whole, must, we think, be the feeling of every candid lover of truth, humor and charity, in the retrospect of his career. But as each tale appears, the same faults are recapitulated, until exaggeration, grotesqueness and absurdity in certain particulars have become as much the critical label attached to the name of DICKENS as "pathos," "humor" and "humanity," which still are and must be his acknowledged attributes. We do not deny that his plots are often too clumsy and complicated; that he frequently gives us caricatures instead of characters, and that his experiments in the more refined social and female delineations are, in some respects, artistic failures; but, while admitting this, we must protest against the too literal criticism of such a writer. There are people, very good and intelligent, who not only have no sense of humor themselves, but act as a damper on that of others; never having associated with free and frank dealers therein, who talk in a dramatic, a facetious, an ironical, or exaggerated, in a word, a humorous way, for pastime, they cannot understand or appreciate any rollicking play of fancy and feeling, and consequently condemn as absurd and irrational what is addressed purely to a sense of the ridiculous. Such minds can never do justice either to the intent or spirit of a writer like DICKENS. But Mrs. Gamp, Toots, the Dodger and Bunsby are so true to the humorous instinct in its normal development, that they have long ago been adopted into the popular vocabulary as precedents. It is true that the use of a physical peculiarity—Miss Dartle's scar, Carker's teeth, Panck's puffing, the neck of this one, the hair of another, and the nose of a third— is a kind of dramatic trick, but it is none the less founded in nature; for nothing is more common than, among intimates, to designate familiar acquaintances and humorously to allude to them by reference to some oddity of manner, person, or phraseology; and, though sometimes carried too far by DICKENS, it is often used with humorous skill as a means of characterization.

250   *Charles Dickens's* Our Mutual Friend

To reach the average sympathies of humanity, the *sensation* and the *sentiment* of a scene, an experience and a character must be incarnated—made real; and this process and power belongs to CHARLES DICKENS in an eminent degree, and with an original relish and relation. He has exercised it indirectly to celebrate humane and hearty, to unveil sinister and selfish characters; and directly to lay bare, expose, reveal and force upon attention the abuses of authority and the social neglect which mars and bids fair to master the prosperity and peace of his country. The circumlocution office, the workhouse, the boarding-school, and many other patent enormities have been made, as it were, to reveal themselves in detail before the public, so as to forever remove the excuse of ignorance, and to cause the duty of lawgivers and the prosperous to appear in letters of light. He has depicted the economics of London life in all their sense and seemings—from the stolid counting-house to the dustman's mounds, from the law-office to the dolls' dressmaker, from the invisible usurer to the serviceable dun, from the old curiosity-shop to the gaol-brokerage, and from the bone-articulator to the bird-fancier. The nooks and nests of London, its streets, river-side, its riots and rioters, upholstery, deserted and thronged domains, its outcasts and autocrats, its reprobates and benefactors, its Jews and pickpockets, priests, heroes, saints, harlequins, its very atmosphere, as by him drawn, defined, colored to the life, in a word, the sensation and sentiment thereof, live in vital relief on his pages. The truth and humor of his *Sketches of London Life and Character* first drew public attention to his skill and promise in the columns of a newspaper, and the same local aptitude is manifest in some of the best descriptive portions of his last novel.

As a tragic writer there is often rare power in his creations, but less of the nature and more of the melo-dramatic; exquisitely pathetic in describing a dying child, his mature villains, however impressively drawn, are less original; Sykes, Ralph Nickleby and Headstone are too unrelieved in their criminal consciousness and action, though full of the tragic intensity of remorse. Although eccentricity is the means and medium, in no small degree, of his reformatory literary achievements, considering the monotonous coloring and unpicturesque routine of English life, we know not if a more efficient agency could be pressed into such noble service. And let it be ever remembered that, as in the dawn, so in the meridian of his career, the philosophy of life DICKENS unfolds is Shakespearean, not only in its free and faithful dealing with the elemental and the persuasive in human nature and life, but in the advocacy and illustration of that wholesome faith in realities, that acceptance in a cheerful spirit of things as they are, with a steadfast and holy purpose to ameliorate them, which is the only practical faith for wise and loving hearts.

(CC) From "The Literary Year," London Review, December 30, 1865, p. 716

It would be both impracticable and superfluous for us even to glance in this summary at all the novels which have been published during the year, and of which the larger number were destined to nothing more than a few weeks' flimsy existence in the circulating libraries. We can only select the most special examples

Appendix 3: Contemporary Reviews of Our Mutual Friend   251

of the art; and of these the chief is undoubtedly Mr. Dickens's last story, "Our Mutual Friend." We alluded to the work in our last year's Literary Supplement, eight parts having then appeared; but it has been completed during the present year, and in October was given to the public in the form of two volumes.[6] A close critical examination will not fail to detect some serious faults in the construction of this tale, and in the conception and development of two or three of the characters; but in none of its author's works have there been more admirable examples of his knowledge of life and of the human heart, while the old mastery over humour and pathos, and the old picturesqueness in scenery and accessories, are as evident as in any of those earlier stories which have now become classics.

[Remainder discusses other literary works from 1865.]

(DD) From "Literary Intelligence, and Notes on New Books," United States Service Magazine, *January 1866, p. 76*

From Messrs. Peterson, of Philadelphia, we have received Charles Dickens's very successful novel, "Our Mutual Friend." In none of his earlier works has he depicted a greater number of queer "types of mankind" than in this, and we incline to believe it his best work since "Oliver Twist." True to his instinct, he again attacks national shams with great success. But the chief merit of the book is the originality of his characters, and the unabated interest which they excite in the reader to their end. Who does not know a Veneering, a Podsnap, a Mrs. Laimule?[7] But dear old Boffin is above all praise. Silas Wegg will live forever, and the Dolls' dress-makers deserve to, also. As usual, the hero is the least interesting of the characters; but "the lovely woman" atones for him, and R. W. is a perfect picture. R. W.'s return from the clandestine marriage to the bosom of his family, is one of the best bits of humor Dickens ever wrote. The Petersons have published it in cheap pamphlet form, and also in a fine two-volume edition, which is worthy a place in every library.

[Remainder consists of reviews and notices of other recently published books.]

(EE) From "Retrospect of Literature, Art, and Science, in 1865," The Annual Register, *1866, Part 1, p. 323*

Among the works of fiction which have issued from the press, Mr. Dickens's work, "Our Mutual Friend," must first be mentioned, as its author, from the reputation of his previous works, is *facile princeps* among living writers of fiction. It must be admitted that Mr. Dickens has not in this his latest effort satisfied in all respects the expectations of his ardent admirers. But we can scarcely be surprised at this, for no writer is always—if we may use an illogical but expressive phrase—equal to

---

[6]   "The Literary Year" essay for 1864 only noticed Dickens's book, deferring commentary until it should be complete. Like other plain notices of publication, it has therefore been omitted from this Appendix.

[7]   Presumably Lammle, but appears as above.

252   *Charles Dickens's* Our Mutual Friend

himself. That Mr. Dickens still possesses the qualities which enabled him to write the "Pickwick Papers," the "Old Curiosity Shop," and "Martin Chuzzlewit," three books so very different *inter se*, yet such proud monuments of the work of one great and original genius, we do not at all doubt; but a novel, especially a novel worthy of Dickens, is a creation; and writers, like artists, are sometimes unable at the desired moment to summon to their aid their highest inventive powers. In the creation of characters, however, Mr. Dickens is still as fertile as ever; it is in the artistic completeness of the picture, if any thing, that he is deficient. "Our Mutual Friend" came out in a serial form, and was completed and reprinted in full during the year of which we are now writing.

[Remainder discusses other literary works and artistic achievements during 1865.]

(FF) From "Literary Notices," Godey's Lady's Book and Magazine, February 1866, p. 187

We last month announced the appearance of this work, complete in two volumes. Since then we have had time to give the second volume the careful attention it deserves. Dickens is certainly no longer the Dickens who wrote Pickwick, but to our mind he is far better; more serious and thoughtful; more earnest in his life-labor of fraternizing the different classes of society. Shoddy doesn't like "Our Mutual Friend:" it sees too true a reflection of itself in the Veneerings. Podsnapdom don't appreciate it of course, and puts away both book and author with a wave of the hand, declaring "he writes about such low people; such people as we have nothing to do with, and don't want to know anything about." But we can say truly that there is nothing but the best of kindly teachings and the purest of morals in his work, while his satire is legitimate in both subject and object.

[Remainder consists of reviews and notices of other recently published books.]

Appendix 4
Selected Bibliography of Editions
of *Our Mutual Friend*

This Appendix provides a bibliography—not exhaustive, as I shall explain—of editions of *Our Mutual Friend* since 1864–65. So many editions of Dickens's work have appeared over the years, including the great many pirated ones published in America and elsewhere during the nineteenth century, and including also any number of issues and reissues that called themselves "editions" but bear no textual differences from other or earlier editions, that it seems both impossible and unnecessary to account for every appearance of *Our Mutual Friend* during the last 150 years. To provide just one example, Walter E. Smith has noted the following of an "edition" published by T.B. Peterson and Brothers of Philadelphia in November 1865:

> This subedition of *Our Mutual Friend* was published, by arrangement with Harper Brothers, on November 11, 1865, probably a few hours after Harper's edition. The work was published in octavo and duodecimo formats in various styles and so-called editions, including a Paper Cover Edition (8 vo, ill. $1.00), an Illustrated Octavo Edition (cloth, $2.50), an Illustrated Duodecimo Edition (2 vols., $4.00), and a People's Duodecimo Edition (cloth, $2.50).[1]

Over the next few years, Peterson continued to publish new impressions in these formats, including in their "Cheap Editions for the Millions" and as a "Green Cloth Edition."[2] And this is just one example involving a single American publisher. In short, *Our Mutual Friend* has been published countless times in innumerable forms, and even Brattin and Hornback passed on compiling a truly exhaustive list in their *Annotated Bibliography* in 1984.

Taking my cues from their work, and drawing partly from both their bibliography and Heaman's update of it in 2003, I offer here a partial bibliography of English and American editions of *Our Mutual Friend*, including information regarding who illustrated the edition and who introduced it, when such information applies. Omitted here are film, television, and radio adaptations—simply because there have been so few of these, and I discuss the principal ones in Chapter 5—and also audio, web, and ebook editions, which are now so numerous and varied that they defy meaningful bibliographic work. Scores of such audio and/or electronic works have appeared just since 2000, and their limitless polymorphism, amid the growing popularity of products like the Kindle, the Nook, and other devices, creates quite the scholarly tangle.

---

[1] Smith, *Charles Dickens: A Bibliography of His First American Editions*, p. 395.
[2] Ibid.

254   *Charles Dickens's* Our Mutual Friend

With these qualifications, the editions that I have included appear chronologically, and the bibliography is divided into the following three categories: 1) editions published during Dickens's lifetime, omitting reprints and reissues from the same publisher; 2) editions published by Chapman and Hall between 1870 and 1913, when their British copyright for *The Mystery of Edwin Drood* expired;[3] and 3) editions published since 1870 that include new textual or critical material, such as illustrations or a substantive introduction. When possible, I have included information about illustrations, introductions, afterwords, and other relevant textual and critical apparatus.

Editions Published during Dickens's Lifetime

20 parts, Marcus Stone (illust.) (London: Chapman and Hall, May 1864–November 1865).

4 vols, Marcus Stone (illust.) (Leipzig: Bernhard Tauchnitz, 1864–65).

20 parts, Marcus Stone (illust.) (*Harper's New Monthly Magazine*, 29–32, June 1864–December 1865).

4 vols, Marcus Stone (illust.) (New York: John Bradburn, October 1864 and February, July, and December 1865).

2 vols, Marcus Stone (illust.) (London: Chapman and Hall, February and November 1865).

2 vols, Marcus Stone (illust.) (New York: Harper and Brothers, February and November 1865).

1 vol., Marcus Stone (illust.) (New York: Harper and Brothers, 1865).

1 vol., Uniform Edition, Marcus Stone (illust.) (Philadelphia: T.B. Peterson and Brothers, 1865).

2 vols, Uniform Duodecimo Edition, Marcus Stone (illust.) (Philadelphia: T.B. Peterson and Brothers, 1865).

4 vols, Household Edition, F.O.C. Darley (illust.) (New York: Hurd and Houghton, 1866).

1 vol., Cheap Edition, A. Boyd Houghton (frontispiece illust.) (London: Chapman and Hall, 1867).

1 vol., Diamond Edition, Sol Eytinge, Jr. (illust.) (Boston: Ticknor and Fields, 1867).

1 vol., Author's Edition, Sol Eytinge, Jr. (illust.) (Philadelphia: Porter & Coates, 1867).

2 vols, Library Edition, Marcus Stone (illust.) (London: Chapman and Hall; Boston: Fields, Osgood, and Company, 1867).

---

[3]   I have chosen to track Chapman and Hall's editions through 1913 rather than through 1907, the last year they held copyright for *Our Mutual Friend*, because they issued in 1913 one final edition—the Universal Illustrated Edition—as the copyright for *The Mystery of Edwin Drood* expired. The edition was presumably meant to preempt all those other publishers who would soon compete with them to print and sell Dickens's "complete" works.

Appendix 4: Selected Bibliography of Editions of Our Mutual Friend   255

1 vol., Charles Dickens Edition, Marcus Stone (illust.) (London: Chapman and
Hall, 1868).

Editions Published by Chapman and Hall, 1870–1913

1 vol., Household Edition, James Mahoney (illust.) (London: Chapman and Hall
[also New York: Harper and Brothers], 1875).
2 vols, Second Illustrated Library Edition, Marcus Stone (illust.) (London:
Chapman and Hall, [1873–76]).
2 vols, De luxe Edition, Marcus Stone (illust.) (London: Chapman and Hall,
[1881–82]).
2 vols, Gadshill Edition, Andrew Lang (intro.), Marcus Stone (illust.) (London:
Chapman and Hall, 1897–98).
2 vols, De luxe Edition, [Luxury reprint of the 1897–98 Gadshill], Andrew Lang
(intro.), Marcus Stone (illust.) (London: Chapman and Hall, 1903).
1 vol., Biographical Edition, Arthur Waugh (intro.), Marcus Stone (illust.)
(London: Chapman and Hall, 1903).
1 vol., Authentic Edition, Marcus Stone (illust.) (London: Chapman and Hall,
[1900–1908]).
1 vol., Fireside Edition, Marcus Stone (illust.) (London: Chapman and Hall,
[1903–1907]).
2 vols, National Edition, B.W. Matz (ed.), Marcus Stone (illust.) (London:
Chapman and Hall, [1906–1907]).
2 vols, Centenary Edition, Marcus Stone (illust.) (London: Chapman and Hall,
[1910–11]).
1 vol., Universal Edition, Marcus Stone (illust.) (London: Chapman and Hall [also
New York: Charles Scribner's Sons], [1913–1914]).

Editions with New Textual or Critical Material since 1870

2 vols, New Library Edition, Edwin Percy Whipple (intro.) (Boston: Houghton
Mifflin, 1894).
1 vol., Macmillan Edition, Charles Dickens, Jr. (ed.), Marcus Stone (illust.) (New
York: Macmillan and Co., 1895).
1 vol., Everyman Edition, G.K. Chesterton (intro.) (London: J.M. Dent and Sons;
New York: E.P. Dutton and Co., 1907).
1 vol., Imperial Edition, George Gissing (intro.), F.G. Kitton (illust.) (London:
Gresham Publishing Company, 1908).
2 vols, Waverley Edition, William De Morgan (intro.), Charles Pears (illust.), Fred
Barnard (frontispiece illust.) (London: Waverley Book Co., 1913).
1 vol., Nonesuch Dickens, Arthur Waugh, Walter Dexter, Thomas Hatton, and
Hugh Walpole (eds), Marcus Stone (illust.) (Bloomsbury: Nonesuch, 1938).

1 vol., Great Illustrated Classics Edition, Allen Klots, Jr. (intro.), Marcus Stone, F.O.C. Darley, and James Mahoney (illusts) (New York: Dodd, Mead, and Company, 1951).

1 vol., New Oxford Illustrated Dickens Edition, E. Salter Davies (intro.), Marcus Stone (illust.) (London: Oxford University Press, 1952).

1 vol., Collins Edition, Jerome K. Jerome (intro.) (London: Collins, 1955).

1 vol., Macdonald Illustrated Classics Edition, J.B. Priestley (intro.), Marcus Stone (illust.) (London: Macdonald, 1957).

1 vol., Heritage Press Edition, John T. Winterrich (intro.), Lynd Ward (illust.) (New York: Heritage Press, 1957).

1 vol., Modern Library Edition, Monroe Engel (intro.) (New York: Random House, 1960).

1 vol., Signet Classic Edition, J. Hillis Miller (afterword) (New York: New American Library of World Literature, 1964).

2 vols, Centennial Edition, E. Salter Davies (intro.) (Geneva: Edito-Service S. A., [1969–71]).

1 vol., Penguin Edition, Stephen Gill (intro.) (Harmondsworth: Penguin Books, 1971).

1 vol., Bounty Edition, Harriet Weitzner (intro.) (New York: Bounty, 1978).

1 vol., Oxford World's Classics Edition, Michael Cotsell (intro.) (Oxford; New York: Oxford University Press, 1983).

1 vol., New Oxford Illustrated Edition, Andrew Sanders (intro.), Marcus Stone (illust.) (London: David Campbell [also Everyman Edition. New York: A.A. Knopf], 1994).

1 vol., Penguin Edition, Adrian Poole (intro.), Marcus Stone (illust.) (Harmondsworth: Penguin Books, 1997).

1 vol., Wordsworth Classics Edition, Deborah Wynne (intro.), Marcus Stone (illust.) (London: Wordsworth, 1997).

1 vol., Everyman Edition, Joel Brattin (intro.), Marcus Stone (illust.) (London: J.M. Dent, 2000).

1 vol., Modern Library Classics Edition, Richard T. Gaughan (intro.) (New York: Modern Library, 2002).

1 vol., Vintage Classics Edition, Nick Hornby (intro.), (London: Vintage Books, 2010).

Bibliography

Manuscript/Archival Sources

New York Public Library, Henry W. and Albert A. Berg Collection of English and American Literature, Agreement between Dickens and Edward and Frederic Chapman, for the writing and publishing of the serial Our mutual friend, for the sum of £6000, dated Nov. 21, 1863.
New York Public Library, Henry W. and Albert A. Berg Collection of English and American Literature, *Our Mutual Friend* by Charles Dickens, Copy 4.
New York Public Library, Henry W. and Albert A. Berg Collection of English and American Literature, *Our Mutual Friend* by Charles Dickens, Proof sheets, with the author's ms. corrections.
Pierpont Morgan Library, Department of Literary and Historical Manuscripts, MA 1202/1203, *Our Mutual Friend* by Charles Dickens, Original autograph manuscript with innumerable erasures and corrections.

Printed Primary Sources

Dickens, Charles, [Untitled notice], *All the Year Round* (November 26, 1859): 95.
———, *Bleak House* (Nicola Bradbury, ed., London: Penguin, 1996).
———, *Book of Memoranda* (Fred Kaplan, ed., New York: Astor, Lenox and Tilden Foundations, 1981).
———, *The Dent Uniform Edition of Dickens' Journalism* (4 vols, Michael Slater, ed., London: J.M. Dent, 1994–2000).
———, *Great Expectations* (Edgar Rosenberg, ed., New York; London: W.W. Norton, 1999).
———, *The Letters of Charles Dickens* (12 vols, Madeline House, Graham Storey, and Kathleen Tillotson, eds, Oxford: Clarendon Press, 1965–2002).
———, *Little Dorrit* (Harvey Peter Sucksmith, ed., Oxford: Clarendon, 1979).
———, *Our Mutual Friend* (4 vols, New York: John Bradburn, 1864–65).
———, *Our Mutual Friend* (2 vols, London: Chapman and Hall, 1865).
———, *Our Mutual Friend* (E. Salter Davies, ed., London: Oxford University Press, 1967).
———, *Our Mutual Friend* (Michael Cotsell, ed., London: Oxford University Press, 1983).
———, *Our Mutual Friend* (Adrian Poole, ed., London; New York: Penguin, 1997).
———, *Our Mutual Friend* (New York: Vintage, 2011).
———, *The Public Readings* (Philip Collins, ed., Oxford: Clarendon, 1975).
Page, Norman (ed.), *Charles Dickens: Family History* (5 vols, London: Routledge, 1999).

Contemporary Reviews of *Our Mutual Friend*

"Charles Dickens," *Reader*, 6 (December 9, 1865): 647.

[Chorley, Henry], "*Our Mutual Friend*," *Athenaeum* (October 28, 1865): 569–70.

[Dallas, E.S.], "*Our Mutual Friend*," *Times* (November 29, 1865): 6.

"Dickens and Depravity," *New York Evangelist* (November 9, 1865): 6.

[Forster, John], "*Our Mutual Friend*," *Examiner* (October 28, 1865): 681–2.

[Guernsey, Alfred Hudson], "Editor's Easy Chair," *Harper's New Monthly Magazine*, 29 (June 1864): 131–5.

———, "Editor's Easy Chair," *Harper's New Monthly Magazine*, 29 (August 1864): 405–9.

———, "Editor's Easy Chair," *Harper's New Monthly Magazine*, 31 (November 1865): 806–10.

H.[owells], W.[illiam] D.[ean], "*Our Mutual Friend*," *The Round Table: A Saturday Review of Politics, Finance, Literature, Society* (December 2, 1865): 200–201.

[James, Henry], "*Our Mutual Friend*," *The Nation* (December 21, 1865): 786–7.

"Literary. Charles Dickens' Last Novel," *New York Times* (December 14, 1865): 4–5.

"Literary Intelligence, and Notes on New Books," *United States Service Magazine* (January 1866): 76.

"Literary Notices," *Godey's Lady's Book and Magazine* (April 1865): 373–5.

"Literary Notices," *Godey's Lady's Book and Magazine* (February 1866): 187–90.

"The Literary Year," *London Review* (December 30, 1865): 712–22.

"Miscellanea," *Reader* (June 11, 1864): 745–7.

"Mr. Dickens's New Story," *London Review*, 8 (April 30, 1864): 473–4.

"Mr. Dickens's Romance of a Dust-heap," *Eclectic and Congregational Review*, 9 (November 1865): 455–76.

"New Books," *New York Times* (November 22, 1865): 4.

"Our Weekly Gossip," *Athenaeum* (April 30, 1864): 613–4.

"Retrospect of Literature, Art, and Science, in 1865," in *The Annual Register; A Review of Public Events at Home and Abroad, for the Year 1865* (Part 1, London: Rivingtons, 1866).

"Reviews of Books—*Our Mutual Friend*," *London Review*, 11 (October 28, 1865): 467–8.

"Reviews—*Our Mutual Friend*," *Saturday Review* (November 11, 1865): 612–3.

"Short Notices. *Our Mutual Friend* [No. 2]," *London Review*, 8 (June 11, 1864): 633–4.

"Short Notices. *Our Mutual Friend* [No. 3]," *London Review*, 9 (July 2, 1864): 25–6.

"Short Notices. *Our Mutual Friend* [No. 4]," *London Review*, 9 (August 6, 1864): 162–3.

"Short Notices. *Our Mutual Friend* [No. 5]," *London Review*, 9 (September 3, 1864): 273–4.

Bibliography

"Short Notices. *Our Mutual Friend* [No. 6]," *London Review*, 9 (October 1, 1864): 386.

"Short Notices. *Our Mutual Friend* [No. 7]," *London Review*, 9 (November 5, 1864): 518.

"Short Notices. *Our Mutual Friend* [No. 8]," *London Review*, 9 (December 3, 1864): 622–3.

"Short Notices. *Our Mutual Friend* [No. 9]," *London Review*, 10 (January 7, 1865): 22–3.

"Short Notices. *Our Mutual Friend* [No. 10]," *London Review*, 10 (February 4, 1865): 156–7.

"Short Notices. *Our Mutual Friend* [No. 11]," *London Review*, 10 (March 4, 1865): 258–9.

"Short Notices. *Our Mutual Friend* [No. 12]," *London Review*, 10 (April 8, 1865): 389.

"Short Notices. *Our Mutual Friend* [No. 13]," *London Review*, 10 (May 6, 1865): 492–3.

"Short Notices. *Our Mutual Friend* [No. 14]," *London Review*, 10 (June 3, 1865): 594–6.

"Short Notices. *Our Mutual Friend* [No. 15]," *London Review*, 11 (July 8, 1865): 49.

"Short Notices. *Our Mutual Friend* [No. 16]," *London Review*, 11 (August 5, 1865): 153.

"Short Notices. *Our Mutual Friend* [No. 17]," *London Review*, 11 (September 2, 1865): 260–1.

"Short Notices. *Our Mutual Friend* [No. 18]," *London Review*, 11 (October 7, 1865): 395–6.

[Wise, John Richard de Capel], "Belles Lettres," *Westminster Review*, 85 (April 1866): 582–98.

Secondary Sources

Ackroyd, Peter, *Dickens* (New York: Harper Collins, 1990).

[Advertisement for Harper and Brothers, *Our Mutual Friend*], *The Round Table: A Saturday Review of Politics, Finance, Literature, Society*, 9 (November 18, 1865): 176.

Allen, Michael, *Charles Dickens and the Blacking Factory* (St. Leonards: Oxford-Stockley, 2011).

Andrews, Malcolm, *Charles Dickens and His Performing Selves: Dickens and the Public Readings* (Oxford: Oxford University Press, 2006).

[Bagehot, Walter], "Charles Dickens," *National Review*, 7 (October 1858): 458–86.

Baker, Ernest A., *The History of the English Novel* (vol. 7, New York: Barnes and Noble, 1936).

Bevington, Merle Mowbray, *The* Saturday Review *1855–1868: Representative Educated Opinion in Victorian England* (New York: AMS Press, 1966).

Bowen, John, *Other Dickens* (Oxford: Oxford University Press, 2000).

Brattin, Joel, "Dickens' Creation of Bradley Headstone," *Dickens Studies Annual*, 14 (1985): 147–65.

———, "'I will not have my words misconstrued': The Text of *Our Mutual Friend*," *Dickens Quarterly*, 15/3 (1998): 167–76.

Brattin, Joel, and Bert G. Hornback, Our Mutual Friend*: An Annotated Bibliography* (New York: Garland, 1984).

Bredsdorff, Elias, *Hans Andersen and Charles Dickens: A Friendship and Its Dissolution* (Copenhagen: Rosenkilde and Batter, 1956).

Buckler, William E., "*Once a Week* under Samuel Lucas, 1859–65," *PMLA*, 67/7 (1952): 924–41.

Casey, Ellen Miller, "'Boz has got the Town by the ear': Dickens and the *Athenaeum* Critics," *Dickens Studies Annual*, 33 (2003): 159–90.

"Chapter of Accidents," *Examiner* (June 17, 1865): 383.

"Charles Dickens," *Punch* (June 18, 1870): 244.

"Charles Dickens' *Great Expectations*," *Eclectic Review*, 1 [New series] (October 1861): 458–77.

"Charles Dickens Relieving the Sufferers at the Fatal Railway Accident Near Staplehurst," *Penny Illustrated Paper* (June 24, 1865): 1.

Chaudhuri, Brahma, "Dickens and the *Critic*," *Victorian Periodicals Review*, 21/4 (1988): 139–44.

Chesterton, G.K., *Charles Dickens* (Ware: Wordsworth Editions Limited, 2007).

Chorley, Henry, "Mr. Charles Dickens," *Athenaeum* (June 18, 1870): 804–5.

Cockburn, Lord Henry, *Life of Lord Jeffrey* (2 vols, Philadelphia: J.B. Lippincott, 1857).

Cohen, Jane R., *Charles Dickens and His Original Illustrators* (Columbus: Ohio State University Press, 1980).

Collins, Philip, "Dickens's Self-estimate: Some New Evidence," in Robert B. Partlow (ed.), *Dickens the Craftsman: Strategies of Presentation* (Carbondale: Southern Illinois University Press, 1970).

——— (ed.), *Dickens: The Critical Heritage* (London: Routledge and Kegan Paul, 1971).

Cotsell, Michael, *The Companion to* Our Mutual Friend (London: Allen and Unwin, 1986).

Dahl, Christopher C., "Fitzjames Stephen, Charles Dickens, and Double Reviewing," *Victorian Periodicals Review*, 14/2 (1981): 51–8.

[Dallas, E. S.], "*Great Expectations*," *Times* (October 17, 1861): 6.

Dexter, Walter, "When Found—," *Dickensian*, 31 (Winter 1934): 1–3.

———, "When Found—," *Dickensian*, 40 (March 1944): 55–9.

Dickens, Charles, Jr., "Personal," *All the Year Round* (July 2, 1870): 97.

"Dickens World," Home page, *Dickens World* (Web, August 11, 2012).

"Dreadful Railway Accident at Staplehurst," *Times* (June 10, 1865): 9.

Eliot, Simon, *Some Patterns and Trends in British Publishing 1800–1919* (London: Bibliographical Society, 1994).

Bibliography   261

Elwin, Malcolm, *Charles Reade* (London: Jonathan Cape, 1931).

Flood, Alison, "*Great Expectations* Voted Readers' Favourite Dickens Novel," *Guardian* (Web, October 3, 2011).

Ford, George H., *Dickens and His Readers: Aspects of Novel-Criticism since 1836* (Princeton: Princeton University Press, 1955).

———, "Dickens in the 1960s," *Dickensian*, 66 (May 1970): 163–82.

Forster, John, *The Life of Charles Dickens* (J.W.T. Ley, ed., London: Cecil Palmer, 1928).

Gissing, George, *Charles Dickens, A Critical Study* (New York: Dodd, Mead and Co., 1912).

Grass, Sean, "Commodity and Identity in *Great Expectations*," *Victorian Literature and Culture*, 40/2 (2012): 617–41.

"The Grave of Charles Dickens," *Punch* (June 25, 1870): 253.

Grubb, Gerald, "Some Unpublished Correspondence of Dickens and Chapman and Hall," *Boston University Studies in English*, 1 (1955): 98–127.

[Hamley, E.B.], "Remonstrance with Dickens," *Blackwood's Edinburgh Magazine*, 81 (April 1857): 490–503.

Harte, Bret, "Dickens in Camp," *Overland Monthly*, 5/1 (July 1870): 90.

Harvey, John R., *Victorian Novelists and Their Illustrators* (New York: New York University Press, 1971).

Hatton, Thomas, and Arthur H. Cleaver, *A Bibliography of the Periodical Works of Charles Dickens* (London: Chapman and Hall, 1933).

[Hayward, Abraham], [Unsigned review of *The Pickwick Papers*, *Sketches by Boz*, and *Sketches by Boz* (Second Series)], *Quarterly Review*, 59 (October 1837): 484–518.

Heaman, Robert J., "*Our Mutual Friend*: An Annotated Bibliography, Supplement I—1984–2000," *Dickens Studies Annual*, 33 (2003): 425–506.

Hill, T.W., "Dickensian Biography," *Dickensian*, 47 (1951): 10–15; 72–9.

[Horne, Richard H.], "Dust: or Ugliness Redeemed," *Household Words*, 1 (July 13, 1850): 379–84.

Howells, William Dean, *Criticism and Fiction* (New York: Harper and Brothers, 1891).

James, Henry, *The Tragic Muse* (2 vols, New York: Charles Scribner's Sons, 1908).

———, *Views and Reviews* (Boston: Ball, 1908).

Jerrold, Blanchard, "Charles Dickens. In Memoriam," *Gentleman's Magazine*, 229 (July 1870): 228–41.

John, Juliet, *Dickens and Mass Culture* (Oxford: Oxford University Press, 2010).

Johnson, Edgar, *Charles Dickens: His Tragedy and Triumph* (2 vols, New York: Simon and Schuster, 1952).

Jones, Radikha, "Counting Down Dickens' Greatest Novels. Number 5: *Our Mutual Friend*," *Time* (Web, February 1, 2012).

Kaplan, Fred, *Dickens: A Biography* (New York: William Morrow, 1988).

Kitton, Frederic G., *Dickens and His Illustrators* (London: George Redway, 1899).

Leary, Patrick, *The* Punch *Brotherhood: Table Talk and Print Culture in Mid-Victorian London* (London: British Library, 2010).

Leavis, F.R., *The Great Tradition: George Eliot, Henry James, Joseph Conrad* (New York: New York University Press, 1963).

Leavis, F.R., and Q.D. Leavis, *Dickens the Novelist* (New York: Pantheon, 1970).

Leavis, Q.D., *Fiction and the Reading Public* (London: Chatto and Windus, 1965).

Lester, Valerie Browne, *Phiz, the Man Who Drew Dickens* (London: Chatto and Windus, 2004).

Levin, Martin, "Cool Readings," *The Globe and Mail* (Web, July 1, 2012).

Lewes, George Henry, "Literature," *Leader* (December 11, 1852): 1189–92.

———, "Dickens in Relation to Criticism," *Fortnightly Review*, 17 (February 1, 1872): 141–54.

Liddle, Dallas, "Salesmen, Sportsmen, Mentors: Anonymity and Mid-Victorian Theories of Journalism," *Victorian Studies*, 41/1 (1997): 31–68.

[Lister, Thomas Henry], [Unsigned review of *Sketches by Boz* (First and Second Series), *The Pickwick Papers*, *Nicholas Nickleby*, and *Oliver Twist*], *Edinburgh Review*, 68 (October 1838): 75–97.

[McCarthy, Justin], "Modern Novelists: Charles Dickens," *Westminster Review*, 26 (October 1864): 414–41.

Marcus, Steven, *Dickens, from Pickwick to Dombey* (New York: Basic Books, 1965).

Mazzeno, Laurence W., *The Dickens Industry: Critical Perspectives 1836–2005* (Rochester: Camden House, 2008).

Meynell, Alice, "Charles Dickens as Man of Letters," *Atlantic Monthly*, 91 (January 1903): 52–9.

Milne, James, "How Dickens Sells," *The Book Monthly*, 3 (1906): 773–6.

Morris, Mowbray, "Charles Dickens," *Fortnightly Review*, 32 (December 1, 1882): 762–79.

Morse, Robert, "*Our Mutual Friend*," *Partisan Review*, 16/3 (1949): 277–89.

"Mr. Dickens's Last Novel," *Dublin University Magazine*, 58 (December 1861): 685–93.

Mullan, John, "John Mullan's 10 of the Best: Wills," *Guardian* (Web, July 6, 2012).

Murry, John Middleton, "Books of the Day: The Dickens Revival," *Times* (May 19, 1922): 16.

Nayder, Lillian, *The Other Dickens: A Life of Catherine Hogarth* (Ithaca: Cornell University Press, 2011).

O'Hea, Michael, "Hidden Harmony: Marcus Stone's Wrapper Design for *Our Mutual Friend*," *Dickensian*, 91 (Winter 1995): 198–208.

[Oliphant, Margaret], "Sensation Novels," *Blackwood's Edinburgh Magazine*, 91 (May 1862): 564–84.

Orwell, George, *Dickens, Dali and Others: Studies in Popular Culture* (New York: Reynal and Hitchcock, 1946).

Page, Norman (ed.), *Charles Dickens:* Hard Times, Great Expectations, *and* Our Mutual Friend, *A Casebook* (New York: Palgrave Macmillan, 1979).

Patten, Robert, *Charles Dickens and His Publishers* (Oxford: Oxford University Press, 1978).

―――. *Charles Dickens and "Boz": The Birth of the Industrial-Age Author* (Cambridge: Cambridge University Press, 2012).

Quiller-Couch, Arthur, *Charles Dickens and Other Victorians* (Cambridge: Cambridge University Press, 1925).

Reade, Charles, *Very Hard Cash*, in *All the Year Round* (August 1, 1863): 529–36.

Rose, Mark, *Authors and Owners: The Invention of Copyright* (Cambridge: Harvard University Press, 1993).

Rotkin, Charlotte, "The *Athenaeum* Reviews *Little Dorrit*," *Victorian Periodicals Review*, 23/1 (1990): 25–8.

Saintsbury, George, *Corrected Impressions: Essays on Victorian Writers* (London: William Heinemann, 1895).

Santayana, George, "Dickens," in *Soliloquies in England and Later Soliloquies* (New York: Charles Scribner's Sons, 1922).

Scoggin, Daniel, "A Speculative Resurrection: Death, Money, and the Vampiric Economy of *Our Mutual Friend*," *Victorian Literature and Culture*, 30/1 (2002): 99–125.

Sell-Sandoval, Kathleen, "In the Marketplace: Dickens, the Critics, and the Gendering of Authorship," *Dickens Quarterly*, 17/4 (2000): 224–35.

Shaw, George Bernard, *Shaw on Dickens* (Dan H. Laurence and Martin Quinn, eds, New York: Ungar, 1985).

Slater, Michael, "1920–1940 'Superior Folk' and Scandalmongers," *Dickensian*, 66 (May 1970): 121–42.

―――, *Dickens and Women* (Stanford: Stanford University Press, 1983).

―――, *Charles Dickens* (New Haven: Yale University Press, 2009).

―――, *The Great Charles Dickens Scandal* (New Haven: Yale University Press, 2012).

Smith, Walter E., *Charles Dickens in the Original Cloth: A Bibliographic Catalogue* (2 vols, Los Angeles: Heritage Bookshop, 1982).

―――, *Charles Dickens: A Bibliography of His First American Editions 1836– 1870 with Photographic Reproductions of Bindings and Title Pages, the Novels with* Sketches by Boz (Calabasas: David Brass Rare Books, 2012).

Staples, Leslie C., "When Found—," *Dickensian*, 55 (January 1959): 3–4.

[Stephen, James Fitzjames], "The License of Modern Novelists," *Edinburgh Review*, 106 (July 1857): 124–56.

―――, "*A Tale of Two Cities*," *Saturday Review* (December 17, 1859): 741–3.

Stephen, Leslie, "Dickens, Charles," in *The Dictionary of National Biography* (vol. 5, Sir Leslie Stephen and Sir Sidney Lee, eds, London: Oxford University Press, 1921).

Stevenson, Lionel, "Dickens's Dark Novels, 1851–1857," *Sewanee Review*, 51/3 (1943): 398–409.

Stevenson, Robert Louis, "Some Gentlemen in Fiction," *Scribner's*, 3 (June 1888): 764–8.

Storey, Gladys, *Dickens and Daughter* (London: Frederick Muller, 1939).

Sutherland, John, *Victorian Novelists and Publishers* (Chicago: University of Chicago Press, 1976).

————, "Dickens, Reade and *Hard Cash*," *Dickensian*, 81 (Spring 1985): 5–12.

————, "*Cornhill*'s Sales and Payments: The First Decade," *Victorian Periodicals Review*, 19/3 (1986): 106–8.

————, "A Note on the Text," in *Armadale* by Wilkie Collins (London: Penguin, 1995).

Swinburne, Algernon, "Charles Dickens," in *The Complete Works of Algernon Charles Swinburne* (vol. 14, Edmund Gosse and Thomas James Wise, eds, London: William Heinemann; New York: Gabriel Wells, 1926).

Tomalin, Claire, *The Invisible Woman: The Story of Nelly Ternan and Charles Dickens* (New York: Alfred A. Knopf, 1991).

————, *Charles Dickens: A Life* (New York: Penguin, 2011).

Trilling, Lionel, *The Opposing Self* (New York: Viking, 1955).

Trollope, Anthony, *An Autobiography* (Oxford: Oxford University Press, 1980).

————, *The Letters of Anthony Trollope* (2 vols, N. John Hall, ed., Stanford: Stanford University Press, 1983).

[Unsigned leader on Dickens's death], *Times* (June 13, 1870): 11.

[Unsigned review of *Great Expectations*], *Saturday Review* (July 20, 1861): 69–70.

[Unsigned review of *The Pickwick Papers*], *Athenaeum* (December 3, 1836): 841–3.

Vaughan, William, "Facsimile Versus White Line: An Anglo-German Disparity," in Paul Goldman and Simon Cooke (eds), *Reading Victorian Illustration, 1855–1875: Spoils of the Lumber Room* (Farnham: Ashgate, 2012).

Waugh, Arthur, *A Hundred Years of Publishing, Being the Story of Chapman & Hall, Ltd.* (London: Chapman and Hall, 1930).

Waugh, Arthur, and Thomas Hatton, *Retrospectus and Prospectus: The Nonesuch Dickens* (Bloomsbury: Nonesuch Press, 1937).

Weedon, Alexis, *Victorian Publishing: The Economics of Book Production for a Mass Market, 1836–1916* (Farnham: Ashgate, 2003).

"When Found—," *Dickensian*, 75 (Fall 1979): 180–3.

White, Edmund, Antonia Fraser, and David Lodge, "Novelists Pick Their Favourite Dickens," *Telegraph* (Web, January 7, 2012).

Wilson, Edmund, *The Wound and the Bow* (Cambridge: Houghton Mifflin, 1941).

Woolf, Virginia, *The Diary of Virginia Woolf* (vol. 5, Anne Olivier Bell, ed., London: Hogarth Press, 1984).

Wright, Thomas, *The Life of Charles Dickens* (London: Herbert Jenkins, 1935).

Index

Ackroyd, Peter 9n, 15n, 16n, 20n, 22n, 23n, 27, 51–2, 98, 101–2
Ainsworth, William Harrison 104, 106
Albert, Prince Consort 44
All the Year Round, see Dickens, Charles, *All the Year Round*
Allen, Michael 72n
Allen, Michelle 149
America, *see* United States
Andersen, Hans Christian 101–3
Andrews, Malcolm 20n, 24n, 27n, 28, 44n, 83n
Annual Register 114, 251–2
Aristophanes 119, 195
Aristotle 120, 197
Arnold, Matthew 109, 137
Athenaeum 40n, 95, 97, 100–102, 105 and n, 116, 122n, 129, 171–5, 199–200
Athenaeum Club 35
Atlantic Monthly 137n, 142
Austen, Jane 150, 154
Austin, Alfred 198

Bagehot, Walter 107–10, 114
Baker, Ernest 140
Bayard, Louis 152
Beadnell, Maria (Mrs. Henry Winter) 17
Beeton, Samuel 88
Benham, William, Canon of Canterbury 13n
Bent's Literary Advertiser 86
Bentley, Richard 20n, 32, 72–3, 88, 104n
Bentley's Miscellany 32, 73, 106
Berg copy of *Our Mutual Friend, see* Dickens, Charles, *Our Mutual Friend*, Berg copy
Bevington, Merle Mowbray 109
Blackwood's Edinburgh Magazine 98, 109, 112
Blessington, Lady (Countess Marguerite Gardiner) 104
Bodenheimer, Rosemarie 148

Bonner, Richard 33
Book Monthly, The 133n, 134
Bookman, The 139
Books in Print 150 and n
Bowen, John 131, 135
Bowker's British Books in Print, see British Books in Print
Bradbury and Evans 12, 23, 25, 29–33, 73–4, 80, 83–7, 93, 110
Braddon, Mary Elizabeth 114
Brady, Cheyne 108
Brattin, Joel 6, 8, 57n, 65–6, 95n, 115, 146–51, 152n, 165–6, 169, 253
Bredsdorff, Elias 101n, 102n
British Books in Print (also *Bowker's British Books in Print* and *Whitaker's Books in Print*) 150 and n
British Broadcasting Corporation (BBC) 7, 134, 142, 151–2
Brooks, Shirley 24n
Brown, Hannah (Mrs.) 17, 24, 25n
Brown, Nicola 148
Browne, Hablot K. (Phiz) 2 and n, 33, 47, 198, 202
Buckler, William E. 87n
Buckstone, John 26
Bulwer-Lytton, Sir Edward 34, 61, 102–6, 137, 179, 244–5
Busch, Frederick 151–2

Carlyle, Thomas 28n, 191
Casey, Ellen Miller 105
Cayzer, Elizabeth 148
de Cerjat, William 43, 49
de Cervantes, Miguel 119, 188, 195
Chapman, Edward 78
Chapman, Frederic 31, 45, 74, 78–84, 86, 88, 96
Chapman and Hall 2n, 6, 31–6, 39–41, 44–5, 55, 72–84, 88, 90–96, 112, 133, 141, 166

Charles Scribner's Sons 133
Chaudhuri, Brahma 107n, 108
Chesterton, Gilbert Keith (G.K.) 132, 140,
143, 146
Childs, George W. 165
Chorley, Henry Fothergill (H.F.) 100, 114,
116, 118, 122–6, 129, 169, 171–5
Cleaver, Arthur H. 39n, 79
Cockburn, Lord Henry 105n
Cohen, Jane 46, 55 and n
Collins, Philip 8, 20n, 102n, 106, 112,
114–15, 169–70
Collins, William (Wilkie) 14, 16–19, 24–5,
31–34, 38, 42–5, 58, 82, 90, 93, 98,
111, 114
Armadale 7, 88–9, 94
Frozen Deep, The 14–16, 19, 25, 27,
44, 69, 101
Conrad, Joseph 144
Cooke, Simon 47n
Cornelius, Anne (Brown) 19
Cornhill 33, 45, 87–9, 92–4, 98
Cosens, F.W. 167
Cotsell, Michael 42n, 148–9
Court of Chancery 31, 107–9, 239, 245
Court Circular 22 and n
Coutts, Angelina Georgina Burdett 16 and n,
21–4, 25n, 35, 81
Crimean War 85, 108
Critic 107n, 108
Cruikshank, George 104

Dahl, Christopher C. 104n, 111n
Daily News 98
Dallas, Eneas Sweetland (E.S.) 2, 24n, 53,
56, 97–100, 111–18, 165, 169
relationship with Dickens 99–100
review of *Our Mutual Friend* 44–5, 92,
96–8, 114–18, 126–8, 179–87
Dalziel Brothers 47
Das Kapital (Karl Marx) 135, 139
Davies, E. Salter 145–6
Davis, Eliza 42
Day, William 52–3
Dexter, Walter 13n, 134n, 141n, 142
Dial 137, 141
Dickens, Alfred D'Orsay Tennyson (CD's
son) 33
Dickens, Alfred Lamert (CD's brother) 43–4

Dickens, Catherine Macready (Katey, CD's
daughter) 14, 21, 26, 35, 101n, 139
Dickens, Catherine Thomson Hogarth
(Kate, CD's wife) 12, 16–24, 26,
28–30, 33, 35, 45, 68–9, 101, 129
Dickens, Charles Culliford Boz (Charley,
CD's son) 11, 13–14, 20–21, 26,
129–30
Dickens, Charles John Huffam
All the Year Round 4, 10, 14, 35–6,
45–6, 48–50, 69, 74–5, 86, 90, 92,
96, 100, 107n, 110–11, 129–30, 198
Christmas numbers 41, 44, 48n,
82, 89
circulation and sales 32–4, 43 and n,
77, 82, 87
creation 5, 12, 29–33
American Notes 46, 90 and n, 96,
106–7, 248
Barnaby Rudge 73, 90, 134–5, 141,
151, 244
Battle of Life, The 222
Bleak House 4, 7–8, 25, 41, 69, 74–5,
77, 80–81, 83–5, 90 and n, 92–3,
96, 101, 107–10, 112–14, 121–2,
125, 131–2, 135, 141, 143–6, 150,
152–3, 156–7, 171, 173, 188, 192,
195, 227–8, 237, 240, 244, 246, 248
Book of Memoranda 41–2, 55n
Boots 27
Child's History of England, A 46
Chimes, The 134, 227
Christmas Books 90 and n
Christmas Carol, A 25, 28, 89, 101,
103, 106, 134, 141–2, 151, 154,
156
Cricket on the Hearth, The 20, 222
David Copperfield 2, 4, 8, 16, 25,
44 and n, 72, 74, 81, 90–96, 101,
106, 117, 123–5, 130–35, 141–5,
150, 153, 156, 172–3, 175, 188,
191–2, 194, 200, 236, 242
death 11, 13, 24, 77–9, 95–6, 114,
129–34
Dombey and Son 7, 15, 25, 27–8, 52n,
56, 74–5, 81, 83, 90–91, 93 and n,
95, 106, 109, 131, 135, 140, 145,
189, 193, 244, 246, 248–9
"Dr. Marigold's Prescriptions" 82, 89

editions of his works 133, 253–5
    Charles Dickens edition 75, 95–6, 255
    Cheap edition 25, 46, 87, 90–91, 95, 254
    Library edition 25, 46, 87, 90–91, 93, 96, 112, 254–5
    People's edition 75, 91, 95
film and television adaptations 7, 134 and n, 141–2, 146, 151–3
France, escapes to 43–4, 48, 51, 53, 69, 119
Gad's Hill Place 11, 13–14, 17, 19, 26, 33, 44–6, 49, 51–2, 69, 101–2, 130
Great Expectations 2–5, 8, 11–12, 24, 29, 34, 36, 41, 46, 69, 72, 74, 77, 82, 93, 96, 98, 101, 111–14, 125, 131, 134–5, 139–46, 151–7, 198, 223, 236, 244
Hard Times 8, 32, 72, 84, 95–6, 109–10, 114, 131–5, 138–9, 142–5, 149, 152, 156, 188–9, 218, 227, 240
health problems 4–5, 11, 24, 39, 45, 50–53, 69, 75, 77, 96, 99, 114
Household Words 17–18, 23–4, 29, 32, 42, 84, 103–4, 108, 124, 130, 159, 220–22
    Dickens dissolves 5, 12, 29–31, 110–11
"Hunted Down" 33 and n
"In Memoriam" 45
"Lazy Tour of Two Idle Apprentices" 18–19
Little Dombey 27
Little Dorrit 3, 8, 14, 17, 36, 41–2, 46, 69, 75, 77, 80–81, 84–5, 90–93, 96, 102–5, 108–12, 117, 131–5, 138–46, 153, 155, 192, 242, 244, 248–9
"Magic Fishbone, The" 134
Martin Chuzzlewit 27–8, 81, 83, 90–91, 95, 106–7, 112, 126, 131, 135, 151–3, 172–5, 186–8, 192, 195–6, 240, 244, 246, 249, 252
Master Humphrey's Clock 32, 105–6
Memoirs of Joseph Grimaldi, The 68
"Message from the Sea, A" 82
Mrs. Gamp 27
"Mrs. Lirriper's Legacy" 48–9, 82, 89–90, 172
"Mrs. Lirriper's Lodgings" 44–5, 82, 172

"Mugby Junction" 82
Mystery of Edwin Drood, The 4, 78–9, 96, 129, 133, 140, 254 and n
Nicholas Nickleby 44 and n, 68–9, 72–3, 80, 90, 95, 105, 135, 151, 156, 173, 188–93, 244, 248, 250
Nonesuch letters 142, 144
Old Curiosity Shop, The 41, 90, 95, 101, 106, 109, 134, 139–40, 153, 173, 193, 228, 244, 246, 248, 250, 252
Oliver Twist 2–3, 8, 42, 68–9, 73, 90, 95, 102, 105–6, 121, 131, 134–5, 141–2, 151–6, 173, 240–41, 249, 251
Our Mutual Friend
    Abbey Potterson 62, 207
    advertisements in 6, 39, 55, 80, 83, 91, 94, 166
    advertising for, by Chapman and Hall 6, 40n, 76, 79–80, 95
    Bella Wilfer 2–3, 12, 45, 48, 52, 62, 64–7, 97, 122–6, 152, 154, 172–4, 177, 184, 187, 189, 191, 201–2, 205–19, 222, 230, 237, 241–2, 244, 246
    Berg copy 6–7, 55–6, 62–4, 166–7
    Betty Higden 2, 43, 48, 61, 64, 71, 118, 120–22, 124, 140, 177, 184–6, 197, 205–6, 209, 218, 227–33, 240–41, 245–6
    Boffin, Mr. 2, 4, 48–50, 52, 56–7, 61–8, 71, 92, 116, 120, 123, 125, 153–4, 172, 177, 184, 189–94, 200–216, 219–22, 225, 230–31, 237, 243–4, 247, 251
    Boffin, Mrs. 2, 52, 61–3, 67, 71, 92, 120, 154, 173, 177, 184, 191–3, 201–9, 215–16, 219, 230, 237, 243
    Boots 123, 174, 176, 223–4
    Bradley Headstone 3, 52, 57, 61, 140, 152, 173–4, 179, 184, 189–90, 193–203, 206, 209–13, 217–19, 237, 242, 244–5
    Brewer 123, 174, 176, 223–4
    Charley Hexam 41–2, 57, 62, 148, 189, 200, 203–4, 206, 212, 236
    Charles Dickens edition 95–6
    contemporary reviews 1–3, 7, 44–5, 92, 97–101, 114–28, 169–252

contract for writing, with Chapman and Hall 6, 36, 41, 44, 74–9, 84

contracts for publication in the United States and Germany 34, 80–81, 83

critical reputation since Dickens's death 131–6, 139–40, 145–50

dramatic adaptations 171

Eugene Wrayburn 3–4, 12, 42, 45, 48, 51, 56–7, 60–61, 63n, 65–8, 72, 92, 120–24, 127, 140, 152, 173–6, 184, 189, 192–4, 202–4, 206, 209–13, 217–18, 238–9, 244, 247

Fascination Fledgeby 1, 61, 65, 67, 152–4, 156, 173, 177, 190, 193, 204, 207, 210–11, 213, 224, 242, 245

film and television adaptations 152

Gaffer Hexam 37, 41–2, 59–64, 92, 116, 148, 153, 176, 200, 202–6, 217, 228–9, 236

George Radfoot 62, 172, 205–6

Georgiana Podsnap 57, 189, 196, 201–2, 204, 207–8, 211

illustrations, *see* Stone, Marcus, illustrations to *Our Mutual Friend*

Inspector, Mr. 62, 202, 223, 227, 236

Jenny Wren (also Fanny Cleaver, Doll's Dressmaker) 1, 57, 65, 67–8, 97, 120, 122, 125, 152–4, 173–4, 177, 179, 184, 186, 189, 192–3, 203, 207, 209–13, 219, 242, 245–7, 250

John Harmon (also John Rokesmith, Julius Handford) 2–3, 12, 41–2, 45, 48, 61–4, 67–8, 71, 92, 121–3, 127, 153, 172–4, 189–91, 193, 200–217, 221–2, 230–31, 236, 241, 244

Lady Tippins 42, 123, 174, 176, 183, 189, 192, 199, 203, 223, 239–40

Lammles, the 1, 37, 41–2, 52, 57, 66–7, 120, 122, 152–3, 174, 177–9, 183, 189–93, 196–7, 201–2, 204, 206–11, 213, 219, 224–5, 237, 244–7, 251

literary appropriations 171–2

Little Johnny 3, 140, 205, 218, 230–31, 244–5, 247

Lizzie Hexam 3, 12, 37, 41–2, 45, 48, 56–7, 59, 61–5, 92, 97, 116, 121–2, 140, 148, 151, 173, 176, 184, 189, 193, 200–213, 217–18, 228–9, 235, 238, 241, 244, 247

Lord Snigsworth 181, 223

manuscript 3–7, 10, 36, 38–9, 52–61, 64–8, 97–8, 165

Milveys, the 174, 189, 209, 213, 235

Miss Peecher 61, 206

monthly number plans 56–60, 64, 165

Mortimer Lightwood 60–61, 68, 122–3, 174, 184, 189, 193, 198, 201–2, 205, 207, 209, 212–13

Old Harmon 62–3, 127, 173, 201, 214–15

origins and sources 37–8, 41–3, 50

overwriting and underwriting of monthly numbers 37–8, 47, 52–61, 66–8

Oxford World's Classics edition 57, 65, 150

Penguin edition 57, 65, 119, 150

Pleasant Riderhood 189

Podsnap, Mr. 42, 97–8, 116, 119, 121, 124–5, 152–3, 157, 174, 176, 178–9, 188–9, 195–6, 199, 201–4, 207, 219, 223–7, 229, 241, 244–5, 251

"Postscript, in Lieu of a Preface" 39, 52–3, 120–21, 128, 165–6, 190, 197, 215–16, 219, 227, 238–9, 243

Proof sheets 6–7, 37–8, 40–41, 46–60, 65–7, 123, 165–6

radio adaptations 7, 146, 151, 253

Riah 3, 42, 63, 67–8, 173, 206–7, 210, 213

revisions 3, 5–6, 54–68, 166

Rogue Riderhood 3, 72, 92, 120, 152–3, 179, 189, 193, 202, 205–7, 210–12, 219, 227, 229, 246

sales and circulation figures 6–7, 75, 80–85, 88–97, 99, 116–18, 128, 133–4, 141–2

"Social Chorus" 38, 41, 61–5, 92, 97, 99, 127, 148, 152–3, 180–83
Silas Wegg 4, 57, 61–6, 71–2, 76, 116, 122, 152, 173–4, 177–8, 184, 188, 190–91, 200–205, 208, 210–11, 214–15, 239, 244, 246–7, 251
Sloppy 2, 71, 177, 190, 205–6, 209, 244
Twemlow, Mr. 42, 62, 122–3, 174, 176, 181–3, 199, 202–3, 207, 210, 223–4, 245, 247
Veneerings, the 38, 41, 59, 116, 120–24, 148, 153, 156–7, 174, 176, 181–3, 193, 199–203, 208, 210–11, 219, 223–5, 227, 240–41, 244, 246–7, 251–2
Venus, Mr. 4, 37–9, 48, 54, 58–9, 61, 66, 122, 153, 184, 200, 204, 208, 210–11, 214, 239, 247
Vintage edition 65, 146, 151
Wilfers, the 3–4, 59, 64–5, 116, 121, 152, 172–3, 178, 184, 192–3, 200–201, 205, 207, 212, 229, 240, 246
Young Blight 42
performs in *The Frozen Deep* 14–16
"Personal" statement on his domestic troubles 23, 29–30, 130, 159–60
Pickwick Papers, The 4, 8, 28, 40–41, 45, 52, 68–9, 73, 75, 80, 90–91, 95–6, 99, 101–2, 104–6, 111–12, 118, 122, 131–6, 141, 143, 151, 155–6, 172, 174, 183, 194–5, 198, 216, 220, 243, 246–7, 252
Pictures from Italy 46
Poor Traveller, The 27
popularity 77, 80–82, 84–5, 90–91, 95–6, 98, 101, 104–14, 130, 133–4, 140–42, 149–55, 179, 239, 245, 248–9
public readings 5, 12, 18–20, 24–9, 36, 44–5, 75, 98, 110
relationship with Ellen Ternan, *see* Ternan, Ellen Lawless (Nelly)
separation from Catherine 12–13, 16–24, 26, 28–30, 35
Sketches by Boz 73, 90 and n, 96, 104–5, 250
"Somebody's Luggage" 44, 82, 172

Staplehurst train accident 4, 7, 9–12, 35–6, 38, 51–3, 66, 69, 114, 119–20, 128, 160–63, 197, 219, 237, 246
Tale of Two Cities, A 2, 5, 8, 11–12, 32–4, 74, 77, 96, 110–11, 141–2, 149, 154, 171, 189
Tavistock House 14, 19–20, 26, 33, 38, 42
"Uncommercial Traveller" 34, 95
"Violated Letter" 22, 29
visits to the United States 2, 12, 24, 35, 73, 83, 151
"Wreck of the Golden Mary, The" 14
Dickens, Elizabeth Barrow (CD's mother) 43–5
Dickens Fellowship 137, 156
Dickens, Francis Jeffrey (Frank, CD's son) 33
Dickens, Helen Dobson (CD's sister-in-law) 43, 45
Dickens, Letitia (CD's sister) 45
Dickens, Mary (Mamie, CD's daughter) 14, 18, 24, 26–7, 44, 46, 139
Dickens Studies Annual 146
Dickens, Walter Landor (CD's son) 26, 46
Dickens World 7, 154–5
Dickensian 147, 151–2
Dictionary of National Biography 131, 136
Disraeli, Benjamin 104–5
Dolby, George 151
D'Orsay, Count (Comte) Alfred 104
Dostoevsky, Fyodor 132, 145
Dublin University Magazine 108, 112
Dvorak, Wilfred 147

Eclectic Review (also *Eclectic and Congregational Review*) 111, 115, 118, 124–8, 219–37
Edgeworth, Maria 173
Edinburgh Review 102–5, 109
Edwards, Amelia 90
Egg, Augustus 14, 44–5
ELH: English Literary History 147
Eliot, George (Mary Ann Evans) 93, 114, 132, 135, 137, 144, 150, 245
  Mill on the Floss, The 182
  Romola 7, 88, 94
  Scenes of Clerical Life 109

Eliot, Simon 85n, 87–9
Elwin, Malcolm 43n
Encyclopedia Britannica 133
"Eugene Wrayburn" (film) 134, 152
Evans, Frederick 21, 23–5, 30–31, 35
Evans, Thomas Coke 32
"Everyman's Library," *see* J.M. Dent
Examiner 10n, 97, 100, 104–5, 115, 128,
    169–70, 175–8

Farrer, William 77–8
Fielding, Henry 126, 175, 247–8
Fields, James 96
Fildes, Luke 96
Fitzgerald, Percy 90
Flaubert, Gustave 150
Flood, Alison 153
Ford, George H. 8, 109n, 111, 114, 130n,
    131, 136n, 141–2, 153, 169
Forster, Edward Morgan (E.M.) 130, 139, 150
Forster, John 10, 14, 16–26, 30–32, 34, 36,
    41–5, 49–52, 69, 73, 78, 80–82,
    93, 96n, 98, 105, 107, 111, 114,
    129–30, 155
  advice regarding public readings 25–6
  early friendship with Dickens 104–5
  Life of Charles Dickens 80–82, 97–8,
    114–15, 130, 136
  review of *Our Mutual Friend* for the
    Examiner 97, 100, 114–15, 118,
    125–6, 128, 169–70, 175–8
Fortnightly Review 130, 132
Fraser, Antonia 154
Fraser's Magazine 106
du Fresne, Marc-Joseph Marion 196
Friedman, Stanley 147
Frith, William 36

Gallagher, Catherine 149
Garrick Club 23 and n, 47
Gaskell, Elizabeth 89, 102, 111
Gentleman's Magazine 129
Gibbon, Edward 71, 116, 200–202
Gilbert, Pamela 148
Gissing, George 138–40, 143, 146, 255
Globe and Mail (Canada) 154
Godey's Lady's Book and Magazine 208, 252
von Goethe, Johann Wolfgang 195
Goldman, Paul 47n

Goldsmith, Oliver 247
Greene's Tu Quoque (by John Cooke) 197
Grubb, Gerald 76n, 79n, 87n, 88n
Guardian 153, 154n
Guernsey, Alfred Hudson 169–71, 178–9
Guild of Literature and Art 108

Hamley, E.B. 109
Harper and Brothers (also Harper & Co.)
    39–40, 80–81, 86
Harper's New Monthly Magazine 39–40,
    80, 169–71, 178–9
Harper's Weekly Magazine 34
Harte, Bret 129
Harvey, John R. 46
Harvey, Martin 141
Hatton, Thomas 38n, 39n, 79, 133n
Hayward, Abraham 105–7
Heaman, Robert J. 146–8, 253
Henry W. and Albert A. Berg Collection 6,
    54, 78n, 165–7; *see also* Dickens,
    Charles, *Our Mutual Friend*, Berg
    copy
Hill, Rowland 103–4
Hill, T.W. 13n
Hogarth, Georgina (CD's sister-in-law) 10,
    14–17, 19, 21–9, 43–6, 101
Hogarth, Helen (CD's sister-in-law) 21–3
Hogarth, Mary Scott (CD's sister-in-law)
    16–17, 102
Hogarth, Georgina Thomson (CD's
    mother-in-law) 21–3
Hogarth, William 18
Holmes, Alice M. 151
Holsworth, George 50
Holt, Richard Hutton 110
Hood, Thomas 106
Hornback, Bert G. 8, 115, 146–7, 150–51,
    152n, 165–6, 169, 253
Hornby, Nick 146, 149, 156
Horne, Richard H. 42, 124, 220–22
House, Humphry 144
Household Words, *see* Dickens, Charles,
    Household Words
Howells, William Dean 118, 122–3, 128,
    170, 187–91
Hunt, Leigh 107 and n
Hunt, Thornton 107–8
Hurlbut, Jesse Lyman 151

Ibsen, Henrik 147

J.M. Dent (also J.M. Dent and Sons) 134, 150
Jackson, T.A. 142–3
James, Henry 3, 144
  review of *Our Mutual Friend* 1–2, 7–8, 45, 61, 84, 97, 100, 114–15, 117, 120, 122, 126–7, 132, 169–70, 191–5
Jeffrey, Lord Francis 105
Jerdan, William 104–5
Jerrold, Blanchard 129
Jerrold, Douglas 14, 17, 27, 104
John Bull 29
John, Juliet 110–11, 154n, 155n
Johnson, Edgar 9n, 14, 15n, 16n, 19, 23n, 25n, 26n, 28n, 31n, 35n, 98n, 102n, 104n, 129n, 145–6
Johnstone, Sir Harry 151
Jones, Radhika 154
Joyce, James 143

Kafka, Franz 143
Kaplan, Fred 24n
Kelly, Fanny 15
Kemble, Fanny 15
Kent, Charles 106
Kingsmill, Hugh 142
Kitton, Frederic G. (F.G.) 37n, 46n, 167
Kucich, John 149

Lamb, Charles 247
Landor, Walter Savage 104
Landseer, Edwin 36, 229
Lane, Lauriat 8, 114, 169
Lang, Andrew 133
Laurence, Dan 139n
Leader 107–8
Leary, Patrick 20n, 22, 23n, 30n
Leavis, Frank Raymond (F.R.) 144–5
Leavis, Queenie Dorothy (Q.D.) 144–5
Ledger, Sally 148
Lee, Sir Sidney 131n
Leech, John 24n, 41, 50, 196
Leeds Mercury 136
Lemon, Mark 14, 16, 21, 23, 24n, 35
Lester, Valerie Browne 2n
Lever, Charles 32, 34, 77, 87

Levin, Martin 154
Lewes, George Henry (G.H.) 107–8, 110, 114, 130–32, 137, 139, 145
Lewis, Linda 148
Ley, J.W.T. 13n
Liddle, Dallas 108
Lindsay, Jack 144
Lister, Thomas Henry 105n
Literary Gazette 105
Litvack, Leon 5–6, 115, 148
Lodge, David 154
London Review 97, 116–18, 122, 126–8, 198–219, 250–51
Lover, Samuel 104
Low, Sampson 86

McCarthy, Justin 100, 112–14, 119, 126, 144
McLenan, John 39 and n
Macready, William Charles 15, 27, 43, 77, 103–4
Macrone, John 72, 104
Maine, Henry Sumner 108–9
Mann, Thomas 143
Marcus, Steven 145
Marlowe, James 147
Marryat, Frederick (Captain) 104
Marshalsea prison 72, 142, 155
manuscript of *Our Mutual Friend*, see Dickens, Charles, *Our Mutual Friend*, manuscript
Mazzeno, Laurence 100, 115, 140–41
Mercury (Liverpool) 29
Meredith, George 132
Merryweather, F.S. 50
Metz, Nancy Aycock 148
Meynell, Alice 137 and n
Michaelangelo 116, 200
Michie, Helena 148
Mill, John Stuart 109
Millais, Sir John Everett 24n, 125, 236
Miller, J. Hillis 148
Milne, James 133n, 134, 140, 141n
Missing Link, or, Bible-women in the Homes of the London Poor, The (Ellen Ranyard) 221–2
Mitton, Thomas 9–10
MLA International Bibliography 135, 146–7
Molière (Jean-Baptiste Poquelin) 119, 195
Monod, Sylvère 147

Morgentaler, Goldie 148
Morning Chronicle 29, 72
Morning Herald 29
Morris, Mowbray 132, 134n
Morse, Robert 145
Mott, Dean 141
Mudie, Charles 34, 76–7, 83, 88, 93
Mullan, John 154
Murry, John Middleton 132n, 141

Nation, The 1, 170, 191–5
National Review 109
Nayder, Lillian 16–17, 20n, 23n, 24n
New York Evangelist 237–8
New York Ledger 33 and n
New York Public Library, *see* Henry W.
    and Albert A. Berg Collection of
    English and American Literature
New York Times 117–18, 122, 124–5, 128,
    242–3, 246–50
New York Tribune 29
Nicoll, Sir William 139
Nineteenth-Century Fiction 147
Nineteenth-Century Short Title Catalog 86
Nisbet, Ada 145
Nord, Deborah Epstein 149

O'Hea, Michael 46, 55, 63n, 148
Oliphant, Margaret 112
Once a Week 33, 87, 89–90
Orwell, George 143–4
Ouvry, Frederic 21–3, 29, 31, 52, 77
Oxford English Dictionary 119
Oxford World's Classics, *see* Dickens,
    Charles, *Our Mutual Friend*,
    Oxford World's Classics edition

Page, Norman 8, 11n, 27n, 114–15, 169
Pall Mall Gazette 98
Partisan Review 145
Patten, Robert 6, 30n, 31n, 34n, 35n,
    73 and n, 74n, 75–85, 87n, 89–93,
    95n, 96, 133n, 149
Pearl, Matthew 152
Penguin (also Viking/Penguin), *see*
    Dickens, Charles, *Our Mutual
    Friend*, Penguin edition
Penny Illustrated Paper 10, 163
Phillips, Walter Clarke 137

Pierpont Morgan Library 5, 53, 56–9,
    66–7, 165; *see also* Henry W. and
    Albert A. Berg Collection
Poole, Adrian 119
Poor Laws 2, 43, 64, 120, 122, 124–5, 197,
    218
Poovey, Mary 149
Pope-Hennessey, Una 144
Praed, Winthrop Mackworth 117–18
Proof sheets of *Our Mutual Friend*, *see*
    Dickens, Charles, *Our Mutual
    Friend*, Proof sheets
Proust, Marcel 145
Publishers' Circular 86
Punch 23, 30, 129

Qualls, Barry 148
Quarterly Review 105–7
Quiller-Couch, Arthur ("Q") 137–8

Random House (also Vintage) 65, 146,
    150–51
Reade, Charles 43, 87, 102–3, 111, 114,
    245
Reade, Winwood 198
Reader 116, 118, 121, 128, 200–201,
    243–6
Reynolds, George William MacArthur
    (G.W.M.) 111
Reynolds's Miscellany 111
Roberts, C.E. Bechhofer 13
Robles, Mario Ortiz 150
Rose, Mark 28
Rose, Natalie 148
Rotkin, Charlotte 105n
Round Table, The 81n, 118, 122–3, 170,
    187–91
Routledge, George 86
Routledge's Railway Library 86, 88
de la Rue, Madame Emile (Augusta
    Granet) 16
Russell, Lord John 99
Russell, Sir George 53
Russell, Sir William 45
Ruth, Jennifer 150

Sadoff, Diane 147
Saintsbury, George 136, 140
Sala, George Augustus 90

Sanders, Andrew 148
Santayana, George 137, 141
Saturday Review 100, 108–9, 111–12, 115, 117, 120–21, 124, 126, 238–42
Scoggin, Daniel 149
Scott, Sir Walter 102, 171, 180, 247
Scribner's, *see* Charles Scribner's Sons
Scribner's Magazine 137
Sedgwick, Eve Kosofsky 149
SEL: Studies in English Literature 147
Sell-Sandoval, Kathleen 109–10
Shakespeare Club 104
Shakespeare, William 15, 119, 126, 138, 171, 175, 182, 188, 195, 200, 214, 224, 247, 250
Shattuck, Harriette R. 151
Shaw, George Bernard 135, 138–40, 143, 146, 156
Sidney, Sir Philip 171
Slater, Michael 9n, 13, 14n, 16n, 19n, 20n, 23n, 32n, 98, 100, 104n, 105n, 129n, 141–2
Smiley, Jane 153
Smith, Arthur 22, 29, 31
Smith, Elder and Co. 88
Smith, George 33, 87–9, 93–4
Smith, Sydney 104–5
Smith, Walter E. 39n, 253
Smith, William Henry (W.H.) 76–7, 79, 83, 86
Staples, Leslie C. 152n
Stephen, Sir James Fitzjames 102–4, 107–11, 145
Stephen, Sir Leslie 107–8, 131, 136, 145
Sterne, Laurence 105, 172, 247–8
Stevenson, Lionel 144
Stevenson, Robert Louis 137, 140, 143
Stewart, Garrett 147
Stone, Frank 2n, 44
Stone, Harry 56–7
Stone, Marcus 2 and n, 6, 46–7, 166
  "Bird of Prey, The" 55, 63–4
  illustrations to *Our Mutual Friend* 39–40, 46–53, 117, 148, 166–7, 198, 202, 205, 207, 210
  inspires Mr. Venus 37–8, 46
  monthly wrapper 39, 46–7, 55–6, 62–3
Storey, Gladys 21n, 101n, 142, 144
Sun 105–6

Surridge, Lisa 148
Sutherland, John 43n, 86, 87n, 88, 89n, 94, 95n
Swift, Jonathan 119, 195
Swinburne, Algernon 137, 140
Symons, Julian 144

T.B. Peterson and Brothers 251, 253
Taine, Henri 244
Talfourd, Thomas 104
Tauchnitz, Baron Bernhard Christian 40, 80
Taylor, Tom 27
Tegg, Thomas 72–3
Telegraph 154
Ternan, Ellen Lawless (Nelly) 5, 7, 11–29, 33, 35–6, 44–5, 49, 51–2, 69, 98, 101, 111, 129 and n, 142, 145, 151, 159–63
Ternan, Frances (Nelly's mother) 14–15, 18, 26, 33
Ternan, Frances (Fanny, Nelly's sister) 15, 26, 33
Ternan, Maria (Nelly's sister) 14–16, 18, 26, 33
Ternan, Thomas (Nelly's father) 15
Thackeray, William Makepeace 23 and n, 24n, 27, 33, 87, 89, 90, 102–4, 106, 135, 137, 156, 171, 187–9, 244–5, 248
  death 35, 45, 114
Thomas, Syd 148
Thompson, John 51
Time (US) 154
Times 3, 9 and n, 23 and n, 44–5, 77, 79, 92, 97–8, 100, 106, 108, 111–12, 115–16, 126, 129, 132n, 141, 159–62, 169, 179–87, 197
Tolstoy, Leo 1, 132, 145
Tomalin, Claire 9n, 13, 14n, 15, 16n, 17n, 19n, 20n, 51n, 104n, 129n, 151
Tomlinson, H.M. 132
Townshend, Chauncy Hare 98
Trilling, Lionel 145–6
Trollope, Anthony 7, 88 and n, 93–4, 114, 135–7, 156, 182, 245
Trollope, Thomas 90
Turgenev, Ivan 132

Uncle John (John Baldwin Buckstone) 16

United States 1, 4, 6–8, 15, 32–3, 39–40,
53–5, 66, 80–81, 83, 95, 100, 106,
114–18, 122–5, 128–9, 137, 151,
154, 162, 165–7, 169–70, 187–95,
208, 218, 237, 242–3, 246–53
Civil War, and effect on British
publishing 1, 6–7, 75–6, 86–8, 96,
100, 118
Dickens's visits to 2, 12, 24, 35, 73, 83
rumors of Dickens's domestic scandal
in 23, 29
sales of Dickens's works in 87, 133–4,
141–2, 150–51
United States Service Magazine 251

Vaughan, William 47n, 64n
Victoria, Queen 14 and n
Victorian Newsletter 147
Viking/Penguin, *see* Penguin
Vintage, *see* Random House

Ward, Lock & Tyler 88
Warren's Blacking 72 and n
Watson, Honourable Lavinia Jane Quin
(Mrs. Richard) 20
Waugh, Arthur 38, 133–4, 141
Waverley Book Co. 133, 139

Weedon, Alexis 85–6, 88n
Weintraub, Stanley 147
Weller, Christiana 16–17, 137n
Wellesley, Arthur, Duke of Wellington 85
Westminster Review 100, 112–14, 115, 117,
119–21, 124, 126, 128, 169, 195–8
*Whitaker's Books in Print, see British
Books in Print*
White, Edmund 154
Whitehead, Charles 104
Whitman, Walt 117–18, 243
Wigan, Alfred 15
Wilde, Oscar 132, 150
William Clowes and Sons 52, 54–5, 60, 65,
80, 166
Wills, W.H. 10, 14, 19, 23, 30–34, 48–9,
51–3, 80–81, 86, 99
Wilson, Edmund 11, 132, 142–5
Wise, John Richard de Capel 119–20, 124,
169, 195–8
Wood, Ellen (Mrs. Henry) 87, 90, 114
Woolf, Virginia 132 and n, 139
Wordsworth Press 150
Wordsworth, William 137, 229
Wright, Thomas 13 and n, 142–4

Yates, Edmund 23 and n, 69